SEARCH FOR THE SAIPH

by
PP Corcoran

Cover Design by The Gilded Quill
www.thegildedquill.co.uk

Published by Castrum Press
www.castrumpress.com

DEDICATION

In memory of George Turkington.

CHAPTER ONE

THE HAPPY WANDERER

GARUNDA – 49.41 LIGHT YEARS FROM EARTH

"Chief Engineer Logan reports we're ready to fold, Captain. Port control has given us the green light and wishes us a safe journey."

"Very well, Robards, let's be on our way. 'Time and tide wait for no man.'"

Richard Boswell smiled at the quizzical look his young navigator gave him at his use of the ancient phrase before turning his attention to the controls.

The journey from Garunda to Alona was split into ten folds of 5000 light year legs each. As the ship emerged at the end of each leg, it contacted navigation buoys placed by the navy's survey command and verified its position. The whole trip would take around ten hours, incorporating the mandatory two-hour shutdown for normal service, inspection, and any minor adjustments the gravity drive needed between such long folds.

The Happy Wanderer accelerated steadily under the push of its ion drive, its massive bulk of 1.8 million tons picking up speed until it finally reached three-quarters the speed of light.

"Three. Two. One. Fold!" Robards called.

They shifted into fold space with an almost-imperceptible shiver that ran the length of the ship.

A second, stronger vibration indicated their return to normal space.

Alarm bells rang.

Throughout the ship, the "FIRE" alarm signs flashed, their urgent blinking mirrored in the captain's display, demanding Richard's attention.

What the hell! Richard quickly brought up the ship's schematic. Fire in the engine room. The sound of bulkhead doors clanging shut reached his ears and the normally constant hum of the air conditioning died as it automatically shut down to prevent the spread of smoke. Richard overrode the alarm on the bridge, silencing it.

First Officer Yoshi Marona turned to Richard. "No reply from the engine room, Captain. I think I should head down there."

Richard desperately wanted to go himself, but his place was on the bridge. He reined in his impulses and calmly released his first officer.

"Off you go, Yoshi. Scare up what crew you can along the way and give the chief all the help she needs."

The majority of functions on ships like the Happy Wanderer were fully automated. She ran with a skeleton crew of just fifteen. Most of this crew worked in engineering, which just happened to be the seat of the fire.

Yoshi nodded and headed for the bridge exit.

"Yoshi!"

The first officer turned toward his captain.

"You be careful now. Take no chances, or your wife will never forgive me!"

8

Yoshi flashed Richard a toothy grin and disappeared down the corridor, heading for the engine room at a dead run.

Richard turned to his next order of business. "Sitrep, Robards!"

"Captain, on re-emergence into normal space, we continued on course at just under a quarter the speed of light..." he tapped the controls as he spoke. "The engine controls are unresponsive and my board shows the engines went on automatic shutdown at the first indication of fire. My systems are running on emergency power and I have minimal active sensor systems."

"Kennedy," Richard addressed his young communications officer, who was busy tapping keys at her workstation; so focused on the screen she was studying, she seemed unaware of her surroundings. Richard raised his voice. "Kennedy!" Still he garnered no response.

"Lorna!" Richard shouted.

Lorna Kennedy jumped as if stuck with a cattle prod. "Yes, sir!" she squeaked.

"Take a deep breath and calm yourself. We have a job to do, keep focused. OK?"

Lorna's cheeks flushed with embarrassment, her first real emergency at the age of twenty-one and she was acting like a scared five-year-old. She shook herself. *Yes, it's my first deep-space voyage, yes, I've only been here fourteen days and don't know the crew, but where did that bubbly, confident communications officer go!? Get a grip on yourself, woman, you're meant to be an officer!* In a stronger voice she replied, "Yes, sir. Sorry, sir. It won't happen again."

"I'm sure it won't. Now, lock onto the navigation buoy and download a message to it. Instruct it to launch its emergency communications drone back to Garunda and inform Port Control we have a fire in the engine room, we're currently adrift at the first way-marker, and we're declaring an emergency and request assistance as soon as possible."

"That's the thing, sir. I've been trying to raise the buoy, but the rear whisker laser mount isn't responding to commands or any of my computer fault interrogations. The bow mount can't traverse far enough to see the buoy and get a lock."

Richard mulled the problem. Each of the navigation buoys contained a communications drone equipped with its own gravity drive. The drones on this run were programmed to head for either Garunda or Alona, whichever was the closest. Any ship in distress could download a message to the drone and launch it automatically, then sit back and await rescue. Now that wasn't an option.

"Kennedy, warm up the emergency drone. Download our current logs but don't launch until we hear back from the First Officer."

The *Happy Wanderer*, like every commercial starship, was required to carry at least one communications drone. After the incident with the TDF *Vasco De Gamma*, where it ended up 50,000 light years from its intended destination, it seemed like a prudent requirement. Well, thought Richard, how right they were.

Lorna was tapping at her keyboard again, happy to have a purpose.

The attention tone beeped in the captain's display and Richard activated the pick-up. It revealed the image of Yoshi in a hard vacuum suit. A sense of dreadful foreboding twisted his stomach. "Go ahead, Yoshi."

"Captain, I've reached the bulkhead at Engineering. The tell-tale signs on this side of the door show it's over

1800 degrees in there. I can't get a visual as the cameras are down. But…" Richard saw Yoshi's look of despair as he shook his head, "I'm sorry, sir, there's no way any of the engineering crew could've survived."

"No way?" Richard responded, rhetorically, as he processed the likely deaths of his crew.

Yoshi shook his head slowly, sharing his captain's pain. "No. I can't see it, sir."

Richard lowered his head, rubbing his forehead gently. Chief Engineer Michelle Logan and he had been friends for almost thirty years, since he had joined Zurich Lines. They had crewed the long-haul cargo runs from the asteroid belt to the inner planets; they were godparents to each other's children. Now, in an instant, she was gone. How was he going to break the news to her husband?

Yoshi's tinny voice jolted his captain back to the present. "With your permission, sir, I'm gonna seal the next bulkhead back from Engineering and then pump out the air from between the two — use it like an air lock. If the fire's consumed all the oxygen in Engineering then there's no point in giving it the fuel to re-ignite."

"Sounds like a good plan, Yoshi."

"I'll enter Engineering and open it to space to allow the heat to dissipate before resealing and re-pressurizing it, before I do a proper damage estimate."

"How long do you think till you can get in and give me a provisional damage report?"

"Not long, sir. We're already suited up here. Give me twenty minutes and I should know what we're facing."

"OK, Yoshi. Permission granted and I'll expect to hear from you in twenty." Richard cut the link and turned to the waiting Robards and Kennedy. "We wait," he said simply.

It was the longest twenty minutes of his life. Richard alternated between hope and dread. Surely there was a chance someone could have survived? There were emergency suits stored in Engineering in case of a coolant leak or sudden depressurization. A suit's internal oxygen supply was good for up to an hour. Some of the crew may have reached them in time. These thoughts were swiftly quashed by reality; there was no chance anyone could survive an 1800 degree fire that would have enveloped the entire space in seconds...

True to Yoshi's word, the captain's console beeped for attention just over twenty minutes later. At the touch of a control, Yoshi's face appeared, sweat streaming from his brow and a worried look on his face. Richard steeled himself for the news he knew, in his heart of hearts, was coming.

"I take it the news isn't good, Yoshi?"

"I'm sorry, sir... We've failed to locate any survivors. The heat was too intense. It's horrific down here. Without proper forensic analysis, I can't even identify the remains of the crew."

Nausea welled in the captain as all hope for the missing men and women dissipated. Now his next priority was his surviving crew, and he pushed aside his queasiness. "What about the machinery, Yoshi?"

"To put it mildly, Captain, we're well and truly screwed. All the computer gel packs are destroyed. That wouldn't be too much of a problem as we have enough spares to replace the more important ones and get the engineering computers back up and running if only..." Richard frowned as Yoshi continued, "the heat from the fire has warped everything in here. I could probably cobble something together to get the control mechanisms working but the actual physical parts of the drive are damaged. I'm afraid there's nothing we have on board that could replace them... Sorry, sir."

"Understood, Yoshi. Get your men clear and seal the door."

"Yes, sir. And sir…"

"Yes, Yoshi?"

"I'm sorry about Logan."

The captain's vision blurred as tears filled his eyes. "Thanks, Yoshi."

Yoshi nodded curtly and cut the link.

Richard gave his eyes a quick rub, hoping that neither Robards nor Kennedy noticed and if they did, they would politely ignore it; he still had a ship to get home.

He quickly glanced at the ship's clock, fifty minutes – on this course at a quarter of the speed of light. Richard calculated they'd traveled 225 million kilometers from the position they'd entered normal space and with every passing second were moving a further 75,000 kilometers from the shipping lane. As long as a rescue ship had his base course and speed they should still find him without too much trouble.

"Kennedy, please update the logs on our communications drone with our current position, heading and speed. Download the First Officer's report and request immediate assistance. Launch the drone as soon as you're ready, please."

Kennedy busied herself at her console and Richard sat back as he calculated how long a rescue vessel would take to reach their location. The shaking of Lorna Kennedy's head caught his attention.

"Problem, Kennedy?"

"Um… yes, sir. The drone accepted the downloads and the command to launch. But my board shows a red light from the launch bay doors. They appear to be stuck."

Richard conjured an image of the launch bay doors in his mind. Positioned just forward of the rear whisker laser communications mount. The laser mount that also wasn't responding. Damn! What else can go wrong? The captain punched the link to Yoshi. The image of his First Officer halfway out of his pressure suit filled his display.

"Sorry, Yoshi, you're not finished yet. The launch bay doors for the Comms drone are stuck. Probably damaged by the fire. I need you and someone else to go free them so we can get the drone out and get some help."

Yoshi had paused while removing his bulky suit. He started shrugging it back on, his brow wrinkled in thought. "Either the hatch controls are fried or the hatch mechanism itself has been warped by the heat. I may have to cut the hatch away and release the drone manually, I don't see another way around it."

"Do whatever's needed, Yoshi, but the sooner we get the drone out, the sooner we get some help."

"Understood, Captain. I'll let you know what I find." And with that, Yoshi cut the link, thinking that it never rains but it pours.

#

On the exterior hull Yoshi regarded the hatch in front of him and wished he wasn't always right. Just as he'd thought; the hatch covering the communications drone bay was partially opened and jammed. Most likely the bay door rams had suffered catastrophic damage. The drone was intact, though a minor miracle. Their first piece of good luck.

No sense hanging about out here, I may as well get to work, thought Yoshi, as he carefully held the plasma cutting torch at arm's length and ignited it. The flame was designed to cut through anything up to and including battle armor, any mistake and it would make very short work of his suit. That mistake would take Yoshi's day from bad to fatal in a heartbeat.

He'd only been working a few minutes and already the plasma torch had easily cut through one of the four rams that operated the bay doors. Yoshi looked up to ensure that the crew member with him was safely out of the arc of the plasma torch while he moved to reposition himself to start on the next ram. He was confronted with the crew member's back.

"Hey Browne, are you with me?"

Yoshi got no reply. He turned the plasma torch off and secured it to the hull, by the bay doors, using the magnetic strap. He walked over to Browne. As he edged closer, he noticed the small hole in the back of her helmet.

"Oh God, no!" Yoshi moved as quickly as he could in his cumbersome suit to check Browne from the front and was confronted by another neat hole in the faceplate. The suit encased a now-dead Browne.

"No!" Despair filled Yoshi as the rational part of his brain tried to figure out what had happened. Had a micro-meteorite hit her? If so, shouldn't the faceplate be completely or at least partially shattered? Movement over Browne's now stiff shoulder caught Yoshi's eye. What the...

The short laser blast from the rifle of the armored figure passed right through Yoshi's chest.

The shot destroyed the integrity of the suit, the electronics controlling the magnetic boots failed, the atmosphere rushed out, the sum result was that Yoshi was lifted clear of the *Happy Wanderer*'s hull. Yoshi's brain, thankfully, began to shut down just as he saw dozens of armored figures scurrying toward the open airlock and entering the ship.

15

#

The screaming alarm on Lorna's console drew all eyes to it. She silenced it and briefly interrogated the computer to confirm its readings. Without raising her head, she shouted: "Dutchman! Dutchman!" It was the call no captain wanted to hear. "I have a crew member off the hull and moving away at speed. Suit beacon is coming in strong and I'm getting good telemetry. Bio readings show…" Lorna's voice faded as her throat closed over. My God, no! Not Yoshi! She slouched in her seat, dropped her head into her hands, and sobbed.

Richard left his seat and gently moved the sobbing young woman to one side. His worst fears were realized; on the display, a red circled icon with the name "MARONA" flashed.

The fire damage at the rear of the ship meant Yoshi had already been over 200 meters from the *Happy Wanderer*'s hull and moving away at 40 kilometers per hour when the mid-ship sensors picked it up. It didn't matter anyway, the suit's bio-sensors showed that Yoshi was already dead.

Richard's eyes fixed on the flashing icon of his dead first officer as he addressed Robards. "Robards, suit up. Browne's still out there, and with the stern sensors down, we don't know her status, she may need your help."

As Robards stood to comply, the bridge doors opened. Richard looked up and was confronted by the sight of a group of armored figures rushing onto the bridge.

Robards reacted faster than his captain, he lunged for the nearest intruder only to be viciously beaten into unconsciousness with a few swings of a rifle butt. As Robards fell to the deck, Richard instinctively placed himself between his Comms officer and the invaders. An uneasy standoff held for what seemed an age, it was

16

broken only when a commanding figure entered the bridge.

This one was different. The entire left arm of his armored suit was painted red and a strange symbol adorned his chest plate. It looked like a black circle covering the entire chest with a red X the size of a man's hand in the middle. The figure held an ugly-looking pistol loosely in its right hand.

The other intruders parted like a wave in front of him. Could this one be the leader? Richard's brain finally caught up, and as he drank in the shape and colors of the armor, recognition slowly dawned. Images of these suits had been carried by every media channel throughout the Commonwealth. Richard furtively glanced at the large red button protected by the clear plastic cover on the arm of his command chair. The button that would purge all the navigation computers aboard the Happy Wanderer, denying an enemy the locations of the Commonwealth home systems. Richard tried to calculate the time it would take to get to the chair before the intruders either cut him down or beat him unconscious, like the bleeding Robards.

The alien commander caught Richard's gaze and followed it to its target, the captain's chair. It turned back to Richard, lifted its right hand, and without hesitation shot Richard and Lorna with two easy jerks of its armored fingers.

'The Others' were in command of the Happy Wanderer and its navigation computer. The Others' had every coordinate of every world known to man.

CHAPTER TWO

THE SHRINE

DURAV – 172 LIGHT YEARS FROM EARTH

As his ship entered orbit, Narath gazed lovingly at Durav, the planet of his birth and home of the Chosen People. In the 2500 cycles since the Creator had gifted them with this new home, they had worked tirelessly in his name. The dark rings of the massive orbital structures supporting the shipbuilding yards contrasted starkly with the bright white clouds that covered most of the planet. Durav was a cold and harsh world. The people overcame all the odds and considered it a testament of their strength of faith in the Creator.

With his guidance, the people overcame all that nature threw at them, he endowed gifts on them that allowed their population to rapidly expand and spread across the surface of Durav. The Creator needed warriors to fight against the spawn of evil. Engineers to build the ships to carry them and the weapons for them to use in his name. Females to provide the young to be trained as the Creator saw fit.

For as long as he could remember, Narath had trained as a warrior and had risen steadily through the ranks. Until now.

A twin tone sounded throughout the ship, the surface shuttle departure was imminent. With one final look at the cloud-covered world below him, Narath headed for the waiting shuttle and his fate.

On the journey to the surface, Narath didn't bother to activate his viewing screen. He knew from long experience that the thick clouds obscured everything. The pilots were completely reliant on their instruments, having no visual references to guide them. Through his seat, Narath could feel the vibration of the shuttle engines increase in their fight to slow the rapidly descending shuttle as it closed on its destination. With a sharp jolt, the shuttle touched down and Narath released his restraints and headed for the door. It opened at the touch of a control from a crew member, allowing Narath to step out into a driving snowstorm.

The snow flurries reduced visibility to just a few feet, though he barely noticed. Narath pulled his blood-red warrior's cloak closer around his shoulders more out of habit than because of the cold as his battle armor was as comfortable to him on this bare, windswept mountain as in the vacuum of space. He wasted no time moving from the landing pad to the ancient beaten path that ran along the steep mountainside leading to the High Coltus; the place where the Chosen People received physical and spiritual guidance from the Creator in their "Ehita," their holy mission to hunt and exterminate the spawn of evil and make the universe pure enough for the Creator's return.

Narath felt a renewed surge of pride in his warriors' recent success, despite suffering heavy losses in their attempt to eradicate the heretics in Sector 14. The small flotilla he'd initially sent to the sector's life-bearing planet had never returned. The ships he'd sent to investigate brought disturbing news. A new enemy had entered the fray, one with sufficiently advanced technology to rival that of Durav.

In response, Narath had sought out the council of the Lesser Coltus, a smaller shrine to the Creator that every Fleet Base and Command Ship carried to allow the faithful to hear the Creator's wishes and with this guidance, Narath formulated a plan to send the full force of the Sector 14 fleet against the heretics.

The fleet was to slowly gather its strength while hiding behind a small dwarf planet in the heretics' system and arrive in small groups to prevent detection from their surveillance platforms. The initial stages of the operation went well, but a ship belonging to the heretics discovered the fleet and transmitted a warning signal before they could be destroyed. The fleet was forced to attack before Narath arrived with the final battle group. On his arrival, Narath found the heretics had been engaged in battle and, to his despair, the Lesser Coltus commanded him to remain at a distance as he watched his fleet's annihilation.

The Lesser Coltus decreed they must return home and seek the Creator's personal guidance. Accordingly, Narath ordered the remaining ships to return to the naval base in Sector 14 and continue harassment operations against the heretics' star system. It was while Narath was en route that the Creator intervened and presented him with a chance to redeem himself.

They detected a heretic's cargo ship and Narath saw his opportunity. He led his warriors in their assault of the ship and managed to capture it and its valuable computers intact.

Through a break in the falling snow, Narath caught sight of the cave's entrance, an impressive sight that never failed to fill him with awe when he considered that this unassuming crack in the mountainside was actually the entrance to his people's most holy shrine. The entrance was flanked by two warriors in battle armor. Their cloaks, the same color as Narath's, whipped in the wind, their ancient targath blades rested point down but were ready for instant use. The Guardians of the High Coltus. Day and night these dedicated warriors stood ready to challenge anyone approaching the High Coltus. At Narath's advance, a Guardian's sword swept up and an evil-looking blade pointed at his chest as the warrior called out his challenge.

"What do you seek, pilgrim?"

Narath removed his helmet and cradled it under his left arm, he felt the frozen air batter at his face, the breathing slits on his neck automatically closed over as the driving snow attempted to force its way in.

"I am Ipes Narath and I come seeking the guidance of the High Coltus." Narath spread his cloak to reveal his armored chest adorned with a simple black circle and a red X at its center.

The guard took a moment as his suits' systems interrogated Narath's and confirmed that he was indeed an "Ipes," a warrior in command of one of the fleets of the Chosen People in their Ehita of purification.

The guardian's targath resumed its point-down position. "Enter Ipes and may the Creator's blessings be upon you."

"And on you."

Narath stepped past the guards and entered the dimly lit cave, the electrostatic field that kept the weather at bay washed over his body.

The rise in temperature was tangible as Narath made his way to the rear of the cave, passing the sacred reliefs on the walls that told the familiar story of the Creator's return to Balach, the original planet of their people.

The Creator had intended to bring his people to Aseena, the land of the bountiful and never-ending beauty, but on his return to Balach, he found the Chosen People had fallen from grace under the heretics' influence. He unleashed a pestilence on Balach and only those of a pure heart survived. The Creator demonstrated his love and compassion for those found to be pure and brought them to a new world, Durav, to start afresh. The Creator set them a task to test their faith and physical bodies, but in his generosity he also gave them the High Coltus, where they were welcome to commune with him and seek his guidance. He proffered gifts that allowed them to travel amongst the stars, seeking out the spawn of evil and purifying the universe. When the Ehita was complete, the Creator would come again and take his people to Aseena.

As he passed the reliefs, Narath reverently ran his armored fingers over them.

Narath was forced to duck his head slightly as he entered a narrow tunnel at the rear of the cave, which sloped sharply downward into the heart of the mountain. Its walls were so smooth, they could have been cut with a modern laser cutter. He marveled at the greatness of the Creator.

The tunnel leveled out and Narath made out the slow melodic tones of people at prayer. The tunnel opened into a large chamber lit by flickering candles.

By the dim light, Narath saw almost 100 people spread around the chamber, kneeling with their foreheads resting on the chamber floor, hands locked behind their necks softly touching the small amber gem at the base of the skull, the symbol of the Chosen People. When a female discovered she was pregnant, she attended the local Atistes, house of the Creator, where the house leader passed a Gift Stone, the Creator's blessing, over her womb. If the child was pure of heart, on its birth a small amber gem would glint at the base of its skull. If, however, the newborn had been tainted by the spawn of evil, the gem was missing and the child was put to death immediately. A rare occurrence, but not unknown. A reminder to the Chosen that the spawn of evil was still attempting to bring about their fall from grace and tempt them away from the path of Ethita.

Narath's attention returned to the many pilgrims around him. A few had noticed the arrival of an Ipes and moved a respectful distance away. Some had come of their own free will to commune with the Creator, while others had felt the Creator call to them. No matter the reason, the Creator, through the High Coltus, spoke to their minds directly, filling them with either guidance to aid their daily lives or knowledge to aid them in their holy mission. A warm, pleasant feeling spread through Narath and he let out a small gasp as the strong, fatherly tones of the Creator spoke to him.

Blessings be upon you.

Narath dropped to his knees, assuming the position of apostasy, his fingers lightly touching the gemstone at the base of his skull. He closed his eyes and concentrated on formulating his reply. *I am Ipes Narath. Warrior of the Creator. I bear news of the Ehita.*

Continue, Ipes.

Narath's nervousness grew. The Creator was loving but strong. Failure in the Ehita could be met with instant execution. Only the spawn of evil could hide from the all-knowing Creator, hence the reason for the Ehita – to eradicate the heretics.

Narath confessed: *I have failed you. My fleet was destroyed at the hands of a new and powerful group of heretics. I can ask only for your forgiveness in the hope that you will allow me to continue to serve.*

Failure is unacceptable, Ipes!

Narath's muscles spasmed as pain spread through his skull to the tips of his fingers and toes, he rolled on the cavern floor before the pain began to subside. He lay gasping for breath as images flashed through his mind. The dispatching of the battle group to destroy life on the planet. The news of its destruction at the hands of the new heretics. His consultation with the Lesser Coltus and the plan to mass his forces for another assault on the planet. The subsequent battle. The destruction of his fleet and finally his capture of the heretic cargo ship and its computers.

Maps of star systems flew by at a rate that Narath could not hope to follow. The complete contents of the ships navigation computers swiftly followed by schematics from the engineering database.

You are redeemed, Ipes. You followed your guidance correctly, albeit the heretics hid from my gaze.

The warmth of the Creator once again flowed through Narath as he felt the Creator's satisfaction.

The heretics' reach is further than expected. The Chosen must be resolute and focus on the Ehita more than ever. However, I shall provide. You will have the tools you need. You will strike at the heart of heretics and you, Ipes, with my guidance, shall lead the Chosen to victory.

Narath felt tears of joy as once again the love of the Creator flooded him.

Henceforth, you are known as Tama Narath, the Hand of the Creator. You will recall all the fleets of the Chosen, for there is much to be done. I shall bless you with knowledge. You will defeat the heretics and clear the way for the Chosen to enter Aseena.

Images of new engine designs and weapons flooded into Narath's mind. In his periphery, he was aware of the Creator speaking to others. Weapons engineers and shipbuilders received their own gifts.

Go now Tama, you have much to do and time is short. The Creator's return is at hand.

Narath got to his feet, filled with a newfound sense of purpose. He bathed in the Creator's love. The Creator would use him to crush the heretics once and for all.

Narath made his way back up the tunnel to his waiting shuttle, his head filled with images of the nuclear fire that he would bring to the home of the heretics. A predatory smile appeared on his lips.

CHAPTER THREE

LET THE JOURNEY BEGIN

CHARON BASE – ORBIT OF PLUTO – SOL SYSTEM

Rear Admiral Christos Papadomas, commander of Survey Flotilla One, or SurvFlot One, sat in the main briefing room of Charon Base. He let his mind wander as he reflected that this is where it all began. Just a few short years ago he'd sat in this same briefing room as an ordinary captain.

Christos shook his head slowly. Five years? Only five years since he and his colleagues, the other three captains and four marine majors, were ignorant of what was to bring them to Charon, the largest satellite orbiting the dwarf planet Pluto at the outer reaches of the solar system. They had no idea they would go on to command Earth's most advanced ships, the Vanguards, and visit stars that scientists had until then only dreamed of; discovering new friends and new enemies in the process. Christos felt a level of satisfaction as he thought of his own role in it. He'd concentrated his efforts on saving the memory of a dead civilization on Delta Pavonis, which ultimately aided the discovery of what was to become Earth's first colony amongst the stars, Janus.

A smile crossed Christos' face as he reminisced about what he thought was his greatest achievement so far;

first contact with the indigenous race of Messier 54, the Baldies. He almost laughed out loud as he pondered the slang term given to the people of Alona and recalled how much it had irritated Ambassador Schamu, the Commonwealth's envoy there.

First contact hadn't gone exactly to plan, though. The Commonwealth had known the Baldies (Christos mentally kicked himself), the Alona, had space faring ability and Christos had taken Survey Flotilla One to Messier 54 to thoroughly survey the system and gather intelligence on the Alona before making first contact. Unexpectedly, he'd happened upon an Alona ship in distress and that had changed everything.

The ship was venting atmosphere with no chance of rescue by another Alona craft, Christos couldn't stand by and let them die. He ordered one of his own ships to intercept and rescue them. Ambassador Schamu had been unhappy with the manner in which events unfolded but understood there was little else Christos could have done. In any case, he wasn't slow in exploiting the opening that Christos had given him by saving the stricken vessel's survivors and returning them to Alona. An audience with Emperor Paxt quickly followed, at which he gave his permission for Schamu to establish a Commonwealth embassy and lo and behold, diplomatic relations were opened. Although some secrets had been kept from the Alona.

They didn't know about The Others. The top levels of the Commonwealth decided that since there was no evidence of The Others traveling the 50,000 light years required to reach Alona, what they didn't yet know wouldn't hurt them. This particular decision didn't sit well with Christos.

The briefing room doors opened and Christos grinned as he saw his former second-in-command of TDF

Jacques Cartier, Bruce Torrance, sporting some new rear admiral rings. Christos bounded from his seat and grabbed Bruce's hand, shaking it vigorously.

"Damn, Bruce, it's good to see you and congratulations on a well-deserved promotion! I wondered who was gonna get SurvFlot Two. You wait till I tell Kayla about this."

The smile on Bruce's face was easily a match for Christos'. "Maybe the promotion will tempt that woman away from you at last! You never did deserve her. I swear you must have got her drunk the night you proposed to get her to say yes."

Christos threw back his head and laughed. "Ha. She's had nearly twenty years to change her mind and she's still here, so it must be the longest hangover in history." Another loud laugh followed, it was only then that Christos noticed the other man still standing in the doorway, also in the uniform of a rear admiral.

Christos quickly released Bruce's hand and stuck it out to the newcomer.

"My apologies, Admiral. Rear Admiral Christos Papadomas, commander Survey Flotilla One."

The thin, slightly balding man took Christos' hand with a surprisingly strong grip. "Gavin Glandinning. Commander Survey Flotilla Three." Gavin gave Christos a lopsided grin. "Or what there is of it."

Glandinning? The name was vaguely familiar. Christos was about to inquire further when the door slid open again and in stepped a legend amongst the survey command rank and file, Vice Admiral David Catney. Now Christos was confused, and by the way Glandinning's mouth dropped open, he was even more surprised than Christos.

As a captain, Catney had commanded Earth's very first interstellar ship, the TDF *Marco Polo*. His crew identified and located the energy source which led directly to the discovery of the Rubicon cave, home of the Saiph database. Catney went on to help design the Vanguard survey ships before becoming the personal choice of the Joint Chiefs to revamp the naval academy. The restructuring was necessary to enable the navy to cope with the huge influx of personnel who had joined up after the true nature of the Others became apparent.

The last Christos heard, Catney had been tapped to head the working group responsible for the integration of the TDF, the fledgling Garundan navy and the small but powerful Persai fleet, into one joint Commonwealth Navy. No easy task.

What the hell is David Catney doing here and where's Admiral Vadis? Christos had expected Vadis to make an appearance, he was, after all, the man who'd led Survey Command through its formative years. Catney took a seat at the head of the small briefing table and waved a hand at the remaining seats, indicating to the others to sit.

"OK, let's get right to it. Admiral Vadis has been requested by the Joint Chiefs to assume command of the Office of Naval Intelligence, effective immediately. The fallout from his sudden departure is that I'm the only rear admiral on the list for promotion who's intimately familiar with the workings of Survey Command so…" Catney let out a small chuckle as he looked at the other admirals. "I got an early promotion to vice admiral and a one-way ticket to the outer reaches of the solar system." His words received chuckles and congratulations from the others.

"Thank you, thank you," Catney smiled around the table. "So, to business. I'm not a big stickler for the rank thing, besides, we're all admirals here, so, in private, I expect first names only and please, each of you, speak your mind freely. In public we play the game and present a united front. Understood?"

The three admirals nodded. Christos felt a renewed admiration for this legend who was now also his new commander; a straight-talking man who didn't expect his immediate subordinates to carry out his orders like automatons.

"Good. Now, the reason I've called you together. The Joint Chiefs have decided that it's time to let Survey Command get on with its primary role, that is, surveying new systems and making peaceful contact with any spacefaring civilizations we find. It's been over a year since the Second Battle of Garunda and the fleet has not only made good the losses it suffered but is further along in its planned expansion than anyone thought possible. Third Fleet in Garunda had first dibs on new ship construction and has already received the first of the new Bismarck class battleships. With the general fleet expansion, the Joint Chiefs believe we now have sufficient strength to begin the planned reorganization."

Catney touched a control on his PAD and a wire diagram appeared in the holo cube in the center of the table.

"The integration of Persai, Garundan, and Terran forces is continuing apace. The Joint Chiefs now have a Garundan and Persai member. They've formed a Combined Joint Chiefs of Staff who report directly to the Commonwealth Council on matters that affect Commonwealth-wide issues. In matters pertaining to national security, the Chiefs still report directly to their respective national governments. Fleet deployment from here on in will be as follows: First Fleet under Admiral Jing will consist of three battle forces designated BatFor 1.1, 1.2, and 1.3 and they will be home ported at Earth. Second Fleet consisting of BatFor 2.1, 2.2, and 2.3 will be home ported in Janus under the command of Admiral Lewis. Third Fleet consisting of BatFor 3.1, 3.2, and 3.3 will be home ported in Garunda under Admiral Radford. Fourth Fleet consisting of BatFor 4.1, 4.2, and 4.3 will be home ported in Pars under the command of Force Leader Taras. Fifth Fleet will be a joint Navy and Marine force broken up into five Marine Expeditionary Brigades of around 14,500 sailors and marines. Each MEB can work as an independent entity or combine to form a Marine Expeditionary Force. Each MEB will be allocated by the Joint Chiefs as and when requested by a Fleet Commander and will be held in Earth space until required."

Catney paused in his brief to let all of this sink in.

Torrence was the first to ask the obvious question. "So where does that leave us?"

Catney touched a control on his PAD, the section of the wire diagram showing Sixth Fleet expanded and a list of smaller sub-units filled the holo cube.

"Welcome to Sixth Fleet the new home of Survey Command."

Christos ran his eye down Sixth Fleet's organizational structure. David Catney was going to be a busy man.

"If I'm reading this right, David, you're not only in charge of Survey Command but whatever 'Training Afloat' is."

Catney gave a short sigh. "The Joint Chiefs, in their wisdom, decided to accept one of my recommendations to expand the naval academy's current curriculum to include a short period of training cruises on frigate-sized ships for graduates prior to releasing them into the fleet. A core of experienced officers and ratings will flesh out the crews of cadets and make sure they don't do too much damage as they terrorize other ships during their training cruises."

Laughter filled the room. Each of the admirals remembered their own first cruises and some of their more memorable mistakes.

"I nearly blew up my first ship when I accidentally allowed the reactor core to run away," smiled Glandinning.

Catney looked at him with a horrified face. "And they let you near my engine room on the *Marco Polo*. How'd we ever manage to get home in one piece?"

Glandinning shrugged and that lopsided smile was back on his face. "Luck?"

Christos finally placed the name "Gavin Glandinning." He'd been Catney's engineering officer on the *Marco Polo* during its first voyage. It occurred to Christos that Glandinning would have been a lieutenant junior grade on that voyage and here he was, what? Nine years later? As a rear admiral. Christos felt his head spin. Nine years from lieutenant to admiral? Even with the rapid expansion of Earth's military forces, he was hard-pressed to explain promotion so quickly.

Christos racked his brain to remember the last time he'd read or heard anything which mentioned Glandinning and came up empty. It seemed that following the successful return of the *Marco Polo* the young lieutenant had dropped off the world. Christos glanced at the youthful-looking admiral and made a mental note to ask him about it sometime, although he suspected the dark world of naval intelligence may be involved. Things just didn't add up. Christos' musings were put on hold as Catney continued his briefing.

"That brings me to the meat of the subject. Survey Command and your roles. It's the intention of the Joint Chiefs that Survey Command will, with all haste, make and execute plans to visit those systems identified in the Saiph database as having had a measure of Saiph interference with the DNA of life on planets within the system."

In the holo cube, the wire diagram was replaced with a list of twelve planets, their names in yellow lettering.

"From the Saiph database, we know they visited twelve planets, including Earth. Now, if we remove Earth and Garunda…"

In the holo cube, the two planets moved to a new column that now bore the legend "Commonwealth," where they joined the new home of the Persai, named after their original planet Pars, and the Earth colony Janus. As they did so, the lettering of their names changed to blue.

"We know the original Pars was destroyed by the Others around 2038 AD."

Pars, with the word 'original' in brackets, moved to a column bearing the legend "Destroyed" in black.

"Alona has not yet joined the Commonwealth and as far as we know remains undetected by the Others."

Alona changed color to blue and moved to a column with the legend 'Neutrals.'

"Delta Pavonis was one of the objectives of the original Vanguard surveys and sadly it suffered an extinction level event destroying virtually all life on the planet," Catney spared a look for Christos. It had been his ship, the *Jacques Cartier*, that had arrived at Delta Pavonis only to find that less than twenty years before an asteroid had struck the planet, causing massive tidal waves and enveloping the planet in a cloud of unbreathable CO_2. Catney remembered the images that the *Jacques Cartier* had brought home of a still-partially functioning near-orbit satellite system. Massive skyscrapers destroyed by mile-high waves. An entire civilization wiped from the universe.

Delta Pavonis moved to the "Destroyed" column.

"That brings us to 70 Ophiuchi, where the *Henry Hudson* originally encountered the Others. The Joint Chiefs are classing that as enemy occupied and between you and me they have a few surprises in mind for its residents but that's for another time."

A column bearing the legend "Enemy Occupied" in red appeared, with 70 Ophiuchi below it.

"Now that leaves us with seven systems. Luckily for us, the Persai have placed surveillance platforms in these systems over the last few decades and if we factor in the data from them, that leaves us with this:"

The remaining seven systems broke into two columns. One highlighted in purple entitled "Life Bearing" and the other in white entitled "Unknown." Below Life Bearing were listed Gamma Leporis, Regulus 4, 16 Cygniz, 23 Librae, and Algol 3. Below Unknown were Tau Eridani and 9 Ceti.

"From the Persai data, we know that artificial energy sources have been detected in these five systems. Unfortunately the data isn't good enough to give us a true picture of what's going on in each of these systems so Christos and Bruce, this is where you come in…"

Christos felt his ears prick up and sat a little straighter in his seat. Out of the corner of his eye he caught the same reaction from Torrence.

"Now I don't need to remind you that the Joint Chiefs believe that one of these systems is more than likely the home system of the Others."

Catney took the time to meet the eyes of each man in the room as the implied danger remained unstated.

"It's my intention to dispatch a survey flotilla to each of the systems showing artificial readings. Dispatched in order of those showing the highest level of energy output. Christos, you have seniority amongst the flotilla commanders so I'm assigning you Algol 3."

Christos gave a sharp nod and stared intently at the words Algol 3 in the holo cube as if just by looking at the name he could discern what awaited him and his crews there.

"Bruce, you get 23 Librae. I want you both to plan for a covert reconnaissance. It's my understanding that you'll have a full diplomatic team on board who will handle any first contact situations but your initial brief is to get in and get out without detection. Your planned departure date is to be no later than thirty days from today. Understood?"

Christos and Torrence replied in unison. "Understood."

Catney gave them both a smile. "Yeah, I thought you would. Gavin, don't worry, I haven't forgotten you."

Throughout the briefing, Gavin Glandinning had remained silent, Christos had almost forgotten he was even present.

"What's the current status of SurvFlot Three, Gavin?"

With a barely noticeable pause Glandinning replied, "Non task-worthy. Currently I have only two of my three Vanguards, a single Talos command variant light cruiser and none of my assigned Persai ships. My last request to Survey Command indicated that I could expect to receive my third Vanguard in two weeks' time, with the second Talos following in approximately a month. They were unable to tell me when to expect the Persai. In my opinion, SurvFlot Three will reach a limited task-worthy state when it receives the second Talos cruiser."

Christos was surprised at Glandinning's admission that his flotilla was not task-worthy. It was a hard thing for a commanding officer to admit, but after hearing that SurvFlot Three was barely at half strength Christos agreed it was the right thing to do.

Again a brief smile crossed Catney's lips. "That's my assessment too, Gavin. So, provided your second cruiser arrives on time, I want you to plan on taking an under-strength flotilla to the two systems that aren't showing any artificial energy sources, Tau Eridani and 9 Ceti. I know SurvFlot Three's still an organizational disaster zone, but do your best. I expect you to be ready to deploy thirty days after the arrival of the second cruiser. If you think you're going to be ready before that, great, but it's your call and if you feel you need longer, I'll back your decision."

Glandinning gave an imperceptible nod as Catney clapped his hands together with a bang.

"One last thing before we wrap up. As I'm doing double duty with the setup of the training flotillas as well as Survey Command, I'll have to leave the majority of the day-to-day work to my staff. But not everything can be handled by staff members, so Christos, you get the short straw. You're now my designated second-in-command when it comes to all things survey."

Christos' groan escaped his lips as Bruce Torrance tried, and failed, to suppress a snort of laughter. He knew exactly how much Christos hated paperwork.

"Now, I suggest we head to the Flag Dining Room for some lunch."

Catney caught Glandinning's eye as they stood to leave. They both slowed to allow Christos and Bruce to get a few paces ahead, then Catney leaned in close. Keeping his voice conspiratorially low, he asked

Glandinning what he'd been dying to ask since the meeting commenced.

"So, Gavin, how were things on Zarmina?"

Glandinning furtively glanced at the two men walking down the corridor in front of them, ensuring they were out of earshot before answering.

"Cold. But on schedule. Maybe another eighteen months and we should be ready for field testing."

"So why did they send you to Survey Command of all places? Surely you'd have been better off staying on Zarmina?"

Glandinning shrugged. "Someone felt I lacked command experience and if the project came to a point where it was required, then it needed someone with combat experience. Putting me in command of a BatFor ahead of the normal promotion chain would have brought too much attention so it was the lesser of two evils, I'd be less noticeable in survey."

"I hope so… Well, you're here now and I for one am glad to have you." Catney slapped Glandinning across his shoulder blades, "Let's eat!"

Catney quelled the unease that welled in his stomach, he had an innate dislike for covert intelligence ops, they didn't sit well with him, and life was much easier when it was not colored by shades of gray. Black Ops were never his cup of tea but Gavin Glandinning had taken to them like a duck to water and strangely, he was already missing the cloak and dagger world. Gavin gave a mental shrug as he brought his thoughts back to the present and the mission ahead.

CHAPTER FOUR

THE DINNER PARTY

TDF *CUTLASS* – CHARON BASE – SOL SYSTEM

When David Catney saddled him with the second-in-command job at Survey Command, Christos originally thought it would mostly involve him initialing and sending stuff on its merry way to some middle-ranking staff officer who dealt with the nitty-gritty. That thought lasted until Christos realized how much paperwork it took to run Survey Command.

Christos was now spending so much time doing the jobs Catney passed off that he was becoming reliant on his own flag captain, Vusumuzi Mkhize, to do the bulk of the organizational work within SurvFlot One. It was work that Christos felt he should be doing himself, but there simply weren't enough hours in the day.

Only another two weeks before the expected departure date for SurvFlot One and Two, time was short, and it seemed there was still so much to do before Christos left for the lunar colony to snatch a few days with his family before whisking off to Algol 3.

An attention chime sounded on his computer, Christos glanced at the time; Twenty-two thirty-five. There weren't many who'd call him at this time of night. Christos happily flipped aside a random memo entitled, "Accidental Pollution of Alien Civilizations by

Improper Waste Disposal during Surface Surveys and its Possible Effects on Cultures not as Advanced as the Commonwealth" – *who wrote these things*? Christos' face brightened when the face of Vusumuzi Mkhize appeared in the memo's place.

"And to what do I owe the pleasure of a call from my faithful minion at this ungodly hour, Vusumuzi?" queried Christos in a light tone. Vusumuzi didn't reply immediately and Christos saw that for once there was no reciprocal smile on his usually happy face.

"Sorry to disturb you so late, Admiral, but a delicate matter has been brought to my attention..." Vusumuzi paused, unsure to how to continue. He wrinkled his forehead as he searched for appropriate words.

"Just spit it out, Vusumuzi, or we'll be here all night."

Vusumuzi straightened his shoulders slightly and his features became neutral. "As per your orders, I've ensured that, where possible, every crew member gets a period of home leave before our planned departure. By the time we leave for Algol 3, ninety percent of all military personnel within the flotilla will've had the opportunity to visit their families."

Vusumuzi paused, waiting for the obvious response. Christos looked at him blankly until realization dawned. Vusumuzi had no control over the diplomatic personnel of the flotilla, they came under the direct control of Ambassador Schamu, unless there was a military priority. By emphasizing the word "military," Vusumuzi was trying to tell Christos something without criticizing the Ambassador. Christos took the bait.

"And what's the leave state of the diplomatic personnel, Captain?"

"To my knowledge, no member of the diplomatic staff has requested space on any personnel shuttles except for diplomatic purposes."

Christos couldn't believe what he was hearing. The mission to Algol 3, like every other survey mission, was virtually open-ended. It could be months before the flotilla returned to Commonwealth space, so it had become common practice amongst survey crews to visit family and friends before they left on these long voyages. Obviously the Diplomatic Corps had never heard of this particular practice. Although Christos was in overall command of the mission, he really couldn't usurp Ambassador Schamu's authority and order that the diplomatic personnel be granted leave. A suggestion that the ambassador may wish to visit his own family before departing might do the trick.

"Captain, I'd be grateful if you could find out if the ambassador is available for a private breakfast tomorrow morning. I have some matters to discuss with him in relation to our upcoming mission that I'd prefer to do in person."

At last, the smile returned to Vusumuzi's face. "I'm sure he'll make the time, Admiral. Would zero seven thirty hours suit?"

Christos kept his face deadpan. "Perhaps we should make it zero seven hundred, Captain. I'm sure he has a busy day planned and I wouldn't want to impinge on it."

A short laugh escaped Vusumuzi. "I'm sure you wouldn't, sir. Zero seven hundred hours it is. Goodnight, sir."

"And goodnight to you too, Vusumuzi." With the link cut, Christos returned to the enthralling memo on waste disposal.

#

At precisely 0700 hours a single elongated tone alerted Christos to the arrival of a visitor in his quarters. The visitor's identity was verified by the marine stationed at the entrance twenty-four hours a day, whether Christos was present or not. A naval tradition that Christos hadn't fully appreciated until he rose to flag rank himself and realized how many unwanted visitors the intimidating marine sentry dissuaded. But this visitor was expected and Christos still wasn't sure how to handle him.

"No sense putting him off, he's here now," Christos muttered as he activated the link to the sentry. "If that's Ambassador Schamu, please show him in. Thank you."

The bulkhead door slid open with a soft hiss. Christos marveled at how neat and fastidious Nicholas Schamu managed to look at this time of day. The creases of his suit trousers would've done a marine on parade proud and his black patent-leather shoes glinted like highly polished glass. Christos wondered, not for the first time, if Nicholas had smuggled his personal manservant on board. Suppressing an urge to shake his head, he allowed a broad smile to crease his face as he stood to greet his guest.

"I'm so glad you could join me, Nicholas. Sorry for the early hour. But with the work load generated by our upcoming mission and the additional responsibilities Admiral Catney has given me, it seems I spend most of my day behind my desk. I thought it important to fit in time to get your personal assessment of your staff's readiness." Christos smiled as he continued, "You know how some staffers are prone to exaggerate readiness or gloss over minor problems rather than irritate their superiors. I prefer to get a true evaluation from the horse's mouth, so to speak."

Before Nicholas could reply, there was a gentle knock on the frame of the bulkhead separating the seating area from the dining area. Christos turned and saw his steward, Petty Officer Bryan Walcott, standing resplendent in his white jacket, mess blue trousers and shoes shining so brightly that Christos was sure they could give Nicholas' a run for their money.

PO Walcott's role was another naval tradition that Christos had always thought anachronistic, but since his promotion he honestly didn't know how he could've managed with simple personal chores – – like moving his belongings from his old office on Charon Base to the newly refitted Cutlass. He'd left his old quarters in the morning, by the end of the day when he retired to his new ones, there was a fresh uniform laid out, an evening meal awaiting him, and a copy of his agenda for the following day. The petty officer had become an integral part of Christos' well-oiled command machine and it was Walcott who'd made the arrangements with the officers' mess for this morning's working breakfast.

"Breakfast is ready, sir."

"Thank you, Bryan. Shall we, Nicholas?"

Christos ushered Nicholas into the small dining area, even on a cruiser the size of Cutlass, space was at a premium. Christos was a firm believer that his officers should not have any special privileges, he observed the same rules and made no exceptions for himself, even for food.

Nevertheless, Walcott had worked magic. The crisp white tablecloth was spotless. The plates, bearing the ship's crest, and polished cutlery were laid with millimeter precision. Christos took his seat and Walcott hovered at his shoulder with a pot of steaming coffee, which he proceeded to pour into a battered, over-sized china mug. As Walcott approached Nicholas, the ambassador held up his hand.

"Could I trouble you for some ice water? I find that hot beverages at the start of the day dull my thinking until at least lunch." Walcott nodded and left the room. Christos drew Nicholas into an innocuous conversation about the diplomatic staff and managed to make it last throughout the remainder of the meal. A fact he was proud of since he actually had no interest whatsoever in the aforementioned staff, so long as when they folded out for Algol 3 they had their act together.

As the meal came to a close and Walcott topped up his coffee, Christos decided the time had come to broach the true reason for the meeting.

"Your department seems well prepared for whatever eventualities we may encounter Nicholas, may I tell Captain Mkhize to expect the requests for outbound shuttles to be with him shortly?"

Nicholas gave Christos a blank look as he set his glass on the table. "Excuse my ignorance Christos, but why would my staff require shuttles? We've completed all our preparations for departure, unless anything urgently requires a staff member's presence off-ship then Captain Mkhize has no need to arrange any additional shuttle time."

Christos' mug stopped its ascent to his lips as he realized for the first time that it had simply never occurred to Nicholas that his staff may wish to visit their families before leaving for the mission. Christos recovered quickly and took a sip of his coffee to give him a few seconds to work out how he was going to tackle Nicholas' apparent ignorance without embarrassing the ambassador.

"Hmm. That could present me with a quandary, Nicholas." By the look on Nicholas's face, Christos knew he had no idea what he was saying. "As you know, I firmly believe that my officers and I get no extra privileges above any crewman's expectations. It's long been a navy tradition that before a long voyage, such as the one to Algol 3 could be, that each and every crew member be allowed a short amount of shore leave to visit their families or to spend as they wish. In a spirit of fairness, I've enforced this rule on my officers as well. I myself am traveling to the lunar colonies tomorrow to spend a couple of days with my wife and daughters." Christos swore he could see a faint glimmer of understanding in Nicholas's eyes. Just one more gentle push. "I need every part of this flotilla to work together, naval and diplomatic, and I'd hate the tradition of shore leave to generate resentment between personnel. Perhaps I should've consulted you earlier and we could've avoided this situation. My apologies, Nicholas."

Nicholas waved off the apology. "No need, Christos, this is a minor hiccup which I can easily rectify. I'll get my staff on it first thing and you can tell Captain Mkhize to expect a request for shuttles presently." Nicholas pulled out a small PAD and began to type.

Behind Nicholas, Walcott desperately tried to suppress a large grin, which got wider as Christos flung him a withering look.

"I'm in your debt, Nicholas. As I said, I'm traveling to the lunar colonies tomorrow, if it's of any use to you, it's my understanding there are spare seats that you or your staff could avail themselves of?"

Nicholas paused momentarily, as if checking an internal diary. "My sister's vacationing with her

44

husband's family this time of year, but I suppose I could visit my brother, he lives in the lunar colony."

Christos stood and walked around the small table, beaming. "Well that's that, then, you can travel with me tomorrow." Before he had time to think, Christos added. "Why don't you join me and my family for dinner some time? I'm sure my wife will be delighted. I know my eldest, Philippa, will be. She's planning a career in the diplomatic corps when she finishes university."

Nicholas seemed slightly taken aback by the offer but recovered quickly. "That's a generous offer Christos, and I look forward to it. Now, if you'll excuse me, I have a few pressing issues to deal with before leaving the office for a few days."

Christos walked Nicholas to the door, as it closed behind him he turned and was greeted by Walcott clapping his hands slowly in admiration. "Well played, sir, well played indeed."

Christos took a small bow before seating himself at his desk, wondering how he was going to tell Kayla he was bringing a stuffy, self-important aristocrat to dinner on one of the only two nights he'd set aside just for the family.

#

LUNAR COLONY - SOL SYSTEM

Surreptitiously gazing at Kayla, Christos still had to pinch himself to believe his luck. Neither her beauty nor cleverness had diminished over the two decades (and three children) since Kayla had finally agreed to marry him.

They'd grown up on the island of Crete in the capital city of Heraklion and met in high school. In school, Christos was physically strong, representing the school in wrestling, but he'd been an average student with

45

only one goal. To join the Terran Defense Forces and travel amongst the stars. Kayla, on the other hand, had always been smart, if shy. As she entered her teens she was gangly and awkward in company.

It was Ms. Zika, his mathematics teacher, who suggested he join the study group to bring up his very average grades and it was here that he met Kayla. At first he couldn't see past the shy, awkward shell of a girl, but as time went on, he began to see her differently. Christos' grades rose sharply under her patient, reserved teaching style while Kayla's social ineptness dissipated as Christos, appreciative of her help, took her under his wing and introduced her to his social circles. Kayla's confidence grew, assisted in some part by the jealousy of her classmates that she got to spend so much time in the company of the best-looking boy in school.

During that year they grew closer. It was only as the summer recess beckoned and Christos was due to go to the White Mountains to spend the summer working on his uncle's farm that he realized Kayla had shed her awkwardness and stick-thin figure and had turned into a slender, confident young lady. It was the longest summer of Christos' life. When he eagerly returned to school in the autumn, he was accosted by the sight of Kayla surrounded by every hot-blooded male in the school, apparently they'd noticed her too. Christos could have kicked himself. He'd missed his chance, he should have made the effort to see her over the summer, no matter how busy the farm was. His heart sank as he turned away, despondent. Then he heard his name. He turned and the image of what he saw burned into his memories.

It was Kayla, running toward him, with the biggest, warmest smile, she ran into his arms and he didn't let go. At the tender age of sixteen, Christos Papadomas

46

knew he wouldn't waste another summer, or autumn or winter or spring, there would never be another woman for him. Over the next two years they were inseparable, until the moment they both dreaded. On his eighteenth birthday Christos enrolled in the navy.

Christos had made no secret of his ambition to travel to the stars, but it meant leaving Kayla behind. What if she forgot him, or worse, met someone else? It should have been his happiest day, to finally realize his dream, so why had he felt so miserable when he'd signed his name on the dotted line? He'd returned home to find Kayla sitting on the doorstep. He was dumbstruck. He'd stood in front of her, looked down at the awkward girl who had become a beautiful woman. He instantly regretted his decision to join up with every fiber of his being. There was only one thing to do. He would go back to the recruitment office and withdraw his application. Anything to stay with Kayla.

The front door opened and there stood the five-foot-one powerhouse that was Philippa Papadomas. No one had ever summoned up the courage to argue with eighty-one-year-old Grandma Papadomas. She looked up at the towering frame of her grandson and then at the tearful girl sitting on the step. Grandma Papadomas placed a wrinkled hand on the head of the distraught Kayla and pointed her bony finger toward Christos.

"If you don't marry this girl, then you're a bigger idiot than your father! I told him the same thing with your mother. Men! Without a woman to tell them what to do, they would never get anything done!"

Christos looked at his grandma, then at Kayla's upturned face. The tears glinting in her beautiful eyes. Christos dropped to one knee and rubbed his sweaty palms before taking Kayla's hand in both of his.

"Kayla Condos. Will you do me the great honor of being my wife?"

Kayla bounced up and flung her arms around the kneeling Christos, nearly knocking him over. Blinking away tears, Kayla said throatily:

"Yes, Christos. Yes! Yes! Yes!"

Grandma Papadomas was forced to clear her throat several times before Christos released his embrace. A smiling Grandma Papadomas extended her hand to Christos and in her open palm lay the wedding ring that she had refused to remove since her own beloved husband passed, nine years earlier.

"No engagement is complete without a ring and I know that your grandpa would want you to have this."

Christos mouthed a silent "thank you" to her as he slipped the ring onto Kayla's finger.

Within the month they were married. Christos headed off to naval training and Kayla started her medical training. Two years later, they were blessed with their daughter. Sadly, Grandma Papadomas passed before her birth and at Kayla's urging their first child was named Philippa.

Kayla easily obtained her medical degree while being a full-time mother to Philippa and Maia, their second daughter. She graduated summa cum laude and received offers from the top four teaching hospitals on the planet. She turned them all down in favor of packing her growing family off to the lunar colonies so as to be closer to the naval bases and Christos.

As for Christos, his natural talents suited naval life. He had a gift that was quickly recognized by his senior officers. Within ten years, Christos reached the rank of Chief Warrant Officer, specializing in engineering and astrogation. Christos resisted repeated calls for him to take a mustang commission, where an enlisted man is offered the opportunity to attend officer training school and gain his commission. Christos firmly believed he needed to get to grips with the nuts and bolts of being a sailor before making the move to the world of an officer. It had taken a particularly persuasive officer, who had enlisted the aid of Kayla, to eventually get Christos to accept a commission. When the Gravity Drive was invented, it put Christos in the enviable position of commanding the ships that traveled the stars.

A sharp pain in his lower ribs brought him crashing back to the present.

"Dad, will you stop staring at Mom like some lovesick teenager? It's embarrassing."

Christos swatted at Philippa's passing head, but she side-stepped him. Walking up to her mother, she reached past her and grabbed an almond from the countertop where Kayla prepared an almond cake. Christos was struck by the likeness his eldest bore to her mother at the same age.

Eighteen in only another two months and with the beauty that worried every father, Christos thanked God she was also blessed with her mother's brains. It seemed the only thing that Christos had contributed to his daughter's DNA was the thirst to journey to the stars, although Philippa had every intention of doing it in her own way. She had her eye on joining the Diplomatic Corps after completing college. A career plan that Christos considered might benefit from his invitation to Ambassador Nicholas Schamu.

Kayla didn't even bat an eyelid when Christos casually mentioned, over a glass of the most expensive white wine he could find at short notice, that he'd invited Schamu to join them for dinner on one of the two nights he had at home before leaving for Algol 3 for probably months. Christos knew she would be pissed, hence the expensive wine. But it hadn't worked. Although Kayla remained silent, he saw the disappointment in her eyes and knew he was in the doghouse.

The chime of the front doorbell was quickly followed by the sight of a mini-tornado flying across the living room with a cry of "I'll get it!" from Christos' youngest, Odysseia. All of nine years old, Odysseia thought it was her duty to greet every visitor to the Papadomas household. Christos secretly suspected she hoped that it would be some pimply singer from her latest favorite sound-alike pop band. Odysseia seemed so certain that one day it would be her latest pop heartthrob, she'd placed a stool by the intercom so that her face came level with the screen. Christos moved quietly into the living room and leaned against the wall where he could get a good view of the intercom's screen.

"Papadomas residence, how may I help you?" Odysseia said in her best adult voice, fooling no one.

Christos could see the image of Nicholas Schamu, completely nonplussed by the formal, if slightly squeaky, voice.

"Ambassador Nicholas Schamu, member of the Diplomatic Corps and representative of the Commonwealth Union of Planets requesting admittance."

Christos put a hand over his mouth to prevent himself from letting out the laugh that was threatening escape. Odysseia jumped from the stool and headed back to her room to watch the latest vid from whoever was in fashion. In passing she waved a hand at the front door.

"Daddy, it's for you."

This time a laugh did escape as Christos stepped to the intercom and pressed the door release key. The front door slid open and there stood Nicholas Schamu, resplendent in yet another immaculate suit. *How many of these things does he own?* Christos wondered.

"Thank you for coming, Nicholas."

"My pleasure, Christos." Nicholas handed him a bottle of wine. "I seem to remember your wife enjoys white wine. I hope she finds this a suitable gift."

Christos knew nothing about wine and the bottle was only decorated with a simple white label. He didn't think Nicholas was a cheapskate, but the wine could have come from any store in the mall. Whatever, he was sure Kayla would need it to get through a meal with Nicholas. Philippa stuck her head around the corner, her mouth half-open as if to speak. She took one look at Nicholas and his immaculate suit, grimaced, then stepped back around the corner.

Philippa glanced down at her fashionable trousers and T-shirt and decided she was way too underdressed for the occasion and fled for her bedroom.

"I seem to have scared the young lady off," Nicholas said in a deadpan tone.

"Nah, she's probably just realized that she may end up in front of you for a job interview in the near future and has decided she best try and impress you right from the start! Come on, let me introduce you to my wife."

Christos walked across the small living room and entered the kitchen.

"Kayla, may I introduce Nicholas Schamu? And look, he brought wine." Christos cheerfully held up the bottle. His smile froze as his wife's eyes fixated on the label. She made a two-handed grab for it and dragged it in front of her disbelieving eyes. Kayla twisted the bottle so she could check the label again, convinced she must be mistaken. Her eyes slowly widened.

51

"I hope you'll find this a suitable Riesling, Mrs. Papadomas? It's from my own cellar and has been allowed to age for the last five years."

Kayla tore her eyes away from the bottle. "Please call me Kayla, Mister Ambassador."

"Kayla, it is then, but I'm in your home tonight so it's only right for you to call me Nicholas."

A rustling at the entrance to the kitchen was followed by a small "Ahem."

Christos put a supporting hand on the wall, there stood before him was Philippa in one of her mothers' best evening gowns. A hint of carefully applied makeup accentuated her prominent cheekbones complemented with a light touch of lipstick. Her hair was drawn back into a ponytail that hung down her back almost to her waist. Who is this impostor and where is my Philippa? When in hell did my tomboy teenager turn into this elegant young woman? I'm arranging a few marines to act as bodyguards. Female marines.

Kayla playfully punched him on the shoulder as she walked past and gave her eldest a small hug.

"Nicholas, this is my daughter, Philippa. Philippa's already received an early acceptance to Harvard to study political science."

"That's quite impressive, Philippa. Your father tells me you have ambitions within the Diplomatic Corps when you graduate. Let me assure you, it's a most rewarding career. If you wish, and with your parents' permission of course, I'd be happy to discuss suitable additional courses which may assist you."

Philippa smiled with barely concealed joy. An opportunity to actually quiz a man who had been the Commonwealth's ambassador to another sentient species!

Christos had used this brief conversation to recover from his shocked realization that little girls eventually grow into young women. Now he said, "I'm sure that won't be a problem but I believe your mother would like you to set the table or we'll all go hungry."

Philippa threw her father a petulant glance before vanishing into the dining room, from where there was an immediate sound of oohs and aahs as Maia pumped her sister for information on their esteemed guest. I'm going to have to watch that one as well in the not too distant future, thought Christos.

"Nicholas, I'm remiss in my duties as host, can I offer you a drink?"

"A small dry gin, if you have one, would hit the spot. I've just spent the day being bored to distraction by my brother."

Christos rummaged in the liquor cabinet before finding the gin cunningly hidden behind every other bottle in there.

"Ah yes, you did mention your brother was here in the lunar colonies. Although I can't recall what you said he did here?"

"I'm surprised your wife hasn't met him. He waxed lyrical today about how he'd secured extra funding for a new space medicine wing at the colonies' teaching hospital."

Kayla arched an eyebrow when she heard that. "Oh your brother works in the governor's office? You remember Christos, I told you about the new grant we got to expand my research."

Nicholas took the glass of gin. "All day William's been bragging about how the new wing will make the lunar colony the envy of the system. I haven't seen the man for eight years and honestly, I'd happily not see him again for another eight."

"Well he's right, the governor's been championing our research ever since it was decided to set up a center of excellence in the solar system. Quite a few of the major hospitals on Earth were vying for the funding. A bit of a feather in the cap for the governor. What does your brother do for him?"

Nicholas looked confused. "Do for him? William *is* the governor."

A loud belly laugh erupted from Christos at the sight of the dapper ambassador looking at his wife incredulously, as if his brother could be anything but the governor, while Kayla just stood there with her mouth open.

Regaining control of himself, Christos gestured toward the dining room.

"Perhaps we should be seated while Kayla composes herself. I must congratulate you Nicholas, it's been a few years since I saw my wife completely dumbstruck."

Throughout the meal, Philippa pumped Nicholas for advice and tips as well as getting him to regale her with in-depth accounts of his previous diplomatic missions. With dinner over, much to the chagrin of her eldest who insisted she was an adult under Commonwealth law, Kayla sent the girls to wash the dishes while the adults settled in the living room.

"Perhaps a glass of Riesling, Nicholas?"

"Only the one Kayla, our shuttle has an early departure slot and I promised William I'd look over a proposal for him before I left."

Christos was surprised that the wine was actually corked with an old-fashioned cork and not a self-sealing microfiber. It took him a bit of time to find a corkscrew in the kitchen. When he returned, it was to the sound of his wife's gurgling laughter. He had to give Kayla credit, she could play hostess with the best of them. But he could tell by the look on her face that the laughter was genuine.

Christos put on his best commanding face. "OK, you two, what's going on in here?"

Kayla's voice sounded like that of a child caught stealing from the cookie jar. "Oh nothing, my love. Come on, pass that wine, I've been dying to taste it."

Christos passed the glasses.

"Now remember, Christos, savor the flavor, don't just gulp it down," cautioned Kayla.

Savor the flavor. It's only a glass of white wine, for God's sake. He brought the glass to his lips, took a sip, closed his eyes, tilted his head back and then as loud as he could he gargled the wine before swallowing it. Letting out a loud satisfied "ah," he looked toward his wife, expecting to see a pretend scowl on her face and ready to berate him for his childish behavior. What he actually saw was a look of complete shock. Uh-oh. Christos glanced across at Nicholas who was failing miserably in his attempt to hide an amused smile behind his glass.

"Christos Papadomas. That wine is over 7000 credits a bottle and you gargled it like salt water. Nicholas I can only say sorry for my husband's lack of maturity."

"Kayla, it's not very often that I see an admiral in fear of anything, but at this moment, the said admiral is shaking in his boots!" Nicholas placed his glass on the table and rose to his feet. "Unfortunately I must bid you goodnight. Thank you, Kayla, for a lovely meal and the hospitality of your home. And as for you, Christos..." Nicholas gave him a smug look. "I shall leave you to your fate."

Christos walked him to the door were Nicholas thanked him again before leaving. As Christos sealed the door he could swear he heard him whistling. Now he only had to placate his wife. Like that was going to happen.

CHAPTER FIVE

FATEFUL DECISION

CARSON CITY – EARTH – SOL SYSTEM

It was late on a Friday evening and the sun was slowly setting behind the Sierra Nevada Mountains. From his office on the 58th floor of the Naval Intelligence Service building in Carson City, Ensign Terrance Wilson was oblivious to the view. He hunched his shoulders in concentration as he ran the information again. Nope, it still wasn't working for him. Young Ensign Wilson was a creature of logic. Give him a puzzle and he would sit perfectly still, run the problem through his head and only move when he had the solution. His father told him it ran in the family and would jokingly compare him to Aunt Elizabeth. But this time Wilson couldn't quite get the parts of this puzzle to fit. A frown creased is forehead as once more he looked at the data displayed in the holo cube in front of him.

The subject of his consternation was time. He'd had been tasked with analyzing masses of information generated by the researchers in the various fields studying the Saiph database recovered from the Rubicon Cavern and putting it into chronological order. An earlier mistake by Patricia Bath misinterpreted the destruction of the Saiph as millions of years before when in fact it was a thousand. The powers that be did not want a reoccurrence of that error, hence Terrence's current role.

Terrance was chosen for the job for two reasons. Firstly he had an eidetic memory, better known as a photographic memory, and secondly, Terrence thought this was the real reason, Commander Bryer Anderson, Terrence's department head, was the laziest officer that Terrence had ever had the misfortune to meet in his so far short career.

Another of young Terrance's annoying habits, at least to his superiors wanting answers in a hurry, was his thoroughness. It hadn't occurred to him to seek permission to stray outside his proscribed parameters, he'd simply expanded his examination to include everything he considered relevant. This incorporated all the current reports on the 'Others'' physical make-up and reports on recovered technology and tactics. For comparison Terrence added to the mix the same information about Humans, Garundans, Persai and the Alonas. It was the results of these comparisons that puzzled him.

Sitting back in his chair, Wilson closed his eyes and blocked out the world around him as he chewed over the facts.

One. There was no doubt that Humans, Garundans, Persai, Alonas and the Others all shared common DNA strain, thus proving Saiph tinkering.

Two. It was the Others who destroyed the home world of the Saiph, destroyed the original home of the Persai and attempted to destroy Garunda.

Three. The reason behind the Others attacks was as yet unknown.

Four. But for the discovery of the Rubicon Cave and the Saiph database it contained and the discovery of a similar database on Pars, then both humans and Persai would've been incapable of matching the Others' weaponry.

Here is where it gets interesting, thought Terrance. Using these four facts as a starting point he was able to formulate further questions.

One. If the Others destroyed the Saiph a thousand years ago, why had neither their star drive or weapon technology advanced so far beyond human capability that they simply crushed us, swatting us as if man were an irritating fly?

Two. Average out where human, Persai, Garundan, Alonan and the extinct race from Delta Pavonis had been and you came up with an interesting answer. All five races had been within a couple of hundred year's development level of each other. So... how come the Others, with no input from the Saiph, had independently developed star travel over 700 years before anyone else but hadn't managed to progress any further since then?

No matter how many times Wilson ran this problem the answer eluded him.

The incessant beeping of his wrist com brought him out of his trance. A quick tap of the com silenced the alarm as he checked the clock on the wall. *Twenty hundred hours? Dammit! I'm late for Maggie, on a Friday night too!* There would be hell to pay. *Hmm maybe a nice bunch of flowers would help*? Terrance powered down his terminal, conducted his usual security routine and locked all sensitive documents away. One last check to ensure he hadn't missed anything and he left. He had a family lunch on Sunday. Aunt Elizabeth was visiting and bringing her fiancé with her. Terrance chuckled to himself at the thought of Aunt Elizabeth, *a fiancé at her age?*

As he headed for the elevator Terrence couldn't prevent the same questions running over and over in his head. Perhaps he could ask Aunt Elizabeth for her thoughts, she was a Rear Admiral after all.

#

"You see the problem Aunt Elizabeth? No matter how I reassemble the data it still leaves the question of how the Others advanced so rapidly then come to a grinding halt? I just can't explain it." Terrance threw his hands up then sat back in his chair on the lawn of his father's house.

Across from him Aunt Elizabeth or more correctly Rear Admiral Elizabeth Wilson (hatchet man for none other than General Joyce, Chairman of the Joint Chiefs of Staff) regarded her young nephew over her iced tea and smiled to herself at his obvious frustration.

"Have you shared this with your department head? Maybe they have access to information that you don't." said Elizabeth soothingly.

The snort that emanated from Terrance spoke volumes about his regard for his superior. "Commander Anderson believes that I'm wasting my time…" Terrance looked pleadingly at Elizabeth as his next sentence came out in a rush.

"But I know that I'm not! I don't know why, but I know it is important! We're missing something here. Put aside all the facts pointing to the near parallel evolution of all the races tinkered with by the Saiph, with the exception of the Others. Every sixty days the Others probe Admiral Radford's defenses. It's like clockwork! You'd think that after the first couple of ships were destroyed they'd change tactics? But no! Every sixty days, along they come. Who does that? No human admiral would continue to send his crew to certain death. The only logical reason that I can think of, is that it pins our forces in Garunda and that is plain, cold-blooded."

Elizabeth Wilson had spent long enough dealing with the machinations of the large unwieldy machine of the Terran Defense Force to know how frustrated Terrance must be. He was trying to convey his logic to his superiors but it was falling on deaf ears. *The thing is, his logic is undeniable,* thought Elizabeth, she was convinced he had valid questions that needed further investigation. It surprised her more that no one had actually asked these questions before but with the rapid expansion of the TDF, the formation of the Commonwealth and the mad rush to build bigger and better weapons to counter the Others' threat, some things were simply overlooked and this was one of them.

"Look Terrance, I'll tell you what. Why don't you put your ideas into a report and forward it to me on Monday. I'll take a good, hard look at it and see what I can do, OK?"

Relief flooded the young ensign's face. "Thanks Aunt Elizabeth, I'd appreciate that."

Elizabeth leaned over and patted him reassuringly on the knee. "Now why don't you run along and see if you can rescue Maggie from your mother before the baby pictures start coming out."

With Terrence gone Elizabeth leaned back in her chair and wondered how a young ensign could have stumbled onto the question which could determine the fundamental reason for the Others' drive to destroy all remnants of the Saiph. *And why the hell did this Commander Anderson not realize the importance of it? Idiot!*

Well her job was to seek out and identify anything that was hindering the war effort and it sure seemed that Commander Anderson needed a swift kick up the rear.

Elizabeth activated her direct link to the office of the Joint Chiefs.

"Joint Chiefs. Colonel Harrison speaking. How may I help you ma'am?"

"Colonel I'd like you to pull a personnel file for me. A Commander Anderson currently stationed with Naval Intelligence, Carson City."

"Yes ma'am. I can have that for you in about twenty minutes. Would you like that forwarded to your personal PAD or shall I forward that to your office for Monday morning?"

Elizabeth glanced around the garden at her family and friends enjoying the late summer sunshine. This was the first time that Robert's and her own schedules had coincided to allow them to visit her sister and allow Elizabeth to show off her fiancé since their engagement.

"Is the meeting of the Combined Joint Chiefs still set for next Wednesday?"

"Yes ma'am."

Well that settles that then.

"Send it to my PAD thanks."

"Yes ma'am."

Elizabeth cut the link and stood up with a small sigh of resignation. Time to find Robert and tell him she had some work to do.

#

CENTRAL COMMAND - MONT SALÈVE – EARTH

Keyton took his seat as Chairman of the Joint Chiefs of Staff of the Terran Defense Force at a small conference table in a room adjacent to the main operations room of Central Command, buried deep inside Mont Salève, south of Geneva, from here the TDF and newly formed Joint Commonwealth Forces were controlled. While waiting for the remaining seats to fill, Keyton reflected on how much his life, and that of the entire human race, had changed in the decade or so since the invention of the Gravity Drive that had brought the stars within man's reach.

It was now widely known that in man's distant past, a race known as the Saiph visited Earth and engineered human DNA, ensuring that humanity became the dominant species on the planet. Seemingly unstoppable, the Saiph had also incorporated some of their own DNA into humans.

The Saiph database, found during initial explorations, listed other worlds where the Saiph had interfered in the natural order of things to ensure that a specific species, carrying Saiph DNA, became the dominant species. Out there, on eleven of these worlds, species carrying DNA similar to that of humans, cousins if you like, were going about their daily business. However, it was another piece of gleaned information that really caused concern amongst the politicians and military alike; the Saiph had been at war with a race they identified as "the Others" and they were losing.

President Coston had gone before the citizens of the Terran Republic with a historic announcement. She explained in detail the impact of Saiph engineering on human development; the existence of the Others and the threat they might pose to an Earth with limited defense forces.

No one predicted the public reaction.

Instead of ensuing panic, millions of men and women stepped forward to serve their planet and defend it. Therefore, in the largest military build-up in human history, the Terran Defense Force grew from little more than a coastguard to a true force to be reckoned with, just in a few short years. The First Battle of Garunda tested the mettle of the fledgling TDF and it wasn't found wanting. It earned humanity its first allies in the battle against the Others. The Persai revealed themselves after more than a century in hiding and, seeing an opportunity for an alliance against the Others, they shared their technology. Many were wary of this new race and felt threatened by their technological superiority, but a single event changed this. The massacre on Delta Pavonis. The murder of 264 scientists was the turning point in race relations. The Commonwealth Union of Planets was born, not only a military alliance but also a political one. The distant cousins were now united under one banner to face the Others and ensure their own survival and a joint future.

A small chime interrupted Keyton's reverie as the door to the briefing room slid open. A sleek, deep-ebony, furred figure entered; Force Leader Tolas, the Persai representative on the Combined Joint Chiefs. His almost eight feet of height only served to emphasize the small stature of Razna Holan, the Garundan admiral, who was barely five-foot-four. His light green, scaled skin and the constantly moving yellow-brown eyes could not have been more contrasting to the towering Persai and his distinctly canine features. Their animated conversation halted as they noticed the seated Keyton waiting for them.

Keyton wrinkled his forehead in a frown as he stood to greet his fellows, he worried that the heated discussion did not bode well for the meeting to order the joint Commonwealth forces into their first offensive operation.

"I gather by your... tête-à-tête, that we have no agreement as yet?"

Razna's head fell back in an open-mouthed silent laugh, characteristic of his people. "On the contrary, Keyton. Tolas and I are in total agreement. You are perfectly correct there are, at present, only two points of contact between the forces of the Others and Commonwealth forces. Admiral Radford's plan to locate the enemy base from which the harassing raids on Garundan space are being carried out is perfectly sound but, and I think we all agree on this point, it may take some time for his plan to come to fruition." Keyton and Tolas remained silent; they knew this was true. "The problem I see is one that's confronted us since the beginning of time. We must wrestle the initiative from the enemy. We must dictate to him how the conflict progresses. He must not dictate to us. We don't know the extent of space controlled by the Others or the resources they can bring to the conflict." Razna's voice rose an octave as he voiced his concerns. "We must know these things so we can devise a winning strategy or the war could drag on for years."

"I agree," growled Tolas, "if we cannot identify the enemy's star systems we will stumble in the dark and hope to bump into them. I'm concerned the Others haven't attempted another assault on Garunda. I fear they're amassing forces and will attack in overwhelming numbers."

Keyton tapped a request into his PAD; the holo cube above the table burst into life as it brilliantly displayed the current force levels of Third Fleet. "OK, let's take a look at what we've got." Keyton pointed at the 3D image display. "Third Fleet has received its first Bismarck battleships and has priority on munitions and repair facilities. The Viper weapons platforms and Sherlock detection platforms surrounding Garunda are now up to scratch and are comparable to those protecting Earth. Ground-based Planetary Defense Centers are coming on-line at a rate of one a month and with their grazers and HVMs I am confident that Garunda could repel any attack."

"And Razna, remember your Baasa guided missile destroyers are equivalent to the human Agis class and add another layer of defense against missile threats" added Tolas.

Razna nodded in agreement. Pars and Garunda had similar skill shortages. Pars had implemented population control and compensated their workforce with technology; Garunda simply did not have skilled crewmembers and were unable to provide crews for larger-sized vessels such as cruisers. The Persai stepped in and offered them ship designs that relied heavily on computer control, much more so than any human ship, but it allowed the Garundans to crew more ships with less crew. Built for small crews and designed for specific needs, the Baasa-guided missile destroyers were perfect for the new Garundan naval academy graduates.

Keyton cleared his throat. "Gentlemen if I may, I'd like to focus on the point of today's meeting. So... Do we agree that Garunda is as secure as we can make it?"

"Agreed."

"Agreed," Razna nodded a little reluctantly.

"And we agree that Pars, Earth, Janus and Alona have seen no evidence of any enemy activity?" Keyton's compatriots nodded their agreement.

Keyton let out a small, apprehensive breath. "That leaves us 70 Ophiuchi..." Another touch of his PAD and the order of battle of the Third Fleet in the holo cube disappeared, replaced with an image of a small, yellowish world orbiting 70 Ophiuchi some 16.59 light years from Earth. "For the past three weeks, Persai ships have been, under stealth, probing the system for any sign of enemy activity." In the display, five small red icons appeared in a loose circle around a larger icon. "Tolas, if you please." Keyton handed over the talk.

"From our analysis, I'm confident the five smaller returns are a single Goshawk anti-missile ship and three Buzzard class battleships. The fifth ship is a bit of a mystery, we haven't seen its type before, and although it's larger than both the Goshawk and Buzzards, it has a lower energy signature. The analysts believe it's a cargo ship of some description and I have no reason to disagree."

"That would certainly fit the data as I read it," commented Razna.

Keyton, seeing the same data, also agreed. "What of the other ship? The one the Others are spread around."

"Ah…" Tolas touched a control on his PAD, the image of the central icon magnified until it filled the holo cube.

Keyton allowed his eyes to absorb the image for a moment. It was a very impressive, if not completed, orbital structure. It looked like a giant starfish. There were five legs joined by a central hub. Beside the image was a small chart of dimensions showing the true scale of the build. The central hub was nearly one kilometer in diameter and each of the legs extended out another 900 meters. Keyton could actually make out small groups of workers on the outer skin, looking like ants.

"That, I think we can all agree, is a starship repair facility. It may incorporate a fleet base and we think it's eighty-five percent complete. Comparing the build progress over the past three weeks, we predict its completion within fifty to ninety days. When does it become operational? Well… your guess is as good as mine… but if I were in charge, I'd want it operational immediately after completion."

A fifty-to-ninety day window before the base may be operational. Keyton gave a silent whistle.

"What about the enemy base on the surface?" Razna queried.

Tolas worked his PAD and the image of the space station shrunk until it was only a point in space hovering over a now rotating planet. As they watched, a small, blinking red icon came into view by the planetary rotation. The rotation took the blinking icon directly beneath the fixed space station until it disappeared out of view.

"The Others have built the space station so that the surface base passes directly below it once every planetary day. Approximately every twenty-six hours."

"Have the Persai ships observed any weapons platforms in orbit?"

Tolas shook his head. "None have been observed but," he snorted, "that doesn't mean there aren't any."

Keyton pushed himself up from his chair and paced slowly around the table, deep in thought. The Others could have an operational fleet base in the next two to three months. God only knew how many ships they would base there. So... five enemy ships in orbit, one of which is a cargo ship; no orbiting weapons platforms, we think, and a surface base with a short time window for attack in a twenty-six hour timeframe... mmm... He continued his pacing for a few more seconds before coming to a decision; he stopped and turned to face Razna and Tolas.

"We must consider an assault on the space station before it becomes operational. If the assault is successful, we must follow it with a ground assault on the surface base. Our objective must be to secure any intelligence it contains. Time is short. If the analysts believe the fleet base could be completed within as little as fifty days, we must strike before then."

Tolas and Razna both knew the risks such an attack entailed, but neither could come up with a valid argument as to why it shouldn't be launched.

Razna sat up a little straighter in his seat and his face was set. "I agree. Tolas?"

The Persai used one elongated finger to scratch behind his left ear as he considered his answer. He could see no other way to gain the initiative from the Others. He considered the risks of achieving the destruction of what was obviously going to be a major fleet base, its supporting surface facilities and the potential bonus of gleaning intelligence from the facilities computer core against the odds of success. He came to a conclusion, slapping his hand hard on the table, he said, "Very well. Attack we must."

Keyton tapped his wrist comm and a disembodied, heavily accented voice answered his summons.

"Communications. Commander Petrovic."

"Commander. Signal the *Dark Horse* and the *Chromite*. My compliments to Admiral Ricco and Brigadier General Pak and request that they report to Central Command at their earliest convenience."

#

CARSON CITY - EARTH – SOL SYSTEM

Commander Bryer Anderson approached his office on the eighty fourth and second from top floor of the Naval Intelligence Service Headquarters in Carson City with crisp steps. Anderson's starched blue uniform with its three gold cuff rings crowned by a gold five-pointed star gleamed. His non-regulation tailored uniform managed to conceal the small paunch that seemed to expand annually. His gold name tag, exactly level with his lapel, announced his name to all. Unusually for an officer in a time of war, even one involved in intelligence, Anderson failed to display any awards or citations related to combat operations. For some unexplained reason, Bryer Anderson had never found himself attached to a unit that was about to go into

69

combat. He'd managed to call in a few favors and had been appointed as Fleet Intelligence Officer for Third Fleet where he'd quickly cleaned house of all those who didn't toe the party line. Free thinking by your underlings was only something that got department heads into trouble and he had stepped on it with a vengeance. Junior officers needed a strong, hands-on approach and after only a short time with Third Fleet, where he caught the eye of Admiral Radford, he was rewarded with a move to headquarters and placed in charge of a newly founded department of Special Projects Research, which forwarded all its reports directly to the office of the CNI. Of course Anderson ensured that every report came through him first, making whatever amendments he deemed necessary before copying the report upstairs with his signature as the author. After all, he did have to rewrite the majority of the reports, so it was mostly his work and he deserved the credit.

The top floor of the building was reserved solely for those working directly for Admiral Aleksandr Vadis, Chief of Naval Intelligence. The one underneath was reserved for heads of the major departments, but after repeated calls to the commander responsible for allocating office space it had taken the promise of a crate of expensive bourbon and dinner at one of the city's most exclusive restaurants to secure Anderson an office suite. It wasn't a corner office, but it would do.

On entering his outer office, it took him a moment to realize that CPO Mundy was missing from her desk. Where was that infernal woman? She knew that today was dry-cleaning day and he had a golf date with Senator Mackenzie this afternoon. Scowling, he walked through the open door into his office, never stopping to wonder why the inner office door was open. The sight of someone perched on the corner of his mahogany, hand-polished desk, enjoying the view, brought him to a halt. The interloper was dressed in the uniform of the day, standard khaki. Probably some secretary who had come to deliver hard-copy material and couldn't resist seeing how her betters were rightfully treated. How dare she enter his office without his permission? Anderson's face flushed with rage. *That lazy bitch Mundy will find herself counting paper clips for the rest of her naval career for not being at her post,* Bryer promised himself.

"Who the hell are you and what are you doing in my office?"

Without turning, a soft female voice answered him. "Perhaps, Commander you should know to whom you're speaking before using profanity to a senior officer."

As the woman turned to face him, the single silver star of a rear admiral glinted on her collar.

Anderson sprang to attention. "Apologies, Admiral. I didn't recognize you, Admiral...?"

"Wilson."

Anderson felt his chest tighten. Admiral Wilson worked directly for the Chairman of the Joint Chiefs and she cut a swathe through officers of not only the navy but of every armed service in her quest for efficiency and an end to corruption at all levels.

"My secretary failed to notify me we had a meeting this morning. I shall be sure to suitably rebuke her for this oversight. Again, please accept my apologies."

Elizabeth Wilson regarded the overweight commander with eyes that would have bored holes in the toughest battle armor. "It would appear, Commander, that you are incorrectly dressed. I believe you should be in standard khaki, unless there's a reason why you're wearing dress blues?"

Anderson managed a spluttered reply. "I... I... I have an important meeting with Senator Mackenzie this afternoon and instead of going home to get changed, I came to work ready." Anderson fixed his most ingratiating smile on his ruddy face. A trickle of sweat ran down the side of his face. He fought the urge to wipe it off. Wilson still hadn't released him from the position of attention. *The bitch is enjoying showing me who's boss*, thought Anderson.

If at all possible, Wilson's eyes hardened even more. "Is that so, Commander? So would you say you're aware of everything that goes on in your department?"

Anderson's sense of self-preservation had never let him down and now it was sounding alarm bells in his head. "I assure you, Admiral, that I personally vet any and all material before it leaves this department."

"Do you? And does your management style also include suppressing information that could prove vital to our understanding of the war?"

His mind raced. Suppress information? What the hell was she getting at? Then the penny dropped. Wilson. Wilson! Surely she couldn't be related to that awkward ensign? The one who'd bombarded him with fanciful tales about how the Others should've crushed the Commonwealth by now and that somehow the combined intelligence apparatus of the Union had failed to ask the right questions, whereas he, a lowly ensign, had asked the right ones. It had taken a direct order from Anderson and the threat of disciplinary action to shut him up. So he'd gone to a powerful relation, none other than the chairman's hatchet woman, with his lunacy and she had, of course, rushed to his defense. Nepotism at its worst.

"I'm sure in your time, Admiral, you've come across junior officers who've been… let's say, over-enthusiastic about an idea and it's taken a more experienced hand to guide them in the right direction."

Wilson couldn't believe what she was hearing. The basis of good intelligence was to collect all available information and then follow it to its ultimate conclusion for better or worse, not just to tailor it to what you thought your superiors wanted to hear. Generals directing a war needed to know all the facts or mistakes were made. And mistakes in war meant dead seamen, soldiers, and marines. For the first time in her life, Elizabeth Wilson felt something snap inside her.

It was at that instant that Bryer Anderson realized he just might have created the end of his naval career. Wilson's steely stare had been replaced with one that he misinterpreted as one of triumph. *The bitch is going to crucify me to save the skin of her pathetic ensign.*

His face recoiled in horror as Elizabeth closed the distance between them. So close that he could feel the spittle hit his face as she said the words that rang his career's death knell:

"Consider yourself beached, Commander Anderson, with immediate effect. The Judge Advocate General's office will prepare papers for dereliction of duty, conspiracy to suppress vital information in time of war and anything else that I can think of. Now get out of my sight before I help you from the building via your office window!"

Anderson staggered backwards under her verbal assault and as she finished he virtually fled the office. CPO Mundy was sitting at her desk as he went past. A large smile on her face. *Laugh all you want, Mundy, but I'll wipe that smile off your face. I don't forget an enemy. I have friends and Senator Mackenzie is just one of them. My father hasn't built a shipping empire without making some connections and I'm not afraid to call in a few of his favors.*

CHAPTER SIX

ADVANCE

EARTH ORBIT - SOL SYSTEM

The flag bridge of the TDF *Furious* hummed with subdued activity. Rear Admiral Analisa Chavez felt apprehension welling in her as she cast a furtive glance at the countdown clock on the far wall. Ten minutes to zero hour. Analisa forced herself to relax. The last five weeks had passed in a blur of planning sessions and operations orders. Her staff had worked like demons to bring BatFor 5.1 up to full combat readiness. The ships under her command had exercised as single units, then progressed through squadron maneuvers till they could work within their respective battle force or be chopped to Admiral Ricco's BatFor 5.2 with no loss of command and control. Analisa had thought that the move to the command of one of Fifth Fleet's battle forces was a snub after having commanded a battle force, in what many regarded, as the fighting fleet but as zero hour approached and she was about to take part in her, and the Commonwealth's, first offensive operation, she had to admit that she wouldn't want to be anywhere else.

A blinking light in her tactical holo cube caught her eye and she recognized it as belonging to her personal link to Admiral Ricco on his ship, TDF *Dark Horse*. Pressing a stud on her chair's armrest, she accepted the call. The slightly chubby, gray-bearded face of Stephano Ricco filled one quarter of the holo cube. Stephano had been one of the many retired officers who had been reactivated under the program conceived and run by the then-Admiral Olaf Helsett before his promotion to Secretary of Defense. Maybe it was because Stephano appeared older than his actual years that he always reminded Analisa of her grandfather. It wasn't a physical resemblance, far from it. Analisa was of old Mexican stock, her skin tone was a warm golden brown and her features were soft and smooth, whereas Stephano Ricco was unmistakably Italian. The high forehead and prominent hooked nose wouldn't be out of place on an ancient Roman coin. But no matter, his soft tones and warm smile exuded confidence and right now, Analisa was glad to share in it. The depth of experience he brought as commander of Operation Lightning Strike was something they all felt was the reason they were ready within the timescale the Combined Chiefs had set. Operation Lighting Strike. Analisa wondered again who had thought that name up.

"So Analisa, are we ready?"

With a quick scan of her tactical repeater, she gave him her most dazzling of smiles. "Ready in all respects, Admiral."

Stephano's face settled into the sort of look that an elderly uncle would give his wayward niece. "How many times do I have to remind you, Analisa, that in private I'd really prefer you to call me Stephano?"

Analisa pursed her lips and gave a small shrug. "I'm sorry, Admiral it just seems... disrespectful."

Stephano wagged a large forefinger at her. "Well Analisa, I'll make a deal with you. When we get back from this I'll take you to my house on the slopes of the

Apennine Mountains and get my wife to make you some of her famous Fettuccine Alfredo. But on one condition..." Stephano's finger pointed directly at her as if it rode a laser beam. "You call me Stephano from now on."

Analisa had to use her hand to mask her laugh. "It's a deal Admiral... Stephano."

A short klaxon sounded throughout the *Furious,* warning all hands that the move to fold space was imminent. There must have been a similar sound aboard the *Dark Horse* as Stephano glanced away for a moment before returning his attention to Analisa.

"Time to go, Analisa. Good luck."

"Good luck to you too, Stephano."

#

TDF *CHROMITE* - EARTH ORBIT – SOL SYSTEM

Brigadier General Dong Pak watched BatFor 5.1 and 5.2 disappear into fold space from his seat in the Operations Room aboard the TDF *Chromite* and sent a small prayer to his ancestors to keep the crews safe as they went into harm's way. Pak commanded the First Marine Expeditionary Brigade that was the ground element of Operation Lightning Strike.

He was responsible for the 14,500 marines and sailors dispersed into a Command Element (CE) incorporating his communications, intelligence, military police, naval gunfire support, and force reconnaissance units. Then came the Ground Combat Element (GCE) of three reinforced infantry battalions complete with integral armor, anti-air, artillery, and support elements. The Aviation Combat Element (ACE) was his primary means of getting from orbit onto the surface of a planet with their thirty-five Reapers for close support. Seventy Buffalos to ferry his troops and thirty-five Gigants were needed to move their heavy equipment. Last but not least, his Logistics Combat Element (LCE), heavy engineering, medical, transport, and the thousand and one other things needed to keep a force the size of the First MEB operating. And just to add a little more complexity to it all the entire force was spread over seven Excalibur class assault ships. One may as well have been trying to herd a swarm of bees as try to bring all the different elements of his command together, but with a marine's stoic endurance, he'd cajoled and sometimes downright threatened some with physical violence to get his command ready for this operation in the limited time available. And they had done it.

Pak initiated a link and in his holo cube the faces of his battalion commanders and the commander of the ACE and LCE appeared.

"Marines. The naval big guns have departed for 70 Ophiuchi and if things go according to plan and Murphy keeps his nose out, I fully expect to give the order for First Marine to fold in around one hour's time. Colonel Mills."

In the holo cube, the still features of Colonel Karen Mills looked steadily back at him through ice-blue eyes.

"By the time we arrive in orbit, I want the marines of the first drop loaded in the shuttles and ready to go. The first drop will be going in blind but you'll have every Reaper on call to support you. When initial contact with the enemy is made, the navy will move ships into position to support you with gunfire. You just keep calling the targets and the navy will hit them from orbit with kinetic energy weapons. It's imperative that you prioritize air defense sites. You and your marines will approach on the surface, but I intend to drop the follow-on waves right onto the enemy's heads."

Pak took one more look at his commanders. "OK. Let's get this thing done. Colonel Mills, if you could remain a moment."

As the link to the other marines was terminated, Pak allowed a small frown to furrow his brow. "Sorry to give you the job of first through the door Karen, but you're the most experienced battalion commander I have and your fitness reports put the others in the shade. R-and-D promised us something special to give us a closer look at the base before you arrived, but the tech weenies failed to produce so what's waiting for you? I have no idea. I need marines I can rely on to get down and force the door for the rest of us."

Karen Mills said nothing for a heartbeat then a brilliant white smile split her face. "Force the door, sir? I intend to kick it in around their ears before they know I'm there and then kick their ass up around their ears too!"

Karen's smile was infectious and Pak felt the muscles either side of his mouth twitch. Shaking his head slowly, he regarded the still smiling Karen. "Semper Fi Colonel."

"Oo-rah sir."

Pak terminated the link.

#

70 OPHIUCHI - 16.59 LIGHT YEARS FROM EARTH

TDF *Furious* rocked as another multi-megaton warhead exploded a few tens of kilometers off the port bow. The restraints of Analisa's seat held her in place and she rode the bucking battleship as smoothly as any rodeo rider. Her tactical repeater showed another swarm of enemy missiles closing on BatFor 5.2 and the list of damaged ships continued to grow.

"How are those repairs coming on?"

"Damage control reports that the control lines to the forward laser turrets are completely fried. Estimated time before they have a working bypass is eleven minutes, Admiral."

Eleven minutes. Crap! BatFor 5.2 would be lucky to make it another five minutes, never mind eleven. "Order the Agis destroyers to screen…" Analisa briefly checked the tactical repeater again. "One-eight-seven mark twenty-four. That should put them between us and Force Alfa. How long before we get good targeting locks on Force Bravo?"

"Admiral Ricco has ordered the *Lissa* to fold to within 250,000 kilometers of the space station and supply targeting data. Our missiles are in the tubes and ready to fire on receipt of the targeting package."

The icon for the Vulcan class heavy cruiser *Port Huron* began blinking an attention-grabbing red in the holo cube before winking out of existence. Analisa gripped the arms of her seat and cursed the god Murphy. BatFor 5.1 and 5.2 had dropped out of fold space less than one million kilometers from the enemy space station, and its group of accompanying ships, in orbit around 70 Ophiuchi. Designated Force Alfa. Admiral Ricco's plan had been to hold the fleet outside the reach of the enemy's missile and energy weapons envelopes and bombard them with Gravity Drive (GD) missiles. Unfortunately, Murphy interfered. As the human ships exited fold space they found that an enemy battle group of three Buzzard class battleships and a single Goshawk anti-missile ship, were virtually directly behind them at a range of only 360,000 kilometers. There'd only been time for the light cruiser TDF *Yakaze* to get a single, pitiful warning off before she was reduced to atoms by the impact of multiple nuclear-tipped missiles. Every threat receiver in the fleet had begun screaming for attention. Three more human ships had taken damage to their drive systems before they were able to maneuver sufficiently for their main armament to come into play and lash the enemy with missile and grazer fire.

Any element of surprise evaporated with the first missile launch from this unexpected group of enemy ships, Force Bravo. Analisa's brain went into overdrive as she forced herself to examine the radically changed situation while the battle raged on around her. The damaged ships couldn't reenter fold space and escape, consequently, the fleet didn't have the option of abandoning the operation and returning home with its proverbial tail between its legs. Destroying the space station was still the priority.

The fleet now faced twice as many enemy ships as was expected but the balance of force still remained with them, despite their casualties. Coldly and clinically, she put her plan together and forwarded it to Stephano for approval. Stephano never got it.

A cry from tactical and Analisa's head snapped back to the tactical holo cube in time to see the *Dark Horse*, Stephano Ricco, and its crew of 950 men and women die as the combined fire of the three Buzzards blew through her battle armor. The *Dark Horse* and her crew became nothing more than expanding plasma. Analisa inherited command of the embattled human fleet.

"Communications. Resend my amended ops plan to the fleet and tell me when all ships have acknowledged. Has the *Lissa* folded?"

Hands flew over controls as Analisa's orders were transmitted to the fleet.

"*Lissa* is away and fleet acknowledges your orders. All ships report ready to maneuver on your command. Agis destroyers moving to screen our casualties but the rate of enemy fire is swamping their command and control."

Analisa cleared all emotion from her voice. People were going to die following her but it was a price that had to be paid. "Fleet order. Execute! Execute!"

The professionalism that five weeks of regimented training drilled into the fleet now paid dividends. As one, BatFor 5.1 and 5.2 swung about unmasking the evil-looking snouts of their main grazers. Fire control computers blinked from red to green. On five battle ships, eighteen heavy cruisers, and twenty-one light cruisers fingers pressed down on firing studs. The vengeance of the fleet descended on their enemy in the form of grazer and plasma fire. Armor resisted the initial onslaught but soon crumpled under its irresistible weight. Force Bravo ceased to exist, except as pieces of wreckage spinning off into the depths of the universe.

The flag bridge seemed deathly still as people took stock of the sudden and violent struggle that had almost overwhelmed them. Analisa took a deep breath and mentally shook herself. Their mission was incomplete.

"Tactical. Have we received the targeting data from *Lissa*?"

"The targeting package is uploading from the drone now. All targets are verified and *Lissa* is standing by to send any required corrections on GD missile emergence from fold space."

A bared-teeth, carnivorous smile spread across Analisa's face. "Push the package to the fleet and fire when ready."

"Aye-aye, ma'am… fleet acknowledges receipt of the targeting package… missiles away." 875 nuclear tipped, gravity drive missiles left their launch tubes and accelerated away, entering fold space a few seconds later only to reenter normal space a fraction of a second later, where they received some minor course corrections from the waiting *Lissa* before reentering fold space and almost immediately returning to normal space less than ten kilometers from their intended targets.

Nothing made of blood and bone could react in time to fire on the speeding missiles but the onboard computers of the hovering enemy ships and the space station tried. Laser emplacements were still swiveling to face the threat when the first missiles impacted their targets, ripping them to pieces.

Analisa leaned closer into her holo cube, as if she could will the missiles onto their targets. Without taking her eyes from the display, she called out to her tactical officer. "Ready a second strike and launch when ready. I want those ships and that space station to be nothing but cosmic dust."

Anticipating such an order, crews throughout the fleet had rushed to reload the launch tubes after the first barrage of missiles. The second wave was already in the tubes when they received the order to reload.

"Fleet reports ready... missiles away."

The *Lissa* was a quarter of a million kilometers from the target area but still her crew were forced to dim the viewers, their sensors went off-line momentarily, as the space around the Others' one-time massive orbital construction, and its protective starships, became a scene from hell's own cauldron. Tens, then hundreds, then thousands of nuclear detonations brought the heat of a star's core down on them. When, once again, *Lissa's* sensor suites came back online, there was no trace of the enemy ships or the orbiting base that was to have been their new home.

On the *Furious,* Analisa turned to her waiting bridge crew as she felt the cold anger slowly release her from its vengeful grip. "Communications! Launch a courier drone and inform Brigadier Pak that he may enter 70 Ophiuchi space unopposed and begin his assault as planned."

#

SURFACE OF 70 OPHIUCHI

The constant bouncing of the assault shuttle, as its terrain following radar maintained it at just ten meters off 70 Ophiuchi's surface at a touch below Mach one shook the fillings in the teeth of Karen Mills. Whatever you wanted to call it, Karen just hoped that the pilots were not totally relying on the computers to fly this bucket of bolts. The idea of running into the ground, or into any of the rocky outcroppings that flashed past the speeding Buffalo, really wouldn't make her day.

"One minute to the Landing Zone, Colonel. Reapers have completed a fly past. There are no signs of enemy activity," called her pilot.

Well, it looks like we got in clean! Thought Karen. The LZ was located some 20 kilometers from the Others' base. Distant enough that it should be over the radar horizon, limiting the chances of the enemy detecting the approaching shuttles whose map-of-the-earth flying would have kept them hidden amongst the ground clutter. It didn't appear that the enemy had deployed any form of over-the-horizon radar, at least none that the Reapers sniffed out.

A deep bass tone sounded in Karen's helmet. Thirty-second warning, she thought, arrival at the LZ was imminent. She stood and turned to face the front of the shuttle as the Load Master activated a switch opening the troop doors on either side of the shuttle. Karen got a brief glimpse of sandy-colored terrain flashing by before the view disappeared in a cloud of dust as the pilots braked sharply. With a noticeable bounce, the Buffalo was down.

"Go! Go! Go!" The screaming of the Load Master in her ear was all the incentive needed as she and the other twenty marines piled out through the troop doors. Karen ran ten paces then went down on one knee, rifle up and scanned for targets. Behind her the Buffalo's engines screamed as it dragged itself back into the air, the pilots pivoted it ninety degrees in place and applied the power clearing the LZ for the Gigants, which were only sixty seconds behind.

Satisfied that nothing was about to pop out of the ground and take a shot at her, Karen lowered her rifle slightly and took a quick look around. The LZ swarmed with the marines of the 24th Marine Battalion. Officers and NCOs ran around urging the marines into firing positions. A small blinking blue diamond in the heads-up display of her Wraith combat suit showed the location of the follow-on wave of Gigant heavy lift shuttles, carrying her heavy weapons as they followed the same route in that the Buffalos had used. Each Gigant had its own dedicated Reaper as escort. Once the Gigant delivered its payload, its Reaper escort would peel off and join the flights of other Reapers providing top cover for the marines.

Just then, a flight of three Reapers flew low over the landing zone, their thin bodies, swept wings, and double rear-vertical stabilizers were a reassuring sight. But not as much as the HVMs that hung under each wing or the snouts of rapid-fire plasma cannon that ran along the side of the pilots' canopy.

Karen continued to scan the landing zone with a professional eye as the double tone of an incoming call sounded in her helmet. "Go for Mills."

"Colonel." It was Major Louis Mesnard, her Executive Officer. "The company commanders tell me that each company is down intact and have taken up defensive positions around the LZ awaiting the Gigants."

"OK, let's get the scouts out and troops loaded up on the Kangas when they arrive. Scorpions are to take flanking positions and I want the Rattlers ready to give supporting fire at the drop of a hat."

"Roger that. What about the navy?"

"General Pak has assured me they'll be there if we need them."

Louis let out a small chuckle. "Marines lead the way."

The arrival of the first Gigant cut short any reply. As the Gigant swept in, its rear clamshell cargo bay doors were already opening. The Gigant had barely come to a stop as the first of the Kanga Armored Fighting Vehicles disembarked. The lethal-looking rapid-fire plasma cannon, mounted in the small turret, was searching for targets as the driver steadied it on its hover motors before heading in the direction of Alfa Company. Each Kanga could hold a complete section of Wraith-suited marines and its armor was resistant to small-arms fire and some heavier lasers. Its rapid-fire plasma cannon meant that it could deliver its marine cargo right on top of a well-defended enemy position while providing its own fire support. As Karen looked on, a second, then a third Kanga exited from the Gigant and made their way over to Alfa Company. Another Gigant began to disgorge the scouts Scorpion Armored Reconnaissance Vehicles. Smaller than the Kangas, the Scorpion was designed to observe rather than fight. The Scorpion carried a varied sensor package, which would allow her scouts to hopefully spot the enemy well before they located Karen's marines. To aid them in that task, each Scorpion incorporated a Chameleon unit. A bigger version of the same technology used in the Wraith combat suits the Chameleon unit was designed to avoid electronic and optical devices allowing the Scorpions to approach extremely close to an enemy position without detection.

The last of the Gigants touched down and Karen's heaviest firepower arrived: The Rattler Main Battle Tank. The Rattler was so massive that even the giant Gigant could only carry one per trip, but Karen was willing to accept the payoff between bringing more, lighter equipment versus one piece of heavier hardware. The Rattler carried a five- centimeter grazer that could blow a hole in anything that got within range. Added to that was a pair of electromagnetic rail guns mounted on either side of the heavily armored turret. Each rail gun could send a stream of two tungsten alloy rounds towards a target at Mach 7. With a 360-degree arc of fire, any airborne or surface threat would meet a very rapid end if it came into the sightline of a Rattler. Karen may only have two platoons of them, but six Rattlers should be enough for the job.

"How long till we're ready to move, Louis? We're an awfully big target just sitting here."

"The last Gigant flight is five minutes out, so say fifteen minutes till the last company is loaded up and rolling."

"Good work, Louis. I'm heading over to A Company if you would meet me there when the command Kanga is offloaded." Karen cut the link. Things were going smoothly so far, she just hoped they'd stay that way.

#

The inside of the command Kanga was cramped with Karen, Louis, the two signalers, and the bank of displays arrayed along one wall. Karen leaned forward and stared intently at the feed the Kanga was receiving from the Scorpions of the scout platoon. Louis sat silently beside her but she had worked with him long enough to know that he was thinking the same as she was... Damn those walls looked big!

"What do you think, Louis?"

"I'm thinking I should've listened to my mother and joined my father working on the vineyard."

Without turning from the displays, Karen gave Louis a friendly punch on his armored shoulder.

"And miss the opportunity to lead a charge against a fifty meter high wall topped by laser turrets. Hah! If only she knew the fun you were about to have."

Louis gave the grinning colonel a side-long glance as a small grin broke his own studied features. "Yeah, imagine! So – we go with a full-frontal then?"

The moment of levity passed as Karen's face hardened once more. "I honestly don't see another option, Louis. The scouts are telling us that the Others have cleared an area around the base out as far as a kilometer. The minute we leave these canyons they'll pick us up on any surveillance radar they have. We have eyes on those laser turrets that are spaced every 200 meters along the perimeter wall, God only knows what else they have that they can throw at us." Not for the first time that day, Karen cursed the tech weenies who had promised but failed to deliver surveillance equipment with genuine stealth properties that could have given her a better look beyond those imposing walls of the Others' base.

Louis wrung his armored hands. "I don't like it, but you're right."

"Decision made then. As soon as the shooting starts I want the Dragonfly surveillance drones up. We need to know ASAP where their heavy weapons and anti-air sites are." Karen highlighted a point on the wall directly

88

below one of the laser turrets. "The Rattlers will concentrate their fire at this point. I want them to punch a hole big enough to get a battleship through, then move their fire east and west and expand the breach. Reapers are to engage the remaining laser turrets moving outward from that point or any targets of opportunity. As soon as the Rattlers take the wall under fire, the Kangas will race for the wall. Troops will remain mounted until the last possible moment. Alfa Company will take point with Bravo and Charlie taking up flanking positions. I want you to remain here with Delta as my ready reserve. Whistle up the Naval Gunfire Support Team, I'll take them with me."

Karen reached for her helmet, but a hand on her arm stopped her and she looked into the questioning eyes of Louis.

"And where will you be?"

Karen gave him the same smile that she had bestowed on General Pak. "With Alfa Company, of course. Now stop being such an old woman!"

Karen punched the control that released the rear hatch of the Kanga, she bent low and sealed her helmet before exiting the AFV and setting off at a steady jog toward Alfa Company.

#

"Advance!" That single word of command brought six Rattler Main Battle Tanks over the lip of the canyon in line. As soon as each Rattler's five centimeter grazer cleared the canyon, they began to fire on the designated point on the wall surrounding the Others' base. Each grazer had an output of three terawatts, when all six Rattlers fired on the same point not even spaceship battle armor could withstand the impact. With the sound of rolling thunder, a ten meter section of the wall blew inward, bringing the laser turret mounted above it crashing down.

The Kangas of Alfa Company raced forward at their top speed of 120 kilometers per hour, firing their plasma cannon at the remaining laser turrets as they went. Bravo and Charlie Company spread out to the flanks, taking more laser turrets under fire as the Rattlers settled into a steady barrage, gradually increasing the size of the breach in the defensive wall.

In increasing volume, the marines began taking return fire from the enemy positions atop the wall. The plasma cannon of the Kangas was simply not powerful enough to penetrate the laser turret's armor. A flight of Reapers screamed in low over the battlefield and HVMs streaked away from under their wings. A fraction of a second later, three laser turrets exploded as the HVMs struck home. The Reapers switched to guns and their plasma cannon stitched the tops of the wall, killing anything that was in the open. As the Reapers pulled up, all three were suddenly swatted from the sky as if by a giant hand, pieces of wreckage falling onto the buildings beyond the wall.

Karen Mills, in the lead Alfa Company AFV, witnessed the destruction of the Reapers as she sped toward the breach in the wall. She brought up the feed from the scout's Scorpions. The Scorpions' sophisticated detection systems quickly triangulated the source of the fire that had brought down the Reapers. From the data it looked like a heavy laser area denial system – similar to that used by the navy to stop incoming missiles. Karen opened a link to the Naval Gunfire Support Team who was traveling in one of the other Alfa Company Kangas.

"I'm sending you a set of coordinates and I want you to put metal down on it ASAP." Without waiting for a reply she cut the link and initiated another to Louis in the command carrier. "Louis, are the Dragonflies up yet?"

"You should be getting something in a few seconds. I've prioritized the area from which that anti-air came from to see if we can identify whether it's a fixed position or mobile. If they have one site, I have no doubt they have others."

"Good thinking, Louis, the navy should be targeting the source of the laser fire now…"

With a bright flash of light and a thunderclap, something, moving faster than the human eye could follow, slammed into the area from which the laser had fired with seemingly pinpoint precision. Debris rose far into the air and coalesced into a large mushroom cloud. But this was no nuclear strike.

As soon as the marines had begun their assault, the battleship TDF *Bloodhound* moved into low orbit above the Others' base. When the call for naval gunfire support came, the *Bloodhound* launched a Kinetic Energy Missile or KEM. The KEM was a six meter long missile made of tungsten alloy. Each KEM was, basically, a long pole of metal with a small guidance computer in its tail section and a powerful chemical rocket motor that accelerated the missile to a speed of 11,000 meters per second. The impact of a KEM on target is the equivalent of 120 tons of TNT.

The site of the laser defense system was now just a large, smoking crater.

Karen's Kanga reached the breach and slowed to a halt, plasma cannon firing at enemy soldiers beyond the wall. A second Kanga began to climb over the rubble of what had once been a fifty meter high wall. As it reached the top of the pile, it exposed its underside:

from within the base a high-intensity laser stabbed out, striking the Kanga's vulnerable belly, cutting through it like a hot knife through butter and lancing into the interior troop bay. The Kanga's turret blew off as the laser exploded through the vehicle. The rear troop doors burst open and badly injured marines piled out; only to be cut down by withering enemy fire as they desperately sought cover.

"Everybody out! We need to clear those buildings or the attack will stall!" Karen shouted over her link. She followed the last of the marines out and bounded over the rubble, keeping low to avoid enemy fire as the marines clambered over the mass of broken concrete and steel. As Karen reached the top of the rubble pile, she showed no hesitation, she carried her momentum forward and fired at enemy soldiers as they appeared at windows and doorways.

The marines of Alfa Company began the long and arduous task of clearing one building at a time. They were soon joined by their fellow marines of Bravo and Charlie Companies. Slowly and surely they pushed the enemy out of their positions. As they pushed deeper into the base, Louis Mesnard kept a steady rain of KEMs falling as he used the Dragonflies to identify more of the laser aerial defense sites and any enemy strong points.

Sheltering in a doorway, Karen took time to assess the situation. Her whole battalion was now invested within the enemy base. They had formed a good strong pocket that she felt she could hold for the time being. Louis assured her that the KEMs had taken out the enemy anti-air sites and the marines had control of the skies above the base. OK! Time to get some reinforcements down here and finish the job! Karen activated her link to Louis.

"Go for Mesnard."

"Louis. Contact General Pak, inform him that I'm satisfied we have a sufficiently secure area for him to begin his drop. I'd recommend…" Karen caught movement out of the corner of her eye and as she turned she saw an enemy soldier lob a small metal can toward her. Instinctively, she spun away, seeking the cover of the wall as she fired two shots from the hip and caught the enemy in the chest. The plasma grenade exploded just short of the doorway where Karen had been standing a moment earlier.

The green blue plasma boiled out of the doorway, catching Karen's lower left leg. She screamed in pain. 10,000 degree heat melted her Wraith armor and burned her flesh and bone.

The Wraith suit's onboard computer reacted instantly; sealing off her lower limb and pumping a massive amount of pain suppressors into her system. Thankfully, Karen was unconscious before she hit the ground. The onboard computer quickly assessed Karen's injuries, calculating that the suit alone could not deal with them. It initiated a distress beacon on the medical channel, calling for immediate medevac.

Louis saw the beacon on his display. Shit! He cursed before assuming command of the battalion and ordering his AFV forward into the battle. An unconscious Karen was recovered by corpsmen who quickly placed her in an AFV headed for the Aid Station. Around her the battle raged on as two more battalions of marines dropped from orbit to join the fray. The marines' victory was only a matter of time now.

#

TDF *FURIOUS* - ORBITING OPHIUCHI 70

"White Spot! White Spot! I have multiple nuclear detonations on the planetary surface."

Analisa Chavez bolted from her seat and pushed the tactical officer to one side, running her eyes over his read-outs. As she scanned the instruments, the flare of another nuclear detonation registered on the display. The detonations were located in or around the enemy surface base. Everyone on the bridge knew the marines were not equipped with nuclear weapons.

"Communications, get me General Pak on the surface. I want to know what the hell is going on down there!"

Hands flew over controls as the lieutenant at communications raced to comply. After a few moments, she slowly moved her hands away from her console and turned to Analisa, her face deathly pale. "Admiral. I'm unable to raise General Pak or anybody on his staff. The links are a complete mess. The only response I'm getting is from the 24th Marines Aid Post who are reporting multiple nuclear detonations from the direction of the Others' base and that they are receiving automated distress calls from hundreds of Wraith suits. They are requesting urgent additional medical personnel and equipment."

Analisa blanked out the horrified looks from the bridge crew as her mind reeled from the shock. The 24th Marines Aid Post was located at their original Landing Zone, twenty kilometers from the enemy base. They must have been outside of the blast radius of the nukes, but three whole battalions of marines hadn't. Had the Others been so desperate that they had used nuclear weapons to not only kill the attacking marines but destroy themselves and their base as well? Analisa became aware that the bridge crew were still staring at her, awaiting her orders.

"Communications. Contact the hospital ship Nightingale and tell them to expect mass casualties." Analisa summoned her Operations Officer with a quick wave of her hand. Commander Patrick Malloy was the man who made Analisa's plans reality.

"Patrick, I want you to personally coordinate with each of the marine assault ships. Find out what surviving shuttles we have that are capable of lifting the wounded. Redeploy medical personnel to whatever sick bay the Chief Medical Officer on the Nightingale deems appropriate..." Analisa stopped and looked up into Patrick's eyes. "This isn't going to be pretty. I suspect the marines have taken an awful lot of casualties today so don't be surprised if they are very angry. I need you to keep it together and get this done. Anything or anyone gets in your way you refer them directly to me but try not to step on too many toes."

"Understood, Admiral."

Analisa gave him a brief smile. "And find out who the surviving senior officer is, will you?"

With an affirmative nod, Malloy headed towards the communications officer to begin his mammoth task of making some sense out of the chaos.

CHAPTER SEVEN

COUNTING THE COST

CENTRAL COMMAND – MONT SALÈVE
EARTH – SOL SYTEM

The mood within Central Command was one of dumbfounded shock. Keyton Joyce stared, without seeing, at the latest casualty figures from the assault on the Others' base in 70 Ophiuchi, which now reached over 11,000 dead and wounded. Three quarters of those were from the marine landing element. The 21st Marine Battalion had been wiped out to a man.

The battalion had been aboard its assault shuttles, only a few seconds out from landing, when the Others began detonating their nuclear demolition charges. Not even an armored assault shuttle could survive in such close proximity to a nuclear blast.

How there were any survivors from those marines on the ground was a mystery. Some were lucky enough to have been in the shadow of a substantial building which protected them from the initial blast and their Wraith suits had done the rest. Even then, not one marine came out of the enemy base unscathed. And despite the herculean efforts of the combat medics, doctors, and nurses aboard the orbiting hospital ships, many a marine had succumbed to his injuries.

The surviving senior officer was seriously injured herself but Colonel Karen Mills, despite losing a leg to a plasma grenade, discharged herself from the small field aid post on the planet's surface and, along with the fleet Operations Officer, she coordinated the recovery of every last one of her marines before allowing herself to be transported to a fleet ship for treatment. The story went that Mills had actually threatened two naval officers with a plasma rifle if they attempted to relieve her before she saw the final marine to safety. From what Keyton heard on the grapevine that particular story was true, although he noted in Admiral Chavez's citation for the Navy Cross that that particular incident was missing.

Keyton forced himself to return his attention to the document currently displayed before him. His various aides had worked overtime to prepare him for his appearance before an emergency meeting of the Armed Services Oversight Committee. Its chairman, Senator Katria Dikul, had been most vocal in her criticism of the Combined Joint Chiefs' decision to launch the attack on 70 Ophiuchi, taking great pains to point out that it had been an all-human affair with no elements of either the Persai or Garundan military taking part. Keyton was getting whiffs of xenophobia and was determined to stamp them out before they could endanger the integrity of the joint Commonwealth forces. This was going to be a long war and each of the Commonwealth planets needed to have complete faith in the other if they were going to survive it.

Well, whatever the politicians thought of Earth's allies, Keyton, for one, had complete faith in them or he wouldn't have dispatched Admiral Razna Holan to Zarmina. His role was to find the promised technical innovations that may have reduced the casualty figures he kept running through his head and, he feared, would haunt him for some time to come.

A soft knock on the door reminded Keyton that it was time to head for the Senate building. Damn, he hated politicians.

#

GLIESE 581G - 20.3 LIGHT YEARS FROM EARTH

Gliese 581G circled its red dwarf star in a slow and steady orbit. With the star producing only some 0.2 percent the visible light of Earth's own sun, Gliese was virtually undetectable in the night sky, even though it was only 20.3 light years from Earth.

The argument that Gliese may have habitable planets had been raging amongst the various astronomical groups since the early 21st century and it hadn't been settled until the TDF sent a destroyer to visit the system. What it found hadn't entirely settled the argument as the findings were immediately classified.

The Combined Joint Chiefs had been looking for somewhere to establish a top-secret weapons research facility, well away from prying eyes, and Gliese 581G (or Zarmina as a scientist in the past had once labeled it) was ideal. With a mass approximately three times that of Earth it orbited its star every thirty-seven days and found itself well within the habitable zone which, for a red dwarf, was a lot closer to its star, hence Zarmina found itself tidally locked with one half of the planet forever in darkness.

Of the remaining six planets in the system, Gliese C and D both lay within the habitable zone, but C appeared to have formed beyond the frost line before moving into a closer orbit of its star, due to planetary migration, and it was composed mainly of ice, similar to Sol's own Ganymede. Planet D, on the other hand, suffered from a runaway greenhouse effect much like

98

Venus and although on the outer edge of the habitable zone, surface temperatures were recorded as high as four hundred degrees Celsius.

What sealed Zarmina as the location for the research base, however, was the discovery of the system's massive comet belt. At least ten times the size of that found in the Sol system it extended from twenty-five to sixty AUs from the star. It was this comet belt that held the necessary ingredients for some of the more complex and, if you paid any heed to mainstream scientists, far-fetched ideas that Doctor Jeff Moore and his research group had thought up, taking ideas from the methodical research that Persai scientists did on the Saiph database and good old human ingenuity. It was to see the fruits of their labors that brought Admiral Holan to Zarmina.

As the courier boat reentered normal space, the first thing that struck Holan was the complete lack of anything other than naturally occurring background radiation. Holan knew that on the planet below there was a facility containing over 6000 of the Commonwealth's best and brightest. Never mind the self-contained orbital shipyard and construction facilities that built and supplied the facility with anything it needed. It was decided at an early planning stage that the fewer people who knew of its existence the better, the ability to be completely self-sufficient had been a priority from the outset. Hiding the massive amount of funding required to build, equip, and maintain it had called for some… creative accounting.

The physical security surrounding the facility was at a minimum. The idea being that Zarmina would rely more on guile than guns. Those who visited the facility held only the highest of security clearances and were never told the actual location of it. Any ship traveling to

Zarmina was piloted by select crews who kept the coordinates of the planet in their heads. Nothing was recorded electronically. As far as any navigation computer on any ship within the Commonwealth was concerned, Zarmina simply did not exist.

Holan caught fleeting glimpses of large orbital structures in the darkness, passing close by, as his ship dropped lower, until finally it kissed the thin atmosphere of the planet. He shifted uncomfortably in his seat and adjusted his harness as he realized his pilots were flying using only their own eyes and passive instruments. At least any pilot error would hopefully end in a quick death, he thought.

The gentle vibration of the engines increased as the pilots applied more power, slowing their headlong plunge into darkness. A faint whistling steadily rose in volume as the ship passed through the thickening atmosphere. *Well, at least we didn't hit anything in orbit,* Holan said to himself. *All we have to do now is avoid plowing into the planet's surface.* Holan felt his restraints hugging him to his seat as the small courier ship slowed further. His seat's monitor displayed a view from the bow camera and Holan was able to make out a faint blinking light directly ahead. As the ship got closer the light got brighter and expanded into a well-lit landing pad, apparently situated in the middle of a barren, rock-strewn plain. No other artificial constructs could be seen in the blazing light of the pad. The landing gear rumbled as it extended and, soft as a feather, the little ship touched down. In contrast, the ship juddered on its skids as the entire landing pad began to drop below the surface. The landing lights extinguishing as it did so and the surface of Zarmina returned once more to its perpetual darkness.

The landing pad seemed to drop into the heart of the planet, but Holan knew that they had, in fact, only traveled 100 meters below the surface before coming to a halt. Holan released his seat restraints and stood as a crew member appeared from the cockpit to stand by the exit hatch. Quickly the tell-tale light changed from red to green as the pumps replaced the Zarmina atmosphere with one more suitable to both Holan's and human lungs. When the indicator went green, the crew member punched the hatch release and stood back, allowing Holan to exit first. With a mumbled thanks, the diminutive admiral stepped out into the large hanger carved from the rock of the planet before his eyes focused on the small group waiting for him at the foot of the ramp.

"Welcome to Zarmina, Admiral Holan," said a smiling, slightly overweight man wearing a one-piece coverall, with more pockets than Holan had ever seen on a single item of clothing. Each of the plentiful pockets seemed to be stuffed to capacity, this only served to make him look like some sort of maintenance man instead of the head of the Commonwealth's premier research facility.

Holan made his way down the short ramp and extended his hand to shake that of the waiting human.

"Glad to be here, Doctor Moore. The Combined Joint Chiefs are anxious to see what progress you have made."

Jeff gave Holan an enthusiastic smile as he absently rubbed at the lenses of his wire-rimmed glasses. "Oh, I think you'll be pleasantly surprised, Admiral. Perhaps a short tour of the facility before a full briefing on our progress would be in order?" Jeff let out a short laugh. "And the opportunity to see where your money has gone, of course."

"Please lead on, Doctor," replied Holan graciously as they headed for the landing bay exit, trailed by the small group of scientists who all started talking at the same time about their pet project.

#

The peace and quiet of Jeff's office was a blessing to Holan's tired ears. Jeff's idea of a short tour hadn't proven to be the same as Holan's. The admiral was glad he'd worn his most comfortable boots as he felt that he had been up and down each and every corridor in the facility at least once, probably twice. Keyton Joyce hadn't been kidding when he had told Holan that once Doctor Moore started on a subject he was interested in, he forgot to stop talking or, as the tour had progressed, walking. It seemed to have completely escaped the good doctor's notice that he was at least two feet taller than the Garundan admiral so for every step he took, Holan had been forced to take two. The subtle hints dropped by Moore's staff about possibly slowing the pace or curtailing the tour fell on deaf ears. The final stop of the tour, Jeff's office, had come none too soon for Holan who dropped into the comfortable chair with a barely hidden sigh of relief.

The rich smell of freshly brewed coffee filled the office as the door slid shut behind Jeff. An audible sigh left Jeff as he sat in the battered swivel chair opposite Holan and passed over the glass of ice water the admiral had requested. Lifting a steaming mug of his own to his lips, Jeff's eyes closed and his features softened as he took a moment to savor the aroma from the beans. Opening his eyes again he caught the quizzical look on Holan's reptilian face.

"My apologies, Admiral, but I'm afraid I have a weak spot for this particular blend. Have for as long as I can remember, in fact, and my mother ensures I always

102

have an ample supply no matter where I find myself – a small packet of the stuff arrives every month like clockwork."

Holan noted that while he had been talking, Jeff's eyes moved to a small hologram cube on his desk displaying an image of a smiling Jeff Moore with an older man and woman who flanked him as they stood in front of a heavily wooded lake shore.

Holan pointed out the image. "Your parents?"

Jeff shifted slightly in his seat as if the question made him uncomfortable. "Yes it is. They've retired to a small place in British Columbia. I don't get to see them too much being stuck out here in Zarmina, but we keep in touch by video mail pretty regularly."

Sensing Jeff's discomfort, Holan quickly returned the subject to the object of his visit.

"So Doctor, I must say that the facility is very impressive."

"Thank you, Admiral. The Persai mining engineers were certainly able to show our own engineers a few tricks they hadn't thought of before, it cut the construction time and got us up and running well ahead of schedule."

"So, where exactly are you in terms of anything we might find useful? We'd hoped that the new surveillance drones would be available for the operations at 70 Ophiuchi."

The expression on Jeff's face hardened as Holan mentioned the assault on the enemy stronghold. Jeff had been privy to the after-action reports and was as struck by the casualty figures as the Combined Joint Chiefs. A few touches of the keyboard integrated into his desktop and a hologram above the desk sprung to life. On it was a sleek missile shape. A shape that looked remarkably like a communications drone except for the expanded bulbous head with prominent curved protrusions.

"I think this is what you're looking for, Admiral. This is what we're calling the S – R – D." Jeff paused between the annunciations of each letter. "The Stealthy Reconnaissance Drone." He went on to explain, "It has a fully functional Gravity Drive which will allow it to be launched from well beyond any enemy detection range. The body comprises the best Persai stealth material, which, in tests, have allowed it to approach to within 200 kilometers of our current best active and passive sensors without detection. The reconnaissance package on board is based on the package currently installed on our own orbital defense platforms but is probably a generation, if not two, beyond them. Give me a month or two and we'll be able to start making deliveries to the fleet."

Holan regarded the SRD with hungry eyes and spoke without taking his eyes from the image. "How have you managed to make such rapid progress, Doctor?"

Jeff was warming to the subject now and a gleam came to his eye. "I'd remind you, Admiral, that the Persai have had more than a 150 years to study the Saiph database. They were held back purely by their need to hide themselves from the Others, so instead of physically developing their advances, they simply stuck to theory. By marrying these theories with human engineers and giving them the resources of this facility, it's like Christmas every day for them." A large grin appeared on Jeff's face. "To such an extent I've been forced to restrict the working hours of some of the scientists and engineers to stop them burning out."

Holan finally switched his gaze back to Jeff. "Is there anything else we can expect to be available in the near future?"

Jeff's forehead wrinkled as he considered the admiral's question. After a brief moment, his fingers stroked the desk's keyboard again and a number of schematics replaced the image of the SRD in the holo cube. "I'm fairly certain we aren't that far from workable applications of these items, Admiral. I think I can safely say that the closest to actual practical use is the micro-fusion generators. They're basically an upgraded model of the fusion generators we currently use to supply power to things like the SRD and communications drones but should be able to generate up to a ten-fold increase in usable power. We envisage them being used as power supplies for small, more powerful weapons packages. Possibly to arm ships such as couriers, which at the moment don't have the spare power to support offensive weaponry or to upgrade orbital weapons platforms, although it requires upgrading the actual weapons package itself, it's not an insurmountable problem."

The idea of armed couriers appealed to Holan. At the moment, the couriers' ion and gravity drive required the entire output from their power sources, so they were unarmed. Presently the only way to arm them was to increase their size to allow a larger fusion generator to be fitted and that was detrimental to the speed and maneuverability they required to complete their mission.

Jeff was getting into his stride again and his eyes gleamed as his words rushed out.

"If you liked that, Admiral, then the next couple of items should be right up your alley... What if I were to tell you that I could protect your ships from enemy lasers?"

Holan's jaw dropped as he looked at the smug face of Jeff looking back at him from the opposite side of the desk. "Go on, Doctor."

"Expanding on the Persai research into stealth materials, we have been looking into meta-materials. The same sort of stuff that the Chameleon units use to channel certain wavelengths of light around an object such as a ship or a Wraith-suited marine."

Admiral Holan may have come from a Garunda that, until a few years ago, had been using steam engines, but his IQ was still above 120, allowing him to grasp the new sciences quickly but only to a level where he understood the practice not necessarily the theory behind them. "I have a grasp of how the Chameleon suit works, Doctor, but how does that lead to protecting our ships from laser fire?"

"Picture a straw going into a glass of water. The parts above and below the water point in slightly different directions. That's a positive refractive index, and is the case for nearly all materials. A negative refractive index occurs if you try to stick the straw into the water and it bounces back at the exact but opposite angle of entrance. Now, imagine the straw is instead a powerful laser. A ship made of conventional materials struck by such a laser would be sliced in half. But a ship made with meta-materials would reflect the beam. And the more powerful the beam, the stronger the reflection." Jeff leaned back in his chair as he watched the admiral absorb what he'd just said.

Holan's mind raced with the possibilities. "Is this actually possible? Not just a fanciful theory?"

Jeff touched a key and in the holo cube one of the schematics expanded till it filled the whole display. "Meet the TDF *Horizon*. She's one of four stripped-out older style Talos cruisers that the admiralty was kind enough to deliver to us instead of scrapping. We've been using the *Horizon* and her three sister ships as test beds for our gravity drive and advanced weaponry theories to see if the engineers can make them work in practice. Each ship's been coated in the meta-materials developed here and re-equipped with micro fusion generators to power them. We've also installed our latest Artificial Intelligences, even more advanced than those found on your own Garundan Bassa-guided missile destroyers. So far we've had great success and expect to be able to field test at full power in six to eight months. Combine these ships with the research we're doing into the development of anti-matter warheads for the next generation of GD anti-ship missiles and you have a ship the size of a cruiser which packs a punch bigger than our most advanced Bismarck battleship."

"We never realized you'd made such astounding progress, Doctor. These advances could change the entire face of warfare. With the tactical advantage that our GD missiles already give us over the Others, they've been forced to rely on closing with our ships and getting into beam weapon range, but with your meta-materials, even that advantage will be negated. We'd be virtually impervious to all they could throw at us!"

Jeff could see the enthusiasm in the admiral's face and felt it was time for a note of caution. "I remind you, Admiral; although I hold out great hope for these developments, necessity is sometimes the mother of invention and I cannot guarantee that the Others, once faced with our next generation of weaponry, won't find a way to circumnavigate it. Granted, it'll initially give you the upper hand, but for how long? I don't think anyone can predict that."

"I think it's time for me to bid my farewell, Doctor. My fellow Combined Joint Chiefs and I thank you for your work and I'm eager to brief them on your progress." Holan stood as Jeff came to shake his hand before they made their way to the door.

"I'll pass your praise on to my staff, Admiral, thank you." And with that the diminutive admiral walked down the corridor toward his waiting ship his head full of ideas on how to employ the new concepts Jeff had revealed to him.

CHAPTER EIGHT

THE ALGOL PARADOX

TDF *CUTLASS* – ALGOL 3
92.8 LIGHT YEARS FROM EARTH

The briefing room of TDF *Cutlass* was not the largest of spaces. Attendance was restricted to essential personnel and the flotilla captains appeared by hologram. Although both measures served to reduce the numbers, the room still seemed cramped to Christos as he watched the busy bees of department heads vie for a seat.

SurvFlot One had arrived at the edge of the Algol 3 system only two hours earlier; the initial readings from the system made the hairs on the back of Christos' neck stand on end and caused untold consternation amongst the various scientists spread throughout the flotilla. Unexplained energy readings had been detected, scattered throughout the entire system. Christos had been loathe to send any of his Vanguards or Kulas in for a closer look until his science section got a better handle as to what the source of the energy readings could be, so, for the moment, SurvFlot One hung on the fringes of the system and waited. Now, at last, the civilian scientists had come to a consensus and were willing to put forward their initial findings.

Christos waited impatiently as Doctor Walter Kernaghan, Chief Physicist and civilian head of the science section, prepared his presentation. Normally Christos would have made his impatience known but Walter Kernaghan had been a member of the crew of the original gravity drive ship, the *Marco Polo*. For the past few years, Walter had worked for Research and Development but when David Catney assumed command of Survey Command, Walter opted to return with him and had jumped at the opportunity to head up the science section of SurvFlot One.

Walter used a finger to push his archaic bifocal glasses back into place as another former crew member of the *Marco Polo* clucked around him like a mother hen. Doctor Amanda Allenby, Chief Xenobiologist, was at least ten years younger than Walter but rumor had it that ever since the *Marco Polo* expedition they were inseparable. It was inevitable when Walter came aboard the *Cutlass* that he was accompanied by Amanda. Not that Christos complained. Having two scientists with their pedigree on board for this mission was a definite bonus. From what Christos had been told by Vusumuzi Mkhize, it was Amanda who had breathed down the various scientists' necks to come up with an explanation for the strange energy readings, while Walter reviewed each theory and sent it back for further investigation or vetoed it.

Walter rapped on the briefing room table to get everyone's attention, he eyed the seated officers and scientists over the top of his glasses like a senior professor presiding over a lecture theater of students before fixing his attention on Christos.

"If I may, Admiral?"

Christos couldn't help but let a brief smile play on his lips as the physicist sought his permission to begin the lecture… sorry, briefing. With an almost imperceptible nod, he sat back to listen to the scientists' conclusions.

"Before I get into our theory behind the energy sources, I would like to quickly go over the data we've so far amassed on this system." Amanda touched a control and the holo cube sprang to life to show a compact triple-star system.

"Algol A is a blue-white main sequence star with a mass approximately 3.59 times that of Sol and about 2.88 times its diameter, with a luminosity ninety-eight times that of Sol and a fast rotational velocity of sixty five kilometers per second. Algol B, as you can see, is an orange-red star and was actually once the most massive star in this system but has now become a cool, low-mass subgiant in which tidal forces from Algol A have distorted the swollen outer gas envelope of the star, so it now forms a teardrop shape. That brings me to Algol C. A bluish-white main sequence dwarf star with a mass 1.67 times that of Sol, a diameter 1.7 times Sol and a luminosity 4.1 times that of Sol." Amanda touched another control and a yellow elliptical band appeared around the three stars.

"Due to the fact that this is a triple star system, we would expect to find any planet where liquid water on the surface could be found would be around fourteen Astronomical Units out from the system center, or roughly somewhere between the orbit of Saturn and Uranus in our own system and its planetary year would be equivalent to twenty-seven Earth years."

Walter paused and viewed the audience over the top of his glasses, which had slipped down his nose. Christos got that sitting in a lecture feeling again.

"Now we get to the interesting part, ladies and gentlemen. Any planet that we could expect to find in the Goldilocks zone would be a very young planet, even if it was capable of retaining surface water. By our understanding of evolution, any life on the planet is most likely to be a single cell anaerobic bacteria, which would be constantly under bombardment by meteorites and comets very similar to Earth in the first billion years or so of its existence…Which does not explain this!"

With a touch of the control panel, Amanda brought up a planet the color of a blue and white marble. If Christos didn't know better, he would swear he was looking at a picture of Earth from high orbit. He looked around and saw he wasn't the only one taken aback by this seemingly impossible planet. A planet human science said shouldn't, no, couldn't exist! But there it was, all the same. And around it floated pinpoints of light mixed with darker spots highlighted against the planet's swirling white clouds.

Walter Kernaghan had a sense of the showman in him and reveled in the shocked faces of his audience for a few moments before Amanda cleared her throat loudly, her hint for him to continue.

"I see that many of you are intrigued by the pinpoints of light which appear to be surrounding the planet and the darker shapes which are in obvious orbit of it, but if I could keep your attention for a few minutes more, I'll come back to the darker shapes in a moment. I would like, firstly, to cover the objects that are not only surrounding the planet but, we've found, extend throughout the entire system. Especially near large asteroid fields. Amanda, if you would be so kind…"

The image zoomed in on one of the bright, firefly-like objects to reveal kilometer after kilometer of solar panels.

"There must be hundreds of square kilometers of solar panels on that thing," muttered one of the young staffers on Ambassador Schamu's staff.

"Not hundreds, young lady, thousands. And in the middle of each massive field of solar panels is a spherical gamma ray laser."

The staffer gave Walter a confused look. "But to what end?"

The smile returned to Walter's lips as he answered her question lightly. "Why, to make black holes of course."

The room descended into total silence as the gathered scientists, navy personnel, and diplomats took in what Walter had just said. The silence was shattered by a clamor of voices shouting questions or dismissals at Walter. Christos gave them a few seconds to get it out of their systems, then caught Mkhize's eye. The captain understood the unspoken order as he slowly rose to his feet before bringing his balled fist down on the table with the sound of an angry god.

"Silence!" Mkhize gave the assembled gathering a withering look. Daring someone to defy his instruction. None did.

From his seat at the head of the table, Christos addressed Walter in a calm, detached voice. "Please continue, Doctor."

Walter gave Christos a perfunctory nod before turning to face the questioning audience.

"Before the period in Earth's history which became known as World War Three, it was theorized that by using solar panels, one could slowly charge a spherical gamma ray laser over a number of years. When the laser was eventually discharged it would do so with the equivalent of a million metric tons of mass. This mass would be released into a converging spherical shell of protons. As the shell implodes, the energy becomes so dense that its own gravity focuses it to a single point and a black hole is formed."

Christos wasn't the only one wondering why you would want to create a black hole. "But for what purpose, Doctor?"

"Well, on forming, the black hole would immediately begin to release the energy which was used to form it. If the black hole could be placed at the center of a parabolic electron gas mirror that would reflect all the energy radiated from the black hole in one direction it could quite easily be used to propel a starship up to near the speed of light. Particle beams would be attached to the ship behind the black hole which would be used to simultaneously feed the black hole and propel it along with the ship."

Ambassador Schamu appeared unconvinced. "Surely Doctor you can't simply drag a massive black hole around space with you?"

The smile on Walter's face said everything. "A black hole of around a million tons would be about the size of one thousandth the size of a proton… So, why not? Obviously creating and harnessing black holes is no easy feat, but the laws of physics certainly allow for it."

Ambassador Schamu shook his head slowly, still unconvinced. "So what makes you think that that's what these," Schamu indicated the thousands of square kilometers of solar panels, "contraptions are for?"

"Ah! I'm glad you asked. Black holes send out a very distinct form of radiation. We call it Hawking radiation. Amanda, if you could bring up the next image please."

The image of the solar panels was replaced by that of an unfamiliar starship. A large central body with what could only be described as the double blades of opened scissors protruding from the front and extending away from it. The entire ship was dull, gun-metal gray and edged in midnight blue. The artist in Christos appreciated its flowing lines tapering to the points of the parallel sloping blades, but to the navy man in Christos it looked like a nasty piece of hardware.

"We have counted fifteen ships in orbit around the planet and each of them is giving off Hawking radiation." Walter sat with a smug look on his face as the room once more burst into loud discussion.

#

Christos was happy to leave the ongoing, and very vocal, discussion in the briefing room for the relative quiet of his own quarters. It gave him time to think through Walter's conclusions. Not for the first time, he wished he had some of those new stealthy reconnaissance probes that the eggheads at Research and Development kept promising. He would've given his right hand for a few close readings of the planet to either confirm or deny the conclusions.

Christos' musings were interrupted by a single elongated tone, signaling that someone was requesting entry. Christos answered the call. "Who is it, Corporal?"

"Ambassador Schamu wishes to speak to the admiral, sir."

Christos' eyes rolled. What did he want? Was his dinner wine chilled to the incorrect temperature again?

"Let him in, Corporal."

The main bulkhead door slid aside and Nicholas Schamu strutted into Christos' private quarters with a somber expression on his face, a look that Christos found unusual on a man who usually displayed about as much expression as a professional card shark.

"Something troubling you, Nicholas?" Christos inquired guardedly.

Nicholas didn't answer immediately, which was indeed unusual. Christos had only just gotten used to Nicholas's condoning aristocratic tone, though even

115

after hosting the man in his home, Christos was still unsure of how to take the dapper ambassador.

At Christos' question, the distracted Nicholas seemed to at last register his presence.

"My apologies Christos, but something that Doctor Kernaghan pointed out during his eloquent briefing has been bothering me. Before I go to my staff with it, I thought it prudent to speak with the flotilla commander."

Running an idea past me? That's a first, thought Christos, but he held his tongue as Nicholas took the other only comfortable seat in the room.

"Perhaps a cup of coffee before we begin, Nicholas? It'll give you a few moments to organize your thoughts."

"That would be kind, Christos. Perhaps some Longjing tea if you have it?"

Christos kept his face deadpan as he tapped his wrist comm, he requested coffee and the rare tea from his steward, Walcott. Walcott had been in the game long enough, Christos was sure, to have done his research into the favorite beverages of all the admiral's likely callers and had stocked the kitchen appropriately.

The two men made small talk while they awaited their drinks, which dutifully arrived less than five minutes later. Once Walcott retreated from the room, Christos broke the ice.

"So what did Doctor Kernaghan say that has you so perturbed, Nicholas?"

Nicholas closed his eyes as he enjoyed the smell and taste of the ridiculously expensive green tea before setting his cup back on the bone-china saucer. Christos' own coffee was served in an oversized mug that the crew of his first command had given him – a joke on the amount of coffee he regularly consumed, which was enough to keep any other human being awake for a week, according to his first XO.

Nicholas responded to Christos' question. "One of the many points that the good doctor raised was that he believed the planet, around which the ships are clustered, should not be possible; not in its current advanced state, at any rate. At this stage in its development it should be hard-pressed to support bacteria, never mind a civilization which has harnessed black holes as a form of propulsion."

Christos had to admit he had some concerns over the advanced development of the planet himself, he also had a feeling that Nicholas had more to say.

"Anything else from the brief that's bothering you, Nicholas?"

Nicholas took another sip of his tea and a contented look came over his face as the warm liquid calmed him momentarily.

"If we take the doctor's assumptions as fact, i.e., the planet cannot possibly be in such an advanced state naturally, then we must extrapolate that the planet's been artificially accelerated in its development; that some type of terra forming has brought the planet to its current state."

Christos saw the pieces fall into place, he had a good idea where Nicholas was heading. "Go on."

"It infers that whoever is in control of the ships currently orbiting the planet is also responsible for the terra forming, which leads me to an uncomfortable conclusion, which may also prove a problem for you."

Christos feared he shared Nicholas' uncomfortable conclusion.

"My point, Christos, is that the original inhabitants of the planet, the ones that we have traveled so far to find, may no longer exist and instead we are facing a new

117

species that have either conquered, absorbed, or simply eradicated the species that the Saiph intended to become the predominant species on the planet."

Nicholas sat back in his chair and sipped his tea, while Christos silently drank his coffee, trying to come up with a plausible argument to Nicholas' well thought-out reasoning.

In the end he didn't have to. The wail of the battle station's call reverberated throughout the *Cutlass*. Christos jumped to his feet, punching his direct link to Mkhize.

The face of his flag captain appeared instantly in the holo cube.

"Twelve bogeys approaching the flotilla at high sub-light speed, Admiral. Tactical has designated them Bogey One and has put them seventy-nine minutes out from our current location…"

Something out of the holo's pickup caused Mkhize to turn away for a few seconds.

"Second group of bogeys detected. Tactical is still firming up their numbers but they are now designated Bogey Two. ETA eighty-four minutes. Bogey Two is coming in from the opposite direction to Bogey One. It looks like they're trying a pincer movement. Communication drones are downloading now and will be ready to dispatch back to Survey Command at your order. Shall I prepare the flotilla to fold back to Earth space?"

Christos didn't reply immediately as he thought through his options, completely ignoring Nicholas, who stood next to him, still holding his teacup. Two separate groups of unknown ships were approaching the flotilla at high speed. He could interpret this as an aggressive move but in the same breath, if Commonwealth forces had detected a group of unknown ships in their space, how would they react? No doubt in the same fashion. When it came down to it, Christos' orders had been to find out what happened to the race the Saiph had visited in this star system, the ships currently charging toward him were the only ones who could answer that. Even if the beings on these ships weren't the original occupants of the planet, surely it was Survey Command's job to make peaceful contact with alien species and extend the hand of friendship... Decision made!

"Mkhize, plot a fold back to Earth space, but don't execute. Ensure that all ships of the flotilla are weapons tight and remain that way unless they either receive an express order to change their weapons state from the flagship or are fired upon. Begin transmitting on all frequencies in Saiph, Terran, Garundan, and Persai that we have no aggressive intentions and only wish peaceful relations. Download my orders to the drones, then get them away. I'll be on the flag bridge in a few minutes."

Mkhize gave Christos a sharp nod and cut the link.

Turning to face Nicholas, he raised his mug in mock salute.

"It would appear that your diplomacy skills will be needed shortly, Nicholas. Perhaps you would like to finish your tea before accompanying me to the flag bridge?"

For only the second time that he could remember, Christos saw a real smile touch Nicholas' lips.

"One must have a decent cup of tea before what may turn out to be lengthy negotiations. Keeps the throat from going dry at the most inopportune moment, you see."

A short laugh escaped Christos. "Indeed, Nicholas. Indeed."

"Tactical. Status of Bogey One and Two?"

"Admiral. Bogey One has come to a halt at half a million kilometers from the edge of the flotilla directly between us and the planet. Bogey Two is slowing and I believe it will also hold at the half-million- kilometer point."

"Communications, any reply to our transmissions?"

"Negative, Admiral. We are continuing to transmit on all frequencies but have received no reply. As per your orders, we've not attempted whisker laser contact."

Christos unconsciously tapped his fingers on the armrest of his chair as he tried to fathom the intentions of the unknown ships. Was Bogey One waiting on the arrival of the reinforcements of Bogey Two before launching an attack? Tactical were telling him that each group of bogeys were made up of the same compliment of ships. A large ship roughly one and a half times the size of the TDF's own Bismarck class battleship, the largest warship the Commonwealth fielded at present. *The Bureau of Design may need to rethink that one*, thought Christos. Three ships slightly smaller than a Bismarck. Six ships roughly equivalent to the Vulcan heavy cruiser and two that weighed in somewhere between the Bismarck and the Vulcan. When you considered both sets of bogeys together, his small flotilla was vastly inferior in tonnage and, he had no doubt, firepower. Christos consoled himself that, so far, no one had fired a shot in anger.

"Well, what do you think, Nicholas?" asked Christos, as he turned to the ambassador sitting in a chair off to one side of his own command chair.

Without hesitation, Nicholas replied. "It would appear that we have ourselves a standoff. Neither side is willing to make the first move so, with the admiral's permission, may I suggest that we be the first to initiate contact?"

Christos' left eyebrow arched as he gave Nicholas a quizzical look. "And pray tell Nicholas, how you suggest we do that? We're already broadcasting our peaceful intent and have been doing so for over an hour without as much as a break in the static from those ships."

The slight ambassador took a sip of his tea. *Tea?* Thought Christos. *Where the hell did he get that from on my flag bridge?*

"I'd be willing to board a shuttle craft with a single aide and minimal crew and fly out to a halfway point between our ships and theirs and see what sort of reaction we get."

Christos was dumbfounded and struggled to get a reply out. "Are you crazy? We have no idea what their intentions are. They could open fire on us at any moment and you wouldn't stand a chance in a shuttle if we start lobbing nuclear warheads and grazers around the place. No. It's out of the question."

Nicholas' expression had remained unchanged throughout Christos' outburst. "Do you have a better idea?"

#

Christos tracked the progress of the shuttle on his tactical display as it departed *Cutlass* and slowly approached the midpoint between SurvFlot One and Bogey One. Christos had held the shuttle's departure until Bogey Two had taken up station, as predicted by the tactical officer, a half million kilometers diagonally opposite from Bogey One. If both groups of ships fired on his small flotilla, there was no doubt in Christos' mind that he was going to take a beating before his ships could escape into fold space.

121

"Shuttle has reached midpoint, Admiral," called the officer at tactical.

And now we wait.

Five minutes passed. Ten minutes passed with no movement from the ships around SurvFlot One. As fifteen minutes approached the tactical officer's board lit up.

"Vampire! Vampire! Missile launch from the heavy ship at the center of Bogey One…"

Shit! I knew I shouldn't have let him go. Christos mentally kicked himself. *Time to get the hell out of dodge before the shooting really starts. Nicholas knew I wouldn't have time to recover the shuttle without taking casualties.*

"Communications. Send to the flotilla fire plan Charlie on my command…"

The shout from tactical stopped Christos in mid-sentence.

"Standby! Computer is now calling it four small craft, not missiles… Wow, look at their acceleration and maneuverability."

"Communications. Belay that order. The flotilla is to remain at weapons tight… and for God's sake get confirmation from every ship, we don't need to start a war unintentionally."

In his holo cube repeater Christos brought up the tactical display and watched the acceleration rates of those four small craft. One look at the speed of them and he understood how the computer was initially fooled into thinking it was a missile launch. Boy, those things could move! Their pilots were performing an intricate weaving maneuver that would give any fire control computer a headache if it tried to lock onto them. Odd that a battleship would carry small craft with that kind of performance capacity. Sure the marines had their Reapers, but they were primarily a close support type, designed for use within atmosphere but only carried on the specially modified marine assault ships of the Excalibur class. Yes, they could operate in space but those fast little ships would put them to shame; if they engaged them in space Christos, unfortunately, knew who he'd put his money on in a fight, and it wasn't the Reapers.

The small craft zipped toward the ambassador's shuttle then streaked past before deftly reversing course and settling into a box formation with the shuttle at its center. The small craft to the right and above the shuttles cockpit began blinking what on a TDF ship would be navigation lights and its pilot edged the little ship forward slowly.

Christos punched a control on his armrest and Nicholas' completely nonplussed face appeared in the now split holo cube.

"Well you wanted a reply Nicholas and it looks like you got one. Now what?"

"It would appear they wish us to join them aboard that rather impressive vessel."

"It's your call, Nicholas, just remember, Kayla would never forgive me if anything happened to her favorite aristocrat."

"If, for whatever reason, I fail to return, you can inform your dear wife that I have bequeathed my entire fine wine collection to her on the stipulation that you are never to gargle with it ever again."

Christos chuckled at the thought of the look on his wife's face if she was ever released into Nicholas' wine cellar. She would set up house in there, given the opportunity. "Good luck, Nicholas."

#

Terminating the link to Christos, Nicholas released a small sigh after ensuring, of course, that his aide, a twenty-something waif of a girl who had volunteered to accompany him, undoubtedly out of some innate sense of adventure on what he was sure the majority of the diplomatic staff thought was a fool's errand, if not tantamount to suicide, couldn't hear. *Well*, thought Nicholas, *nothing was ever achieved by those who were not willing to make sacrifices.* The fact that the sacrifice in this case may very well be his own life, his aide's life and that of the pilot and copilot was something that Nicholas never let enter his mind. Nicholas activated his link to the pilot.

"If you would be so good as to follow the lead of our escort, please."

Even through the bulkhead separating the passenger area from the flight deck, Nicholas was sure he could hear the pilot cursing. No matter, the shuttle edged forward and with that the small craft that had blinked its lights dropped into position directly in front of the shuttle while the remaining three small craft reoriented themselves into a triangular formation. The leading small craft accelerated gently until they were amongst the larger vessels facing the Commonwealth flotilla. Nicholas could only admire the various ships' sleek design as an architect would appreciate a fine building. Each ship was the same gun-metal gray color edged in midnight blue.

The shuttle passed through the ranks of the gray ships, Nicholas noted the snouts of protruding weapon points and rows of what he guessed to be missile tubes. These ships may be pleasing to the eye but the weapons emplacements showed that they also had a more deadly purpose. A sharp intake of breath from his aide dragged Nicholas' eyes from the passing warships and back to his seat display, which showed the view from the pick up on the nose of the shuttle. They were approaching the mother ship, for the small craft and its bulk blocked out the starlight as the shuttle slipped between the twin pylons, which stretched out from the main bulk of the behemoth. The shuttle slowed its pace in line with the lead escort, and as he watched, the skin of the vessel appeared to split and a bright shaft of light bathed the shuttle.

The largest set of bulkhead doors Nicholas had ever seen slowly opened like the jaws of a predatory beast to reveal a cavernous hanger, lined on either side by double rows of small craft identical to the ones escorting the Commonwealth shuttle. There had to be at least 100 of the nimble craft. Each had what Nicholas supposed was ground crew working on or around them, they didn't appear to be wearing any form of vacuum suit to protect them. How was that possible? A slight jolt answered his question moments later as the shuttle passed through some form of invisible barrier that must protect the hanger bay from the ravages of space. *Now that's interesting and I bet very useful.*

The pilot brought the shuttle to a hover above a set of blinking lights on the deck and with a deft touch of the controls, brought the shuttle slowly down, settling it on the deck plates without even a noticeable jolt. *He must be out to impress our hosts, as must you Nicholas.*

Nicholas released his restraints and stood, smoothing the imaginary creases from his jacket as he did so. He turned to his aide who was still seated and gawking out of the shuttle window.

"Excuse me, Miss?"

His question startled the young woman, who tried to stand without releasing her seat restraints, managing only to rise a few millimeters before the locking mechanism kicked in and held her fast to the seat.

Realizing her mistake, she tapped the release and stood, her face reddening in embarrassment.

"Eh. Kelly sir. Kelly Johanson."

Nicholas looked her up and down, inspecting her with the eye of a drill sergeant.

"It would appear that we have arrived at our destination, Miss Johanson. I would remind you that initial contact with these people will leave an impression that will set the tone for all future negotiations, so I will ask you again. Are you prepared for whatever awaits us? Or do you wish to remain aboard the shuttle?"

Something seemed to change within the young woman as Kelly stood, just that little bit straighter, lifting her chin while her eyes fixed on Nicholas'. "Let's do this."

Nicholas regarded her a moment longer before turning without another word to the shuttle's personnel door and keying in the open sequence. The door slid to one side with a slight hiss of hydraulics, and Nicholas and Kelly were bathed in the harsh light of the hanger. The small ramp extended and without hesitation Nicholas walked down onto the hangar floor, Kelly following closely on his heels. At the base of the ramp, Nicholas halted and waited. They didn't have long to wait.

A bulkhead at the side of the hangar, nearest the shuttle, split open and a pair of what Nicholas assumed to be crew member approached them. From a distance they looked remarkably human-like; two arms, two legs, one head. But then it struck Nicholas that these aliens were thinner and taller than humans. Out of the corner of his eye, he noted that Kelly was managing to control her features... or she was totally petrified and going into shock. *How embarrassing if she faints.*

126

Kelly was indeed petrified but there was no way in hell she was going to show it to that stuffy martinet beside her. Kelly had never worked directly with Ambassador Schamu, but the horror stories made her think twice about volunteering to be his aide on what her coworkers had called a suicide mission. The flight on the shuttle had only served to reinforce her impression of Schamu. She had no doubt that when he actually spoke to these aliens he already had some forms for them to fill out. In triplicate, undoubtedly.

Kelly's undivided attention was re-focused on the two aliens as, with precision that a marine would envy, they came to a halt only a couple of meters in front of her. Both dressed in identical stylized uniforms. The same gun-metal gray as their ship with trims of midnight blue running down each arm. Kelly was forced to crane her neck slightly to maintain eye contact with the two aliens. She wondered if Schamu had noticed how human-like they looked. Their two eyes were closer together than a human's, separated by what was unmistakably a nose and a mouth located below it. Kelly had to suppress a laugh as she realized that both aliens' pale blonde hair was styled in what could only be described as bob haircuts. Each could've passed for a stretched human – if it wasn't for the pattern of dark spots, about the size of a freckle. They ran from the top of their skulls down to their eyes, completely encircling them before continuing down either side of their jaws where they joined.

The alien on the right raised its arms and in its hand was a small electronic device, which began to emit a high-pitched whine. The alien stepped forward and waved the device firstly across Kelly and then Nicholas before pulling another, larger device from a pouch on its belt and touching the two together. After a few seconds the larger device beeped and a small display flickered to life and Nicholas could see undecipherable symbols scrolling across the small screen. The alien holding the device gave what Nicholas would've described, if it'd been a human being, an incredulous look before stepping forward and repeating the procedure. Again the larger device scrolled the undecipherable symbols but this time when the scrolling symbols came to a halt the alien turned the screen to the second alien who, throughout the whole procedure, stood unmoving. Its inscrutable gaze fixed on the two human diplomats.

It appeared to Nicholas that it was this alien who was in charge, Nicholas prepared to address it, when without warning it swapped places so it was now standing in front of Kelly. The unexpected move surprised Nicholas, but not as much as Kelly, she managed not to let the surprise show on her face only by squeezing her balled fists tightly while keeping them locked at her sides.

As unexpected as this move had been, what happened next completely blindsided Kelly. In unison, the aliens bowed deeply at the waist and raised their outstretched arms to shoulder level. The alien in charge spoke, Nicholas' and Kelly's ear bugs translating instantly.

"Welcome, daughter of the Progenitors. We of the Benii have long awaited your arrival and are ready to pledge our allegiance in the struggle against the destroyers of worlds." The words were formulated in perfect Saiph.

Nicholas Schamu had not gotten to the dizzy heights of ambassador within the Diplomatic Corps without the ability to think on his feet; the change of position after the device had examined them. The use of the word "daughter." Nicholas was willing to bet that this was a matriarchy. A quick glance at Kelly told him that she was still trying to comprehend these words. The aliens remained in their posture, heads down, arms extended, obviously awaiting a reply. With as minimal movement as possible Nicholas nudged Kelly's elbow. That seemed to be all she needed to recover from the shock.

Kelly mimicked, as best she was able, the posture of the aliens and Nicholas followed suit. Seemingly satisfied, the two aliens once again stood erect.

"I am High Commander Botac, commander of the Combined Forces of the Benii Federation. This is Admiral Yula, and you stand aboard the Benii carrier Koslla. Flagship of our naval forces."

Kelly's stomach was doing somersaults. Ambassador Schamu was the one meant to be negotiating, she was only here to take notes, damn it! But no. Schamu was just standing there... silently. Kelly could have screamed at him. *Relax, Kelly, take a breath... you can do this.*

"I am Kelly Johanson. I am a diplomat with the Commonwealth Union of Planets and I come to you in the hope that we may establish a peaceful relationship with the Benii." Kelly hoped that the translation program in her PAD did its job properly and hadn't just told her hosts something like she thought they had ugly haircuts.

"Do you have news of the war?"

Kelly hesitated and her eyes widened in surprise. *How could the Benii know of the Commonwealth's war against the Others?* Kelly decided to play coy.

"The war, Commander?"

Now it was Botac's turn to hesitate.

"Once we of the Benii discovered the crashed ship of the Progenitors, it took our archaeologists nearly a generation to decipher its writings. But once we did, we learned the Progenitors were at war with an implacable foe, who it seems, if they discovered any world visited by the Progenitors, would destroy it and all life on it, with no hesitation. Our scientists redoubled their efforts to discover the secrets of the Progenitors' technology, but much of it was simply beyond us, so we developed our own less-advanced weapons and drives. I see from your own arrival here that you have conquered the problem of interstellar travel. We were forced to rely on generation ships to establish ourselves on other worlds…"

"You have spread to other planets outside your own star system?" interrupted Nicholas.

Both Botac and her companion reacted as if Nicholas had slapped them across the face.

Nicholas scrambled to recover the situation. "My apologies, Commander…"

Botac cut him off with a chopping motion as she addressed Kelly. "I see that your Commonwealth has the same problem as we Benii. Men who do not know their place. More and more men think they can speak without permission in the presence of their betters."

Kelly turned to Nicholas with a mischievous grin. She was beginning to enjoy this. "Please forgive him, Commander. I shall ensure that I have a conversation with him later reminding him of his position in society." Turning back to Botac, she continued. "Tell me of these worlds, if you will?"

"May I suggest we retire to more comfortable surroundings to continue our conversation?"

"Of course, Commander. If I may, I would like to bring my secretary to take notes?"

Botac eyed Nicholas like a misbehaving puppy. "As you wish, Kelly Johanson. If you would like to accompany me?"

Botac gestured to the entrance through which she and Yula had entered the hanger bay and Nicholas ensured he kept a respectful distance behind the small group of females.

The return journey on the shuttle was excruciating for Kelly. Following the initial meeting in the hanger bay with Botac and Yula, where Ambassador Schamu had been forced to take a back seat, he hadn't uttered another word. Whenever Kelly tried to make eye contact with him he had pointedly ignored her. When they returned to the shuttle he sat in his seat and when Kelly tried to explain her actions he simply held up a hand to stop her. The twenty-minute flight to the *Cutlass* was the longest twenty minutes of her life. Schamu busily tapped away on his PAD, *probably arranging for my removal from the mission,* Kelly thought glumly.

The shuttle shuddered lightly as it landed on the *Cutlass* and Schamu stood to leave. Kelly remained in her seat, close to tears at the thought of being sent home in disgrace.

As he reached the personnel hatch, Schamu paused and turned to face the still-seated Kelly.

"Miss Johanson. I must say that your performance today was…" Nicholas looked down at his immaculate suit and brushed an imaginary piece of lint from his sleeve, "remarkable."

Kelly's brain could hardly process Schamu's words and he was still talking.

"You coped excellently with the rather radical turn of events, thrusting you into the position of assuming leadership of our negotiations with the Benii. As such, from this point you will be our primary negotiator. Before each meeting, I will give you a list of points that I wish covered but how you do so will be entirely up to you. I've taken the liberty of forwarding to your PAD a list of suitable candidates for your new staff. At this juncture, I believe it would be wise to keep all staff who are likely to have contact with the Benii restricted to females, but I would like you to introduce Garundan and Persai females at the earliest possible moment, to show the Benii that we are truly a pan-species alliance. Any questions?"

Kelly was in a state of shock. Not trusting her voice to reply, she simply nodded.

"Good. I will personally brief Admiral Papadomas but I expect he'll want you to brief a joint naval and diplomatic meeting as soon as possible. I suggest you be ready in…" Schamu referred to the archaic gold pocket watch he always carried. The sound of its cover snapping shut brought Kelly's head up, straight into the smiling face of Nicholas Schamu. She recognized that mischievous smile. It was the same one she had given him back in the hanger bay. God she hated karma.

"Two hours." And with that, Schamu exited the shuttle and was gone, leaving Kelly muttering words that would have made the best marine gunnery sergeant turn red.

#

Christos looked over the top of his battered mug at the dapper ambassador sipping his Longjing tea. Christos lowered his mug and rested it on the armrest of his equally battered leather chair.

"A race that has colonized two other star systems, equipped with carriers and star fighters all powered by black holes. If I hadn't seen it with my own eyes I wouldn't have believed it." Christos allowed himself a soft chuckle. "The tech weenies are going to wet themselves."

"Indeed, Christos. From the discovery of a wrecked Saiph starship they have, in a mere 400 years, gone from pre-industrialization to interstellar travel. A prodigious achievement."

Christos shook his head slowly as he contemplated the look on the faces of the Joint Chiefs back home, never mind the male politicians. A society where females were dominant. Now that was something his wife would appreciate and his daughters would love.

"So the Saiph had been establishing a meteor defense shield around the planet when they met their untimely end?"

"It would seem so, Christos. It fits with the data compiled by our own people and explains why life survived on a planet that, otherwise, should have met its end a long time ago. When the Saiph ship was uncovered, it caused turmoil. I gather there were a number of wars over the years, until the Benii were able to translate the Saiph language, at which point they became aware of their position in the universe and the fact that the Others were out there intent on destroying all life. The Benii became as determined to survive as we did after our world wars and by reverse engineering as much of the Saiph technology as they could, they developed rudimentary space flight. With single-minded determination, they went on to build a fleet of generational ships which they sent to their nearest neighboring star system likely to have a planet capable of supporting life. An orange dwarf star 4.1 light years distant. The journey took the ship over 150 years but they made it, and established a colony they called Baut. By that time they had mastered black holes as a power source, however, they were discontented with just one colony; so they dispatched a second colony fleet to a G-type main sequence star, thirteen light years distant, where they established Gossol. Both colonies, as far as the home system is aware, are flourishing."

"Wow… that really is quite an achievement. If we hadn't invented the Gravity Drive we too would've gone down the generational ship route – if we ever wanted to visit the stars." Christos took a gulp of coffee before asking the question he knew both of them had avoided.

"So what do you think the people back home are going to think of a race which is armed to the teeth and has been training for a fight with the Others for nearly half a millennium?"

Nicholas regarded Christos over the top of his cup. "I would say that the prospect of a well-armed, well-motivated, well-trained fighting force with an institutional hatred for the Others would make some salivate. Some, on the other hand, may regard them as a bit of a loose cannon and be glad that they don't have the ability to get from one star system to another in a hurry."

That was the issue Christos had found himself considering ever since Nicholas sat down and began recounting his meeting with the Benii.

"So what do you think our next step should be?"

A frown of concentration creased Nicholas' forehead before he answered.

"I have already arranged for Miss Johanson to continue to lead the negotiations; I have shortlisted some senior female staff to assist her, although I expect it may not be too long before High Commander Botac will request a tour of the *Cutlass* and realize that the majority of our senior officers are male. That's a hurdle we'll cross when we come to it. In the meantime, I suggest we request a diplomatic courier dispatched here with an all-female crew."

Christos cocked his head. "For what purpose?"

"Even with the Benii's most advanced ship, it still takes them nearly a decade to make a round trip to Baut. As a sign of our friendship, why don't we put the courier ship at their disposal and suggest that they invite the leaders of Baut and Gossol to a summit aboard *Cutlass*?"

Christos mulled it over, it certainly sounded good, easier to break the news that their system of female superiority wasn't applicable to the Commonwealth; if they were to be allies, there was no sense in hiding it from them much longer.

"OK, Nicholas, I'll get the request off as soon as the briefing is over. Talking of which, I think it's time we made our way down there and hear what Miss Johanson has to say. By the way, don't you think that two hours was a little short to prepare a briefing for the staff?"

"I would have made it an hour but Mr. Walcott serves such a delightful Longjing that I just couldn't resist a second cup."

Christos sometimes couldn't tell when Nicholas was being serious or sarcastic.

CHAPTER NINE

SOMEBODY ELSE'S WAR

FLAGE BRIDGE – TDF *RAPIER* – CHARON BASE ORBIT OF PLUTO – SOL SYSTEM

Rear Admiral Bruce Torrance allowed himself a moment of satisfaction as the ships of SurvFlot Two slowly pulled away from Charon Base and headed for clear space before engaging their gravity drives sending them on their way to 23 Librae, 83.7 light years from Earth. Like the majority of the star systems visited by the Saiph, information on 23 Librae was sketchy. Observations identified it as a G5 V-type star, a main sequence star that gave off the yellow hue typical of G-types. It was approximately 107 percent the size of Earth's sun but much older, somewhere between 8.4 and 11.1 billion years old.

The Persai observation platform established there were seven planets in orbit around the star. Two of these planets had been identified by human astronomers as far back as 1999; one a gas giant much like Saturn but 1.6 times its mass; and in 2009 a second Saturn-like planet was discovered but it wasn't until the Persai shared their platforms data with the rest of the Commonwealth that astronomers were able to get a definitive structure for the star system, and what they found was remarkable. Two planets were orbiting the star in a region that indicated they had liquid water on their surface and could be fully capable of bearing life. This was not the first star system that the Commonwealth had come across with more than one life-bearing planet in a single star system. Messier 54 had two such planets, Alona and Geta. But what made 23 Librae different was the Persai data that led scientists to believe that there were, in fact, two intelligent races in this one star system, each of which had evolved independently of the other. The xenobiologists were already expounding theories as to what differences or similarities they may find. *Well, time to find out*, thought Bruce.

"Communications. Has the flotilla reported ready?"

"All ships report ready to fold, Admiral."

"Very well. Navigation. When you're ready."

"Aye-aye, sir. Three...Two...One...Fold!"

The familiar feeling of dislocation with the real world washed over Bruce, it passed as SurvFlot Two exited fold space and the collision alarm began to wail... all hell broke loose.

"Navigation. Status report!" shouted Bruce as his fingers flew over his own controls to bring up the navigational plot on his chair's holo cube, but the young lieutenant at the navigator's position got there before him. Bruce felt his seat restraints cut into his shoulders and waist as TDF *Rapier* rolled hard and its compensators fought to correct the sudden maneuver. The restraints slackened as the compensators caught up and Bruce's brain began to analyze the data rolling across his repeater. Had they inadvertently arrived in an asteroid field? The Persai platform had shown this area of space located between two of the outermost planets well clear of any obstructions.

Bruce had to shout to be heard over the wailing alarm. "Communications! Update on the status of the flotilla please! I want to know if we've suffered any damage ASAP," he paused before adding, "and will someone kill that damned alarm!"

Before the officer could answer, *Rapier* was rocked to her keel, Bruce felt his restraints bite once more. That was no asteroid impact, somebody was firing at them! Bruce's brain went into overdrive and he began snapping orders in rapid-fire succession.

"Communications! Weapons free, flotilla-wide. Tactical – I need to know what the hell is going on here and quickly. Navigation – plot us a course out of here and standby to fold."

"Admiral…" the tactical officer called. "Sensors are showing a single bogey at a range of… 5000 kilometers. The bogey fired some form of particle beam weapon at us. Engineering reports we suffered minimal damage. Bogey is maneuvering. I believe it is attempting to get broadside onto the *Ericson*. Possibly to bring its full armament to bear."

Ericson was one of Bruce's three Vanguard survey ships, designed primarily for stealthy survey missions, not for combat. A particle beam that could rock a heavy cruiser like the *Rapier* could do a lot of damage to the much smaller *Ericson*. Any decision Bruce may have made was muted a few seconds later as the bogey fired and three particle beams hit the *Ericson*'s rear quarter. It turned its engineering section into a mass of twisted metal and venting atmosphere.

In Bruce's tactical display, the icon for the *Ericson* began to blink blood-red. "Communications, warn that ship off. Tactical, move the *Claymore* and the *Mosi* into position to support the *Ericson*. If it looks like that bogey is about to fire again, I want it wiped from space."

"Sir! I have Captain Ray on secure link."

Bruce punched a control and the face of Foster Ray, captain of the *Ericson*, appeared in the holo cube.

"What's the damage, Foster?" Bruce saw the smoke-shrouded bridge behind Foster and heard the background shouts of officers trying to regain control of their ship.

Foster shook his head slowly. "Not good, Admiral. Engineering is gone. Damage control can't even get in to check for survivors and I fear the worst. Without engineering I have no propulsion and we're operating on emergency power for life support. Weapons control is damaged but my XO believes that given a few hours he can have that back on line, but the power lines to the reactors are pretty much shot and that's not a job we can repair without yard help..." Foster looked at Bruce with dejection. Foster knew that his ship was finished. It would only take one more broadside from the bogey to kill Foster and his remaining crew.

"Captain, wipe your computers, set your scuttling charges and abandon ship." Bruce could see that Foster wanted to argue with him but Foster knew the reality of the situation and his shoulders slumped in resignation.

"Aye-aye sir."

Bruce cut the link and turned to the tactical officer. "OK, Guns, what's the bogey up to?"

"Bogey's creeping closer to the *Ericson*. Power readings indicate that its weapons systems are still powered up. Computer has identified at least three heavy particle beam emitters, although from their configuration I'd bet there is at least another two we haven't identified yet. The armor of our cruisers should be able to handle the beam's output but unfortunately as seen by the damage to the *Ericson* it's easily a match for our lighter units. Bogey's approximately the size of an Agis class destroyer. As far as propulsion goes, it's shown it's capable of moving at a quarter the speed of light during maneuvers. Engineering is analyzing the power readings and will hopefully be able to give us a better estimate of its design limits. As far as its intentions, I'd guess it's trying to get as close to the *Ericson* as it can so it can use it as a shield to stop us firing on it."

That all made sense. On the tactical repeater Bruce saw smaller icons begin to shoot away from the *Ericson*. That would be the life pods containing the surviving crew. The bogey shifted its position and before anyone could react it was amongst the scattering life pods and magnetic grapples shot out from its hull and snared four of the pods and began reeling them in remorselessly. Whoever crewed the bogey now had hostages.

#

The next hour seemed to crawl by. All the remaining life pods from the *Ericson* had been recovered and their occupants were safely aboard the *Claymore* and *Mosi*. All except the four taken aboard the ship which had fired on the *Ericson*. Their current situation was unknown. The bogey had just sat still in space, making no attempt to move or to communicate with the Commonwealth flotilla that now surrounded it.

Bruce stared at the image in his repeater. The snub nose of the bogey had two large particle beam projectors protruding from it. The sleek shape and gray color scheme reminded Bruce of a shark. Small boxes disturbed the smooth skin at regular intervals. Fire and control points for its weapons systems theorized the Tactical Officer. At regular intervals along the waist were smaller weapons points. Small enough to be area denial weapons or anti-missile weapons. Near the rear of the ship there was a cluster of weapons points, presumably to defend the drive system, which was housed in what could only be described as an inverted fin that dropped some twenty metres below the main body of the ship. All in all, it made for a lethal-looking ship.

Bruce smacked his hand on his armrest in frustration. He knew next to nothing about the ship that held his men. Although he hadn't ordered it, he knew that in the marine spaces they were already preparing contingency plans to storm the ship and rescue the captives but without a lot more intelligence a rescue mission was worse than foolhardy. All attempts at communication with the bogey had failed. If there was no movement soon, Bruce would be forced to send in his marines. He would not leave people behind.

"Admiral, incoming call from the bogey."

Bruce span to his holo cube and an image coalesced. A young, obviously frightened crew member appeared. A nasty-looking welt on her right cheek. Her survival suit showed the name Childers, A. Bruce felt his anger rise at the sight of the injured crew member and it took all his willpower to keep it in check.

"Childers, are you all right?"

The crew member glanced at something or someone outside of the camera's field of view before replying and Bruce saw the fear in her eyes. "Admiral…sir. There are three of us here. Lieutenant Medina's life pod must have been damaged." Childers' eyes dropped to the floor for a second and when she looked back up there was the glint of a tear. "She was dead when they opened her pod."

Bruce could tell that the young woman was struggling to hold it together.

"It's OK, Childers, there was nothing you could do. What about the other two with you? How are they?"

Childers' face broke into a satisfied smile. "PO Gambee came out fighting, sir. It took five of them just to hold him down. They tied him up but he's OK. Crew member Yong isn't in a good way though, sir. He wasn't conscious when they took him out of the life pod and I don't know where they took him...I don't know if he's still alive, sir." Childers started to tremble and Bruce could see that she was on the verge of losing it.

"Childers, you need to hold it together. I promise you, we will get you out of there. You and Gambee and Young. I'm not leaving here without you. Do you understand me, Childers?"

The trembling slowly subsided and Childers wiped at her eyes. "Yes, sir."

"What about your captors, Childers? What can you tell me about them?"

A fleeting confused expression passed over the crew member's face. "Sir... I got the feeling that they expected someone else when they opened the life pod's hatch. When the hatch opened they dragged me out and I thought it was all over." Childers touched the large welt on her cheek. "That's how I got this. I banged my face on the pod bulkhead on the way out. I always was a bit clumsy." A small smile came to her lips. "But sir, when they got a good look at me they seemed... startled. That's when PO Gambee started struggling with them and they just tied me up and dumped me in a cell with the PO. We had a couple of visitors. I think one of them was a doctor of some kind because he took skin and blood samples but otherwise they've left us alone. When they came to my cell this time and dragged me out I thought... I thought it was all over, sir but then they stuck me in front of this contraption and linked me to you. I don't get it, sir. They haven't spoken to us at all. I... I don't know what they want me to say?"

Bruce didn't get the chance to ask another question as the image of the crew member cut away and was replaced with that of a gray-skinned, lightly scaled alien. The large bulbous head shaped like an oval ball, the jet-black eyes set widely apart and what looked like breathing holes set high in the forehead. A small slit below the eyes lay slightly open.

The alien stared into the camera lens as if searching deep into Bruce's soul before the small slit opened wide and a deep growling tone escaped its lip-less mouth. The image disappeared as the link was cut.

"Admiral we're receiving a data packet from the bogey. I'll forward it to linguistics for analysis but from my initial take, I'd say that it's a language file."

Bruce sat back in his chair and considered this turn of events. The aliens had three of his crew members and two of them appeared to be unharmed. How Yong was faring was unknown. Now the aliens had sent a language file. Were they trying to establish a dialog with him? Childers had said it appeared the aliens were surprised when they had found her in the life pod, so who had they been expecting?

"Communications, compile an English language packet and transmit it to the bogey. Tactical, I want a complete sensor sweep of this system. Primarily I want to know if our friends out there are the only space-faring race."

Bruce touched a control on his armrest and after a slight pause, he was connected to Ambassador Isa, head of SurvFlot Two's diplomatic mission. "Ambassador, there's been an interesting development in our standoff with the bogey and I would like to discuss it with you as I believe that it may fall more within your purview than mine."

Amber Isa cocked one fine eyebrow above heavy-lidded eyes. "Do we have an update on the crew members from the life pods?" Her softly spoken question was edged with concern.

The image of the bruised face of Childers came fleetingly to Bruce's mind as took a small breath before answering. "As far as we know, we have one fatality but the other three are alive."

Amber looked into the gaunt face of Bruce for a moment, his usual self-assuredness had taken a knock but beneath it, Amber could see his resolve hardening into something else. A determination to secure the release of his people. "And how can I be of assistance, Admiral?"

"It was something Childers said to me. That when the life pods were opened the aliens seemed surprised. Like they'd been expecting to find someone else inside. Ambassador, I think they fired on us more by knee-jerk reaction rather than by intention. I think we've wandered into someone else's war."

#

The anxiety was easy to read on Bruce's face as Amber made her final preparations for what they both hoped would be the first step in releasing the three captured crew member. Amber's face was one of studied calm. Years of service in the Diplomatic Corps had given her the ability to keep all emotion from her expression but that didn't mean that she didn't feel her chest tightening. The linguists had been working feverishly to make sense of the language packet that had been transmitted to the *Rapier*. The linguists assured Bruce and Amber they were confident they had made enough headway that a limited conversation was possible and that any two-way conversation would only increase their understanding of the aliens' language.

Amber gave Bruce a small smile. "Well, here goes nothing."

Bruce gave her a small nod. "Communications. Open a link to the bogey."

Amber let her neutral expression return as the holo cube sprang to life and she was confronted with the image of the gray-skinned alien. The computer's facial recognition software identified the alien as the same one Bruce had seen earlier. *Unless they're all identical,* thought Amber.

"Greetings, sir. I am Ambassador Amber Isa and I represent a group of planets called the Commonwealth Union of Planets."

There was a long pause as the alien stood stock-still saying nothing in reply. Amber began to wonder if the linguistic program had failed to interpret her message. After what seemed an eternity, the slit below the alien's eyes began to move and in Amber's ear bug a broken, unemotional computer-generated voice said, "Greetings Ambassador Amber Isa of... unknown...planet. Apologies. Death. Hurt. Mistake. Forgive. Thought you Deres... unknown... Enemy."

Out of range of the pickup Bruce slapped his armrest with a balled fist. *Damn, I was right. They thought we were someone else.*

"We are not your enemy, sir. All we wish are the return of our people and we will leave in peace."

Obviously the computers on the bogey were working on the interpretation just as the ones on *Rapier* as this time the alien's reply came quicker.

"I will return unknown crew member unknown worry you take revenge unknown trust you."

145

In the holo cube the alien raised its arms revealing its large hands, thin pieces of skin linked each of its fingers, like those on a frog's feet. Amber kept her face expressionless but inside she allowed herself a smile as she counted the fingers. Five. No doubt about it, these aliens were the descendants of Saiph DNA manipulation. Exactly what SurvFlot Two had been sent to find. When Amber had been selected as head of the diplomatic mission she felt it was the culmination of her career. The opportunity to go into space and establish relations with alien races which carried the same genetic material as humans. Long-lost relatives of humanity. In that moment, Amber realized that she only had one choice if she was to earn the trust of these aliens.

"I suggest a trade, sir. The crew member for me. I will be your guarantee of safety."

Bruce Torrance's jaw dropped and he began to protest but a look from Amber stopped him. She understood that she couldn't secure the release of the crew member without offering something in return and what would signal trust more than her offer?

"That would be acceptable."

Amber gave a satisfied nod. "Expect me shortly and thank you, sir."

The link was cut and Amber turned to Bruce. The relief at the prospect of the release of his crew member mixed with apprehension over the deal that Amber had just struck with the alien. Bruce regarded her for a few moments before his face broke into a wide grin.

"Ambassador, excuse my turn of phrase, but you have got a big set of stones."

Amber returned his grin. "Admiral, sometimes you just have to roll the dice and see where they land."

#

The shuttle that had delivered Amber to the motionless bogey had undocked and was accelerating away when the incoming signal icon lit up in Bruce's holo cube. Accepting the signal the face of Doctor Novak, the *Rapier*'s chief medical officer, appeared.

"You'll be glad to hear that apart from a few cuts and bruises, both Childers and Gambee are fine."

"What about Yong?"

"Crew member Yong has suffered a fractured skull so I've kept him unconscious for the moment until I can get him back to sick bay and get a bone weaver on him but there doesn't appear to be any brain damage so he should be fine in a week or so, just a headache."

A sense of relief washed over Bruce, which was quickly replaced with one of unease as he remembered that the ambassador was now a hostage of the aliens.

"How did the aliens treat the ambassador?"

"From what I could see, with respect..." The doctor chuckled. "Although the look on Wilder's face was one for the books."

Aubrey Wilder had been... persuaded to accompany Amber aboard the alien ship. When the head of the linguistics department had heard of Amber's deal, he petitioned Bruce to allow someone from his department to go with her. His argument was based on the point that the ambassador was fully reliant on the interpretation software loaded onto her PAD and, as he had pointed out, there was always the chance the PAD could fail. Wouldn't it be better if a trained linguist accompanied the ambassador? Bruce wasn't happy with the suggestion of giving the aliens a second hostage but he could see the merit and reluctantly agreed. Aubrey Wilder hadn't been too enamored with the idea either, but when Bruce mentioned the words "promotion" and "academic credit," the young linguist agreed. Now

Bruce was wondering if Wilder was beginning to regret his decision.

"Thank you, Doctor. Let me know as soon as you have anything new on Yong's condition."

Bruce cut the link and sat back in his command chair. His stomach let out a quiet rumble and he realized he hadn't eaten since they'd arrived in system. Bruce checked the clock on his repeater. Had it only been three hours? Perhaps a sandwich from the galley? Bruce settled in for a long wait.

#

"I swear to you Aubrey, if you throw up, I will personally kick your ass!"

"Sorry Ambassador, but I've never been in a situation like this. I work in an office."

Another pitiful moan escaped Aubrey, and Amber Isa regretted her decision to bring him along. When they had docked with the alien ship, Amber had been the first to step through the airlock with Doctor Novak close on her heels. Awaiting her was crew member Childers, a vacant stare fixed on her face. Two of the gray-skinned aliens had Gambee's arms pinned by his sides and he looked like he was ready to throw them off at any moment and start fighting again. From a side corridor, what looked like a hospital gurney was wheeled in by another alien. On the gurney lay an unconscious Yong, the cover over his chest rising and falling at a steady rate. Gambee's muscles tensed and the aliens holding him tightened their grip.

"Petty Officer, relax. I'm here to get you and the others home and any rash action will only delay that," intoned Amber loud enough to be heard across space. Gambee gave a curt nod and forced himself to relax.

A single alien in a one-piece brilliant white coverall belted at the waist stepped forward. A stylized golden

148

sunburst was emblazoned on the right side of his chest and he held a small black box-like device in his webbed hand. He raised the box to his mouth and began to speak into it quietly. From a hidden speaker in the device came out slow, monotone English.

"Ambassador Amber Isa, I am Ship Master Ussa and I greet you in the name of the Nilmerg. Sorry for damage to ship and bodies. Was mistake. Believe you Deres. Mistake. Give back bodies."

Ussa made an awkward arm motion at the Nilmerg pushing the gurney and he wheeled it into the center of the room before retreating.

Amber spoke without turning away from Ussa. "Doctor, if you would be so kind."

Novak cautiously walked forward and ran his medical PAD quickly over the unconscious Yong. "Looks like a skull fracture, but I'll know more when we get back to the *Rapier*'s medical bay." Two medical orderlies moved forward transferring Yong onto a hovering med bed, its built-in instrumentation coming to life as it detected a casualty. Novak tapped a few controls on his PAD and the bed administered a mild sedative. "That should keep him comfortable for the journey. Let's get him aboard the shuttle."

One of the orderlies gave the med bed a gentle nudge and it moved off in the direction of the waiting shuttle with the second orderly and Novak trailing behind. With Yong safely on his way to the shuttle, Ussa motioned to the Nilmergs restraining Gambee. Both Nilmergs released him and took a step back. Gambee flexed his arms and began to say something but Amber cut him off.

"Not a word, Petty Officer. Get aboard the shuttle. Now!"

Gambee gave her a sullen look before reluctantly walking towards the airlock. "Aye-aye ma'am."

That only left Childers. Amber called to her softly. "Childers." No reaction. "Angie." The use of her first name provoked a reaction in the young crew member. Bruce had been right. The whole ordeal of having her ship shot out from under her, the mad scramble for the life pods, being taken hostage by aliens, seeing her dead officer and watching her crew mates being either beaten by the aliens or removed unconscious had just been too much for her. Amber marveled that she had managed to last as long as she had.

Amber looked towards Ussa for permission and he made that strange arm motion again. Amber walked slowly forward and put an arm around Childers' shoulders. "Come on Angie, let's get you home."

Childers looked into the ambassador's face as the trembling set in and her eyes filled with tears. "Home?"

Amber hugged her gently. "Yes, home. I need you to walk Angie, can you do that?"

Together they shuffled forward to the airlock where one of the orderlies had returned from securing Yong aboard the shuttle. He gently took Childers from the ambassador. Amber went to step away but Childers gripped her arm with surprising strength.

"Thank you. Thank you for coming for us."

Amber gave her a small smile and patted her hand gently. "The admiral was very insistent." With that, the orderly carefully walked Childers into the airlock. Shaking herself mentally Amber walked as confidently as she could back the few paces until she once again stood opposite Ussa. Behind her, she heard the airlock close and with a jolt the shuttle disconnected itself and began its journey back toward the *Rapier*.

Quiet descended on the space as human ambassador and her nervous linguist faced Ship Master Ussa. The seconds passed slowly. Ussa stood stock-still, his two large black eyes unblinking. *That's if they do blink of course,* thought Amber. *Well, we just can't stand here forever, someone has to make the first move.*

"As I promised Ship Master, I have remained in exchange for our hostages. So, where do we go from here?"

"Ambassador not prisoner. Trust shown. Guest now."

"Perhaps we could talk about..."

A high-pitched triple beep came from behind her and the Nilmergs' reactions were lightning-fast as hands dropped to leg holsters and evil-looking stubby weapons appeared.

Ussa shouted something at his crew and each froze in place but the weapons still pointed towards Amber. No, she realized, they weren't pointed at her. They were pointed at something behind her. Wilder. What had that idiot done?

Amber raised her arms above her head, hoping the Nilmergs would recognize it as an act of surrender and in a loud stage whisper called out to Aubrey, "Whatever you're doing Aubrey, I strongly suggest you stop it or we're both going to end up dead."

When the linguist didn't answer, Amber slowly turned her head to see what he was doing, only to find him busily tapping away at his PAD.

"Aubrey, you need to stop whatever you're doing now, do you hear me?"

Aubrey continued tapping away for another few seconds then stopped and his face came up with a smile that spread from ear to ear. "Got it." It took him a moment to realize that Amber had her hands above her head and that every Nilmerg in the room was pointing something nasty at him.

"Oh dear. Eh…"

"Very slowly put the PAD on the deck, Aubrey, and step away from it, OK?"

Instead of obeying, Aubrey touched a single key on his PAD and in her ear Amber felt the familiar gentle tingling of her ear bug activating and clear as day a voice could be heard.

"No one will fire unless specifically instructed by me. There have been enough mistakes already and I will not go down in our history as the ship master who started another war."

While Amber had been concentrating on her dialogue with Ussa, Aubrey had been busily refining the interpretation software on his PAD, unaware of events going on around him. The triple beep emitted by the PAD was the sound of his success. Unfortunately, it had almost got both of them killed.

"Aubrey, tell me you can get your software to run on Ussa's little box of tricks."

"Not a chance, Ambassador. I have no idea how their systems are set up."

Amber felt the hope fade.

"But what I can do is download it to an external bone pick up that he could wear. A bit bulkier than an ear bug, it bypasses the ear canal and sends the sound vibrations directly into whatever equivalent bone structure they have for converting sound to vibration, but with a little trial and error it should be just as effective."

Amber was still trying to figure out how to ask Ussa to wear the bone pick up when he walked right up to Aubrey and stretched out his open hand. Ussa had obviously been following their conversation as best he could. Aubrey got to work. Pulling a pick up from his top pocket, he placed it carefully onto his PAD. A few seconds later, Aubrey's PAD emitted a small beep and he placed the pick-up in Ussa's hand. With a swift motion the Nilmerg commander rotated his arm at the elbow and placed the pick up beside a small flap of skin just behind his lower jaw. Amber gave it a few seconds, crossing the fingers of her outstretched hands.

"Can you understand me, Ship Master?"

Ussa's took a small step backwards and his hand went to the pick-up. "Yes Ambassador, I hear you clearly. A moment please." Ussa pivoted to face his crew, all still with their weapons aimed at Aubrey. "Holster your weapons." With obvious reluctance, they did as ordered.

"Now that we can understand each other properly, Ambassador, let my express my deep regret for the confusion which led to us firing on your ship. In way of an explanation we have been at war with the Deres for more than four generations and your ship's sudden arrival... well, to be honest, we thought it was a new Deres weapon with which to ambush us."

"Understandable, Ship Master. If I had been at war for so long then I may have reacted in the same fashion. But if I may ask, who are the Deres?"

CHAPTER TEN

AN AUDIENCE WITH THE EMPEROR

ALONA – MESSIER 54
50,000 LIGHT YEARS FROM EARTH

TDF *Southern Cross* emerged into the vast nothingness of space and immediately the ship's systems began to probe the space around it.

"Looks like we've arrived in clear space, sir. Instruments show that the nearest objects look to be the rings of the gas giant at 1800 mark three six. Distance is just a hair over 260,000 kilometers."

Lieutenant Commander Bob Straits let out a satisfied grunt. He had commanded the *Southern Cross* since she had left the Janus ship yards eleven months before and since then she had been bouncing between the four planets of the Commonwealth nonstop, but this was the first time that he had made the voyage out to Messier 54 and after a journey of 50,000 light years the ship had arrived exactly where the navigation officer had said it should. Pretty impressive. Not that he was going to tell Nichol Lacroix that. The bridge of the small courier ship was cramped enough without having to contend with her massive Gallic ego bragging about how good she was.

"OK Mark, contact Alona port approach control and identify us. Apologize for our unannounced arrival but explain that we're a diplomatic courier with urgent dispatches for the Commonwealth embassy. We're holding at the outer system marker and request permission to fold to the inner marker where we'll proceed to an orbital insertion using sub-light drive only."

"Got it. We should get a reply in about three hours at this distance depending on how on the ball the controllers are today."

"Fine, let's do a bit of housekeeping while we wait. I'm not too happy with those upgrades to the sensors, could you run a full diagnostic and tell the chief we're still getting that intermittent warning light from the fusion injectors? We're going to be here a while so I'm happy if he takes nonessential power offline to have a look at it as long as we're ready to go again when we get the green light from port approach."

Bob sat back in his chair and brought up the latest ship's engineering report while the first officer set about the systems diagnostic.

An hour later, Bob was immersed in the latest paper on theoretical advanced engine design when a blinking amber icon in the display caught his attention. That was odd. Bob tapped the icon and his display filled with sensor data. According to this there were multiple engine sources closing on the *Southern Cross*.

"Mark…"

"I see it, sir. The sources are partially hidden by the gas giants rings. Give me a minute, the computer is running the data now."

One minute became two as the computer worked away, trying to identify the engine signatures.

Mark pushed himself back from his console with a low hum and scratched his jaw.

When he didn't say anything further, Bob got up and stepped over to him. "What have you got, Mark?"

Mark pointed at a slow, repeating wave on his display. "The computer says that's a gravity drive. Problem is, it doesn't exactly match any gravity drive used by the Commonwealth. Don't get me wrong, it's not far off a match. The closest I have is a commercial version of a Talos light cruiser drive, but it looks to have been modified somehow. Whoever it is, there are five distinct drive sources and they're closing on us so we should be able to get a better sensor reading as they do. To be honest with you, skipper, I don't think they know we're even here."

TDF *Southern Cross* was only fifty meters long and six at the beam. With most of her power systems offline while the chief inspected the fusion injectors, *Southern Cross* was a proverbial hole in space. Bob brought up the projected course of the unknown ships. If they kept to it, the closest of the five should pass within 40,000 kilometers of him in about nine minutes. A bit too close for comfort.

"Get Nichol back up here double time. I want her to plot us a course at an angle away from those ships. Use only the docking thrusters to maneuver and I want the primary sensor array to face them all the way. Whoever they are, I want as much detail on them as we can get and tell the chief to get the drive buttoned up again. If these guys turn out to be unfriendly, I want to be able to hightail it out of here."

#

The next quarter of an hour was the longest in Bob Strait's life. Once again, Nichol had proved how good a navigator she was as she maneuvered the small courier away from the oncoming ships with aplomb. Bob had been forced to wipe the sweat from his eyes as the five unknown ships, all the size of light cruisers, powered past him in perfect formation, completely unaware of the *Southern Cross*. His ship's computers recorded every detail of their cigar-shaped superstructure and passive sensors absorbed every erg of energy the ships emanated. The likely power output of the four ominous-looking grazers clustered around the cruiser's nose and the smaller snouts of the particle beam emitters spaced along the length of the hull had Bob squirming in his seat. Just one hit from one of those particle beams would rip the *Southern Cross* apart, never mind the grazers. But it was one particular image that was still floating in Bob's display. On the flank of each of the cruisers, just below a raised command structure, was emblazoned a winged beast, the talons of its four extended legs grabbing the sword that passed through its body. The symbol of the Imperial Alonan Navy. A navy that didn't have access to certain aspects of Commonwealth technology as it had refused to join the Union of Planets. One of those technologies was the gravity drive.

"Nichol, plot us a course for home and fold when you're ready. The dispatches can wait."

GENEVA - EARTH - SOL SYSTEM

The quarterly meeting of the Commonwealth Union of Planets leaders had been a series of briefings by preening politicians, eager to get as much media exposure for themselves and the political parties they represented as possible. Rebecca Coston unconsciously massaged her right hand and forearm. She must have shaken hundreds of hands today as the aforementioned politicians vied for a moment with the twenty-fourth president of the Terran Republic and a sound bite, which the media would replay on the various news

157

channels. Accompanied only by her ever-present protection detail, Rebecca left her office via a side door, which led to a small room where she entered a waiting elevator. She found the quiet of the elevator a refreshing change as it dropped down through the core of the mega-scraper that housed the multitude of departments required to run a planet-wide government. The ride from her office passed in silence as Rebecca collected her thoughts for the forthcoming private meeting with the other heads of state. The elevator reached ground level but didn't slow its descent. When the doors eventually opened, Rebecca stepped onto a small platform five stories below ground.

Waiting to greet her was Patricia Bath. Rebecca had recognized the urgent need to have an adviser who could distill into bite-sized pieces the massive amounts of information being generated on a daily basis by the ever-growing diplomatic, science, and military arms of the Commonwealth, and when Rebecca approached her old friend Aaron Beckett and her science adviser Valerie Hayes, both of them came up with the same name. Patricia Bath. Rebecca was promptly impressed by the young woman's organizational skills and in no time at all Patricia had cut a swathe through the various department heads who insisted they be allowed to brief the president personally. Anyone who refused to comply with the new adviser's rules found themselves getting a personal call from Rebecca's Chief of Staff, Clement Bradshaw. Anyone who was stupid enough to cross swords with Clement very quickly found themselves on the losing end of an argument they wished they'd never started. Word spread fast that Patricia Bath had the ear of the president and top aides so Patricia's new guidelines were implemented with only mumbled complaint.

"Madam President, I've loaded a short brief on each of the points that you asked for onto this PAD."

Taking the PAD with a weary smile, Rebecca nodded her thanks as both women entered the waiting train carriage and sank into its comfortable seats. The maglev raced along the underground tunnel connecting her office building in Geneva with the sprawling underground facility known simply as Central Command. The eighteen kilometer long tunnel allowed the president to leave her office and be in the heart of Central Command within minutes. Safe from anything but multiple nuclear strikes.

The maglev slowed smoothly from its 300 kilometer per hour headlong rush as it approached the first of a set of armored blast doors, which rolled aside, allowing the carriage to pass before resealing the tunnel behind it. A second set of blast doors closed behind the maglev, which came to a halt and lowered itself onto the tracks. With a subdued whoosh, the carriage doors opened and a waiting marine colonel escorted the president and her party along brightly lit corridors filled with soldiers, sailors, and marines going about their business. The colonel parted the throng like the bow of some oceanic vessel, never slowing his business-like pace until he reached a set of doors with the simple sign, "Briefing One", above it. Only the presence of two armed ground force soldiers who snapped to attention as the president approached marked the door as being any different from the multitude of others along the route. With a gracious "thank you," Rebecca passed through the doors accompanied only by Patricia. Her protection detail took post outside the room, alongside the silent soldiers.

As the briefing room doors closed behind them, Rebecca stopped for a moment to allow her eyes to adjust to the relative darkness of the room lit only by the ambient light filtering in from "The Pit." The raised briefing room, with a glass wall, offered an impressive view into the operations center that was the beating heart and brain of the Terran Defense Forces. Its constant activity always reminded Rebecca of what it must be like to be at the center of an anthill. Row upon row of displays manned by officers speaking in hushed tones. The largest holo projectors Rebecca had seen anywhere turned the front wall of "The Pit" into a constantly changing montage of numbers, diagrams, and images as priorities changed.

Rebecca returned her attention to the room. Moving to the head of the table in the center of the room, she nodded a welcome to Prime Minister Bezled of Garunda and Chairman Taarov of the Persai, each seated beside their representatives to the Combined Joint Chiefs of Staff.

"Madam President," called General Keyton Joyce from behind a lectern at the far end of the table. "We're ready to start the presentation whenever you are."

"Please do, General, I'm most interested to hear the Joint Chiefs' assessment of recent events."

"As you know, ladies and gentlemen, following the decision to initiate survey missions once more Survey Flotilla One was tasked to Algol 3, Survey Flotilla Two to 23 Librae and Survey Flotilla Three is as yet to deploy but is finishing working up and should be leaving for Tau Eridani within the next seventy-two hours. If I may, I would like to give you all a brief overview of what SurvFlot One and Two found on reaching their respective destinations."

Rebecca glanced across at Bezled and Taarov, who both nodded their assent. "Go ahead, General."

The holo cube above the table came to life with the representation of the Algol 3 system. Its three stars slowly rotating at its center in their odd balancing act. The presence of three stars in the one system led to a confusing series of orbits as each star in turn influenced each of the systems' planets, but highlighted in the holo cube was the single planet of any importance. Benii.

"The revelation of finding another advanced race that was not only aware of the Saiph manipulation in their own past but also fully aware of the potential threat posed to them by the Others came as no real surprise to us. Our analysts had believed it inevitable that we would eventually come across another race who, like the Persai, had either come across the Others or some evidence of the Saiph. The fact that they, without the aid of the gravity drive, had also managed to colonize two other star systems, was unexpected, but on reflection, the Persai had been in the process of establishing extra solar colonies when the Others had destroyed their original home world."

Force Leader Tolas surged to his feet and slammed his fist down on the table, his lips flattened to show teeth. "Something those thrice-cursed Balek will pay for at my hand and the hands of my kin, General!"

Chairman Taarov placed a calming hand on Tolas' arm. "Of that I have no doubt, my friend. But for now, we build our strength ready for the day of vengeance. Continue, General Joyce."

"It would appear Mr. Chairman, that the Benii hold the same sentiments as yourselves toward the Others. Having used the courier ship we dispatched for the use of Ambassador Schamu to establish contact with their two colonies, Baut and Gossol, we found that even though Baut has a relatively harsh environment and life is difficult there, the colonists have managed to build up a significant military force. The second colony, Gossol, has a much more benign environment and though a younger colony, it has also flourished and established a viable tech base which has already produced a number of warships and is in a position to significantly increase production if the Commonwealth was to supply additional resources in the way of automated ship building units." Keyton paused and gave the gathered politicians a deliberate look. "That of course is a political consideration and not a military one. However the ambassador reports that both colonies have asserted their allegiance to the home world and have agreed to be guided by its decisions."

"What is your opinion of the Benii military strength, General?" interjected the Garundan Prime Minister.

The image of a large gun-metal gray ship edged in blue replaced that of the Algol 3 system in the holo cube.

"This is a Benii carrier. It is roughly one and a half times the size of our largest current battleship. However, its armament is radically different. It carries 115 of these…"

In the holo cube appeared a sleek, round-nosed spacecraft. Two stub wings protruded away from the main body and at the tips of each wing sat a long, lance-like weapon. Above and below the main fuselage sat a small turret mounting twin cannon.

"This, ladies and gentlemen, is a Benii space fighter. They call it a Freiba. I believe that is a type of flying insect with a particularly nasty sting. An apt description. The Freiba is specifically configured for fighting in space, rather than our own Reaper, which is primarily configured for atmospheric warfare. These

Freiba are highly maneuverable and incredibly fast. According to Admiral Papadomas' reports he believes that the Freiba could very well swamp the close-in defense systems of any current warship in either the Commonwealth's or the Others' order of battle. They are armed with two concentrated beam emitters, which, individually, would cause superficial damage, but it is the analyst's opinion that a number of strikes will penetrate battle armor and may cause significant damage. Needless to say, the boys and girls in Research and Development are desperate to get their hands on a Freiba."

"It's my understanding, General, that the Benii have already offered the Commonwealth full access to their military technology in return for an alliance against the Others."

"Yes, Madam President, that is correct. I believe Ambassador Schamu is in the process of preparing his suggestions for an initial memorandum of understanding to be put before the Commonwealth Council for approval so that he may open up full treaty negotiations with the long-term view of the Benii joining the Commonwealth as a full partner."

"And what is the opinion of the Joint Chiefs on allowing the Benii into the Commonwealth, General?"

Keyton Joyce took a moment to look at the image of the Benii carrier and the Freiba next to it before answering. "The three planets of the Benii have managed to retain a similar force structure. Incorporating them into the Commonwealth fleets would bring us eight carriers, 920 Freiba space fighters, twenty-four battle ships and thirty-six heavy cruisers. That is the equivalent of all the firepower of First Fleet. The only drawback is that the Benii ships' drive systems limit their ships to high sub-light speeds, but I have it on good authority that with assistance from our scientists working on Zarmina, they could have a working star drive within a few months." Keyton gave a small shrug. "Alternatively, we could just retrofit the Benii fleet with gravity drives, but that would be a major undertaking and I have every confidence in the scientists on Zarmina finding a more acceptable solution. So in short, with the strength of the Others' fleet still an unknown quantity, I would say the more ships we have, the better."

Rebecca felt there was nothing more to be gained at this time by further debate on the Benii question so she moved the briefing on. "What of 23 Librae?"

"That, Madam President, is a completely different matter. Our interpretation of the situation in the system has been based solely on the reports of Ambassador Isa and Admiral Torrance. Militarily, we have already seen the effectiveness of the Nilmerg's weaponry. Our estimate is that they are approximately forty years behind our own current top of the line ships, but if they're able to achieve the element of surprise, as they did in the case of SurvFlot Two, then their weapons can inflict significant damage to our lighter units. Anything above heavy cruiser size would have no difficulty in defeating even a numerically superior Nilmerg force if it came down to it."

"Then Admiral Torrance is to be congratulated in showing restraint in not destroying the Nilmerg, even though he found himself in a difficult situation."

"That he is, Mister Prime Minister." A wry smile appeared on Keyton's face. "I could not guarantee that I would have shown such restraint, but the people in Survey are trained slightly differently from those in charge of the battle fleet and in this instance that paid off."

"Are we any further forward on who these..." Rebecca searched her memory for the name.

"The Deres, ma'am?" Patricia added helpfully.

"Yes, the Deres. I've only had time to scan Ambassador Isa's report but the situation in 23 Librae strikes me as a complicated one."

A schematic of the 23 Librae system appeared in the holo cube. A type G star with two worlds orbiting exactly opposite each other in the Goldilocks zone with a third world just skirting the edge of the life-bearing zone.

"Complicated may be an understatement, Madam President. Ambassador Isa's report indicates that for the majority of their history, the Nilmergs believed they were the sole intelligent species in the universe. Their astronomers had searched the heavens for signs of other life, much as we had done, without success. As time went by, they developed sufficiently to place artificial satellites in orbit and planned and launched unmanned missions to their nearest planetary neighbors. It was one of these probes to the planet on the fringe of the Goldilocks zone that revealed to them the existence of Deres. With Deres orbiting exactly opposite from them, the ambient interference the star generated had hidden any form of electronic emissions from either planet."

Chairman Taarov let out a quiet chuckle. "I bet it came as a bit of a shock to find that what you had been looking for in the stars was actually only a stone's throw away."

"I can imagine it did, Mr. Chairman," agreed Keyton. "The news of another sentient race in their own star system led to the nations of Nilmerg pooling their resources to construct a manned spaceship which was launched with the intention of visiting their neighbors. As the spaceship passed beyond the stars' radio horizon they lost contact with it. This was only to be expected. But the months passed and they heard nothing further from either the ship's automatic systems or the crew, so they decided to launch a second ship, but this time the ship was equipped with a relay satellite which the crew would deploy just on the edge of the radio horizon. This satellite would constantly relay telemetry back to Nilmerg from the ship. As the Nilmerg ship established orbit over what had been identified as the largest populated area ready to deploy its landing unit, the ship relayed back unusual readings which indicated a high level of radiation was present in the atmosphere. A level that couldn't have occurred naturally. The explanation the Nilmerg scientists came up with was that there had been a high-order nuclear explosion in the recent past. Without warning, the feed from the spacecraft was cut. The ground controllers back on Nilmerg initially thought there was some form of technical fault, but as they began to piece the data together, they discovered that the radar on board the ship had caught a fleeting trace of at least two objects launched from the surface of Deres which were on a collision course with the ship. Their conclusion was that their ship was shot down deliberately."

"An act of war?" asked Rebecca.

"Or one of defense, Madam President."

Rebecca gave Keyton an incredulous look. "How so, General? The Nilmerg had made no hostile gestures. Their ships carried no weapons."

With a few taps of his PAD, Keyton brought up a schematic of the original Nilmerg manned ship.

"This was supplied to us by the Nilmerg as proof that the original ship they sent to Deres was, as you pointed out Madam President, unarmed. At first glance no weapon systems are evident, but…"

In the holo cube the schematic expanded until it was centered on the propulsion system.

"Meet a 35-megaton nuclear bomb."

The room was still as the politicians tried to absorb what Keyton was telling them.

Chairman Taarov was the first to recover. "Are you telling us, General, that the Nilmerg deliberately launched a nuclear attack on the Deres? A people they had never even met. That's ludicrous."

"I never said it was deliberate, Mr. Chairman. The Nilmerg used the best of each nations' current space technology to build their manned ships. To get the ship into orbit they used hypergolic fuel. A fuel that is composed of two distinct parts. When the two parts are mixed, they react and are highly combustible. They are also highly corrosive. The Nilmerg knew they couldn't possibly carry enough fuel to make the journey from their home planet to Deres so they developed a very rudimentary nuclear fusion drive. It worked. But in their rush to launch, it was subjected to only minimal testing. I remind you of the radiation traces the second Nilmerg ship detected in the atmosphere before it was destroyed. I submit that the first Nilmerg ship suffered some kind of engineering failure, entered the atmosphere and exploded. If I was a Deres, all I would have seen was an unknown spacecraft entering orbit over a major city then...Bang!... A thirty five megaton nuclear atmospheric detonation."

In her mind's eye, Rebecca saw the blinding flash followed by the fireball and shock wave. When she spoke, her unease was evident as she tried to control her shaking voice.

"What would be the effects of a detonation of that size, General?"

Keyton spoke without consulting his notes, this was something every human commander who studied his own planet's past wars knew by heart. He showed no emotion as he spoke in a hollow tone. "Radiation pulse of 500 Rems out to about three kilometers. Those who receive this level of exposure will suffer between fifty and ninety percent mortality from the acute effects alone. Dying will take between several hours and several weeks. A nuclear fireball's radius will be 4.61 kilometers. The amount of radioactive fallout will depend on whether the fireball makes contact with the surface or not. Out to nine kilometers from the point of the impact, the overpressure will either demolish or severely damage all but the heaviest of concrete buildings. Casualties will rise to 100 percent. Out to twenty one kilometers most residential buildings will collapse. Fatalities will be widespread. Out to sixty kilometers, those not under cover will most likely experience third-degree burns which will leave severe scarring and possibly require amputation."

Of the three races present in the room the Persai had had the power of the atom used on their home world by the Others, but only humans had witnessed the effects of nuclear weapons unleashed on a population center by members of their own race. The pale faces of Rebecca and Keyton aborted any questions that the others may have been about to ask.

Rebecca forced herself to stop thinking of the millions of deaths that humanity had inflicted on itself in the ultimately futile national wars in Earth's recent past and to concentrate on the present.

"I take it the Deres retaliated, General?"

"Yes, ma'am. They had no way of knowing that the explosion was most likely an accident. We believe at this point they hadn't reached a sufficient tech level to develop their own nuclear weapons so they used the only weapon of mass destruction they had. They packed chemical-fueled missiles with a biological weapon, a highly contagious virus, and sent the missiles to Nilmerg. When they reached their targets they deployed their payload. Within a matter of weeks, the first Nilmerg fell sick with an unknown disease, which was fatal in up to eighty percent of those infected. The virus spread like wildfire and in a matter of months it was a global pandemic. Luckily for the Nilmerg, the disease was too efficient. As the casualty rates soared, those who had contracted the virus died so quickly that they didn't get the chance to reach areas that were so far clear of the disease. By the time the virus burned out, over sixty percent of the entire Nilmerg population were dead. The survivors were too scared to make physical contact with each other for fear of reigniting the disease, so it took nearly twenty years before the Nilmerg became a viable space-faring population again. This gave the Deres time to develop their own space force, so when the Nilmerg returned to Deres looking for revenge they were ready. Both sides were so evenly matched that they effectively fought each other to a standstill. The most fitting analogy we've come up with is the trench warfare of World War One. Both sides just batter away at the other in a war of attrition that neither is ever going to win and both will eventually lose."

Prime Minister Bezled cleared his throat quietly. "Are you telling me, General, that both sides are fighting a war they cannot win and that the war was started by accident?"

"I know it seems bizarre, Mr. Prime Minister, but as an impartial observer it would seem to fit. It certainly wouldn't be the first time in human history that a conflict had been started by mistake or by a misinterpretation of the available facts. What are you going to do about it? That is the question before you. The Commonwealth forces could intervene and put a halt to the conflict. As I've already said, the Nilmerg weaponry isn't of such a quality that it would provide a substantial threat to one of our heavier units. That would lead to the conclusion that our ships wouldn't have much to fear from Deres weaponry either. Militarily, we could do it. The question has to be whether or not there is a political will for us to intervene. My own opinion is that an attempt should be made to broker a peace before the Commonwealth even considers getting involved in a war that, frankly, is none of our business."

"Very succinctly put, General," Taarov growled from the far end of the table. "But... and this is an important point I feel, we went to 23 Librae to find out what happened to those peoples that the Saiph had manipulated and we have found them killing each other over an accident." Taarov looked slowly around the room meeting each person's eyes. "Do we not have a moral responsibility to put an end to the fighting? Even for a short time? And allow both sides the opportunity to view the facts from an impartial observer?"

Rebecca took the time to gauge the feeling in the room before replying. "Would you Mr. Chairman and you Mr. Prime Minister be willing to support a decision to instruct Ambassador Isa to make contact with the Deres and attempt to broker a ceasefire with the view to organizing peace talks under the auspices of the Commonwealth?"

The military men had had their say. Now it was up to the politicians to decide on the way forward. A decision that didn't take long.

Prime Minister Bezled was the first to decide. "Garunda agrees."

Taarov nodded slowly. "As does Pars."

Rebecca relaxed slightly as she allowed a smile to cross her face. "Very well, I shall have the appropriate instructions drawn up and dispatched forthwith to the ambassador. Now, General. For the last item on the agenda and one that has been the cause of major concern amongst the Commonwealth Council. The situation in Messier 54."

The image in the holo cube changed to show the close-up taken by the *Southern Cross* of the cruisers bearing the symbol of the Imperial Alonan Navy.

"Madam President, our analysts have been going over the images and data recorded by the *Southern Cross* with a fine-tooth comb and we have little to add from our original analysis which was distributed to the Council. Each of the cruisers comes in slightly heavier than our own Talos light cruisers but we believe the Alonan have gone for a heavier energy weapon armament as opposed to missiles. That may be because they haven't been able to reduce the size of the gravity drive down to a sufficient size to make it practical for missile use. What's interesting though, is that although all of the cruisers are running what appears to be a modified merchant gravity drive, one in particular stands out."

"Oh. How so, General?" asked Taarov.

"The circumstances of how the Alonan have managed to get their hands on gravity drive technology is still under investigation by not only our own Naval Intelligence Service but by the Federal Investigation Bureau. We believe that we may have a break in the investigation."

Rebecca leaned forward, anxious to hear more. "Care to share, General?"

Once more, Keyton touched a control on his PAD and in the holo cube two oscillating waves appeared, one above the other.

"What you're looking at, ladies and gentlemen, is the output of two gravity drives. The top one is of the Alonan cruisers. The bottom one belongs to the Zurich Lines merchant vessel *Sea Hawk*. Now, every gravity drive has an individual signature. A fingerprint, if you like."

The display zoomed in on a single peak on the cruiser's oscillating wave. It wasn't quite as regular as it first appeared.

"That, my experts tell me, is a fault in the drive lining. A small crack, not worth repairing, but that crack makes this cruiser the easiest to identify, and this," the image zoomed out only to zoom in again on the trace of the *Sea Hawk*, "is the same portion of the trace from the *Sea Hawk*. As you can see, they are identical."

"But… that's not possible. Is it?" said an exasperated Bezled.

Keyton shrugged his shoulders. "The experts tell me that the chances of two gravity drives having the exact same signature are in the tens of millions to one."

Taarov weighed in. "Well, surely all we have to do is locate the *Sea Hawk* and recheck her drive. There must be some mistake."

"That, Mr. Chairman, was my first thought. Unfortunately the *Sea Hawk* was removed from service ten months ago and sold for scrap. It should be sitting in a parking orbit alongside the Pathos reclamation yards."

"Should be, General?"

Keyton gave Rebecca a noncommittal look. "I'll be honest with you, Madam President, until we physically check, I'm not holding my breath. I have my best men on the job and I have the utmost confidence that they'll get to the bottom of this."

Rebecca slapped her palm down on the table in frustration. "Well, I think it's high time we found out what the Alona are up to, don't you?"

#

ALONA - MESSIER 54
50,000 LIGHT YEARS FROM EARTH

Aaron Beckett stood patiently in the ante-room outside the throne room of Emperor Paxt the Ninth. Over his decades of diplomatic service, Aaron had been forced to wait at the beck and call of many an important dignitary and he had devised a simple method of keeping himself occupied as he did so. Aaron had noticed that the majority of these types of people liked to surround themselves with magnificent pieces of art. Be those paintings or sculptures. Aaron would start in one corner of whatever room he was waiting in and work his way around each wall, carefully examining each piece of art as he went. With the amount of practice he'd had over the years, he'd actually become a bit of an expert on the subject of fine art and more than once had been able to spot a fake much to the embarrassment of its owner. Aaron was on his third wall when the large double doors opened and a uniformed Alonan usher beckoned him forward.

The imperial palace had been built by the first emperor, Emperor Paxt the First, in the aftermath of the series of wars that had threatened the very existence of the Alonan people. Emperor Paxt at the time of the wars had been a leading general in the army of the Northern Confederation. He'd become sickened by the orders of his political masters who were squandering the lives of his troops, so he led a coup that overthrew the government and took sole command of the nation.

173

Through a series of trusted officers, he reached out to the military leaders of the other major powers, offering to bring about an immediate cessation of hostilities. The politicians of the other powers had witnessed the execution by General Paxt of his predecessors and had been terrified that their own military would follow suit, so they began a series of purges to weed out any officer whom they didn't believe was politically reliable and would not continue the war.

That was when General Paxt decided to go public with his offer to end the war. He broadcast an appeal to the ordinary soldiers to not only do the right thing for themselves, but for their families and for their planet as a whole. In a tide of revolution, the old political houses fell and for the first time in a generation, the planet Alona was at peace. With the politicians out of the picture, the soldiers looked to their officers for guidance, who in turn looked to General Paxt. Paxt seized the moment.

With the skill of the great general he was, he reorganized the various armies into labor battalions who set to work repairing the damage the war had caused. Homes, schools, and hospitals went up in record time. To feed his soldiers, he sent them into the fields, not to forage and steal from the farmers but to provide labor to plant and harvest the crops. The government would take a percentage of the farms' produce to feed the soldiers but whatever was left, the farmer was free to sell to whomever he wished. Borders were dispensed with and with it individual nations were swallowed up into the greater whole. Within a decade, Alona was a radically different place. No one went hungry. No one was cold. People cared what happened to their neighbors and if you ever needed help, of any kind, you found a soldier. A soldier whose duty was no longer just to fight for his people, but to care for them to the best of his ability. None of this would have been possible if it hadn't been for General Paxt. In a show of gratitude and faith in his leadership, the people by popular decree declared him Emperor Paxt the First. In an amazing feat of foresight, Emperor Paxt put in place a law that the position of emperor could never be hereditary. Paxt himself designed the system of government to ensure this. Normal citizens elected District Governors and they in turn elected one of their own as Emperor. But to remind people of their duty to Alona as a whole, it was decided that the only citizens who would have the right to vote would be those who had served in the uniform of the empire for no less than three years. Whatever the Commonwealth thought of the system, it had been in place for over 300 years and nobody seemed interested in changing it.

This was the first time Aaron had been in the imperial palace, located in the hills overlooking the planetary capital of Bozra. As the capital city had grown, it had spread around the walls of the imperial palace so that the palace grounds from above looked like the only greenery in a sea of gray and brown buildings. The building itself covered some 67,000 square meters and was a testament to Alonan architecture. When Emperor Paxt the First had the building commissioned, he ordered that the building was to incorporate art and design from each of the old nations to show that though each of the constituent parts of Alona were individuals, they had come together as a whole. *Great idea,* Aaron thought but the clash of styles could be taxing on the eye.

As Aaron walked in through the ante-room doors and entered the throne room, he was struck by the amount of light in the room. On both sides the walls were made of sheet glass giving spectacular views of the palace gardens. Rather than intimidating a visitor, the sight of so much greenery was relaxing. The exact opposite of what any dictatorial military leader would want. Aaron advanced toward the waiting emperor, seated on a small raised dais at the end of the room. His footsteps deadened by the plush carpet. Apart from the emperor himself, Aaron could only see Grand Admiral Raga and the foreign minister, Minister Hozal, in a room that could easily hold hundreds. A sense of foreboding came over Aaron as he approached the base of the dais and halted at a respectful distance.

"Your Majesty, Minister Hozal, Admiral. The Commonwealth Council is grateful for you making time in your busy schedule to see me."

Emperor Paxt nodded by way of greeting, leaving Hozal to speak for him.

"It is not every day that I receive a call from Ambassador Calvin requesting a personal audience with the emperor himself for a Special Envoy of the Commonwealth. We are intrigued to hear what you have to say. Ambassador Calvin would not be drawn into explaining the reason behind the meeting, just that it was of the utmost urgency that a meeting be arranged at the emperor's earliest convenience. So, here we are, Mr. Beckett."

So you're not going to admit that you know exactly why I'm here. Oh well, I didn't really expect you to straight off the bat.

"A week ago, a Commonwealth courier ship carrying urgent diplomatic mail for our embassy on Alona arrived unexpectedly at your system's outer marker..."

"In violation of the standing agreement between our two governments, Mr. Beckett, as I'm sure you well know, all scheduled arrivals or departures from the Alona system must be cleared through the appropriate authorities. We have no record of any clearance being granted to this courier."

Ah, so you did know I was here about the courier!

"You're quite correct, Minister. But as I'm also sure you're aware there are provisions within the agreement for urgent diplomatic traffic, which this courier was, to make unscheduled arrival in the Alona system as long as they hold at the system's outer marker. Inform approach control of their arrival and wait at the outer marker until given permission to enter the system. Exactly what this courier did. To the letter." Aaron emphasized the last part.

Minister Hozal's face remained impassive but Aaron caught Admiral Raga clench his jaw. *Looks like nobody told the navy about that particular clause. Oops.*

"I seem to remember a courier requesting permission to approach the inner system and then for some unexplained reason it made no further contact with approach control." Hozal gestured toward Admiral Raga. "I believe the navy launched a search and rescue operation in the area of the outer marker in an attempt to locate the courier, believing that it may be in difficulty. An exercise that tied up valuable naval resources for quite some time and at considerable expense, I may add. I take it your courier made it safely back to Commonwealth territory without incident?"

"It did indeed Minister, thank you for your concern," Aaron said graciously.

"In the circumstances, I suppose we can overlook the fact that yet again the courier violated our agreement by not seeking permission to leave the system," Hozal said dismissively.

In the circumstances? Aaron jumped on Hozal's slip.

"And what circumstances would those be, Minister?"

Hozal immediately realized his mistake. "What I meant to say Mr. Beckett was…"

Emperor Paxt raised his hand. "Enough of this verbal maneuvering. Mr. Beckett, ask us what you want to ask and be done with it."

Aaron was caught slightly wrong-footed by the emperor's intervention. He had expected to spend at least another ten minutes playing verbal chess with Hozal before eventually getting to the point but it would seem the emperor was not a man for wasting time.

"Your Majesty. While the courier was holding at the outer marker, it identified five unknown ships equipped with gravity drives approaching its location. The courier's computers could not identify the ships as belonging to any of the members of the Commonwealth and since Alona does not have access to Commonwealth gravity drive technology…"

"Only because you deny us it as part of your policy of refusing the Empire the weapons to protect itself," spat Admiral Raga angrily.

A glance from the emperor silenced him.

Aaron detected an opening.

"Protect yourself from whom, Admiral? Surely you do not believe the Commonwealth has any intention of initiating any form of armed conflict with the Empire. Have we not always be open about our intentions of establishing peaceful trade relations?"

Neither Admiral Raga nor Minister Hozal said anything. Both instead looked toward the Emperor who leaned forward in his seat and pointed an accusing finger at Aaron.

"Your use of the phrase 'open about your intentions' is one I find amusing in the circumstances, Mr. Beckett. If your government wanted to be open with the Empire then perhaps there would be no need for secrets between us."

Aaron's forehead wrinkled in confusion. He didn't like the way this was going. "I'm sorry, your Majesty, you have me at a disadvantage. The Commonwealth has always been open and honest with the Empire."

The Emperor let out a loud *ha*! "So when were you going to tell us about the Others?"

CHAPTER ELEVEN

INVESTIGATIONS

EARTH - SOL SYSTEM

Elizabeth Wilson was having a bitch of a day. When her driver had picked her up from her home on the outskirts of Geneva for the ride to the shuttle port that served the Terran Republic's capital city, she wished she'd passed this particular job off to someone much younger. In the nearly four years that she'd been working for General Keyton Joyce she had to admit there'd only been one time that she had seen him so determined that she get results and that had been when that sniveling wretch Geoffrey Rawson was implicated in a bribery scandal during his short time as Secretary of Defense. That particular waste of rations was now rotting in a cell of the maximum security penal colony orbiting Titan and long may he stay there.

The shuttle port operated around the clock but when Elizabeth had passed through at three o'clock in the morning local time, there was hardly a soul to be seen. Even still, Elizabeth was in civilian clothes and her driver had selected one of the unmarked ground cars for their use. A good thing as the sight of an aging female admiral of naval intelligence may have turned a few heads. The local Federal Investigation Bureau were under express instructions from their director to ensure that there was no security personnel around to ask any questions so when she arrived at the security checkpoint, the two officers on duty suddenly found themselves deep in conversation about some sporting event or other. Similarly in traffic control the duty controller gave permission for the shuttle that was not squawking any identifier permission to depart before, while a senior FIB agent stood looking over his shoulder, he wiped the computer records of the departure. As the agent departed, he dropped a gentle reminder of how federal offenses carried a mandatory five-year sentence. The controller had been working the night shift for nearly a decade but this was the first time he'd had a fed hanging over his shoulder and threatening him with a trip to a penal colony. Whoever or whatever was on that shuttle must be pretty important but you could bet your bottom dollar he wasn't going to say anything.

The Naval Intelligence Service didn't actually own any ships, but when you get a personal call from the Chief of Naval Operations, you tend to just say yes sir, no sir, three bags full sir, so when Lieutenant Commander Kenichi Sutou had received such a call and was told to expect a civilian shuttle craft in the next fifteen minutes, the passenger of which he was to give his total and unquestioning cooperation, he had done just that and the second the CNO cut the link, Sutou had flipped the cover off the large red button that sat alongside his bed. Kenichi hesitated for just a second. This could be nothing, Kenichi he told himself. Like hell! The CNO does not call a lowly destroyer captain in the middle of the night for nothing. Kenichi's finger smashed down on the red button and the battle stations alarm screamed its call to arms throughout the Havoc class destroyer TDF *Sorcerer*. Kenichi ran down the narrow corridor, buttoning his uniform shirt as he went. Sleepy crew member dived out of his way as they too rushed to their posts. As Kenichi approached the bridge bulkhead, a marine leveled his pistol at him until he confirmed the identity of the captain, even then the pistol stayed out but was moved to the more comfortable guns south position. It was unusual for a ship the size of *Sorcerer* to carry its own marines but the Havoc destroyer's main mission was anti-piracy patrols and convoy protection so there was a marine platoon on board to carry out boarding actions. The fact that his was the only ship apart from battle fleet currently in Earth's orbit that was capable of carrying out boarding actions didn't escape Kenichi's notice.

Ensign Milett's face was white as a sheet as Kenichi entered the bridge. It had seemed like the ideal time for the young ensign to get some bridge time while the ship had been safely tucked into orbit. To her credit, she only spared Kenichi a hurried glance before she went back to updating her board as section after section reported ready. As the last section reported ready, Kenichi's XO, Lieutenant Morgan Malek, burst onto the bridge.

"What the hell is going on, skipper? We're in Earth's orbit for Pete's sake."

Ensign Milett was still working the sensors and her voice cut off any reply from Kenichi. "Unidentified shuttle on approach. No IFF being received. ETA four minutes twenty seconds. Computers have a firing solution, sir."

Kenichi held up a finger to stop the question he could see Morgan wanted to ask. "Keep a lock on that shuttle ensign, but do not fire without my express permission. Morgan, you have the bridge. I want to be able to fold out of here in the next five minutes. Get the marines to meet me in the boat bay loaded for bear. They have…" Kenichi's eyes flicked to the bridge clock. "Three and a half minutes. And before you ask I have no idea what's going on either but let's be ready for anything."

Morgan gave him a curt nod and bent to work as Kenichi headed for the *Sorcerer*'s boat bay.

Three minutes later, Kenichi stood at the shoulder of the boat bay petty officer as he checked the tell tales on his board ensuring that the small boat bay, which looked even smaller now the civilian shuttle sat next to the *Sorcerer*'s own two shuttles, was sealed and pressurized. Already in the boat bay were twenty Wraith-suited marines formed up in two ranks with Second Lieutenant Vernetti front and center. She and her marines must sleep in those damn suits to have got here before he did.

Kenichi strode through the boat bay hatch and took post beside Vernetti as the shuttle steps extended and the hatch cracked open. A slim female figure appeared at the top of the steps, pausing to take a good look around the boat bay. Hints of gray in her hair glinted in the bay's lights as she made her way sprightly down the steps. Without Kenichi hearing any word of command, the marines behind him came to attention and presented arms. The female in civilian attire stopped precisely on the yellow deck line that represented the thresh hold of the *Sorcerer*.

"Permission to come aboard, Commander Sutou."

Well she knows who I am, thought Kenichi. "Permission granted ma'am. I and the *Sorcerer* are at your disposal."

The twinkle in her eye caught Kenichi by surprise. "Of course you are, Commander." The smile that hovered on her lips was infectious and Kenichi felt himself smile in return. As she stepped over the yellow line she stuck out her hand and Kenichi took it. "Admiral Elizabeth Wilson, by the way." Elizabeth felt Kenichi stiffen. "Yes I am that Admiral Wilson and you and your crew come highly recommended." Elizabeth released Kenichi's hand and indicated the twenty marines. "Praise which I see is well deserved. Just how much notice of my arrival did you get, by the way?"

"Less than fifteen minutes, Admiral. *Sorcerer* is currently at battle stations, all sections show a green board and we are ready to get under way at your order."

Elizabeth allowed a small chuckle to escape her. "Not too shabby, Commander. Not too shabby at all. Why don't you have Lieutenant Vernetti join us on the bridge and I'll fill you in on the details of our little early morning jaunt."

#

Kenichi Sutou couldn't say he was happy with the admiral's plan but CNO had been explicit. Total and unquestioning cooperation. The fact that Admiral Wilson wanted Kenichi to fold from Earth's orbit and then come out as close to the Pathos reclamation yards as possible was stretching that cooperation. The region of space around the yard was strewn with space junk and if *Sorcerer* came out of fold space in close proximity to said junk it could all be over before the crew knew what hit them. Kenichi had spent quite a few anxious moments going over the fold with his navigator but at last he was ready.

Admiral Wilson had never actually had a ship-board command. Elizabeth had spent her entire naval career in intelligence but by the pained expression on Kenichi's face when she had outlined her plan she could

184

tell that he wasn't too thrilled but he said nothing, just got together with his navigator and started plotting the fold. Lieutenant Vernetti on the other hand, had been grinning from ear to ear when she left the bridge to brief her marines on their role in the operation. Boarding actions were few and far between these days and a federal warrant that authorized the person executing the warrant to use any and all force necessary to secure evidence and suspects was even rarer.

"Excuse me, Admiral, but we're ready to fold. Perhaps you would like to take your seat?"

"Thank you, Commander."

Kenichi took his own seat and muttered a prayer under his breath. "Navigation. Execute!"

"Three. Two. One. Fold!"

Kenichi swallowed as the familiar wave of nausea swept over him, then it was all over and the collision alarms blared their warning.

"Shut that damn sound off! How close navigation?"

Lieutenant Joanie Wiggins slumped in her seat then slowly turned to face Kenichi as a smile crept across her face. "473 meters."

Crap, that was close! Kenichi gave her a big thumbs-up as he activated his link to Vernetti. "Marines away!"

Changing channels, Kenichi called the yard control room. "Pathos control, this is the TDF *Sorcerer*. I am in possession of a federal warrant. You are hereby ordered to open your outer hatches and all personnel are to refrain from operating any computers and gather immediately in the mess. Marines are entering the structure and have orders to use force up to and including lethal force in the execution of the warrant. No further warnings will be given. *Sorcerer* clear."

#

Stacey Vernetti and her marine platoon were all anchored to the hull of the *Sorcerer* by the magnetic clamps of their Wraith suits. When Admiral Wilson explained the importance of the time factor when boarding the yard, Stacey suggested that the marines could save time by pre-positioning along the outer hull of the *Sorcerer* before it entered fold space. Commander Sutou looked like he was going to have a meltdown. No one had ever traveled through fold space attached to an outer hull before. Was it even possible? Stacey calmly pointed out that just because nobody had ever done didn't mean it couldn't be done. There was certainly no technical reason why it couldn't and it would save the marines vital seconds clearing the *Sorcerer*'s airlock. Reluctantly, the commander agreed, and Stacey and twenty marines were the first to witness fold space with their own eyes. There wasn't much to it. One moment she was looking down on a blue-and-white Earth, a brief wave of strangeness, and the next she was looking at the hulking steel form of Pathos yard.

"Marines away!" called Sutou over the link and with that, Stacey pushed off with all her might. The mechanical muscles of her Wraith suit pushing her toward the personnel lock highlighted in her heads-up display. The counter on her flight time flew toward zero and the suit's computer rotated her and bent her knees to take the shock of impact. Bang! She was down and her magnetic clamps secured her to the hull dead on target. Whoever was in the yard's control room followed *Sorcerer*'s instructions, for the airlock in front of her began to open and the marines piled in.

"Team One in the forward airlock."

"Team Two in the rear airlock," said Gunny Sabin. Vernetti would sweep the forward half of the yard and secure the control room and the manager's office while

Gunny Sabin and his team would sweep aft securing the computer core, power plant, and mess hall.

The airlock gained full pressure and the inner hatch slid open. Stacey brought up the yard schematic in her display as she stepped into the corridor, taking a second to orientate herself.

"OK, One Bravo you're this deck, forward two frames and that should be the control room. Alfa we're one frame forward, stairs on our right, one deck up manager's office. Move out."

The marines bounded forward, the sound of their armored feet reverberating down the corridor. Twenty meters and Stacey swung right up the staircase, taking the steps three at a time as the staircase shuddered under her armored weight. Top of the stairs and she caught a fleeting glimpse of a scared male face disappearing behind a closing door. Damn! Stacey ran forward but when she reached the door it was locked. A quick examination showed it to be nonstandard. Someone had removed a bulkhead door from a military grade ship and replaced what would ordinarily have been a door flimsy enough for Stacey's suit to punch through. *The clock's ticking*, Stacey thought.

"Blow it."

Stacey stepped back as the next marine in line pulled a small explosive charge from his leg pouch and attached it to the locking mechanism. In her heads up display a new countdown clock appeared. Five... four...three... In Stacey's ear a warning tone sounded, two... one...Flash! The Wraith suit's computer automatically dimmed her visor and dialed down her external audio but she still felt the whole corridor shake as the charge went off. Without hesitation, Stacey was through the breach and in the office. Movement! Struggling to get off the floor was the male she'd seen just as the office door slammed shut and he had something in his hand. Stacey's hand was already moving before her brain fully recognized the threat. Gun! As if from nowhere, Stacey's PEP side arm appeared in her hand and fired of its own accord, taking the male in the center of the chest. The impact sent him flying back from the desk and slamming into the rear wall of the office, where a small needle laser fell from his hand. PEP still up and ready, Stacey advanced on him using one servo-assisted hand to fling the office desk to one side. Her suit sensors showed him to be unconscious but alive. The Pulsed Energy Projectile infrared laser pulse-emitting pistol created a rapidly expanding plasma on contact with the target. The resulting sound, shock, and electromagnetic waves stunned the target and caused pain and temporary paralysis.

"Corpsman to the manager's office. One civilian casualty."

Stacey moved into the smoke-filled corridor, leaving one of her marines guarding the injured man.

"Team check?"

"Team One Alfa. Control room secured."

"Team Two Alfa. Computer core and power plant secure."

"Team Two Bravo. Mess hall secure. By my count we're short three crew."

"Two Bravo from Two Alfa we have two secured in the power plant I'll have them escorted to you now."

"One Alfa has the third unaccounted for crew member. All crew accounted for. Good work, marines." Stacey switched channels. "Sorcerer. Team One. The yard is secure. One civilian casualty. Non-fatal. Suggest you send over the tech team to the forward airlock and I'll have an escort waiting for them."

"Good job, Marine. Tech team is en route."

On the bridge of the *Sorcerer* Kenichi Sutou let out a deep, gratified sigh as he leaned back in his seat and the stress of the last few minutes evaporated. Admiral Wilson caught his eye and gave him a silent applause.

Maybe now he would find out what this was all about.

#

A loud groan escaped Arnjad Harb as he crawled back to consciousness. His chest hurt like he had been kicked by a horse and his head pounded like the worst hangover he'd ever had. Arnjad made to raise a hand to rub his aching chest only to find that his arm wouldn't move. Arnjad forced his eyelids to open against the harsh light and looked down at his unresponsive arm to see that it was securely strapped to the arm of a chair. What the… Arnjad's mind reran events in his mind's eye. The sudden appearance of the TDF warship off the yard. His mad dash from his quarters to his office. The office door being blown out and the image of the armored marine coming toward him. He'd pulled the needle pistol he always carried and tried to shoot the marine but the pistol had hardly cleared the holster when the marine had shot him and he had receded into darkness. Arnjad had thought he was dead and his nightmare was over. Obviously not.

"Glad to see you're awake at last, Mr. Harb," a gentle voice said.

Arnjad tore his eyes from his bound arm and focused on the elderly female in civilian clothes sitting at the low table opposite him. Arnjad swallowed as he tried to lubricate his dry throat. "I demand to see a lawyer. I have rights." A wry smile was on his face.

A gentle laugh from the woman wasn't what Arnjad had expected and the smile left his face as his self-assuredness was replaced by a growing feeling of

189

unease. "Ah, Arnjad, I see that you're not fully aware of your present situation so let me enlighten you. We, that is, the navy not the FIB, I wouldn't want to get you confused so early in our conversation; executed a federal warrant to search for evidence of treason committed by persons unknown. That treasonable offense was specifically the sale of technology during a period of hostilities which could aid and abet a foreign power..."

"I told you before, lady, I want a lawyer. I ain't telling you nothing till I see him so you're wasting your breath," spat Arnjad.

The woman continued in the same gentle tone as if completely unfazed by his outburst. "As the alleged offense falls under the Defense of the Republic Act, you are not entitled to legal representation during questioning and may be held for as long as is deemed fit by the ranking military officer." The woman stood up and walked toward the cell door where she stopped and turned to face Arnjad. Her face had lost all its gentleness. "That ranking officer would be me. Admiral Elizabeth Wilson. You have been selling gravity drives to the Alonan Empire, Mr. Harb. I have enough evidence from the computer you were trying to destroy to prove it in a court and I'd like to remind you that treason is still a capital offense. Unless, of course, there's something you'd like to share with me that would make it worth my while speaking with the Attorney General and asking him to commute your sentence to life without parole."

The blood drained from Arnjad's face and Elizabeth Wilson smiled sweetly at him. "I'll leave you alone with that thought and when I come back we'll see if you've changed your mind about talking to me."

Arnjad began to shake uncontrollably as the door closed behind Elizabeth.

#

ZURICH - EARTH - SOL SYSTEM

The imposing head offices of Zurich Lines towered over the bustling city of Zurich. It had been designed and built as an edifice for the power of one man. Seaton Anderson. Owner and chairman of the board of Zurich Lines. Seaton had inherited the struggling shipping company on his father's death thirty-five years previously, and with singled-minded determination had built the company up till it was the largest and most lucrative shipping line in the solar system. With the advent of the gravity drive, Seaton had seized the opportunity to make his company the shipping line of choice for the expanding Terran Republic and by doing whatever needed to be done, he secured the massive government contracts that were up for the taking when the Republic began to colonize Janus. Seaton had spent a small fortune funding the war chest of influential politicians and where that didn't work he had people who worked for him who could... shall we say... overcome obstacles. Seaton saw blackmail and payoffs as a legitimate business method and if he was to be entirely truthful with himself he got a certain amount of pleasure out of watching the faces of those more righteous-than-thou senators when he revealed to them that he knew every last one of their dark little secrets. The forming of the Commonwealth had only led to another expansion of the company as Zurich Lines shipped everything from grain to high-tech components to every star system known to man. Every system, except one. The Alonan Empire had refused to join the Commonwealth, so the government had placed strict

191

controls on what could and what could not be exported to the Alonans.

Zurich Lines, along with every other shipping company, had complied with government regulations but last year, Seaton had received a curious message from his manager on Alona requesting that Seaton himself pay a visit to the planet. Seaton's interest was piqued. No manager in his right mind would ever request the company chairman visit in case he found something that displeased him and Seaton had fired many a manager over the smallest infringement of what Seaton believed was best for the company. So under the cover of an inspection tour of all company general offices in the Commonwealth, Seaton left Earth in his private yacht accompanied only by his private secretary and bodyguards. After stopovers in Janus, Garunda, and Pars, Seaton eventually arrived on Alona, where a very nervous manager told Seaton of a meeting he had had with the Alonan Secretary of Trade and another unidentified Alonan who the manager believed to be a military man by the way he carried himself. The Alonans had made an astonishing proposal. If Zurich Lines was able to supply a number of working gravity drives to the Alonan Empire, then they in turn would guarantee that henceforth, all imperial contracts for the next decade would go to Zurich Lines. Seaton sat in the manager's office as he considered the potential profit. The numbers were simply staggering and would secure Zurich Lines' position as the largest shipping line in known space. But the consequences of being caught were also massive. The gravity drive was the single biggest advantage that the Commonwealth had over its enemies and potential rivals alike and the government wasn't likely to look too favorably on it being supplied to the Alonans. On the other hand, Seaton had no doubt that the Empire would get the technology eventually, so why shouldn't he be the one to benefit from supplying it? It would all have to be handled very carefully of course, but Seaton was sure he could find the right men who, for the right price, could handle the job. The manager was told to inform the Alonans that they had a deal and with that, Seaton headed back to Earth, he had some planning to do.

Now, potentially, all those carefully laid plans could be in ruins. The first the outside world knew about the raid on the Pathos yard was when another Zurich Lines ship had arrived at the yard for stripping and its captain had been ordered to return to Earth's orbit. The first thing he did when he reached Earth was contact the home office to see what sort of mix-up had sent him to a yard under quarantine by the navy. Head office had sent a request to the legal department to contact the navy, which it had done at the start of the next business day. The reply from the navy was the reason Seaton was now sitting in the boardroom with his closest advisers. The yard was sealed by order of a federal judge under the power of the Defense of the Republic Act.

"So what do we know?" Seaton gruffly demanded from the small group of directors he had hand-picked to help him run Zurich Lines. A thin, raven-haired woman who sat directly opposite Seaton at the small, ornate conference table cleared her throat. Daya Thomas was director of Zurich Lines Business Information Department, better described as Seaton's own intelligence chief. Since he had taken over the business from his father, Daya had been by his side and was the one person on the board, apart from Seaton, who knew the complete contents of Seaton's private file collection, which gave him so much political and business clout.

"From what we've managed to put together from our sources in traffic control a navy warship the… eh…" Daya tapped on her PAD for the correct information. "The *Sorcerer* informed traffic control at zero four forty-five this morning that it was taking part in an unannounced naval readiness exercise and without waiting for permission entered fold space directly from orbit. At nineteen hundred hours the MV *Wagonmaster* approached the Pathos yard where it was due to be decommissioned. As it reached the yard's outer marker, it was warned off by the *Sorcerer* who informed it the yard was under naval control by order of a federal warrant. I've put out feelers to our people in the federal court to find out who signed the warrant and what its purpose was but so far nothing. It looks like the FIB played this one close to their chests and then got the navy to do their dirty work for them."

Seaton ran his hands through his thinning hair in frustration. "Have we heard anything from Harb?"

"Nothing. The navy isn't allowing any of the yard personnel to communicate with the outside world."

"We need to get some legal advice as to whether they can hold the personnel incommunicado and if so for how long. Get legal on the case right away."

"If I may make a suggestion, Seaton?"

With a wave of his hand, Seaton gave his permission.

"Since the navy carried out the raid on behalf of the FIB, then surely their actions fall under the purview of the Armed Services Oversight Committee which, as you know, is chaired by Senator Dikul, who I believe may owe us a few favors."

Seaton sat for a moment, thinking over Daya's suggestion. He needed to know how much Harb had told the navy about the secret movement of ships to

Alona and to what extent Harb had implicated the company and Seaton himself.

"OK Daya, let's make the senator aware of our interest. The rest of you, business as usual until we know more. Thank you."

Daya made to leave with the others but a gesture from Seaton kept her in her seat. As the door closed behind them, Seaton ensured the electromagnetic door seal was in place before he spoke.

"How much does Harb actually know?"

"Enough," answered Daya without hesitation.

Seaton tapped his index finger on the polished table. He refused to let one man bring down the company he had spent the majority of his adult life building. "Harb will need to be neutralized."

Daya's face was as impassive as stone. "Agreed. And the men who crewed the ships to Alona?"

"Can they be traced back to us?"

"Captain Thackery was the only one who had any direct contact with either Harb or myself. The crew members were recruited by Thackery so they have no direct link to us."

"Thackery will need to be neutralized then."

Daya stood to leave. "I'll make a call. It'll be done by the end of the day."

#

Over the years he'd had so many names that if he was truthful, he actually had to think about what his real name was. The man of medium height, medium build, middle age, and mediocre clothing lay on the flat roof of the apartment block and watched the street below through the lens of his sneaker glasses. He had been on the roof for four hours now and still there was no sign of his target. The target's house had a short driveway leading up to it from the main road and a parking area

195

outside the front entrance to the house. The roof of the apartment block provided a great vantage point over the street and the parking area. The sneaker let out a small beep as it detected movement on the driveway. Sure enough, a ground car was pulling up at the front door of the house. The driver's door opened and the sneaker zoomed in on the driver's face. Target identified. Even after all those hours of lying still, the man rolled over with practiced ease and the sniper rifle came up onto his shoulder as his eye went to the telescopic sight and his finger brushed lightly on the trigger. He continued the roll and was on his feet and dismantling the rifle as he headed for the stairs.

Jake Thackery never felt the single flechette round that penetrated the back of his skull before exploding out of his face.

The FIB team that had been waiting in the street to arrest Thackery was already running up the driveway when they saw Thackery fall to the ground. The first agent to reach him slipped and fell in the pool of spreading blood. Cursing loudly, he activated his wrist comm and called for an ambulance, knowing that it was already too late. The thin pointed steel projectile with its vaned tail had done its job.

#

TDF *SORCERER* - PATHOS YARD – SOL SYSTEM

The door of the cell burst open and two armed marines were through the entranceway and pinning Arnjad against the far wall before he had the chance to fully realize what was going on. Elizabeth Wilson strode in and thrust a PAD into his face. On its display was the face of a smiling, slightly overweight man in the uniform of a merchant captain.

"Do you know this man, Arnjad?"

196

Arnjad attempted to muster a sneer but the pain in his arms where the marines had him pinned turned his efforts into a grimace. "I told you before lady, I ain't telling you nothing until you grant me immunity."

The picture on the PAD changed to show the same man lying face-down in a pool of his own blood.

"This is, sorry, *was* Captain Jake Thackery, late of Zurich Lines and now late of this life. He was killed by a sniper outside his home two hours ago before the FIB had the chance to arrest him."

Arnjad's legs began to tremble of their own accord as Elizabeth went on.

"The communications logs show that you and Thackery spoke on a regular basis and my computer forensic people tell me that someone tried to erase data from the computer core that shows that Thackery has been to Pathos at least a dozen times in the last twelve months. Now why would someone do that, I wonder?"

Arnjad's eyes were still staring at the bloody remains of Thackery only inches from his face. The marines were no longer pinning him to the wall, his legs had gone so weak that the marines were actually holding him up.

"Now, Arnjad, I know that Thackery had been a merchant captain for Zurich Lines until a year ago when he mysteriously quit and has been unemployed since. His bank records show several large payments and he recently purchased the house that someone killed him in front of. Not bad for a man with no gainful employment. I'm betting that Thackery was getting paid to captain the merchant vessels that were delivered to your yard for decommissioning and after they arrived here you logged them in, then Thackery continued on to Alona and you made sure that the records were kept straight." Elizabeth moved the PAD away from Arnjad's face and looked him straight in the eye. Arnjad tried to speak but although his lips moved, no sound came out.

"It seems to me Arnjad, that someone didn't want me talking to the late Captain Thackery. Tying up loose ends, so to speak. And you, Arnjad, are one of those loose ends. So, here's what I'm going to do. Since you don't want to talk to me, I'm going to transfer you to the custody of the FIB and from there you will be moved to a prison of their choosing and held in general population…"

Arnjad's legs gave out from under him and the marines maneuvered him so he sat on the cell's single bed.

"At some point, someone will attempt to tidy up the loose end and maybe they'll be more cooperative."

Arnjad's head began moving from side to side. "You can't do that, they'll kill me!" Arnjad's head came up and he looked at Elizabeth with pleading eyes. "You have to protect me!"

"And why would I do that? Unless of course there's something you want to tell me?"

Arnjad took one more look at the picture of the blood-soaked corpse of Jake Thackery still visible on the PAD Elizabeth held in her hand and began to speak.

CHAPTER TWELVE

IT'S GOOD TO TALK

23 LIBRAE – 83.7 LIGHT YEARS FROM EARTH

Bruce forced himself to relax as *Rapier* crawled towards the blue-green planet. He wasn't the only one feeling apprehensive. The tactical officer looked like he was about to have a meltdown and was concentrating so hard on his readouts that Bruce couldn't remember the last time he'd seen him blink. Bruce understood completely as his own tactical display filled with the returns of what the computer was calling forty-seven destroyer-sized ships formed up in a solid wall directly in front of *Rapier*. Bruce highlighted the center ship in the wall facing him and tapped a control to expand the image. The ship had a bow similar to that of some ancient oceanic vessel. The hull thickened from the bow and about a third of the way along the length of the ship, two large domes, like a lizard's eyeballs, stuck out from the smooth surface. Each of these large domes contained a wicked-looking energy mount. As his eye traced the hull, there was a belt of smaller domes, which completely encircled the diameter of the ship. Tactical had determined these to be radar and lidar systems. Amidships were four even rows of six hatches. Missile launch silos, if he was to hazard a guess. The stern of the ship flared out and partially covered the drive system. The computer put the gross tonnage as 16,000 tons. Slightly heavier than his own Vanguard survey ships. Each of these destroyers had its fire control systems locked onto his flagship and even though he was fairly certain that individually none of them had the firepower to penetrate his battle armor, their combined fire was another thing entirely.

"Guns, let navigation know to cut our forward drive when we reach your estimate of their weapons envelope. Let's not let someone with an itchy trigger finger get too nervous."

"Aye-aye sir. Navigation, hold us at 3000 kilometers."

"Understood. 3000 kilometers. Time to all stop, two minutes."

"So far so good, Admiral," whispered Ambassador Amber Isa from the seat beside Bruce's command chair.

Turning to regard the petite ambassador, Bruce felt his reply catch in his throat as he looked into her brown eyes and upturned face. *Stay focused, Bruce*, he berated himself. "Just remind me again, Ambassador, how you managed to persuade me that approaching a planet we know has been at war with its nearest neighbor for over 100 years in a single ship, unsupported by the remainder of my flotilla, was a good idea?"

Amber's face lit up with a cheery smile. "Well, I could say that you recognized the keen intellect behind the plan, i.e. my own. Or I could reiterate the orders from the Joint Chiefs that you were to assist me in my mission to Deres as much as practically possible. Or..." Amber's smile seemed to widen and her eyes glinted. "You fell for my womanly wiles."

Bruce quickly checked that none of the bridge crew had heard her last comment before he formed his best command face. "Ambassador, I can assure you that I will follow my orders to the letter but I would remind you that those orders specify that my first regard is for the safety of my command and if I get even an inkling that those ships out there present a danger to *Rapier*, we're out of here and you can continue any negotiations over old-style radio."

Amber seemed completely unfazed by Bruce's reaction. In fact, Bruce was certain that her smile had managed to turn even more playful. "You're no fun, Admiral."

Before Bruce could reply, a call from navigation brought his attention back to their current situation. "All stop, Admiral. *Rapier* is holding 3000 kilometers from the nearest Deres vessel."

"Thank you." Bruce spun his whole chair to face Amber. "Well, it looks like you're up, Ambassador. Time to see if your plan will work and if Wilder has managed to interpret the Deres language properly from the data supplied by the Nilmerg."

Amber's demeanor became business-like. "Communications. Transmit the greeting message and follow it up with the language packet, if you please." A fleeting look of uncertainty passed over Amber's face.

This was the first time that Bruce had seen the ambassador show anything but the utmost confidence and without thinking he said quietly, "I'm sure it'll work, Amber."

It took Amber a moment to realize that the admiral had used her first name. In all the time she had been aboard the *Rapier*, he kept things between them on a very formal level and Amber had come to think that that was just his way. Another stuffy marionette. That was until the day she'd seen the true concern he had for his crew when the three survivors of the *Ericson* had been taken hostage. That single incident had forced Amber to reexamine her opinion of Rear Admiral Bruce Torrance. She had seen the way he interacted easily with even the lowest crew member, so why was he always so formal with her? No matter how hard she tried, she was never able to engage him in anything other than discussions about the mission, so she had simply given up and resigned herself to his brusqueness. But now he had called her by her first name when he had seen that she was having self-doubts and its effect had been to make her feel immediately stronger as he showed his faith in her. How odd.

"We're receiving a reply, Madam Ambassador. It's a request to establish visual communications."

Amber's shoulders went back and her chin came up. *Showtime, Amber.* "Go ahead."

A grainy image filled the holo cube and for the first time Amber and Bruce got to see the living face of a Deres. As the comms officer worked to clear up the image, a stern voice boomed around the flag bridge.

"Nilmerg. You are not wanted here. Return to the rest of your murdering kind immediately or we shall destroy you where you stand."

The holo cube cleared and there stood a squat, heavily built figure. The rounded head seemed unnaturally small when compared to the two large, pointed ears on either side of its skull. Bright yellow eyes stared at them, made all the more striking by the green skin darker still than that of the Garundans. A black uniform with several glittering silver bars on the high collar covered the Deres from just below its protruding chin until the image was cut off around the waist.

Amber took a deep breath before beginning in her most pacifying tone. "As you can see, I am not of Nilmerg. I am from the planet Earth and we come in the hope of establishing peaceful relations with the Deres people."

The angry expression on the face of the Deres in the holo cube spoke volumes as the interpretation software rushed to keep up with the conversation.

"Lies! I shall not fall for this trick, Nilmerg. I tell you for the last time to leave Deres space or I shall fire upon you. There shall be no further warning!"

Amber paused, uncertain how to overcome the intransigence of the Deres. Bruce stepped into the holo's pick-up range.

"Sir. I am Rear Admiral Bruce Torrance of the Terran Defense Force. I have no doubt that your instruments show that my ship is more powerful than any of your own, yet I have not powered up my weapons or made any aggressive moves toward you. We have approached your planet slowly so as to show you our good faith. All we ask is that you give us the opportunity to talk with you. Perhaps a face-to-face meeting would convince you that we are not Nilmerg?"

The Deres commander stared at them for a moment. Then, "Standby." And the transmission was cut.

Amber's shoulders slumped as Bruce walked around in front of her. "That didn't go as planned but at least he didn't shoot at us," stated Bruce.

Amber stood and straightened her jacket. "Thank you for the assistance, Admiral. I must say that the Deres commander was probably the most stubborn opponent that I have faced in some time."

A beeping from communications caused them both to face the pick-up. Bruce gave the comms officer a curt nod and the holo cube filled with the image of the same Deres they had spoken to a few moments earlier.

"I cannot allow you to approach the planet any closer. You will follow my flagship to the fourth planet of the system where you shall enter orbit and I shall meet with you on the surface." The Deres leaned closer into the pick-up. "Be warned. Any deviation from my instructions and I will destroy you."

The signal abruptly ceased, leaving Amber and Bruce staring into a blank holo cube.

"Bet he's the life and soul of the party at home," said Bruce.

#

Rapier settled into high orbit around the fourth planet following the tacit instructions received from the lead Deres ship to the letter. Coordinates had been received from the Deres which identified a location on the planet's southern landmass along with the order to send a single shuttle to that location which must contain only the flight crew, Ambassador Isa and Admiral Torrance. Captain Laka, Bruce's flag captain, had expressed his unhappiness that the admiral intended to leave the ship and meet with a group of aliens who had already forcefully expressed their dislike for the *Rapier's* presence in the system. Laka argued that Bruce should at least take along a small marine contingent to ride shotgun but as Amber had pointed out, the Deres wanted Bruce and herself to be the only passengers on the shuttle and getting them to trust her was going to be hard enough without turning up with a bunch of Wraith-suited armed marines. Reluctantly, Bruce had been forced to agree with Amber and he vividly remembered the look of unhappiness on Laka's face as he entered the shuttle for the flight down to the planet.

The short flight passed in almost total silence as Bruce and Amber marshaled their own thoughts for the impending meeting. Bruce stared absently at the passing terrain as it flashed past on his seat's viewer. The slightly too-green ocean soon gave way to a fertile jungle, which in turn gave way to rolling grasslands. The planetologists put the age of Planet Four as roughly the same as the two life-bearing planets in the 23 Librae system. About 3.8 billion years. But Planet Four was located towards the edge of the Goldilocks zone for this type of star so it had a lower mean temperature and although the vegetation appeared lush, the oxygen level in the atmosphere was lower than Earth's, which meant Bruce and Amber would have to wear breathers. A minor inconvenience, and one that Amber worried could hamper her talks with the Deres as a breather encased the nose, mouth and lower portion of the head and neck. Amber wanted the Deres to see her whole face, even if that meant passing out within a few minutes from oxygen starvation. The Chief Medical Officer of *Rapier* had ended her argument with the simple expedient of refusing to allow her to leave the ship if she refused to wear a breather. The look on her face had been that of an unhappy teenager losing an argument with her parents. Bruce couldn't recall ever meeting a more stubborn woman.

"Five minutes to the landing zone, Admiral," called the shuttle pilot.

Across from him, Amber was total calm personified. Her eyes closed as if asleep but there was a tell-tale tapping of her right index finger. Bruce was glad to see he wasn't the only one feeling slightly apprehensive. Perhaps a few words of encouragement would put them both at ease.

"Ambassador."

Amber replied without opening her eyes.

"I assure you, Admiral, there is no need to be nervous."

Bruce felt his mouth fall open and the planned words of encouragement failed to materialize. He wasn't nervous. He wasn't the one tapping his finger. He was trying to put her at ease, not the other way around. Instead, Bruce scrambled for something else to say. "Just reminding you to wear your breather, Ambassador."

Amber's eyelids remained firmly shut but her lips creased in a small smile. "Yes, Dad. I promise I'll be good."

Bruce sat back in exasperation as the shuttle made the final run into the landing zone.

The pilot's voice came back through the intercom. "One minute to landing zone. We're picking up some faint artificial energy readings from the mountain range seventy clicks to starboard. Do you want us to abort, Admiral?"

Bruce brought the readings up on his display. The pilot was right, the readings were very faint. Had the Deres managed to sneak another ship down to the surface and were waiting to ambush them? No, surely not. They knew that *Rapier* had enough firepower to blow any of their ships out of orbit without breaking a sweat.

"Proceed on course but keep an eye on that power source and I want a complete record made of it. Maybe it'll give us some worthwhile data on the Deres power systems that *Rapier* doesn't have already. Keep me appraised if there's any change in its power output or position."

"Aye-aye sir. Thirty seconds to touchdown."

The faint rumble of the landing gear extending was followed seconds later by the gentle tug of his seat restraints, then the slight bounce of touchdown. The crew chief appeared beside the exterior hatch, his breather already attached to his face. Bruce released his buckles and slipped on his breather as he stood awaiting the crew chief's signal that the cabin pressure had equalized with that outside the shuttle and it was safe to crack the hatch. After a few moments, the crew chief still stood patiently beside the hatch, controls unmoving. Bruce turned to see Amber standing to one side, her breather hanging from its straps on the side of her seat.

Bruce shook his head in exasperation. It was like working with a five-year-old! "The crew chief won't open the hatch until he's sure it's safe for all the crew, Ambassador. Emphasis on the *all*."

For a moment it looked like Amber was going to argue with him but she simply shrugged as she recovered her breather and fitted it. Bruce turned back to the crew chief who, although his lower face was completely covered by the breather, Bruce could swear had laughter lines around his eyes. Is it unprofessional if I roll my eyes? He wondered.

The hatch opened and as the ramp extended the first breath of chilled air entered the shuttle. Bruce paused in the hatchway for a moment as his eyes adjusted to the bright natural sunlight. With a reassuring tap of his PEP in its leg holster, he stepped down the ramp closely followed by Amber. The high-pitched sound of screaming turbo fans drew his eyes westward where, low on the horizon, he could make out a dark dot approaching at speed. The dot grew into the shape of a small ship. A thin elongated body with swept forward wings and a tri-fin tail tipped with what looked like engine intakes. The ship changed course slightly, angling over to one side, giving Bruce a good view of the upper wing surfaces and fuselage. A prominent, lozenge-shaped pod sat atop each wing about halfway down its span. Bruce gauged them to be weapons pods of some kind as they had a small circular cutouts on the forward edge but no corresponding cutouts to the rear. Bruce put the ship to be about fifteen meters long. The wide windows of the cockpit high above the conical nose section and smaller porthole-type windows extended the length of the main body. The vertical tail section was adorned with a symbol that Bruce thought resembled a Chinese character but in bright yellow. The ship circled the landing zone once before the two engines on the lower tail sections rotated vertically to change thrust direction and a small bay opened directly below the cockpit to reveal a jet exhaust. The similarity to early Earth vertical takeoff jets was remarkable, thought Bruce, as the jet wash blew dust up from the ground. Amber put her hand up to cover her eyes as Bruce simply closed his eyes and allowed the lighter debris to wash over him and the smell of high octane jet fuel filled his nostrils. So they still rely on carbon fuels to power their smaller ships noted Bruce.

The small dust storm subsided as the high-pitched whining of the turbo fans dropped away and peace returned. Amber was still attempting to clear pieces of loose grass from her clothes as a hatch set directly behind the cockpit opened and a folding set of stairs extended. As soon the steps locked in place, four rifle-toting Deres, wearing the same all-black as the Deres commander, rushed down. Two took up positions a respectable distance from Bruce and Amber, their weapons held loosely in their arms but leaving the two humans in no doubt that it would only take a fraction of a second for them to bring them into a firing position and cut them down where they stood. The remaining two Deres moved off and took positions to the bow and stern of the human shuttle. Presumably to ensure that no one tried to exit the shuttle on its far side. The sight of the armed Deres made Bruce think Captain Laka's suggestion about the marines might not have been such a bad one after all. *Oh well, we're here now.* Bruce consoled himself with the thought that he was pretty handy with a PEP, so at least he might get one shot off before meeting his maker.

Resigning himself to his fate, Bruce waited patiently for the Deres' next move. He didn't have long to wait. One of the rifle-toting Deres raised a hand to his uniform collar and spoke too quietly for Bruce to hear. It may have been too quiet for Bruce to overhear, but whatever the device was the Deres was using traveled on a general signal that the PAD was able to pick up and transmit to the humans. The ear bugs in both Bruce's and Amber's ears came to life. "Marshal Poll. It is true, they are not Nilmerg. I'm not sure what they are. We see only the two of them. The taller one has what I believe to be a weapon but it is holstered. The smaller one appears to be unarmed but I cannot guarantee that it may not have a concealed weapon. What are your orders?"

"Be vigilant Tier, I am coming out with Deputy Lex. Let us see what these aliens have to say."

At the top of the stairs the figure of the squat Deres commander appeared and then stepped respectfully to one side to allow another Deres to exit the shuttle first. This Deres was dressed differently from the others. He was still dressed rather formally but his attire struck Bruce as more civilian than military.

"It looks like you may actually get the chance to talk to someone in their political leadership, Ambassador." Bruce whispered out of the side of his mouth.

"Thank god. I wasn't looking forward to speaking to the commander, he struck me as your typical military Neanderthal.... No offense intended, Admiral."

"None taken, Ambassador. I'm sure after a few days of negotiation you politicians can decide what color the sky is."

"Touché, Admiral."

The two Deres reached the bottom of the steps and approached the waiting humans. They stopped a few feet from them and both sides stood for a few seconds in awkward silence, eying each other up. Amber decided to get things underway.

"Greetings, sir. I am Ambassador Isa representing the Commonwealth Union of Planets and this is Rear Admiral Torrance of the Terran Defense Force, commander of the human ship in orbit above us."

If the two Deres were surprised at being addressed in their own language, neither showed any visible reaction.

"I see your technology allows for your ability to interpret our conversation without the need for bulky computers. Impressive indeed. My name is Aral Lex and this is Marshall Poll, head of our space forces. I myself am a deputy within the House of the People and I have been sent here on the express instructions of Commissioner Malas himself to offer you whatever it requires for you to switch your allegiance from the Nilmerg to the Deres."

Amber and Bruce exchanged a furtive glance before Amber replied. "I believe you are mistaken, Deputy, we are not allies of the Nilmerg. We are explorers who have come to your star system seeking peaceful relations with both the Nilmerg and the Deres. Believe me, Deputy Lex, we harbor no ill will to the people of Deres."

"Then why were your ships escorted from the edge of the system by a Nilmerg warship to their home world?

And why are you here now if not to make demands of us!?" Poll demanded.

"It was sheer coincidence that a Nilmerg warship and not a Deres warship was nearby when we arrived in your system if I ..."

"I do not believe in coincidence, Ambassador." Poll interrupted gruffly. "Like us, the Nilmerg would have detected your vessels approaching the system as, no doubt, you were aware of the presence of the Nilmerg. You chose to meet with them first!"

"That was not our intention, Marshall. Ships of the Commonwealth have the capability of traveling between points in space through a technique called Fold Space. It is impossible to know what awaits you at your point of arrival beyond any general facts you already know about your destination. Detecting a ship near your point of arrival is beyond us."

Bruce winced as Amber revealed key facts about the Commonwealth's star ship design but it was out there now. *Let's hope she doesn't decide to reveal any more of our capabilities.*

Amber's disclosure seemed to stop both Deres in their tracks and Amber saw the mix of fear and admiration in their eyes. She also sensed an opening.

"The Nilmerg are also aware of the capabilities of our ships and their reaction was very similar to your own. I must admit that they too were skeptical of our intentions in your star system. That was until we told them the reason the Commonwealth chose to visit this system as opposed to any other star within easy reach of the Commonwealth."

Both Deres were hanging on every word that Amber was saying. "Have either of you gentlemen ever heard of a species called the Saiph?"

#

Bruce was relaxing in his cabin aboard *Rapier* after the short flight back from the planet's surface. Unbidden, a grin came to his face as he remembered the look on Deputy Lex and Marshall Poll's faces as Amber had recited her story of the Saiph and how they had traveled the stars, spreading their DNA on many worlds. Of how the Commonwealth consisted of descendants of these races and of the missions launched by the Commonwealth to the other worlds to find out what had become them. The best part was the look on Poll's face when he realized that the hated Nilmerg were made of the same stuff he was. Priceless. Bruce thought he was going to choke to death on the spot. Of course they refused to believe any of it without proof but Amber had come prepared. Before leaving the surface she allowed the Deres to take a sample of her DNA for comparison against their own and that of any captured Nilmerg they wished. Her parting shot was one that had the effect of leaving Deputy Lex speechless. Amber explained that prior to leaving Nilmerg to meet with the Deres, she had proposed to them that if both sides were agreeable a temporary halt to hostilities would be immediately imposed with the longer term aim of both sides engaging in peace talks which the Commonwealth was willing to broker. Further, the ships of SurvFlot Two would be deployed as peacekeepers. Both Deres and Nilmerg had the opportunity to get good readings of Admiral Torrance's ships and knew full well they were more than a match for any of their ships that wished to breach the ceasefire. Deputy Lex had promised to take Amber's proposal back to the Commissioner and the House of the People and gain an answer forthwith.

The beeping of the desktop terminal got Bruce's attention. Bruce's brow creased as he noticed the call came from his chief civilian scientist, Doctor Ramesh. A touch of the controls accepted the call and the wrinkled face of Arjit Ramesh appeared. Before Bruce could say anything, Ramesh began talking.

"Sorry to bother you, Admiral but I've been going over the data of the power source you recorded on the planet's surface from your shuttle and I would like your permission to go active on our ground-penetrating radar to get a proper look at the area the power source originated in."

"I'm not sure if that's a good idea, Doctor. Both sides here are on tenterhooks and if our active systems are mistaken for a fire and control radar then we could find ourselves in a shooting war pretty quickly."

"Admiral. You see I must use our active systems if I am to prove or disprove my findings."

Scientists. They're almost as bad as politicians, thought Bruce irritably. *Why can't they just start at the beginning?* "And what findings are those, Doctor?"

"Why, that the power readings are an exact match for those of the Rubicon Cave and there's every chance that there may be another Saiph library buried on this planet."

CHAPTER THIRTEEN

THE COMMITTEE HEARING

GENEVA – EARTH- SOL SYSTEM

The senate committee hearing rooms had been designed with one purpose in mind. That anyone facing the committee on their long, raised bench could not fail to be left in awe of the high and mighty who had demanded their presence.

General Keyton Joyce was suitably unimpressed. In his lifetime, he had faced down pirates who would've cut his throat without a second's hesitation. It was only after his first appearance in front of the Armed Services Oversight Committee that he realized not all pirates belonged in space.

When Keyton had first assumed the post of Chairman of the Joint Chiefs of Staff he had, as he assumed at the time, an adequate experience in dealing with politicos whose only interest was what was best for them, but his first brush with Senator Katria Dikul, Chairman of the oversight committee, had introduced him to a new level of self-serving politician.

In the wake of the Geoffrey Rawson affair, Katria Dikul had somehow managed to maneuver herself into a position where she was able to take virtually complete control of the investigation even though it was being handled by the Justice Department and the FIB.

Dikul and her aides had ensured that she made appearances on every vid news program that had even the most tenuous link with the investigation. At any opportunity she expounded her own views on who was to blame for allowing Rawson to have been able to place his own supporters within the Defense Department. Supporters who had managed to conceal his criminal activities. All the while, Dikul was doing the same with her own people under the auspices of Senate Observers. These so-called observers questioned every action and decision made by staff until, one day, one of them made the mistake of questioning a decision made by the current Secretary of Defense, Olaf Helsett. The observer found himself unceremoniously ejected from the building by the marine guards, closely followed by every senate observer in the building.

Senator Dikul had been furious. Threats of special senate hearings and charges of interference with senate investigations were bandied about in the following days and it had taken direct intervention by President Coston herself on behalf of Olaf to curtail their interference in his running of defense.

That very public act of reminding Dikul of her place had made Rebecca Coston a life-long political enemy and, by association, anyone whom Dikul perceived as a possible ally to Rebecca. Keyton found himself in that group no matter how apolitical he tried to be.

The banging of a large wooden gavel by Dikul signaled the start of the hearing. This ancient form of commencing an important event was closely followed by the more modern sound of a neutral computerized voice saying "Secure" as the Master at Arms activated the anti-surveillance systems built into the room.

Keyton let out a small snort as he reflected on how the expensive anti-surveillance systems were a complete waste of time. Anything said in this room could be revealed without a moment's hesitation by any of the politicians if they thought it would get them a single gram of political capital.

The stentorian sound of Katria Dikul's voice came to Keyton's ears as, not for the first time, he wished he had remained as a line general and never accepted the promotion to the Joint Chiefs.

"Before we start in on the subject of today's unscheduled meeting, I would beg the indulgence of the committee for a few moments. Senator Mackenzie wishes to make a short statement in relation to the committee's findings on our ongoing inquiry into the handling of the debacle at 70 Ophiuchi."

Keyton stiffened and fought to keep his expression neutral. There had been no mention when Keyton had been requested to appear before the committee that the subject of 70 Ophiuchi was on the agenda. Mackenzie was one of Dikul's lackeys and Keyton was sure that anything that he had to say about the assault on 70 Ophiuchi already had Dikul's seal of approval.

The overweight senator at the far right of the bench cleared his throat as he used a silk handkerchief to dab the beads of sweat from his high forehead.

"Thank you, Madam Chairman. Fellow committee members. Since our last meeting I have been working without end to establish the true facts surrounding Admiral Ricco and General Pak's incompetent acts which led to the death of so many of our brave service men and women at 70 Ophiuchi…"

Keyton exploded out of his chair, ignoring the restraining hand of his JAG lawyer. "How dare you, Senator! Admiral Ricco and General Pak died doing their duty to the best of their abilities. No one here could have predicted that an enemy battle group would be in a position to ambush our ships as they emerged from fold space, and their ground troops using nuclear demolition charges to destroy their base while our marines were in the midst of their assault... you simply don't expect an enemy to commit suicide."

Mackenzie looked physically shaken by Keyton's angry retort and was obviously struggling to form a reply when Dikul intervened. Her tone was soft and placating.

"Perhaps we could leave this particular subject to another day, Senator Mackenzie. The events may still be too recent and evocative for us to review subjectively."

"Perhaps you have a point, Madam Chairman," replied Mackenzie, tremulously dabbing once more at the sweat which had become a steady stream on his forehead.

Keyton regained his seat but his thoughts were still filled with the slanderous words of Mackenzie about two men whom he had known personally for years.

"Returning to today's agenda, General. It is the committee's understanding that naval and marine units have been involved in a joint operation with the Justice Department in relation to the procurement by the Empire of Alona of a number of gravity drives."

Keyton took a moment to regain his calm before answering. "Central Command received a request for assistance from the Attorney General in the execution of a sealed federal warrant. The TDF *Sorcerer* and her marine contingent executed said warrant under the direction of a flag officer and officers from the Judge Advocate Generals' office."

"Would you be kind enough to share the specifics of the warrant with us, General?"

Before Keyton replied, the JAG major raised his PAD and used his finger to indicate something on the display. A small frown furrowed Keyton's brow.

"On advice from my attorney, I respectfully decline to answer the chairman's question. Further, I would advise the chairman that as the warrant was sealed she should take the matter up with the Justice Department."

The silence following Keyton's reply seemed to stretch on. Dikul held his eyes steadily but Keyton had a lifetime of practice waiting for the other man to blink first. The tension in the room was finally broken by the blustering, self-righteous voice of Senator Mackenzie.

"I order you to tell us the entire contents of that warrant, Joyce! Does it extend to Seaton Anderson?"

The minute it was out of his mouth, Mackenzie knew he had made a huge mistake. His face paled and his head dropped. Dikul's head swiveled toward Mackenzie like a raptor eyeing up its prey. Her eyes flashed with anger before turning to stone. When her gaze returned to Keyton, his face remained as immobile as before but she knew that Mackenzie's outburst had opened a door that now could never be closed.

#

The roar of laughter that came from Olaf Helsett made the furniture in the Secretary of Defense's office shake. The imposing bulk of the former admiral tipped his chair back and raised his glass in mock salute to Keyton Joyce. Keyton raised his glass in return before taking a sip of the ridiculously expensive whiskey.

"We've got the bitch!"

"Not yet, Mr. Secretary, but that slip by that tub of lard Mackenzie confirmed we have Seaton Anderson worried. I still find it hard to believe that a man with as much to lose as Anderson could be personally involved in the supply of the gravity drives to Alona."

Keyton gave a nonchalant shrug. "But I can't see who else would have the political pull to get Dikul to convene an emergency meeting of the oversight committee."

Olaf allowed his seat to return to the vertical and fixed Keyton with a knowing look.

"If the AG can prove a link between Seaton, Dikul, and Mackenzie it will make Geoffrey Rawson look like an amateur. How is your favorite guard dog coming along with the Pathos yard manager?"

Keyton's features became unreadable. "If you are referring to Admiral Wilson, then her small... eh... chat with the aforementioned Arnjad Harb seems to have provided the AG with enough evidence to go back to a federal judge and get snoop warrants for any and all premises and accounts owned or controlled by Zurich Lines and Anderson."

Olaf's lips pursed and he let out a low whistle. "Wow! The evidence must have been pretty damning if a judge was willing to grant those warrants. Wilson is to be congratulated. You can pass along my personal thanks for that, too."

A sly smile appeared on Keyton's face. "I'll be sure to do that. The next round of flag promotions is due soon and I have it on good authority that the position of Deputy Director of the Office of Naval Intelligence is likely to require filling as its current incumbent is going to be tapped for a position on the Chairman of the Joint Chiefs staff..."

The room furniture took another battering as Olaf's laugh reverberated around the room once more and his pointed finger centered on Keyton.

"You, General Joyce, are a true Machiavellian."

"Everything I've learned has been taught to me by a true master, Mr. Secretary."

"Ha! Groveling will get you far, Keyton. Rest assured, any promotion recommendation of Admiral Wilson will get the highest endorsement of this office."

Olaf placed his empty glass down on his desk and he reverted back to the admiral he used to be. "Now. Back to the business at hand. How goes Radford's operational planning?"

CHAPTER FOURTEEN

ORIGINS

9 CETI - 66.5 LIGHT YEARS FROM EARTH

Gavin Glandinning was beginning to think that some scientists really didn't know how to behave like adults. Just like the Tau Eridani system, the Persai surveillance platform had indicated that there was every chance of finding life in the 9 Ceti system, but it had failed to detect any artificial power sources. The star was a yellow orange main sequence dwarf star a little bigger and brighter than the Earth's sun, but much younger. Somewhere around 600 million years old. The scientists would have expected to find any planet in the Goldilocks zone to have a violently volcanic, rocky crust constantly bombarded by large asteroids and comets but what they had found was a stable planet, slightly larger than Earth, with two moons orbiting it. It was these two moons that were the subject of the heated discussion that reminded Gavin more of a school playground argument than any evenly balanced scientific discussion. Gavin looked across the briefing room table at the slight figure of Ambassador Oslan. The Garundan returned his look with amused eyes. *No help from that corner*, thought Gavin. Instead his eyes sought out Force Leader Homla, SurvFlot Three's second in command. By the look on her face, Homla had had about enough of the bickering scientists as well. Gavin gave her a slight nod and Homla took that as her cue to slap an open palm on the table, bringing all discussion to an instant halt.

"Enough! We have not convened this meeting to waste Admiral Glandinning's time with your childish behavior. What is it you wish to show us?"

Faced by an irate seven-foot-tall Persai who reminded every human in the room of something from a cheap werewolf movie, the assembled scientists were suitably cowed into silence. Doctor Heather Reid was the exact opposite of the towering Persai. Being only five-foot-two in her stocking feet and slightly overweight, her black shoulder-length hair streaked with gray reminded all those who met her of their own grandmother. Her softly spoken Irish brogue had lulled many an unwary astrobiology student into believing that he could win an argument with her by simply being louder and brasher. But behind the gentle features was a mind as sharp as a scalpel and those same students had found themselves tied in knots as she tore their arguments to shreds and sent them packing.

Gavin considered himself lucky to have her as head of his science department but at times, and this was one of them, her willingness to allow others to exhaust their arguments and run out of steam before having her say didn't quite run in tandem with his trained military sense of cutting through the crap and getting to the point. As the scientists retook their seats under Homla's withering gaze, Heather tapped her PAD and the image of the fourth planet of the 9 Ceti system slowly rotated in the holo cube for all to see. The scattered white clouds floating serenely over the large blue oceans and the green continents had been the cause of the active discussions that the various scientists had been having for the last five minutes.

Heather cleared her throat softly, which had the desired effect of turning all eyes in the room on her. "Admiral. Ladies and gentlemen. Since we arrived in this system a week ago, we've been faced with nothing but contradictions. Where we expected to find a volcanically active planet, we have found one that, because of the gravitational forces exerted on it by its twin moons, should for all intents and purposes be teeming with life. Instead what we have in front of us is a world that apart from the very basic insect life required to pollinate the varied plant life, is completely devoid of an animal above the level of small rodents. The oceans are rich in minerals and algae but where are the larger life forms that we have found on every planet known to the Commonwealth?" A worry line creased Heather's forehead. "Something does not add up here and neither I nor my team can explain it. As our survey of the planet continued we followed standard procedure and used ground-penetrating radar to show us any artificial structures that may have been hidden beneath the abundant foliage and this is what we found…"

In the holo cube, the image zoomed in to a point along the coastline of one of the larger continents. The image focused on a large inlet, which would have provided an ideal location for an artificial harbor and, if Gavin was reading the image correctly, that was exactly what the radar return showed.

"For those of you who are not used to interpreting these images, like my good self, I have been assured that what we are looking at is an artificial breakwater. Those regular shapes along the shoreline are docks with buildings spreading along the shore and extending back away from the shore for approximately a kilometer and a half. The computer has identified similar clusters of buildings spread across the whole planet. There is also evidence to suggest that there was a rudimentary road system linking major population centers on this particular continent but not on any of the others. However, there is no doubt that at a point in the recent past, there was a flourishing civilization on this planet. From the evidence, the archaeologists are willing to hazard a guess that it was about the same level as medieval Europe."

Gavin let his gaze drop to the floor as a sour taste filled his mouth. *Oh God, not another one.*

Homla asked the question that she knew everyone in the room wanted an answer to. "Doctor. Are there any signs of an orbital bombardment? Is this another world that the Others are responsible for killing?"

Heather shook her head. "There are no signs of bombardment. Samples returned by shuttles show that there is no sign of anything unusual in the radioactive levels of the atmosphere. Similarly, there are no indications of any natural catastrophe. If there had been major volcanic activity, the atmosphere would show concentrations of tephra, volcanic ash, but again there is nothing. If the planet had been subjected to an asteroid impact, again, there would be evidence, but there is nothing."

Gavin tapped his finger on the table. "Well, if there is no evidence of a natural calamity and no sign of orbital bombardment, can you at least date the ruins and narrow down a window for whatever befell this world?"

"I'll be honest with you, Admiral. Without more data I could speculate about what happened here until I was blue in the face but there is only one way that I could get the data that would give me a definite answer to what happened here."

"And how would you do that, Doctor?"

Heather shrugged her shoulders. "Why, by going down there, of course."

#

Heather felt like she couldn't breathe properly in the bio suit she had insisted that everyone who would be putting their feet on the planet's surface wear. She knew it was only her mind playing tricks on her. The small backpack she wore circulated air at a comfortable room temperature but with a slight over-pressure to ensure that anything which may manage to tear the tough nano-polymer suit wouldn't allow the planet's atmosphere into her suit. Heather looked over at the small marine contingent that the admiral had insisted accompany her science team in their Wraith suits. How they could spend hours on end in those things amazed her. Activating her link, she addressed her small party. "OK, people, let's see if we can get to the bottom of this mystery. I want plant and soil samples from the immediate area and if you can find any insects or animals, all the better. Remember, nothing gets put onto our shuttle without first having been through the mobile lab, understood?"

A series of mumbled "yeses" came back over the link. The second shuttle with the mobile lab sat off to one side. Hermetically sealed against the slightest chance of any contamination, the scientists who manned it could work without the handicap of wearing full bio-suits. *And why didn't I detail myself a cushy job in there,* Heather berated herself. *Because you like to get your hands dirty, that's why.*

Two and a half hours later and Heather was regretting her decision. Her body was telling her there was a fault with the suit's temperature and humidity controls. Her brain was telling her there was nothing wrong with the controls and to just admit that she was getting too old for working in the field. The high-pitched voice of Lindsey Sears erupted into her left ear.

"Doctor Reid, it's Lindsey, could you come into the lab for a moment? I've found something that I think you should see."

The prospect of having to go through a complete decontamination before she could shed the suit wasn't the most appealing of ideas but at least she could take it off for a while. That of course meant she would have to put another suit back on to come back out and then go through the whole decontamination process for a second time but what the hell, a cup of coffee in the relative comfort of the lab sounded good.

"OK Lindsey, I'll be right over."

Heather trudged over to the lab's airlock and opened the outer door. Stepping inside Heather felt the vibration of the small motor that circulated air inside her suit die as the suit sealed itself for what was to come. The scrubbers concealed in the walls automatically came on as the outer door sealed, replacing any oxygen in the airlock with inert argon so only the air already within the suit itself remained. The walls, roof, and floor of the chamber lit up with intense ultraviolet light, killing any microbe that had managed to attach itself to the outside of the suit. As the lighting returned to normal, Heather released the seals of her helmet and suit and dropped the whole thing into the waste chute by the inner door. The complete suit would be flash burned before the ashes were dumped in space on the return trip to the *Triton*.

#

Lindsey Sears may have had a very irritating voice that reminded Heather of fingernails being dragged down a chalkboard, but she was a first-class virologist, so Heather sat patiently as Lindsey walked her through what she had found and no matter how hard she tried, Heather couldn't find fault in her findings. Putting down her cup of cold coffee, Heather gave Lindsey a small pat on her arm as she walked past her and made her way up to the shuttle's small communications console. Sitting down, she took a deep breath as she tried to settle the butterflies that were suddenly flying around in her stomach. Heather steeled herself and activated the link to the *Triton*. A second later the all-business face of a young naval officer filled the display.

"Communications. Lieutenant Dhal. How can I help you, Doctor Reid?"

"I need to speak to the admiral."

The young officer hesitated a moment. "I'm sure Commander Bekker is available, Doctor."

Neil Bekker was Admiral Glandinning's Chief of Staff and would normally have oversight of everything before deciding whether to bother the admiral with it. *Not this time*, thought Heather.

"I need to speak directly with the admiral now, Lieutenant. And I mean right now!"

#

The image in the holo cube looked remarkably like a thin white worm to Gavin Glandinning. "So what am I looking at, Doctor?"

"Admiral, you are looking at what is responsible for there being nothing left on the planet any bigger than a large mouse."

Gavin looked from the doctor with the grating voice to Heather and then back again. "Perhaps you would care to explain, Doctor Sears."

"This, Admiral, is a virus. No scrub that." Lindsey looked upon the thin white image with a distinct triple head and curved tail with respect bordering on admiration. "Admiral, for a virus to spread, it does so in a number of ways. For a communicable disease to spread from an individual host to another individual it could be by droplet contamination. Where one individual coughs or sneezes on another. By direct physical contact, where an infected person touches someone else. By indirect physical contact, where you would touch, say, contaminated soil or a contaminated surface. By airborne transmission, where the microorganism can survive in the air for some time. Fecal or oral transmission, where you are infected usually from contaminated food or water sources. Transmission could also be indirect. Using another vector or organism such as, say, malaria via a mosquito or tapeworm via infected pigs. Most viruses known to us will use only one or possibly two of these methods and are almost always specifically aimed at one particular species. Now this," Lindsey indicated the image in the holo cube, "this little beauty is capable of not only employing all the methods of transmission, but is a cross-species infection and will kill its host within a week of being infected."

Gavin couldn't help but look at the virus in the holo cube with a newfound respect. "Damn. How does nature even come up with something like that?"

"Oh, nature didn't come up with this one, Admiral. This baby was specifically designed."

Gavin's eyes widened in surprise. "Come on, Doctor, be serious. All the data we've seen indicates that the civilization was only at a level equivalent to Earth's medieval period. No way could they have bio-engineered a world-killing virus. And even if they could have, why would you design a virus that would kill your own civilization along with everything else on the planet? You must have made a mistake."

Lindsey looked affronted. "I assure you, Admiral, my findings are correct. Science does not lie."

Before Gavin could retort, Heather interjected.

"Perhaps you should tell him the rest, Lindsey."

Gavin looked at her incredulously. "There's more?"

"As I said, Admiral, there is no way this virus could have occurred naturally. The telltale signs of manipulation are there. Humans experimented with tailor-made viruses in the twentieth and twenty-first centuries and although a leap beyond what they were, the basic ideas behind this virus are easily achievable. What really got my attention was that the computer was able to identify the DNA that the virus was designed to latch onto."

"Well, we know this planet was listed in the Saiph database, so it would seem to me that it wouldn't be too big a leap to expect the virus to be specific to Saiph DNA."

Lindsey gave Gavin a smug look as Heather answered. "Very nearly correct, Admiral. Yes, it was designed to attack Saiph DNA, but more specifically, Saiph DNA which had been spliced with the DNA of the species we know as the Others."

Gavin felt his spine tingle with excitement as he tried to control his voice. "Are you telling me that we're in orbit around the Others' home world?"

Heather nodded as a large smile spread across her face.

Gavin sat back in his seat, his mind racing at the news. After a few moments he activated his link.

"Communications. Lieutenant Dhal."

"Lieutenant, prepare a communications drone for immediate launch… cancel. Make that two drones, destination Survey Command, and stand by for a data packet from Doctor Reid. Mark it Priority One."

Gavin cut the link before Dhal could acknowledge.

"Doctor, I need to know everything you can find out about that planet down there. Anything you need, you just holler. If we don't have it within the flotilla I can guarantee Earth will get it to us ASAP."

#

DURAV - 172 LIGHT YEARS FROM EARTH

It may have been summer in this hemisphere of Durav but at this high altitude the snow still lay on the ground and the ceaseless wind that blew cut you to the bone. None of this seemed to bother Tama Narath as he resolutely trudged up the path worn in the mountainside by many a faithful pilgrim before him. As he reached the cave entrance, the ever-present guardians recited the ancient challenge, their evil-looking targath blades ready to cut down anyone foolish enough to attempt to enter the High Coltus for any reason but to commune with the Creator.

Narath may have been the commander of the largest force the Creator had seen fit to have gathered by the Chosen People in their Ehita against the heretics, but even he was barred from entry into the High Coltus until the guardians were satisfied with his response. Replying with the pilgrim's prayer, they allowed him passage into the relative warmth of the cave and he made his way along the tunnel that led to the heart of the mountain and the High Coltus. As Narath entered the candlelit chamber at the tunnel's end, he felt the warmth of the Creator fill him. Narath went to his knees, placing the fingers of both hands on the Gift

Stone at the base of his skull as he was bathed in the Creator's love.

Blessings be upon you, pilgrim.

I am Tama Narath, Hand of the Creator, and I bring news of the Ehita.

Tell me of your news, Narath.

As the Creator has decreed, I recalled the fleets of the Chosen People and began the process of reequipping them with the gifts the Creator has blessed us with. I am proud to report that although the modifications have taken time, they are now complete and I am preparing to begin the assault that will cleanse the heretics from the stars once and for all.

The feeling of love that flowed from Narath's Gift Stone was an almost physical thing.

You have served me well, Narath. The time of the Creator's return is at hand and as you lead the Chosen People on the Ehita I shall lead you all to Aseena. And what of my gift that will open the way for you to complete your task, Narath?

Narath struggled to gather his thoughts as the Creator's love slowly left his trembling body.

As you commanded, I made that a priority and the last of the units are being deployed as we speak. When I receive confirmation of their deployment, all will be in place and I ask for your blessing to deploy the fleet.

For just a fleeting moment, Narath's head filled with a series of flashing images as the Creator considered every possible variable that may affect the forthcoming battles. Faster than the fastest computer. Never before had Narath been privileged to see into the workings of the Creator's mind.

You have my blessing, Tama Narath. Go forth and sweep all the heretics before you.

Narath felt the Creator leave his mind and shook off the feeling of emptiness that always came over him after

231

communing with the Creator. *But soon I shall enter Aseena and forever stand at the Creator's side.*

Narath stood and straightened his cloak as he strode purposefully back up the tunnel.

CHAPTER FIFTEEN

THE ROCK

ENEMY HELD SPACE – WHITE DWARF SYSTEM 54.2 LIGHT YEARS FROM EARTH

Sergeant Semple glanced at his passive scanners; he was closing fast on the asteroid that held the Others' base, 1800 meters per second, to be precise. With a nudge of his finger on the controls, his specially modified egg released pressurized argon and slowed his ship to a more acceptable speed. This was the bit he hated most. The final approach. Until now he'd relied on the guidance information supplied by the navy pukes. As he closed on the asteroid used as the Others' main naval base in the region, he felt shivers of insecurity run up his spine. Enough! He pulled himself together to concentrate on his job at hand; to land on the rock housing the naval base, disable the defensive batteries and secure the airlocks that the marines of the assault force would use to gain access.

The past two days of traveling through space confined inside his specially adapted Wraith suit, wrapped in a variation of the egg that the marines used for planetary assaults, had little impact on his present worries...not! Five kilometers out. Umbilicals detached. Thrusters engaged. Separation from the egg complete. Semple ran through the checklist. The rock seemed to be approaching very fast... retro thrusters firing; feet hit first; bend the knees... and ... we're down. Semple took a deep breath as he completed Phase One. *You're still alive, Semple!* He smiled wryly.

Semple took a moment to orient himself as his suit's passive sensors soaked up the terrain around him. Yes! It looked like he had landed on the correct asteroid at least. An icon in his heads-up display blinked to a regular beat, indicating the route to his nearest target. The target was a form of area denial weapon; similar to that used by the navy to kill close-in threats, such as missiles, on their terminal attack leg. One of those lasers would do a lot of damage to an approaching assault shuttle. A furtive glance at the countdown clock in the top left of his display informed him he had less than two hours before the assault force arrived. *Time is a-marching!* Semple hoped the Others didn't have any work parties on the surface today, or this mission was blown. He shook his head inside his Wraith suit, resigned to the fact that there was nothing he could do about it now.

With dutiful determination, Semple followed the directions to target icon, wondering how many of his forty fellow Thunder troopers had also made it onto this rock.

#

Colonel Vladimir Egnorov unwittingly mirrored Semple's thoughts. His men were still on strict emissions control, just as they had been since their launch from the navy shuttles three days ago, he had no way of knowing how successful Phase One had been.

The plan devised by Vladimir and Alec Murray was a dichotomy of simplicity and complexity. Using automated reconnaissance probes, launched from stealthy Persai ships beyond the detection range of the Others, they simply used the Others' own tactics against them.

At the second battle of Garunda, the Others coasted into the Garunda system with their drive engines off, allowing them to remain undetected by the Sherlock surveillance platforms as they traveled on a ballistic trajectory. The navy now used this same cunning move to allow its recon probes to infiltrate the heart of the Others' defenses. The probes passed through the system using only their passive systems to collect data. When the navy was sure they were beyond the Others' detection range, the same stealthy Persai ships collected them, extracted the data, and returned it to Third Fleet for analysis. Vladimir and Alec had spent hours poring over the probe data. They identified the majority of the defenses on and around the base and formulated a plan of attack.

A plan that Vladimir was in the midst of, he hoped the Others wouldn't disrupt it. *I'm on this rock now, my only ride home is the navy.* Vladimir shook off his uncertainty and activated his direction to target icon. The green arrow appeared in his heads-up display. 250 meters? *Not far, just need to watch my footing.* Vladimir made a mental note of the cratered and pockmarked surface, it would make his route difficult and time-consuming. The countdown clock told him that the fleet's arrival was in one hour fifty-six minutes and twenty-eight seconds... twenty-seven seconds... twenty-six seconds... Vladimir took off as surefooted as a goat.

Each of the Thunder troopers was assigned an area of responsibility covering approximately four square kilometers of the asteroid's surface. The analysts identified an average of three prospective targets in each of these squares, giving the Thunder troopers about forty minutes to reach and dispense with each target before making their way to the final rally point, where they planned to form up for the assault prior to the fleet's arrival.

Both Vladimir and Alec knew forty minutes was not a huge amount of time, but they also understood the risks; the longer the Thunder troopers deployed on the surface the greater the chance of detection by the Others.

Vladimir covered the ground in good time. Within fifteen minutes, he was lying on his belly observing his target; the cover of an anti-ship missile silo, or so the navy analysts believed. Perhaps "believed" was too strong a word, "assumed" was much more accurate, Vladimir acknowledged, as he uttered out loud: "It could be the cover of a garbage disposal, for all I know." He also knew there was no sense in taking chances.

Vladimir gave the area around the silo a final check for alarms or booby traps before surreptitiously approaching it. With practiced skill, he quickly placed the explosive charges around it and set the timer unit. When initiated, the charges would buckle the silo cover and prevent it from opening, rendering the missiles within useless, he hoped... well, that was the plan.

With a last verification of his work, Vladimir reconfigured his heads-up display to show the route to his next target; a beam weapon projector, of sorts.

One hour nineteen minutes and twelve seconds till fleet arrival... eleven seconds... ten seconds...

#

Three kilometers away, Semple had already completed his second task, the mining of a radar dome. He was now headed for his third and final target. A swift glance at the countdown clock showed fifty-two minutes left. "Hustle, Semple, hustle!" he muttered, it was over 300 meters to the next target, 400 more to the rally point.

Semple crested the edge of a crater, whether it was down to his own haste or sheer bad luck, Semple would never know, but there, scant meters away, were two enemy soldiers and they were staring directly at him.

On instinct, Semple drew his mono-molecular blade in one hand and his pistol in the other. He launched at the startled soldiers as they were confronted with the sight of an eight-foot-tall black shadowy figure coming at them. Their surprise and subsequent inaction was the advantage Semple needed. He fired as he moved, putting two shots into the face plate of the right-hand Other. It shattered and was followed almost instantaneously by an explosive decompression as the air left the suit and propelled the now lifeless body away from him.

Semple didn't have time to observe his handiwork, he had already moved on to his next victim. With as much force as he and his suit could muster, Semple pushed his blade up and under the chin of the second Other. The force of the maneuver lifted the hapless enemy soldier off the ground as Semple buried his knife to the hilt. Death was immediate.

Semple lowered the space-suited body to the ground and glanced around. There was no sign of the first soldier. Its momentum had already carried it out of sight. He hoped it wasn't discovered until after the assault had begun. The question foremost in Semple's mind was whether the Others had been lying in wait for him or whether it was Murphy's Law showing its hand by throwing an unexpected monkey wrench in the works of best-laid plans. Swiftly, Semple checked the vicinity of the base of the crater. Sure enough, there it was, a tool bag secured beside a half-open metal cover.

Relief washed over him. Thank you, God! The enemy he'd just dispatched had been performing routine maintenance, he hoped, as he moved toward the metal cover.

Semple removed the cover completely and shone a light down the shaft it had been encasing. Approximately twenty meters down, there was a second metal cover. *God knows what's down there, but what the hell?* Never one to waste an opportunity, Semple rapidly and efficiently attached an explosive charge to his magnetic grapple and sent it down the shaft. The magnet held the charge securely to the second hatch. Random explosions would only add to the chaos and confusion that could buy the assaulting force enough time to secure the base.

With the explosives in place and the clock ticking, Semple headed to his final target.

Forty-three minutes and ten seconds until fleet arrival, nine seconds... eight seconds... seven seconds...

#

Vladimir lay on his abdomen and used his enhanced optical scanners to assess the brightly lit airlock only 350 meters from him. His ultimate goal. No appearance of any guards but Vladimir easily discerned the ugly protuberance of a plasma weapon emplacement on either side of the airlock.

"I gotta take care of you mothers," he murmured. He had to destroy them before his troopers could advance into the open, otherwise they would be cut down before they achieved more than a few steps.

The plan called for his small force of ten troopers, and three others like it, to take their signal from the arrival of the fleet. On cue, they would attack the four identified air locks on this side of the asteroid and hold them until the arrival of Alec's marines. With the arrival of the reinforcements, they could then force their way into the base and secure it.

Vladimir had reached the rally point without incident and hoped the other Thunder troopers had done the same. A blinking red icon in his display warned him that a whisker laser was requesting his IFF, Identification Friend or Foe. An instruction sent the response and two Thunder troopers emerged from the gloom to take up defensive positions around the edge of the crater.

Over the next ten minutes, the remaining seven Thunder troopers of Vladimir's force arrived at the rally point. All they could do now was wait and hope the fleet was on time.

Twelve minutes and fifty-nine seconds until fleet arrival... fifty-eight seconds... fifty-seven seconds... fifty-six seconds...

#

GARUNDAN SYSTEM – GARUNDA
49.41 LIGHT YEARS FROM EARTH

Vice Admiral John Radford, Commander Third Fleet, prowled the flag bridge of TDF *The Iron Chancellor* like a caged animal. It was the waiting that he hated the most. For what seemed like the hundredth time in the past ten minutes he checked the countdown clock displayed at the top of the main holo cube. It filled the entire center of the flag bridge. The numbers remorselessly marched downwards.

Five minutes and zero seconds... four minutes and fifty-nine seconds... fifty-eight seconds...

The lieutenant at tactical turned to address the admiral. "Fleet reports all ships at battle stations. Colonel Murray reports his marines embarked on the assault shuttles and buttoned up ready for drop."

"Thank you, Lieutenant Alekia. Communication's fleet-wide address. Audio and visual, if you please."

John positioned himself in the center of the flag bridge, clasped his hands behind him, and squared his shoulders as he faced the holo pickup. A nod from the officer at communications told him his image was now being beamed to every ship of the massed Third Fleet.

"Ladies and gentlemen of Third Fleet. Since our first meeting with the Others, we have been on the defensive, reacting to the actions of the enemy like a puppet on a string. But no longer... Now we take the war to them! All of you. Be you human, Persai, or Garundan, have gathered together with one aim... defeating the Others. And today, together, we take that first step. A step that will undoubtedly cost us in blood but one that must be taken. I know that some amongst you are nervous, even fearful, of what faces us when we join battle. Look around you, your crew mates share that feeling. I share that feeling."

John kept his eyes fixed on the pick-up, staring into it as though he was staring into the eyes of the people he was about to send into battle, infusing them with the confidence he wasn't feeling in its entirety.

"All I ask is that you do your duty. May your gods be with you and I'll see you on the other side."

The flag bridge was deathly still as John made his way over to his command chair and punched in a private comm channel. The face of Alec Murray seated in his Wraith suit aboard his assault shuttle appeared in the small holo display.

"Nice speech, John." The beginnings of a smile appeared on John's face as he shrugged his shoulders.

"It felt like the right thing to do. Are you ready for this?" Now it was Alec's turn to give a small smile and chuckle.

"No. But I'm going anyway! Vladimir would never let me live it down if I didn't personally lead the troops. Besides, there's a certain Sergeant Semple on that rock that I'm in debt to and you know how us Scots hate being in someone's debt." A red icon blinked in John's display. Thirty seconds to go... twenty-nine... twenty-eight... John looked again at his friend.

"Good luck, Alec." The Scotsman's grin spread from ear to ear.

"Who needs luck? I've a plasma rifle with a full charge." John cut the link, smiling and shaking his head slowly. The lieutenant at navigation began his countdown.

"Three. Two. One. Fold." Third Fleet vanished from the 31 Aquilae system.

#

ENEMY SPACE - WHITE DWARF SYSTEM
54.2 LIGHT YEARS FROM EARTH

The countdown clock in Vladimir's display hit Zero.

Bang on cue, a small green telltale icon started blinking in Vladimir's display. His suit had detected the arrival of Third Fleet's flagship, *The Iron Chancellor.*

"Suit. Break communications silence and broadcast the go-code to all Thunder units and the Flag. Break. Suit. Thunder Channel. Thunder one-zero, fire at will."

The Thunder troopers around him, with Hand-Held Hyper Velocity Missiles, let loose at the weapons positions on either side of the airlock. In a heartbeat, both positions were torn apart by the missiles impacting at 30,000 kilometers per hour. Even as the missiles struck their targets, Vladimir and his troopers bounded forward, closing the distance to the airlock. Within seconds, they had covered the distance and were stacking up in single file along the right-hand side of the rock surrounding the sunken airlock entrance.

"Breaching charges forward!"

A trooper moved forward on Vladimir's command and slipped a small, but extremely powerful, shaped-charge explosive from each leg pouch, it had been developed exclusively for this operation. Activating the integral magnetic grips, he attached two to the seam where the doors of the airlock met, one high, another low, before stepping back around the protruding rock. Theoretically, the shaped charges directed the explosive force forward so that there was no danger to anyone standing directly behind them, but a soldier of any ilk knew the ever-present risk of malfunction; the experts advised on their safety but they didn't suffer the injuries when their little toy failed to function as advertised. The Thunder troopers didn't take any chances, particularly with an untested high explosive.

"Cover! ... Firing now!"

The troopers anticipated the deep rumble that caused their boots to vibrate, it was followed swiftly by a bright flash. The outer airlock doors were breached. They rushed through the prodigious expanse the explosives had carved and found themselves in a large airlock easily big enough to hold twenty Wraith-suited troopers. Perfect. Vladimir looked at the inner airlock door. *Yeah, a perfect match for the outer door.*

"Breaching charges forward!"

A trooper moved forward and prepped the inner door just as he had the outer one, with more of the same explosive charges, placing one high, one low, in a matter of seconds his task was complete; he retreated as far into the crowded airlock as he could.

"Cover! … Firing now!"

Vladimir's suit rocked with the now-familiar blast but it was accompanied by an unexpected rush of atmosphere, traveling with a formidable force. Like a hurricane, it contained every unsecured nut and bolt from beyond the inner airlock. Vladimir's suit was bombarded by wave after wave of debris, small and large. He caught a glimpse of a few unlucky enemy crew member flying past, wide-eyed. Vladimir could almost hear the screams escaping from their muted open mouths as they were ejected into the cold vacuum of space.

Without warning, the deadly flow of out-rushing air stopped. Vladimir speculated that the automatic bulkhead doors further inside the base had been sealed shut, leaving those trapped to their ignominious fate while preserving the remaining base from the effects of the breach.

Vladimir and his troopers stepped into a small plaza-like area with four corridors branching off of it, apparently leading further into the bowels of the base. Vladimir knew he would leave himself vulnerable to a flanking attack if he moved down any of them. His phase of the assault would be complete as soon as he secured the breach. "Suit. Thunder One Zero. Alfa team secure right flank. Bravo team move left. Find yourselves a good firing position and hunker down. Now we wait for the cavalry."

Vladimir crouched in the doorway of what he thought had once been an office. He paused to check the progress of the other Thunder troopers. He let out a satisfied grunt as he noted that all the demolition charges his troopers had placed on their way to their rendezvous points had functioned successfully. The plan was on track and would diminish enemy fire against the navy as they held position off the naval base before launching Alec Murray's marines. It seemed the Thunder troopers at the three other airlocks had made successful breaches with minimal casualties and were assuming defensive positions to await Murray's men.

Oddly, none of the other teams were reporting any type of enemy counter attack. The enemy didn't appear to realize that with only the small number of Thunder troopers holding the airlocks, this was their best chance to dislodge Vladimir and his men and re-take them. Well, Vladimir wasn't known for looking a gift horse in the mouth, time to give the admiral the good news.

#

John Radford and Third Fleet sprang into existence only 200,000 kilometers from the naval base. Their engines strained to bring them to a halt relative to the base. Third Fleet was already at battle stations. Every weapons system in its mighty arsenal was manned and ready for action.

Extensive planning, using the data from the reconnaissance drones, had allowed John's staff to build a detailed picture of the enemy's defenses. The planning staff devised a complicated fire plan to coordinate his ships' ordnances as one and bring the heaviest weight of fire down on the enemy as quickly as possible.

John forced himself to remain in his seat on the flag bridge of the Bismarck class battleship TDF *The Iron Chancellor*. He was finding it difficult to hold his features in check as the ships of Third Fleet unleashed their combined fury on the Others. Three Bismarck class battleships, six Nemesis class battleships, nine Vulcan heavy cruisers, and nine Talos light cruisers fired as one.

An avalanche of missiles fell on the outer defenses and the smaller asteroids containing them as Third Fleet pummeled them into cosmic dust. Grazers reached out to touch orbiting weapons platforms and the radars that guided them. Wherever the grazers touched there was a

244

brief, intense light like a moth dancing too close to a flame as the platforms succumbed to the massive energy transfer and exploded. The planners hadn't taken any chances. As fire shifted from the weapons platforms and smaller asteroids, it was redirected to targets on the larger asteroid that held the naval base itself. Missile silos and laser defense sites, already crippled by the Thunder troopers' demolition charges, were targeted a second, third, and sometimes fourth time as Third Fleet scoured the surface clean of any threat.

John's eyes never left the tactical holo cube showing the space surrounding Third Fleet and the naval base as the lieutenant at communications spoke.

"Admiral. Thunder reports all breaches successful and requests immediate marine support."

"Understood Lieutenant, inform the marines that they have permission to launch."

"Aye-aye, sir... Marines away."

If at all possible, John stared even more intently into his holo cube as a sprinkling of smaller icons appeared in the heart of Third Fleet and headed for the naval base. Surrounded by the massive armored battleships and cruisers of the fleet were four Excalibur Assault Ships.

Based on the Vulcan heavy cruiser, the Excalibur had been modified to carry a complete assault battalion of 510 marines along with everything they would need to sustain them. The small icons in John's display were the first wave of forty Buffalo assault shuttles, holding 800 marines, heading for the breaches in the naval base's defenses. Twenty Reaper close support craft were riding shotgun, ready to use their quick firing plasma cannon and high velocity missiles to neutralize any threat to the shuttles.

John creased his forehead as he stared into his holo cube. Something wasn't quite right. The recon probes had shown the naval base was heavily defended by missile silos and energy weapons on the asteroid it had been carved into, surrounded by weapon platforms almost thick enough that he could have got out and walked to the base. There were more weapons mounted on the bordering lesser asteroids that also needed dispatching.

OK, Thunder may have destroyed all the defensive systems on this side of the base, Third Fleet had laid down a massive amount of fire on its arrival and neutralized the surviving weapons, but even still... the enemy response should have been greater, Third Fleet wasn't taking enough hits. The enemy reply was... sluggish.

"Tactical. Update on enemy response."

The officer at tactical scanned his readouts quickly, he tapped a few keys updating John's display before turning to face him.

"Admiral. Enemy fire is sporadic and uncoordinated. Our systems show we are being successfully targeted by the enemy fire and control radars which we are destroying in turn with High Speed Anti-Radiation Missiles and grazer fire but it doesn't explain why, if they can target us, their defensive fire is so completely uncoordinated."

The officer paused as if searching for an explanation.

"Sir. If I hazard a guess, I would say that they have suffered significant damage to whatever command and control system they use."

John considered that for a moment. That had been his own gut feeling but right now he had more to worry about than a failure in the enemy's chain of command.

"Let's not look a gift horse in the mouth, Commander, we'll worry about it later," John was cut short by an urgent call.

"Vampire! Vampire! Multiple missiles incoming from the far side of the naval base. A count of 380. Missiles are in search mode. They've been launched blind from the far side of base."

John rapidly snapped his orders out.

"Activate electronic counter measures. Free anti-missile batteries fleet-wide. Move the Agis anti-missile destroyers to a best firing point between the enemy missiles and the shuttles. Agis priority fire is in defense of the marine shuttles, the fleet will have to look after itself."

The marine shuttles didn't turn from the incoming missiles. Their best hope of survival was to get to the surface of the asteroid on the double. John conjured the image of pilots pushing their throttles to the stops, coaxing a fraction more speed out of their already overtaxed engines. He punched in a new command, and in his holo cube the face of Rear Admiral Evans, Co BatFor 3.1, appeared.

"Rhys. I suspect we have enemy ships hiding in the shadow of the asteroid. Maneuver your command until you clear the blind spot. Remember, Thunder have destroyed the base defenses on this side but we can't allow them to take potshots at us with impunity. If one of those missiles gets a lock on a shuttle full of marines, it won't stand a chance."

Evans nodded. "Understood, Admiral. You can count on us. Evans clear."

The face of Evans disappeared and John's attention returned to the tactical problem at hand. Without the Agis destroyers, Third Fleet would inevitably take hits.

"Enemy missiles have acquired targets, Admiral. Looks like they've been programmed to pursue the largest ships. Most are ignoring the shuttles and are heading straight for us. Sensors show a second wave of similar size crossing the radar horizon of the asteroid now. Their search radars are going active."

A tap of a key and the image of Captain Chandra Badal, John's Flag Captain, appeared.

"Admiral," said Chandra with a slight bow of his head.

"Captain. Please feel free to fight as you see fit."

"Thank you, Admiral. Badal clear."

In the holo cube, the icons representing the enemy missiles closed on Third Fleet and John calmly addressed the entire Flag Bridge. "Buckle up people, this is about to get interesting."

John tightened his seat restraints and checked his helmet, still in its rack on the right side of his seat. Images of Force Leader Taminth's untimely death as the bridge of his Persai cruiser Vitaros catastrophically decompressed, flashed unbidden through his mind, he knew only too well the damage caused by laser impact. Once more unto the breach, dear friends, once more, a wry smile crossed John's face as the Shakespearean quote popped into his head.

#

"One minute. Doors opening. Gravity off."

Alec Murray half listened as the Load Master went through his pre-drop ritual. The marine's seats retracted into the walls of the Buffalo assault shuttle as the magnetic restraints activated and became the only thing securing Alec and his marines in place. The Wraith suit automatically straightened each of their legs and locked at the ankles, knees, hips, shoulders, neck, elbows, and wrists. It ensured each marine made a clean exit from the shuttle and didn't become entangled on stray equipment or worse still, another marine.

A female voice came over the pilot's circuit.

"Good luck, marines. Give them hell!"

Christ! I've got to match a face to that voice one of these days. Alec was briefly distracted by the warm honeyed drawl. With a slight click, the velvety voice returned.

"Thirty seconds. Reapers are mowing the road so visibility may be obscured."

The Reapers were blasting plasma cannon, tearing through the asteroid's surface in close proximity to the marines' drop zone. If there were any surviving enemy hiding in ambush for the marines then they would fall victim to the withering Reaper fire. *I hope.* Regrettably, it also blew debris up; with no wind or gravity to disperse it quickly, it could significantly decrease visibility and make spotting the enemy even harder. Alec activated his command link. "Marines. Switch to image intensifier mode." His suit complied and the world around him disintegrated into shades of green and black.

"Drop! Drop! Drop!"

800 marines spat from the bellies of forty Buffalos, split equally into four groups of 200 over the four breach points being held by the Thunder troopers. Alec had time to feel his suit configure for landing then...
Thud! He was down and moving for the rally point. A blinking diamond in his heads-up display showed the entrance to the airlock marked by the Thunder troopers. Alec bounded toward the airlock as fast as his suit would carry him, followed on all sides by his marines who were shaking down into their fire teams as they moved.

On reaching the black, blast damaged doors, Alec halted.

"Suit. Transmit IFF code."

The suit transmitted the encrypted Identify Friend or Foe code. Bursting in behind a group of Thunder troopers armed to the teeth and with itchy trigger fingers could really ruin your day in a hurry.

A triple tone and a solid green square in the top left of his display showed that his IFF had been received and acknowledged by the waiting Thunder troopers. Still, Alec moved through the wrecked doors cautiously. Never trust a machine.

"Good to see you, Alec, thought you were taking a nap out there."

The light tone in Vladimir Ergonov's voice belied his relief at seeing 200 marines arriving to back up his own ten troopers.

Alec let out a small chuckle. "The admiral insisted I finish my breakfast before I left, you know how he is, always mothering us."

The responding laughter was cut short by a wicked blast of plasma fire that removed a large chunk of wall from just above Vladimir's head. Vladimir brushed the rubble from his suit with one armored hand before continuing.

"As you see, the natives are restless. We've managed to hold here without too much trouble. For whatever reason, they haven't managed to get their act together and have been launching sporadic piecemeal attacks rather than waiting to amass their strength and rush us."

Alec mulled that piece of news over for a moment.

"Maybe their larger forces are trapped further inside the base somewhere and we'll come across them as we move deeper?"

"A possibility, Alec. But there's another strange thing. Thunder Three Zero reports that it has prisoners."

Alec shook his head in disbelief. Prisoners? The Others didn't surrender. They fought to the death or committed suicide if they were about to be captured. Real, live prisoners? The intelligence weenies would be falling over themselves to interrogate them. The walls shook from the impact of another plasma blast from further along the corridor, concentrating Alec's attention on their current situation.

"Well, I'm here now, let's get on with it. Why don't you stay here and let the real workers show you how it should be done?"

Vladimir snorted loudly. "And let you take all the credit for Thunder's good work? Not likely! Suit. Thunder command channel. All Thunder call signs advance when they have adequate marine support. Break. Last man in the bar buys the round, Alec." The Thunder troopers moved off, firing down the corridor as they went.

Alec shook his head slowly, smiling, then rose to a crouch and headed off after the Thunder troopers, closely followed by his own marines.

#

FLAG BRIEFING ROOM - TDF *THE IRON CHANCELLOR*

The flag briefing room was filled to capacity and then some. The noise generated by the myriad of voices, human, Garundan, and Persai was deafening as the doors slid open permitting entry to John Radford. He stood on the threshold for a moment; soaking it all in before he crossed it.

In the ten days since Third Fleet successfully carried out the assault on the Others' naval base, there had been little time for anyone to catch their breath. Although the bulk of Third Fleet remained relatively unscathed from

251

the battle; BatFor 3.1 under Admiral Evans had taken a beating.

After following Radford's order to engage the enemy vessels on the far side of the asteroid housing the naval base, Evans led his ships to the projected location of those enemy vessels. He arrived slap-bang in the middle of a deadly mixed force of Vultures, Buzzards, and Goshawks and they were prepared, they benefited from the supporting fire of weapons platforms, which had not been subjected to any suppressive fire.

Realizing the inadequacy of his lighter ships, Evans ordered the cruisers to engage the weapons platforms at longer ranges while his heavier battleships closed and fought at short-range battle. Casualties on both sides had been high. BatFor 3.1 lost one Bismarck and three Nemesis battleships, while one other Bismarck and all the remaining Nemeses suffered significant damage. On the other hand, the enemy had not been so fortunate. With the exception of one badly damaged, but relatively intact, Buzzard, the remaining enemy ships were now an expanding wreckage field.

Evans boarded the intact Buzzard, the computer cores had been turned to piles of melted circuitry and the entire crew was dead, either by battle injury or by their own hand. He was never more aware of how remarkable it was that so many enemy soldiers had been captured on the naval base itself.

"Admiral on deck!" called the first officer to spot him.

The room descended into silence as Radford made his way to his seat at the head of the table. Reaching his chair, he sat and indicated for those around him to do the same.

"Please be seated, ladies and gentlemen."

There was just enough seating even in this large room for the various BatFor commanders and their immediate staff, but Radford insisted that a seat be made available at his immediate right for Colonel Vladimir Egnorov, commander of the Thunder troopers.

Radford cleared his throat before beginning.

"Firstly, my apologies for dragging you away from your commands at such short notice but Commander Hoshino," he inclined his head in the direction of a diminutive Japanese commander in her early fifties a few seats down from him, "has developed some critical intelligence that she wishes to make you aware of personally. Commander, if you please."

Kaya Hoshino was all of five-feet-two inches tall and couldn't have weighed more than ninety-eight pounds soaking wet, but Radford had quickly learned her mind was remarkable. Hoshino had the ability to process information and use the extrapolated data to make leaps of logic that made any state of the art computer seem tardy.

When Radford put his staff together, the Bureau of Personnel saddled him with a micro-managing bureaucrat of an officer, Commander Bryer Anderson, to run his intelligence shop. Said commander had obviously pulled some strings to get himself the prestigious position of Fleet Intelligence Officer. No doubt he had already been eyeing up his next promotion.

After keeping a close watch on how the commander ran or should he say, dictated, the intelligence shop, Radford had had no choice but to send the commander packing.

Radford had been left with a junior lieutenant holding the key post of FIO and, not trusting the Bureau of Personnel not to send another incompetent officer like the last, Radford had sent a request to Admiral Aleksandr Vadis, Chief of the Office of Naval

Intelligence, for his recommendations. Two days later, Commander Hoshino arrived and without any undue fuss quickly and efficiently turned the intelligence shop into what could only be described as a fountain of all knowledge.

"Thank you, Admiral. As you are no doubt aware, my staff and I have pored over the vast amount of information recovered from the enemy base. That data comes from three main sources.

One. The computer cores. They were successfully recovered, in my opinion, due to the actions of Colonel Egnorov, his Thunder troopers and the timely arrival of our own marine support." Vladimir Egnorov shifted in his seat uncomfortably, being singled out for praise during such a high-level meeting was something that didn't happen very often for a lowly colonel.

"The disruption caused by his demolition charges to the enemy command and control system combined with the speed with which the Thunder troopers and marines secured the base, meant the enemy had no time to purge their computer cores. We've gleaned a wealth of information from them. The highlights of which, with the admiral's permission, I will come back to." John gave a confirmatory nod.

"Two. Enemy prisoners." Hoshino paused to look around the room. "For the first time we have enemy prisoners. Our linguists are working on interpreting the Others' language, unfortunately, many of them are sedated as they tend to either attack their interrogators or fall into what our doctors are calling a form of 'psychotic paralysis.' Even through this limited contact, we've been able to ascertain a recognizable rank structure; which to be honest is nothing less than you'd expect in a militarily, regimented organization such as a navy. One discrepancy we have found, however, is that no matter the rank of the individual, they appear to show a definite deference to any prisoner whose armored right arm is painted a distinctive red."

She tapped a control on her PAD and a schematic of the enemy base projected into the holo cube. One area in particular, relatively close to the surface but separated from the main base by a single long corridor was highlighted.

"Now as you can see from this diagram, all the prisoners who were wearing the distinctive red paint were captured in this area. The marines took significant casualties securing it as these soldiers fought particularly ferociously. The Others were eventually captured when our marines used breaching charges to collapse the corridor roof on them and later dug them out.

"The marines moved on to the end of this corridor and here they were confronted with a battle armor bulkhead. On entering the room beyond they found it had already been breached from above. The entire room was open to space and apparently killed all inside. There was also significant damage to what our technicians believe to be an advanced Artificial Intelligence, it is far more advanced than anything we have seen up to now on enemy's side." Hoshino paused for breath and effect, as she wanted the room's full attention. "In addition, this entire room was lined with thermo-baric explosives; and it contained a very powerful ultra-low-frequency transmitter. The control lines for both had been damaged by the breaching charge which, we currently believe, is the reason we have any prisoners at all."

Hoshino's last statement caused a stir and a few murmured words around the room as she paused to see if anyone else could connect the dots.

Radford looked around at the puzzled faces. What seemed obvious to Hoshino had escaped him when she had first put the facts in front of him; there was little point in wasting any more time. "If you would explain, Commander."

Hoshino's lips pursed in disappointment at the lack of appropriate response, they had all missed the obvious. She nodded, "Admiral," before once more addressing the room.

"Please cast your mind back to the First Battle of Garunda when, following the battle, the marines boarded the Others' last remaining ship. The crew put up a stiff resistance to the marines until the point where they reached a battle armor bulkhead. Before they could force their way past the bulkhead and enter the room there was an extremely strong ultra-low-frequency transmission, followed immediately by a thermo-baric explosion. It completely destroyed everything in the room. Every single enemy crew member dropped dead where he stood. There were no survivors. Until now, we have been at a loss to explain why."

Every eye focused on her and she could see from their faces that the pieces were beginning to fall into place.

"I've been examining BatFor 3.1's sensor logs. As Admiral Evans' marines were about to board the ship, a powerful ultra-low-frequency transmission was detected emanating from within. When the marines searched it, they discovered a room behind a battle armor bulkhead, which had been subjected to a thermo-baric explosion.

"In the intelligence game, there is no such thing as coincidence.

"I believe that that room housed an AI which activated the ultra-low-frequency signal which in turn killed every living crew member on that ship before triggering a thermo-baric explosion to destroy all evidence of its own existence."

A deafening silence filled the room as those gathered fathomed the implications of this statement.

"Commander." Force Leader Tciph of the Persai contingent broke the silence. "Are you saying that the Others are controlled by sophisticated computers? That seems… well… far-fetched." Radford cleared his throat, interrupting Hoshino before she could reply.

"I had the same thought, Force Leader, but the intelligence is stacking up to support the commander's assumption. The destruction of the naval base's AI prior to the start of the assault could explain their slow and uncoordinated response to our arrival. The ULF signals are a matter of record as, indeed, are the thermo-baric explosions from both my encounter with them after the First Battle of Garunda and Admiral Evans' fight with them here. The launching of clockwork raids on Garunda, which allowed us to follow them back to this naval base. Add two and two together and the answer is four. I believe that Commander Hoshino certainly has a working hypothesis that fits these facts."

Again the room sunk into silence as they considered Radford's mathematics.

"Hmm, you said you had a third source of information, Commander?" asked Admiral Evans after a few moments.

"If you will bear with me, Admiral, I would like you to consider points one and three together. Sensor records from BatFor 3.1 confirm the ships they engaged here were the same ones that have been harassing Garunda for the past eighteen months.

"But take note of the size of the facilities here. They are no doubt built to service a much larger fleet, which begs the question, where are those other ships now?

257

"During the search of the base, we found items which caused us to re-evaluate the threat the Others may pose to the Commonwealth as a whole." Hoshino fiddled with her PAD, the image of a vaguely familiar computer core, attached to alien machinery, appeared in the holo cube. "This is a human civilian navigational computer recovered from within this base. Its serial numbers allow us to trace it to the cargo ship *The Happy Wanderer*.

"*The Happy Wanderer* was on a scheduled cargo run between Garunda and Pars when she disappeared some nineteen months ago. No sign of the ship was found, despite an extensive search. She was presumed lost with all hands, it now appears that she, and her navigational computer, fell into enemy hands."

The babble of excited talk interrupted Hoshino, she rapped her PAD on the table for attention.

"As I said, we recovered masses of information from their computers. A couple of pieces are from their navigational database." Hoshino touched a control and the schematic of the naval base was replaced by an image of a solar system. A very familiar solar system. Earth's solar system.

A strangled "Jeee...sus... that's Earth!" came from somewhere in the gathered mass.

"Intelligence indicates the enemy have not only identified the location of Earth, but over the last nineteen months have accessed the *Happy Wanderer's* computer. They now possess a complete layout of Commonwealth space."

The babbling began again, almost drowning Hoshino's words; Radford held up his hand to quiet the room and allow her to be heard.

"As I was saying, the Others possess a layout of Commonwealth space, but we now have access to their navigational database." Hoshino tapped her PAD and the image of Earth's solar system vanished. In its place, an unfamiliar solar system sprang into being. Its sun rotating slowly at its center while eleven planets orbited it. Another touch of the PAD and the fourth planet expanded until it filled the entire holo cube. A planet whose surface was mostly hidden from view by a brilliant white cloud. Almost like a magician reaching the pinnacle of his show Hoshino pointed at the image in the holo cube.

"Ladies and gentlemen, I give you the home world of the Others."

Radford could've heard a pin drop. He gave them a few moments to digest... to stare at the white-shrouded globe in the holo cube before he stood. John rested his hands on the table and garnered the entire room's attention.

"OK, people, what we've learned here is a game changer. The enemy knows where our home systems are located, and they have for the better part of a year and a half. As the commander pointed out, this base was designed to accommodate more than the equivalent of a battle group. Only a few elements of that battle group have been harassing Garunda for the past year and a half; it means that their other ships are somewhere else." Radford stood tall. "We've been played, people. The Others have kept us occupied in Garunda while they planned to hit us elsewhere. It's a lot less than nineteen months sailing time from here to Earth, it's my guess they're amassing their forces for an all-out assault on our home systems."

A murmur of agreement ran through the room.

"I've ordered the dispatching of drones to the naval commands of Earth, Janus, Pars, and Garunda. Drones are also on their way to Alona to keep our naval attaché in the loop. It's my intention to return to Garunda at the earliest opportunity and assume a defensive posture until I receive orders to the contrary from the Joint Chiefs."

John looked slowly around the room, making eye contact with each of his subordinate commanders.

"Gentlemen. I suggest you return to your ships. We leave within the hour."

CHAPTER SIXTEEN

ALONA SEE WHAT YOU WANT TO SEE

ALONA SYSTEM – MESSIER 54
50,000 LIGHT YEARS FROM EARTH

Since the all-time low in relations between the
Commonwealth Union of Planets and the Empire
following the discovery that the Empire had purchased
sensitive Commonwealth tech on the black market, the
Alonan Imperial Navy had had its five gravity drive
equipped Vaspar cruisers conducting training cruises at
a much higher tempo than had been previously planned
in order to train up the crews that would eventually
man the remaining six Vaspars that were still under
construction in the specially built naval yard in Alonan
systems Ort cloud. The word was that neither Grand
Admiral Raga or the emperor himself believed for a
second that there was any chance of an armed conflict
with the Commonwealth, but only a fool would not
prepare for a possible worst-case scenario so Captain
Welak and his crew worked hard at perfecting the skills
required to master a gravity drive warship and the
weapon systems that it carried. It didn't help that the
majority of systems were still calibrated in
Commonwealth Standard English and used their
numerical system, but that was just one more obstacle
to be overcome.

"Captain, we're picking something up on the long-range sensors."

Welak activated his display and it flickered to life as it extended out from its position at the side of his chair. On a Commonwealth warship he had no doubt that the captain would have the benefit of a high-resolution holographic display, but Alonan technology still lagged behind that of the Commonwealth, and the mix of advanced and standard tech on board the AIN *Volkar* was a prime example of that.

On the display, a large bright cloud slowly closed on the *Volkar*'s position. "Can you clean it up any?"

"Sorry, sir but the ships are so tightly packed that at this range their energy sources are overlapping. The computers just can't pick out individual ships at this distance."

Welak massaged his temples as if weary. "Do we at least have a likely course for them?"

"Computer is working on it now, sir but it will be a few minutes."

Welak cursed quietly. If only they had Commonwealth computers! But wishing got him nothing, so all he could do was wait. Welak couldn't even call for help. The *Volkar* was over a light year from Alona so the approaching ships would be long gone before any radio transmission reached home and the espionage types hadn't been able to procure any of the Commonwealth communications drones. All he could do was temper his impatience and wait for the computers to spit out their findings.

#

The minutes dragged by but eventually the information popped up on the navigator's screen. "Computer predicts that unless the ships make a radical course correction, they should enter the Alonan system

262

in thirty-six hours, assuming they slow down to sub-light speeds. On entering the system, their earliest time for Alona is seven hours after that. Total time forty-three hours."

Welak stood up, clasped his hands behind his back and began pacing up and down the small bridge. "Do we have a ship count yet?"

The exasperated lieutenant at tactical tapped his keys then sat back in frustration. "Whoever they are, they seem to be running their drives at maximum output. Our sensors are having a hard time burning through the interference. My best guess at the moment is fifty-plus ships in the battleship class with numerous smaller ships surrounding them. As they get closer I should be able to refine that."

Welak knew his next question had to be asked but he also knew he wouldn't like the answer either way. "Are they Commonwealth?"

"Negative, sir. Computers cannot identify the engine type at this time but I've seen enough traces of Commonwealth gravity drives and what I see isn't that."

Welak forced himself to sit back down in his chair and consider his options. He had a force of fifty-plus battleships accompanied by numerous smaller ships with an ETA in the Alonan system of thirty-six hours. His only means of warning home of the impending threat was to fold his ship for home but if he did that they wouldn't know the total composition of the force. Or, remain where he was until his inadequate sensors could pierce the veil of interference and get a good look at the approaching ships. Information that could be vital. But what if his ship wasn't quick enough to get away and it was destroyed? A force that large falling on an unprepared Alona would be a catastrophe.

"Navigator, plot a course for home and fold when ready."

#

The mood in the Imperial Navy's central command was one of heavy somberness. The news of an approaching fleet had roused Grand Admiral Raga from his bed and, in turn, the emperor. Raga stared at the ugly, mammoth vessel, which spouted weapon emplacements along its 1700 meter length in the wall display.

Emperor Paxt broke the silence of the room. "It's them, isn't it, Admiral?"

Raga slowly nodded before answering his emperor in a low, resigned voice. "I fear it is, your Majesty. With your permission, I would like to request the military attaché at the Commonwealth embassy review our data but..."

Emperor Paxt placed a hand on the shoulder of the man whose counsel he had come to rely on. "Can we stop them?" Under his hand he felt his friend's shoulders slouch.

"I've ordered the new cruisers to form a defense line 500,000 kilometers from Alona. The yards are working nonstop to bring the other cruisers on line. Even with their efforts, it would be a miracle if they could get even one more of the cruisers out of the yard in time to make a difference. Our remaining fleet, such as it is, will fight but it would be only a valiant gesture, and they wouldn't stand a chance against the firepower that's headed our way. I'm sorry, your Majesty, but without help, our forces will be defeated and the orbital defense satellites alone won't be enough to stop any form of orbital bombardment."

Paxt released his grip on his friend's shoulder, attempting to hide his own anguish. He turned to a waiting aide. "Get me the Commonwealth embassy. I

264

wish to speak with the ambassador personally on a matter of the utmost importance."

#

EARTH ORBIT - SOL SYSTEM

TDF *Southern Cross* entered Earth space less than five minutes after its communications drone arrived at the inner marker screaming its warning of an imminent emergency arrival. The traffic controllers scrambled to clear the priority approach corridor in the time available. A three million ton cargo hauler made a radical maneuver that her designers would never have believed possible. *Southern Cross'* arrival was followed almost instantly by three tight beam transmissions, two earthbound, the third a simple, plain language message for Earth Port Control that sent the Port Controller himself rushing for the traffic control center. Clear all incoming and outgoing civilian traffic in Earth space and prepare for priority naval traffic!

#

CENTRAL COMMAND
MONT SALÈVE - EARTH - SOL SYSTEM

The day-to-day running of the Commonwealth Union of Planets was overseen by three ministers, one from each of the member planets. Together, they formed the Commonwealth Council. These ministers dealt with the mundane minutia that was generated in something as vast and complex as a union whose members were divided by light years. Although the gravity drive had shrunk these distances to nothing more than an inconvenience, it was still too arduous and time-consuming to refer back every question on minor policy changes to the various home worlds, so each of the three council members had broad discretionary powers to implement policy in the name of their planet. But in exceptional circumstances these three individuals had a

265

power that, though it was always hoped they would never need, was incorporated into the legislation that formed the very basis of the Commonwealth. The power to authorize the emergency deployment of military force.

Deep inside Mont Salève, the Combined Joint Chiefs sat on one side of a table facing in the holo cube, the three members of the Commonwealth Council in their plush, comfortable offices in Geneva. The tension in the room was palatable and tempers were wearing thin.

"May I remind the Council that if the humans had not come to the aid of Garunda when the Others first appeared, then I would not be here right now? Those forces were deployed by a people who, even though they hadn't been asked, knew that it would mean the deaths of their own for a people they had never even met but they did it because it was the moral thing to do!" Admiral Razna Holan nearly shouted at the three politicians.

Minister Yalus replied with the quiet, unemotional voice of one long used to thinking rationally about real politic. "Admiral, I too, remember standing in the street outside of my house and wondering at the flashes of light in the night sky only to find out later that our human cousins had saved us all. Although I agree with your sentiment, Admiral, the Alonan Empire has repeatedly refused membership of the Commonwealth and has gone as far as stealing military secrets from us to further their own agenda."

Keyton Joyce could see that Razna was building up for a retort that may not have been as polite as it could be so out of view of the pick-up he placed a steadying hand on the diminutive admiral's forearm. The man facing them was a politician, so maybe they should attempt to come at this from a different, more political, perspective.

"Ministers. This is a golden opportunity to show the Empire the benefits of membership of the Commonwealth. If we stand back and do not come to their aid in their time of need, how will the Benii, the Nilmerg, and the Deres view us? Would you wish to be associated with a Commonwealth that did not come to your aid in your time of need but would rather leave your entire planet and people to die?"

The three ministers stared back at Keyton for a long moment before Minister Tovana lent across and said something in a low growl to Yalus as only an eight-foot-tall Persai could. In the holo cube, Yalus gave a curt nod before leaning back into the range of the audio pick-up. "One moment please, gentlemen." And the holo cube faded to a mellow yellow, leaving the military men alone for the moment.

"That Yalus is nothing but a sniveling political Katharaz! In days gone by, I would have challenged him to Gallav as a matter of honor and wet my blade with his worthless blood!"

Force Leader Tolas slapped his fellow member of the Combined Joint Chiefs on the back with such force that it knocked him forward in his seat. "And I would be your second. These politicians need to be reminded of their own mortality sometimes."

Before Keyton could add anything, the holo cube chimed and the three council members appeared once again.

Minister Yalus spoke for the council. "In an unanimous decision, under Article 52.4 sub paragraph six of the Commonwealth Union of Planets Charter, the Council authorizes the deployment of such forces as the Combined Joint Chiefs feel necessary to secure the safety of Alona. The authority will remain in place until such time as this decision is either endorsed or revoked by the respective heads of state of the Commonwealth Union of Planets. Good luck, gentlemen."

The holo cube returned to its yellow standby mode as Keyton turned to his fellow Chiefs. "Let's get the orders cut and transmitted to Admiral Jing. We're up against the clock here and you can bet The Others aren't waiting for us."

#

TDF *RESOLUTION* - EARTH ORBIT – SOL SYSTEM

Aboard the TDF *Resolution* Admiral Ai Jing brooded quietly in his chair. Around him the organized chaos that the orders from the Combined Joint Chiefs had unleashed on First Fleet two hours ago had his staff scurrying around the flag bridge like ants but the area around the admiral remained one of calm, as if a physical bubble blocked out the nightmare of trying to move an entire fleet of ships from rest to a war footing in the precious time allowed within the Chiefs' orders. A lone figure was impertinent enough to enter the bubble and approach the most senior fleet admiral of the entire Commonwealth.

"The latest readiness updates are in, Admiral."

"Tell me it's good news, Jamie."

Commodore Jamie Walker, Chief of Staff, First Fleet brought his PAD up and activated the display so Ai could see it. "BatFor 1.4 was the ready BatFor so they report ready in all regards. BatFors 1.1 and 1.3 were preparing for a war games exercise so they were nearly fully manned and the last stragglers are reporting aboard now so they report ready. BatFor 1.2 is hosting the port visit of the Benii carrier Koslla. They're off-loading their visitors as we speak. That leaves us BatFor 1.5. We've caught them in the middle of a maintenance-

and-stand-down cycle so they're only at thirty percent manning. A call has gone out for all crew to repair aboard immediately, but I don't hold out any hope of any of their ships being able to become fully operational in the time window, I'm afraid."

Ai steepled his fingers in front of him as he ran the numbers in his head. If he took BatFor 1.5 out of the equation, that would give him thirty-six Nemesis battleships, forty-two Vulcan heavy cruisers, twenty-four Talos light cruisers and seventy-two Agis destroyers. A formidable force and one that on its own should be able to handle the Others' fleet fast approaching Alona.

"What have we heard from the other fleet commanders?"

"Second Fleets ready BatFor, BatFor 2.2 has moved to full readiness and Admiral Lewis believes that BatFor 2.1 and 2.3 will be ready to deploy within twelve hours."

Too late.

"Third Fleet is out of position. Admiral Radford has BatFor 3.1, 3.2, and 3.4 with him. BatFor 3.1 suffered significant damage but remains operational. BatFor 3.3 remains in Garunda as system defense. Admiral Radford has expressed his concerns about dispatching elements of his fleet to assist in operations in Alona. He is concerned that with the bulk of First Fleet deployed so far from home that if this is part of a general push by the Others, we may not have adequate forces available locally to counter them."

Ai raised as eyebrow. *A valid point, John, and one that hadn't escaped my notice either.*

"What of Fourth Fleet, Jamie?"

"Force Leader Rhon has limited heavy units available. The Persai are still in the process of building and commissioning their first battleships, relying on aid from the TDF if they have to face anything heavier than an oversized enemy task group. He does, however, have a flotilla of cruisers that he can deploy to join us at Alona."

Persai cruisers were well able to punch above their weight, as was demonstrated at the Second Battle of Garunda, and he could do with the additional firepower.

"What does that leave us here in the Sol system?"

"BatFor 5.1 and 5.2. Admiral Chavez is currently in command of both units awaiting a replacement for Admiral Ricco. 5.2 is combat ready but 5.1 is only sixty-five percent effective at this time. Fifth Fleet's marine assault element and its escorts are intact although the same cannot be said for the actual marines, they're still restructuring following 70 Ophiuchi. However, I'm not expecting a requirement for ground combat and if so, I'm assured that Alona will provide any ground units needed. That leaves DesRon 5.8 and 5.9, totaling six Havoc destroyers currently employed as either individual units or in pairs throughout the system on perimeter patrol…Oh yes, I nearly forgot. The Garundan training flotilla is due to arrive in system later today. I was looking forward to seeing their new Baasa destroyers, their specs look impressive."

"Maybe another time, Jamie. OK, this is what I want to happen. BatFor 1.5 is to continue its recall and when complete, chop it to Fifth Fleet under Admiral Chavez. Admiral Lewis is to retain his full strength but be prepared to deploy units to the Sol system. Admiral Radford is right to be concerned that this may be a general push and I don't like leaving Earth so uncovered. Third Fleet is to return to Garunda at the earliest opportunity. Fourth Fleet is to release the cruisers and they are to rendezvous with us at Alona. Order DesRon 5.8 and 5.9 to deploy as individual units and cover as much of their patrol areas as possible. If the Others do come this way, I want Admiral Chavez to have as much notice as possible to call for help."

Jamie's head was bent over his PAD and he tapped away furiously. Ai waited for him to come to a stop and look up.

"Inform the fleet that we fold in twenty minutes, ready or not."

#

TDF *FURIOUS* - EARTH ORBIT - SOL SYSTEM

Analisa Chavez watched quietly from the observation lounge of TDF *Furious* as the last of First Fleet entered fold space and began its 50,000 light year journey to Messier 54 and the defense of the Alonan system. Analisa was under no illusions about what faced them there. The latest intelligence estimates had identified at least fifty-four individual drive sources, thirty of which were confirmed as Buzzard class battleships and if the Others' fleet was anything like their typical structure, you could put good money that at the heart of the oncoming fleet there would be another dozen or so massive 2300 meter long Vultures supported by the Goshawk anti-missile ships. A small shudder ran down her spine as she remembered the devastation that only three Buzzards and a single Goshawk had managed to inflict on her own BatFor 5.1 and 5.2 when they had emerged out of fold space in 70 Ophiuchi and been jumped by the small enemy task force. Losses had been heavy and the face of Stephano Ricco came unbidden into her thoughts as Analisa's vision began to blur with tears. Her hand reached up and her fingers touched the golden cross that hung from a thin chain around her neck. Her mind went back to a late summer's evening

271

on a hillside in the Apennine mountains only a few weeks before, when two women had sat together, watching the sun set. One an admiral who was still coming to terms with the loss of so many men and women under her command and the other a woman who was mourning the loss of the man who had been her husband and companion for over forty years. As night fell, Analisa had bid her farewells but as she went to leave, Rosetta Ricco held out her hand and in it was a small gold cross and its chain.

"My Stephano gave this to me after the birth of our first son and I would like you to have it to remember Stephano by."

Analisa accepted the gift as her eyes misted over. She went to reply but her voice had betrayed her. Instead she wrapped Rosetta in her arms as the tears began to run down her cheeks. The walk back to the ground car, which had taken her to the waiting shuttle, had been a blur. It was only as she stepped from the shuttle into the boat bay of *Furious* that she at last managed to return to her normal self and had immersed herself in rebuilding her badly battered command.

Analisa berated herself for her melancholy and with a newfound sense of purpose, tapped her wrist comm.

"Communications. Lieutenant Hom."

"Lieutenant, track down my staff and let them know I want a briefing on fleet resources remaining in system and suggestions on how best to employ them. Tell them to be prepared to brief me at…" Analisa checked the time on her wrist comm. Damn! It was after midnight. "Zero eight hundred."

"Yes, ma'am, I'll get right on it."

"Chavez clear."

Her staff weren't the only ones that would have a busy night as Analisa headed for her quarters and the mountain of paperwork that had been slowly building up as her command licked its wounds and regained its former strength.

\#

OFFICE OF THE PRESIDENT
GENEVA - EARTH - SOL SYSTEM

The sun was beating down on a Geneva that was enjoying the last hot days of summer before the cooling autumn arrived. Rebecca Coston was enjoying the view of the sailboats on the lake when the intercom beeped for attention. Rebecca dragged herself away from the view and touched a control on her desk.

"Yes, Jim?"

"The delegation from the Benii Federation has arrived, Madam President"

The Commonwealth leadership and the delegation from Benii were due to meet later this afternoon. An early morning call from the foreign affairs liaison requesting a meeting alone with Rebecca on an urgent matter had caused a mild panic in the scheduler's office, but the Benii request had been granted.

"Show them in please, Jim."

As her office doors opened to admit the Benii, Rebecca stepped forward to greet them noticing that there was only the Benii lead delegate, Representative Hoolas, and High Commander Botac. The hairs on the back of Rebecca's neck began to stand up. The Benii had only arrived yesterday and they had been greeted with a full state dinner attended by Rebecca, Prime Minister Bezled and Chairman Taarov. In Rebecca's opinion, the evening had been a resounding success, although it was obvious that the Benii were still finding it hard to come to terms with the fact that the Commonwealth was a society based on gender equality.

Rebecca guided the two Benii over to a small area where some comfortable chairs were arranged around a low coffee table. On hearing of the short notice meeting, two members of the housekeeping staff had appeared and replaced the chairs which normally sat here with ones more suitable for the Benii's elongated frames.

"So, how may I be of assistance, Representative Hoolas?"

Hoolas gave the High Commander a sideways glance before answering. "Madam President we are...eh... concerned over the sudden movement of so many of your warships. Is there something we should be made aware of?"

So that was it. The movement of First Fleet would have been hard to miss, especially when one of your visiting Benii admiral's tour is cut short and they are virtually flung off the ship they were touring. Well, Aaron always said the truth is best in difficult situations.

"The Commonwealth has received a request to come to the assistance of the Empire of Alona. They have detected a large fleet of ships approaching their system and believe them to belong to the species we call the Others..."

"The Destroyers of Worlds are attacking Alona?" blurted out a shocked Hoolas.

"Unfortunately, the intelligence we have received leaves us in no doubt that it is in fact them."

"But Alona is over 50,000 light years from here. From the briefings I have read, their ships are not equipped with engines that would allow them to cover such massive distances without taking inordinate amounts of time to do so," interjected Botac.

Rebecca could only nod in agreement. "I admit that our military leaders are at a loss to explain their presence in Alona. We had believed that the Others were restricted to areas of the galaxy where we already had contact with them but it would appear that we were wrong in our assessments of the extent of their reach."

Representative Hoolas quickly regained her composure. "It would be our understanding, Madam President, that the Commonwealth and Alona do not have a treaty which compels the Commonwealth to come to the aid of Alona if she is attacked."

"That is correct, there is no formal treaty requiring us to intervene but, and the whole of the Commonwealth agrees on this point, there is a moral compulsion for us to prevent an attack which would undoubtedly end in the extinction of the Alonan race."

Representative Hoolas leaned back in her over-sized seat and looked past Rebecca out over the still waters of Lake Geneva and thought how much it reminded her of her home, so far away, and wondered who would come to its aid if the Destroyers of Worlds were to darken its clear-blue skies. Standing, she reached out her hand in a gesture she had seen the humans do the night before. A slightly startled Rebecca took the proffered hand in hers, and slowly shook it.

"Thank you for your time, Madam President. I look forward to our discussions later."

"My pleasure, Madam Representative, and I hope I have managed to lay your concerns to rest."

"Indeed you have."

As Hoolas and Botac left her office, Rebecca had the feeling that the Benii had reached an important decision in their relationship with the Commonwealth.

#

ALONA - MESSIER 54
50,000 LIGHT YEARS FROM EARTH

First Fleet's arrival in the Alonan system was met with a sense of relief from Grand Admiral Raga as he stood in the war room deep below the Imperial Palace. The situation board, which covered one entire wall of the subterranean room, had been split into two separate screens. On one half was the latest update from the Vaspar cruisers, which were taking it in turns to fold out to a position beyond the enemy's weapons range to check on their progress. Against all hope, the Others had slowed their approach and were barely crawling through the outer reaches of the system. That provided no solace to any of the mining colonies that happened to lie in their path. Each had been reduced to radioactive dust by the passing enemy fleet.

The second screen showed the inner system with Alona and Geta slowly orbiting the star at the heart of the system. Alona's orbit meant that it lay in an almost direct path between the enemy fleet and the star. Clustered around Alona were a few, too few, blue icons that represented the remaining Vaspar cruisers and the under-armed and under-powered ships of the Imperial Navy. But with the arrival of the Commonwealth fleet, the odds were turning in favor of Alona.

"Incoming signal from the Commonwealth flagship, sir. He has confirmed that he has orders to engage the enemy and is awaiting your permission to do so."

Raga slapped one balled fist into his open palm as his body bent at the waist as if he could physically reach out and destroy the intruders by sheer force of will only.

"Permission granted."

\#

Ipres Garal leaned heavily on the rail surrounding the control deck of his flagship, *The Creator's Wrath*. Garal had been forced to slow his approach to the heretics' planet as the prey that he was here to destroy had failed to appear but now, now they had arrived and it was time to show these heretics the way of the Ehita and rip their beating hearts from their chests. He only hoped that the Creator blessed Tama Narath and his part of the Creator's plan.

"Tactical. Activate the buoys!"

CHAPTER SEVENTEEN

IN EARTH SPACE

BEYOND THE ORBIT OF PLUTO - SYSTEM

"Watch out for that tumbling motion, Johnny. If that thing hits the arm the wrong way, it'll rip it right off and you can explain that one to the boss."

Johnny Ciotti mumbled something under his breath that didn't sound too complimentary, but his full concentration remained on the slowly tumbling Sherlock platform that he was currently trying to grab with the maintenance shuttle's grapple arm. *Forget the arm*, he thought, that platform is the size of a small ground car and worth more than the entire three-man maintenance crew and the wreck of a shuttle they were aboard put together. *What the hell is it doing so far out here anyway? We're way beyond the surveillance shell.* With a gentle nudge of the joystick, the grapple arm locked onto the platform and Johnny tossed his head back and smiled smugly at Fiona.

"And that will be a beer you owe me."

The look Fiona gave him as she left for the maintenance bay told him he may be waiting a long time for that beer. Shaking his head despondently, Johnny got up from his chair to follow her.

Twenty minutes later, Fiona had the guidance package stripped down and was brandishing a circuit panel with a neat little round hole in it. "Well, there you have it, folks. Looks like a micro-meteorite hit. We should have a spare in the standard maintenance pack we'll have this little puppy back up and working in no time."

Johnny was running his finger down the fault list on his PAD and grimaced as his eyes lit on another fault report. "Hold your horses there, cowboy. Those desk jockeys at Central Command report an intermittent fault in the detection and identification system. Says here this thing is reporting sightings of a Saiph star drive every thirty days on the button and has been for six months now." Johnny's head shook in disgust. "So first they let this thing wonder off all the way out here then ignore another fault for six months. The area controller probably got sick of the same fault blinking on his screen so passed it to us to clear it." Johnny picked up the screw gun and got to work on the panel covering the detection system. *This may take longer than we thought.*

For an hour, Johnny tried everything he knew to find a fault in the detection and identification system but he was damned if he could find one. Admitting defeat, he called Fiona over. "If there's a fault in the detection system, I can't find it. Maybe you'll have better luck."

Fiona swaggered toward him and Johnny braced himself for the sarcastic remarks he knew were coming when the hooting of the collision alarm nearly deafened him. Johnny made for the maintenance bay entrance at a dead run with Fiona hard on his heels. The shuttle wasn't that big. An engineering space, a maintenance bay, and a small living area just behind the cockpit, so it took only seconds for Johnny to arrive in the cramped cockpit where the third member of the crew, Jiri Okoro, was frantically going through the engine start-up sequence with one hand while trying to plot a course back to Earth with the other.

Fiona slipped into the co-pilot's seat and killed the collision alarm. "What's going on, Jiri?"

Jiri never lifted his eyes from the controls. "Shut up, Fiona, I'm trying to concentrate!"

Fiona glanced over her shoulder, her eyebrows drawn together in a mix of worry and confusion. Johnny, who was still standing in the cockpit entranceway, put a hand on Jiri's shoulder.

"Hey, Jiri. What's got you so spooked?"

"Look at the proximity sensor, man!"

Johnny looked at the display on the center console and his heart stopped. Less than 200 kilometers from the tiny shuttle was the largest collection of ships he had ever seen. Johnny was still looking at the display in amazement as he landed on his rear end as Jiri fired up the engines and pushed the throttles through the fire walls to get the shuttle up to fold speed.

#

"I'm sorry, Tama Narath, I failed to detect the small ship on our exit from fold space and now it has escaped."

Narath placed a reassuring hand on the young warrior's shoulder. "Do not worry yourself, it was the Creator's will. Now let us turn to the task at hand. Order the ships carrying the remaining buoys to fold to their targets immediately. Once they are away I want you to send the activation signal to the buoys already in place. The final stages of the Ehita are upon us."

#

EARTH ORBIT - SOL SYSTEM

Aboard the *Furious*, the battle station's alarm shrieked throughout the ship and Analisa Chavez left the remains of her late lunch sitting as she raced for the flag bridge, hurriedly securing her uniform blouse as she did so. As she raced along the corridor heading for the elevator she passed crew members running for their posts. On reaching the elevator, she punched in her override code and the elevator took her directly to the flag bridge. The marine on duty was already opening the bulkhead door as she exited the elevator and she slowed her headlong run as she entered the bridge and stopped in front of the tactical holo cube which filled the center of the bridge.

"Speak to me, people!"

"Admiral, five minutes ago, a maintenance shuttle that had been out beyond the surveillance shell arrived within the inner marker, screaming it had observed an unidentified fleet emerge from fold space. I was about to order one of the Havoc destroyers to head that way to investigate when three bogeys appeared out of fold space and began engaging any ship in range. Before the Viper defense platforms could fire, the bogeys had destroyed at least one freighter and damaged two others. Damage reports are still coming in and I expect more casualties. Central Command went weapons-free on the Vipers who successfully engaged the bogeys and all three are reported destroyed."

Analisa's brain was running at top speed as the holo cube icons representing every Commonwealth ship in Earth orbit were rapidly changing color from the yellow of a ship in orbit to blue as each ship in turn reported ready at battle stations.

"Do we have any idea who they were?"

"Computer made an initial identification but it didn't make sense to me so I have it running again."

Analisa tore her eyes away from the holo cube and zeroed in on the tactical officer. "What do you mean, it didn't make sense?"

The poor lieutenant wilted under her glare as his reply came out in a stutter. "The... the computer initially called the bogeys Buzzards, but that couldn't have been right, the Others don't have gravity drives."

Analisa knew the lieutenant was right. The Others used an alcubierre drive to travel the vast distances involved in interstellar travel. Only the Commonwealth and now Alona had gravity drive technology. *Well, the Others have it now too,* thought Analisa. *And if they do, we have a lot less time to get organized than I thought we did. All our defense plans called for home fleet to fold out to wherever the enemy fleet had been detected and fight a long-range battle with gravity drive missiles, but if the enemy have the ability to use fold space to jump in behind us, we can't afford to leave Earth uncovered, especially with Home Fleet out in Alona. Time to call the cavalry.*

"Communications. Fleet signal. Activate Case Purple. The fleet will adopt defensive positions supported by the fixed orbital defense platforms. Let's get communication drones away to all Commonwealth naval bases, requesting they immediately dispatch ships to our aid. Tactical, get with Central Command, we need to ensure we coordinate our fire with the platforms."

A chorus of aye-ayes came from her staff as they got to work. Analisa forced herself to relax a little. Her communications drones would reach every fleet base within a few minutes and shortly thereafter she knew that every Commonwealth commander would move heaven and earth to get to her aid as quickly as they could. Case Purple was her worst-case scenario where she would augment the firepower of the fleet using the orbital defense platforms and the fixed defenses on the planet below. She couldn't hold forever but she could hold long enough for help to arrive and that was long enough.

"Admiral. The drones. They're all reporting drive failures."

Analisa felt her heart skip a beat. "What? All of them? That's impossible!"

#

"The buoys have been activated, Tama Narath. The heretics can no longer use their gravity drives to escape the Creator's vengeance."

Narath's face contorted into what passed for a satisfied smile, his near-translucent skin wrinkling as his mouth opened and showed sharp pointed teeth. *The Creator's plan is revealing itself as promised. Praise the Creator.* The new drive systems the Creator had revealed to the chosen people had been retrofitted into the ships of the people and they had built the buoys that had been seeded so patiently over the last year in the systems controlled by the heretics. No vessel equipped with the heretics' gravity drive could operate within the disruption field generated by the buoys, the last of which had been emplaced by the three ships which had so selflessly sacrificed themselves in the face of the heretics' planetary defenses. By his calculations, it would take five days for his fleet to reach the planet the heretics of this system called home. It was a pity the buoys' disruption fields affected his own ships' drive as well as that of the heretics, but it was no matter. Narath intended to advance on the planet, mopping up any outpost the heretics may have established in this system. Then he would cleanse their world in nuclear fire. Deactivate the buoys and move onto the next world of the heretics. The one they called Janus. The path of the Ehita was long but Aseena awaited him.

"Order the fleet to advance. Let us put these heretics to the sword. No mercy!"

"No mercy!" cried the crew of the command deck.

Narath regained his seat and pulled his blood-red cloak around him like a comforting shield.

#

MESSIER 54 - 50,000 LIGHT YEARS FROM EARTH

Ai Jing had the ships of First Fleet pushing their sub-light engines to the maximum and already he had a few whose engines had failed under the strain but he pressed on regardless. Shortly after his fleet had arrived in Alona, the Others had activated some sort of dampening field which had extended not only around the two populated planets of the system but out as far as nearly eighty light minutes from the system core. That would be nearly the equivalent of the orbit of Saturn in Earth's solar system. Not only that, but the Others had pre-placed deactivated buoys, so that as soon as the fleet managed to identify the location of one of the buoys and destroy it, another came on and began transmitting its dampening field. Ai knew that finding and destroying each buoy individually was a losing proposition and he simply didn't have the time to waste on it, for there was only one reason he could think of that the Others would have for mounting an attack on Alona. They knew that the Commonwealth would send a fleet to defend Alona and when that fleet arrived, they activated the buoys, effectively trapping it. Ai hoped he was wrong but his tactician's brain knew he wasn't. The Others had trapped him here so they would have a free hand somewhere else. And that somewhere else was Earth. *Well*, Ai thought to himself, *I'm damned if I'm going to stay trapped. I'm going to charge my ships down*

284

your throat, close with you, and kill you with grazers, plasma guns, and anything else I can throw at you! Then once I get beyond the dampening field I'll head home and do the same to your friends there.

"Tactical. How long to weapons range?"

"One zero eight minutes, Admiral."

Ai thought of Analisa Chavez and her depleted forces. *Just hold on, Analisa, I'm coming.*

#

CHARON BASE - ORBIT OF PLUTO – SOL SYSTEM

David Catney had to raise his voice to be heard over the constant rumbling of megaton missile strikes on the surface of Charon a kilometer above his head. "Are the drones away?"

"Yes, Admiral, but we've still received no word from either Central Command or any fleet vessel," shouted the communications officer.

What the hell was going on? It had to be that strange energy field the surface sensors had detected further in system. Whatever it was, it didn't look like Charon Base was going to get any help in time to save it. Charon was composed mostly of ice with a rocky core at its center and with the number of nukes impacting the surface it was only a matter of time before one successfully reached down and destroyed Survey Command.

"What about the mining and processing facilities?"

"Most of them are within the area covered by the energy field so I was forced to resort to old-style laser and radio communication to pass your message to switch off everything which might reveal their position to the enemy." The young lieutenant shrugged her shoulders. "I'm sorry sir, it was the best I could do."

David gave her a lopsided smile. "That's all I could ever ask, Lieutenant. Now I think it's time we got out of here and joined everyone else in a shuttle before our visitors decide to finish us off."

The face of the lieutenant grinning back at him was the last thing David would ever see as a forty-megaton warhead detonated directly over the control room. The overpressure turned the reinforced concrete and steel to dust, ending his life.

#

ALGOL 3 - 92.8 LIGHT YEARS FROM EARTH

The communications drone emerged from fold space 15,000 kilometers from SurFlot One orbiting serenely around the Benii home world in the Algol 3 system as it had been for the past four months while Ambassador Schamu continued diplomatic negotiations with the leaders of the Benii Federation concerning their establishment of full trade and diplomatic relations with the Commonwealth. The drone orientated its laser and began to download its message. Christos Papadomas was in the middle of a conference with Force Leader Verus, second in command of SurFlot One, and his staff was going over the results of the survey missions to Baut and Gossol, the other systems colonized by the Benii, when his wrist comm beeped for attention.

"Papadomas."

The urgent tone of Vusumuzi Mkhize carried through the room. "Emergency signal from Survey Command, Admiral. An enemy fleet identified as the Others consisting of at least fifty capital-sized ships and an estimated sixty-plus ships of other classes has entered the Sol system, using gravity drives and began engaging both TDF and civilian targets. Admiral Catney states that an unknown energy field with multiple point sources extending from the inner system out as far as eighty light minutes may be interfering with his communications drones, as he has been unable to

286

establish contact with any Commonwealth ship within the eighty-light minute bubble. Attempts to alert Janus, Garunda, and Persai have also been unsuccessful…" Christos heard Vusumuzi clear his throat and when his voice came over the link again it was slightly huskier. "Admiral Catney states that Survey Command is currently under attack and he has ordered it evacuated as he believes its destruction imminent. Message ends."

The occupants of the conference room sat in stunned silence as they all tried to digest what Vusumuzi had just said. The Others had found Earth!

Christos shook himself before he began to spit orders out in quick-fire succession. "Vusumuzi. Signal the flotilla. Prepare for immediate departure. I want all the ships that can be prepared to fold for Earth space in the next fifteen minutes. Destination will be the outer marker. It sits at ninety-two light minutes so should be outside this energy field. Get communications drones away to Janus, Garunda, and Persai stating my intentions, also send drones to SurvFlot Two and Three ordering them on my authority to rendezvous with us at the outer marker as soon as possible. Get another drone to Admiral Radford and Third Fleet with my orders and attach the message from Survey Command." Christos took one grim look around the room. "OK, people, let's get to it."

As the room emptied, Christos signaled for Verus to keep her seat. As the door closed behind the last staffer, Christos slumped slightly. "As far as I am aware, no request to activate the Commonwealth common defense treaty has been issued by Earth's government. You've seen the numbers, Verus. At least fifty capital ships and god knows how many smaller ones. The largest ships that my flotilla has are your Vitaros cruisers. Even if Torrance and Glandinning meet up with us at the outer marker, that still only leaves us with fifteen cruisers against an enemy force which outnumbers and outguns us at least ten to one." A small sigh escaped Christos as he averted his eyes from the impassive Verus and began tapping his finger on the conference room table. "The Others have invaded Earth space and I intend to do my damnedest to slow them until help can arrive but it may be a futile gesture and I in good conscience cannot ask the Persai crews amongst the flotilla to follow me on what could be a suicide mission."

The scraping of chair legs tore Christos' gaze from the polished table. Christos looked up to find Verus standing to attention, her eyes fixed on him. "Admiral, you are an honorable man and in your time of need neither I nor any of my fellow Persai would desert you or your people. Together we will defeat these murderers of planets."

Christos could only nod his thanks, not trusting his voice to betray his heartfelt emotions. Verus gave him a bared tooth smile and quickly left the room to return to her own ship. The clock was ticking.

#

9 CETI - 66.5 LIGHT YEARS FROM EARTH

The message that the drone from Survey Command had passed upon its arrival in 9 Ceti had the men and women of SurvFlot Three scrambling to prepare their ships for immediate departure. Gavin Glandinning issued orders for all combat vessels in orbit around the dead planet to plot a course for Earth, but the arrival of the drone with Admiral Papadomas' orders to rendezvous at the outer marker had given him pause. Christos had ordered all ships to gather at the outer marker because he suspected that whatever energy field was blanketing the inner system was affecting communications within that field. Specifically, it was affecting gravity drive drones. Gavin blocked out the sounds of the flag bridge as something tickled a memory in the back of his mind… One of Jeff Moore's pet theories was the possibility of sending out a carrier wave, which would interfere with a gravity drive's ability to generate gravity waves therefore making the drive useless. It seemed that the Others had just proved Jeff's theory for him. Gavin wracked his brain, trying to remember the details of the briefing paper that he had read at Zarmina. Something about having to alter the bandwidth of the gravity wave generator within the gravity drive itself, which would allow a ship to bypass the effects of the interfering carrier wave. Stripping a gravity drive engine down to get access to the wave generator was not something that any chief engineer on board a ship would take upon himself lightly. It required precision tools and an intimate knowledge of the theory of gravity wave generation and preferably the assistance of a major shipyard. Gavin had no doubt his own chief engineer was capable of doing it with his limited resources but time was of the essence here. By Gavin's best estimate, the enemy fleet would be in weapons range of Earth within eighty-four hours. What Gavin needed was a shipyard with top-notch engineers and there was only one place he knew outside the Commonwealth home worlds which had that sort of manpower and equipment. Zarmina! Gavin's fist came crashing down on the arm of his chair, startling the bridge crew.

"Communications. Signal Force Leader Homla that with immediate effect he is to assume command of the flotilla and make his way at best speed to rendezvous with Admiral Papadomas. Navigation. I am about to send you a set of coordinates. Your nav system will attempt to reject them so you will have to enter them manually. Once they are accepted you are to fold us there immediately."

Both officers looked at Gavin as if he had two heads but then answered with aye-ayes and carried out his orders.

Gavin sat back in his seat and considered the repercussions of the orders he had just given. Disregarding a direct order from his superior officer to make his way immediately to Earth's space and then disclosing the coordinates of the Commonwealth's most secret research base. Gavin gave a short chuckle as he wondered which one they would hang him for first.

Gavin was still chuckling as *Triton* entered fold space.

CHAPTER EIGHTEEN

HOLD THE LINE

TDF *FURIOUS* – EARTH ORBIT – SOL SYSTEM

The mood amongst Fifth Fleet was one of resigned fatalism. It had been four days since the invaders had entered the Sol system and began their steady, inexorable advance toward the birthplace of humanity. For Analisa Chavez, the days had seemed to merge into one long, unending series of operational planning meetings and constant harassing demands from her political masters, demanding to know what she was going to do to protect them from the onrushing enemy. After the second day of these messages she had gone directly to the Combined Joint Chiefs and pointed out, rather sarcastically, that she could either organize the defense of the planet or spend her time in a pointless exercise making said politicians feel important.

The terse reply from Central Command that her priority was her operational planning and that all other calls were to be redirected to the Chairman of the Joint Chiefs' office at least removed one drain on her precious time.

The entry tone on her terminal alerted her that she had a visitor. Analisa activated the intercom with one weary hand.

"Yes, Corporal Wellan."

"Commander Malloy, ma'am."

"Thank you, Corporal."

As the door slid aside, the tall, gaunt figure of Patrick Malloy walked in. Analisa couldn't help but notice that the commander's ever-present jauntiness was missing. On closer examination, it was apparent that Malloy's eyes were sunken into his face and his normally pristine uniform was looking unkempt. Bordering on the scruffy. Analisa indicated the comfy seat opposite her own.

"Take a load off, Patrick. You look like hell. When was the last time you slept?"

Patrick sank into the seat with a loud sigh and regarded Analisa with tired eyes. "A lifetime ago, Admiral."

Taking one of the spare cups from the tray that was half-buried under the mountain of PADs on the desk, Analisa filled it to the brim with steaming hot coffee before passing it over to her haggard operations officer.

"Maybe some of this will pick you up. I have no idea what PO Ruiz puts in it but I assure you it does the job."

Patrick took the cup in both hands and raised it to his nose for an appreciative sniff of its deep, burnt aroma before taking a tentative sip. As the coffee flowed down his throat his eyes closed for a second and he released a small sigh of satisfaction.

"Now that is damn good coffee. If I ever become an admiral I may have to steal Ruiz away from you."

Analisa chuckled as she raised her own cup and took a sip. "Over my dead body."

The moment of light heartiness passed as Analisa's thoughts returned to their impending battle with the Others.

"What's the latest update on the enemy's progress?"

Patrick returned his cup to the table and tapped a few controls on the PAD he had brought with him. The holo cube sprang to life with a representation of the inner Sol system.

"The enemy fleet's progress has remained steady. The radio transmission we picked up from Survey Command before we lost contact with it instructing the asteroid mining and industrial complexes to go dark seems to have been followed to the letter. From what take we have from the Sherlock platforms, there are no reports of any of them being attacked unless they happen to have been in the direct path of the enemy advance."

Analisa regarded him over the rim of her cup. "No surprise there, really. No miner or manager would want to do anything that would attract the attention of an enemy warship. What of the larger settlements and bases?"

Patrick shifted uncomfortably in his seat and his face became strangely neutral. "That's another matter entirely. The naval yards around Titan reported several large enemy units shaping a course for them before it went off the air. A similar signal was received from the Boreland habitats. The governor had begun broadcasting surrender messages to the enemy fleet commander, requesting that the colony be considered an open city." Patrick's knuckles turned white as his hold on the PAD tightened and his voice became taut. "Central Command has since confirmed nuclear detonations in and around the area of the colony."

"Oh God." The mix of anger and despair nearly overwhelmed her. It felt like a living thing ripping at her very soul. "The bastards! There was nothing of any military or strategic value there. They were only families trying to have a life...Maybe I should have sent one of the battle groups to cover them… maybe draw the enemy off them…"

Patrick was shaking his head. He desperately wanted to reassure his admiral that she had done the right thing by keeping her forces intact. "Admiral. You know the size of the enemy forces we face better than anyone. A single battle force would have been a futile gesture. Sending them out there would only have condemned them to death and right now we need every ship we can get our hands on." Patrick looked at Analisa. His eyes pleading for her to understand that she had made the right call. Knowing that her decision to harbor her fighting strength for the battle still to come had been the right one. One look into her wretched, pain-filled eyes told him that no matter what he said, the deaths of so many colonists would haunt her for the rest of her life. Attempting to take her mind off the tens of thousands of innocents brutally murdered, Patrick hurriedly continued his brief.

"On the positive side, we now have confirmation that Admiral Radford's Third Fleet reinforced by SurvFlot One, Two and Three have managed to close the gap between themselves and the enemy fleet. Their revised ETA is thirty-seven hours…"

It didn't take Analisa long to do the math in her head. "So we can expect contact with the enemy in twenty-nine hours. That leaves us eight hours to hold against a fleet that out numbers us nearly ten to one. We have no room to maneuver as we have Earth to our back, which allows our opponents free movement around the battlefield and therefore the initiative." A tired grin slowly covered her face. "Well, I would say we have him beaten hands down. What do you think, Patrick?"

Patrick couldn't help but mirror his admiral's grin. "Perhaps we should signal him to surrender now and save us all a lot of work."

Analisa chuckled softly before returning to the subject at hand. "What of the orbital defense platforms both here and around the lunar colonies?"

A touch of the PAD and the area around Earth and lunar orbit expanded. A series of concentric overlapping circles completely covering the Earth and forming a large dome shape around the various lunar colonies. "As you can see, Admiral, the Viper missile and grazer platforms are sown pretty thickly. There isn't a part of Earth's orbit that isn't covered by at least three and in some cases four Vipers. Couple that with the heavy surface-based grazers of the Planetary Defense Centers and it provides a comprehensive defense network. This will be our inner layer and will be controlled by Central Command. I have, however, identified a number of areas where the Vipers were that thickly sown that I felt that removing a single or even two platforms would have only a negligible effect on the shell's defense fire. These spare platforms I have had boosted into a higher orbit and have used to cover the fleet's flanks."

Icons like a sprinkling of stars appeared across the surface of the inner defense zone. Each icon represented a ship and Analisa reflected how few they were.

"Each BatFor has been allocated specific fields of fire in order that we don't waste ammunition by firing more than is required to kill a target."

"How are our ammunition states?" queried Analisa.

"The ships are virtually filled to the hatches with as many HVMs and anti-missile missiles as we could scrounge up. If the enemy continues to operate his dampening field then our GD missiles will be useless. This, for us, will be a completely defensive battle."

"Agreed. Our priority is holding until Third Fleet can arrive and even the odds."

"My biggest worry is that I have no way of knowing whether the enemy will stick to their current approach vector. Any change of direction by them will mean some tricky maneuvering by our own ships to get them into a good defensive position."

Analisa felt herself gnawing at her lower lip. "I understand your concern there, Patrick but there's nothing we can do about that just now. The lack of coverage around the lunar colonies still bothers me though."

Patrick was well aware of how thin the defense fire was around the colonies. "Unfortunately I have found myself in a position of having to rob Peter to pay Paul. The only way I can increase the firepower of the lunar defenses is to take it from the defenses that I need to protect Earth. And to be completely coldhearted about it, the logical conclusion is to protect the many and do what I can for the few."

Analisa knew that Patrick had spent hours agonizing over the deployments of his assets and how best to employ them. He wouldn't have come to Analisa with this plan if it wasn't the one best suited to her orders.

"Having reviewed your deployments, I wholeheartedly concur with them."

A look of relief washed over Patrick's face. He also realized that by approving the plan he had conceived, Analisa was accepting responsibility if it failed.

"So what have we got left to cover?"

Patrick worked his PAD for a few moments before looking up. "Mostly informational stuff coming from Central Command. The Ground Forces have been forced to deploy units to all the major spaceports. Apparently anyone who has access to a ship that can make orbit is trying to get off the planet. Several high profile businessmen and politicians have been arrested in their attempts to leave."

A nasal harrumph escaped Analisa. "Don't these people understand that even if they get off the planet, the gravity drives aren't functioning anywhere in the system? The Others' smaller ships have the speed to hunt them down and blow them out of space. They'd be better off finding themselves a nice deep mine to hide in till this is all over one way or the other." Seeing that Patrick hadn't finished, Analisa gestured for him to continue.

"Last but not least. The Benii carrier has remained in orbit despite repeated warnings from the Department of Defense, the State Department, and even a personal call from the president's office that the space surrounding the Earth may very well soon become a war zone."

Analisa cocked an eyebrow at this. "Are the recovery tugs still attached to the carrier?"

"Yes, ma'am. According to my information, the president has ordered the tug captains to comply with any instructions they receive from the Benii commander. And that includes breaking orbit and heading for a clear area of space not affected by the dampening field to engage their gravity drives and allow the Benii to return home."

How curious, thought Analisa. Maybe they would make a run for it at the last minute to allow their sensors to get the best possible read on the Others' weapons systems. Analisa spared the ancient mariners clock on the wall of her cabin a quick glance. "OK, Patrick, inform the captains that I want an enforced rest period for all watches as of now. Bring the fleet to battle stations at zero seven hundred hours."

Patrick stood to leave with an "aye-aye, ma'am." Analisa stopped him with a raised hand.

"That rest period applies to you too. I need you on top of your game tomorrow."

"Understood, Admiral."

The door slid shut behind him and Analisa caught herself fiddling with the small gold cross around her neck as she reflected on the deployment plan for a final time. *I may not be the most devout believer, but if you're going to intercede then sometime soon would be good.*

#

FLAG BRIDGE – TDF *THE IRON CHANCELLOR* 6.5 HOURS FROM EARTH ORBIT – SOL SYSTEM

The mood amongst Third Fleet was just as dismal as that of the ships around Earth. John Radford sat in his command chair and reviewed his tactical plot for what seemed like the thousandth time in the past hour. In the plot the distance between the oncoming Others and the line of defense established by Fifth Fleet and whatever ships Analisa Chavez had managed to cobble together was narrowing by the second. The countdown in the top right hand corner of the holo cube showed that the enemy would be in weapons range of the moon in twenty-six minutes and no matter how hard John had forced his ships he had still only managed to close the gap to the enemy fleet to six and a half hours. And no matter how many times he reviewed the numbers, Chavez would be hard-pressed to hold long enough for John to come to her aid. *However much good that would do anyway.* Even with the added numbers of Third Fleet, the combined Commonwealth forces would still be outnumbered something like two to one in heavy units and nearly three to one in lighter units. Certainly the

298

fixed defenses of the orbital platforms would massively increase Chavez's firepower, but if the enemy played smart they would sit off at a safe distance and bombard the platforms until they had managed to degrade them to a level where it would be safe to enter their engagement range without suffering significant casualties. If they did that, Fifth Fleet simply didn't have the firepower to hold them up for long. It would be a slaughter. John's fist hammered down on the arm of his chair in frustration and heads on the flag bridge turned to look in his direction. They all shared his frustration because no matter how hard they pushed the engines, by the time Third Fleet managed to reach Earth's orbit, the Others would have reduced the planet to a radioactive wasteland.

#

FLAG BRIDGE - TDF *RESOLUTION* OUTER MARKER – SOL SYSTEM

After what seemed like the longest five days in his life, Ai Jing and First Fleet eventually arrived at the Sol system's outer marker. The courier drones launched by Survey Command had been waiting for them at the third way point and they had borne the news that Ai had prayed he wasn't going to hear. The Others were in the home system and their target was Earth.

First Fleet had already faced the Others in combat as the battered remnants of what had once been the pride of the TDF was witness to. Ai had known that time was his most important factor so his tactics had been simple and brutal. With the brute force of a heavyweight boxer, he had taken the enemy fleet at the run. Using his most powerful battleships to punch a hole through the center of their battle line he had mercilessly raked their ships with missile and grazer fire until there was nothing left of them but floating pieces of shattered wreckage. Ai had lost one Bismarck, eight Nemesis class battleships along with seventeen heavy cruisers, twenty light cruisers and twelve destroyers in his battle to get past the Others' fleet.

Another Nemesis had succumbed to an engineering failure during the final fold to earth space and its chief engineer was desperately trying to repair the damage so the ship could continue on to Earth but it didn't look good. The remainder of First Fleet's units filled the tactical display as Ai orientated the fleet for the final push toward Earth.

A new icon sprang into life in the display, quickly followed by three more. The computer highlighted them in the blinking yellow of unknown types. It appeared that the sensors were having difficulty getting a solid lock on the four ships as it took the computer a few seconds longer than usual before the icons changed to the solid blue of friendly units. The computer identified the lead ship as the TDF *Horizon*. Ai brought up the *Horizon's* details on his display and when he read them, his brow creased in bewilderment. According to the computer, *Horizon* was an older generation Talos cruiser that had been decommissioned. Ai was just about to instruct his comms officer to hail the unidentified ships when he was preempted.

"Admiral, we're being hailed by Admiral Glandinning. He's transmitting a set of fold coordinates and requesting that we follow him there after a five minute lead."

Glandinning! What was the CO of SurvFlot Three doing aboard a decommissioned Talos cruiser instead of on the flag bridge of his own ship? Ai began to get that itch at the back of his neck that told him that something odd was afoot. "Navigation. Plot those coordinates onto my repeater."

In the holo cube, a blinking diamond appeared as the nav officer entered Glandinning's coordinates. Ai sat back and his hands automatically settled into their steepled pose as he processed the meaning of the blinking diamond. The point was on the opposite side of Earth's orbit from the approaching enemy fleet.

"Comms. Put Admiral Glandinning onto my private link, please."

The youthful face of Gavin Glandinning appeared in the holo cube at the side of Ai's chair.

"Admiral Glandinning, perhaps you could enlighten me as to firstly why you are aboard a ship which my records show to be decommissioned, accompanied by three other ships which are similarly listed. And secondly how you expect me to follow you to coordinates which are clearly within the area covered by the Others' dampening field?"

Gavin looked back out of the holo cube at him like a contrite schoolboy. "Well you see, sir, I was aware of certain facts that the other fleet commanders and you may not be aware of..."

It took a physical effort for Ai to control his growing anger at the young admiral. An anger that Glandinning obviously could see, as he hurriedly explained further.

"Before being assigned to SurvFlot Three, I was attached to a research and development base which specialized in drive and weaponry development. I was aware that the director of the base, Doctor Moore and his team, had been using these old cruisers as test beds and one of the things they had been trialing was a Variable Gravity Drive..."

"Get to the point, Admiral, my patience is wearing thin," growled Ai.

In the holo cube, the head of Jeff Moore appeared alongside Gavin's. "The Variable Gravity Drive works on a different frequency to that of the standard Commonwealth drive and I believe it will not be affected by the dampening field so these cruisers can fold to any point within Earth space."

Jeff's statement cut off any protest that Ai was about to come up with. Instead he felt himself leaning forward in his seat, staring intently into the pick-up. "But how does four old cruisers' ability to fold into Earth space help me?"

The grinning face of Gavin answered him. "These four old cruisers have more than one trick up their sleeves, sir. I intend to fold into Earth's space and clear an area big enough for the whole of First Fleet to fold into."

AI looked long and hard into the eyes of the younger admiral and his stare was met with the utmost confidence. "Very well, Admiral Glandinning. You lead and I shall follow. First Fleet will fold in five minutes to your designated coordinates. Jing clear." Ai broke the link and spun to face his comms officer. "Transmit the coordinates to the fleet and tell them to be prepared to fold on my order." The seed of an idea began to germinate in the senior admiral's brain and he leaned back in his seat, his brain blocking out the rush of shouted orders as his bridge crew prepared for the fold. If he came out of fold space at Glandinning's coordinates, the Earth's shadow would hide his ships from any chance of enemy detection. If he timed it just right, the Others would be engaged with Chavez and the fixed orbital platforms, allowing him to swing around and come at them from the flanks, relieving the pressure on Chavez. Would it be enough to allow the combined First and Fifth Fleets to hold until Radford arrived and evened the odds up? Ai ran the numbers in his head but he knew that no matter what, he had no

302

choice in the matter. Chavez couldn't be expected to hold without immediate reinforcements and Radford simply couldn't make it in time. What other choice did he have but to go along with Glandinning's plan?

As the comms officer bent to his task, Ai recited a silent prayer that Glandinning knew what he was doing, because if he didn't, he had just condemned every sailor of First Fleet to death.

#

EARTH SPACE - SOL SYSTEM

"Vampire! Vampire! Multiple enemy launches. Computer is having difficulty getting a good count through the enemy's electronic counter measures but best estimate is 900 plus birds. Looks like the orbital platforms are the initial target as you expected, ma'am."

No great surprise there, thought Analisa. If they lost the support of the platforms, then the ships under her command would be easy pickings for the enemy fleet. Analisa gave herself a shake to shed the melancholy.

"Tactical. Bring up our own ECM and let's see if we can get at least a few of their birds to loose lock. How long until his ships enter the missile envelope of the platforms?"

The officer at tactical tapped a few keys and a faint broken line appeared in Analisa's tactical display. "At his current closing rate, the lead ships should cross into range in three minutes. His first flight of missiles will reach the platforms on or about the same time."

In her display, the tsunami wave of approaching missiles began to crystallize into individual points as her ECM fought with that of the enemy and began to burn through the electronic fog.

"Comms. Fleet signal. Weapons remain tight, let Command Central fight the platforms."

"Vampire! Vampire! Second launch detected. Looks like similar numbers to their first launch. Computer is calling us the target this time."

Well, here we go. Let's just hope that our preparations were good enough. "OK, let's go with Fire Plan Charlie. Weapons free fleet wide." Analisa tightened the straps of her seat and gave her helmet in its rack mounted on the side of the chair a gentle, reassuring pat. *Hopefully I won't need you.*

Patrick Malloy called from his position hovering over the tactical officer. "Enemy ships now within range of the platforms. Central are engaging enemy units with the Viper grazers and using HVMs to counter his missiles."

"Third missile launch detected. Looks like the platforms are the target again."

Analisa's display filled with a third wave of enemy missiles. This one looked to not be as thick as the first two waves. After launching upward of 1800 missiles already, maybe the enemy admiral was becoming more prudent. Or perhaps he's waiting to see the effect of his first two strikes, thought Analisa with a silent chuckle.

Moving at nearly the speed of light, the heavy 15 centimeter grazers of the orbital platforms reached out to hammer the closing enemy fleet. Even over the vast distances involved in space battles, the effect of being struck by even one of these grazers was akin to swatting a fly with a sledgehammer. Each of the Viper platforms may only be capable of firing 100 shots before its power source was exhausted, but whoever was doing the targeting in Central Command had chosen to go for the enemy's heaviest units.

The Others' heavy Vulture battleships were struck by not one. Not two. But three grazers. Battle armor buckled and failed as the grazers struck. The grazers penetrated through to the unprotected ships' innards and wherever they touched steel it immediately became super-heated and expanded into plasma so rapidly that it hardly slowed the progress of the grazer. The grazer only slowed as it met the armor on the far side of the ships hulls. The effect for any ship struck was cataclysmic. Within seconds, eight Vultures had simply ceased to exist. If the Viper platforms had been human then any joy they felt at their success was soon to be squashed as the first wave of enemy missiles reached them.

Now it was time for the second type of Viper platform to come to their defense. Each grazer Viper was accompanied by two other Vipers equipped with nine HVMs. These short-range missiles exploded from their boxes as soon as they detected an enemy missile entering their threat envelope. Unfortunately, no one had ever planned on an enemy who was able to fire so many missiles in a single wave. The defensive HVMs raced outward to meet the threat. Their on-board guidance systems fought to burn through the ECM of their oncoming foes. But in the end it came down to simple numbers. The HVMs were simply swamped by the number of incoming missiles and some got through too close with the grazer Vipers. Computers on board these platforms identified the threat and laser close in defense clusters moved immediately to rapid fire. More enemy missiles were blotted from space, but still they came. Nuclear kiloton warheads exploded and ripped jagged holes in the intricately planned defense zones. On board Furious, Analisa was the first to see the holes appear, but before she could pass any orders, Patrick Malloy had the Garundan Bassa-guided missile destroyers moving to fill the gaps. Patrick turned to face her as if he had felt her eyes upon him and gave her a toothy grin and a quick thumbs up. That was when the second wave hit.

The ships of Fifth Fleet rocked as missile after missile exploded. Discharging pinpoint X-ray lasers which penetrated even the thickest of battle armor. A ship could survive such a single strike as long as it didn't hit anything vital. The missile wave that fell upon Fifth Fleet carried some 300 of these warheads and the effect was nothing short of catastrophic. The Nemesis class battleships Granger and the Yangtze were gone in the blink of an eye. The cruisers Leander, Sphinx, and Hermes suffered more hits than they had the right to survive but although severely damaged, they held their place in formation.

The remainder of the enemy missiles had been a mix of conventional nuclear warheads and ECM missiles. *Furious* rocked as she was battered by wave after wave of close in detonations but her armor held. Analisa spared a moment to look around the bridge and her eyes fell upon the crumpled form of Patrick Malloy lying against the far bulkhead. His face was pale and blood was pouring from his nose, but to Analisa's great relief his chest was still rising and falling in a slow steady rhythm. Analisa cursed herself for not taking the few seconds it would have taken to order him into a seat and strap himself in. Instead her thumb squashed down on her comms link. "Corpsman to the flag bridge."

Returning her attention to her tactical plot, she was relieved to see that the first and second waves of enemy missiles hadn't caused as much damage as they might have. The remaining Viper grazers were still firing although their shot count was nearing full capacity and they would soon have to shut down, forcing Analisa to resort to her own ship's grazer fire. The HVM platforms

306

were another matter entirely. The weight of the first enemy wave had been such that they had fired off the majority of their missiles. A quick look at the display sidebar showed them down to nineteen percent efficiency. Nowhere near enough to stand up to the third wave of enemy missiles which were bearing down on them. Without the HVM fire to interdict the incoming wave the grazer platforms were finished. And if they went, Fifth Fleet was all that stood between the Others and Earth.

"Tactical. Expand our defensive engagement fire to include the Viper platforms and move the remaining Bassas into a position to support your fire plan. What's the ETA on the third wave?"

When there was no immediate reply from Tactical, Analisa searched her plot for the expected wave of missiles herself, only for her eyes to fall upon them in an unexpected place. Damn!

"OK, Tactical, they've tricked us. The third wave is headed for the lunar colonies. Comms let's get a warning out to them. They have…"

"Seven minutes, ma'am," called the officer at tactical.

"Seven minutes until impact."

The blinking light of a priority signal from Central Command caught Analisa's eye and she tapped the accept key. The face that filled her display was, however, not one that she had been expecting.

The impassive face of High Commander Botac looked back at her from the display. "High Commander, I'm afraid I don't have the time to talk to you at the moment, I'm…"

The businesslike voice of the High Commander cut Analisa off in mid-sentence. "Admiral Chavez, on my own authority as the senior Benii officer present and with the blessing of Representative Hoolas, I am placing the resources of the Koslla at your disposal. If you would be so kind as to transmit your IFF codes, my Freiba are arming now for an anti-shipping strike and should be ready to launch within the next ten minutes. It would be inconvenient if your anti-missile defenses mistook them for the enemy."

Analisa caught the eye of the comms officer and gave him a curt nod. "You should have the codes shortly, High Commander. If I may, I will also forward you our recommendations for an initial strike package. I admit that we've never had the benefit of a dedicated space fighter such as your Freibas, but from my briefings they pack a big punch for such a small ship."

Botac's lips curled upwards in a knowing smile. "Believe me, Admiral, the enemy are in for the shock of their soon-to-be-shortened lives. Now if you will excuse me, I need to meet with my planning staff to go over your recommendations. Time is short."

Without another word, Botac cut the link, leaving Analisa with the major headache of preparing for a strike by space fighters that she had never seen in action before.

#

Minutes later, a feral smile crossed her face as she reviewed the updated strike package the Benii had sent to her for approval.

"The Koslla is launching now, ma'am… my god look, at those things move!"

On Analisa's plot, 115 Freiba space fighters formed up into their individual squadrons with the precision that champion ballet dancers would have been proud of and began what the Commonwealth tacticians were calling the Benii dance. An intricate series of maneuvers that were designed to confuse any fire control computer. Moving as fast as an HVM the sleek little fighters speared toward the Others' fleet.

"Time till contact?"

The tactical officer answered without taking his eyes from his plot as he marveled at the seemingly effortless grace of the Benii. "Six minutes at their current rate of closure."

"Time till we enter the enemies energy weapons range?"

This time the officer was forced to check his readouts. "Eleven minutes fifty-two seconds."

"Have we received any updates from Central Command in relation to the strikes on the lunar colonies?"

"Nothing since the original confirmation that the colony defenses had begun engaging the enemy missiles. Sorry, ma'am."

Analisa went to placate the tactical officer but the blinking priority signal light on her display was illuminated again. Maybe the High Commander needed some more information? Pressing the "accept" key, Analisa was confronted by the neutral face of the Chairman of the Combined Joint Chiefs of Staff.

"Admiral Chavez. Fifth Fleet is to immediately advance and engage the enemy."

The shock of the order caused Analisa's face to pale as the blood fled from it and she found that her voice had escaped her as she stammered to get out a reply. "But... But General. If I advance and leave the support of the Viper platforms, the enemy have the opportunity to defeat the fleet in detail. With the fleet gone, the Others can stand off and destroy the Vipers opening a hole in Earth's defenses large enough to allow their missiles through unchallenged. I have no idea how much damage the Freibas are capable of but surely they

309

can't hope to cause so much damage that Fifth Fleet on its own can hope to defeat the remaining enemy ships?"

In the holo cube, the face of Keyton Joyce remained as impassive as ever but his reply said everything his expression didn't. "Who said you would be on your own, Admiral?"

#

Tama Narath strode across the bridge of The Path of the Creator and stopped in front of the main plot. "What are those?"

"The computer is calling them small personnel shuttles, Tama Narath. Could the heretics be trying to board us?"

The idea of the heretics attempting such a thing was not unheard of. It had happened before. Rather than allowing their capture and no doubt torture at the hands of the heretics, one of the ships of the people had followed the direction of their Lesser Coltus and fought till the end or committed suicide so as to not be taken after being disabled in the system the heretics called Garunda.

"Alert the ships guard fleet-wide. Tell them to be prepared to repel boarders."

"Immediately, Tama Narath."

As he continued to watch the display, a satisfied grunt came from the direction of the sensor team.

"Report?"

The smiling face of the sensor team leader turned to face him. "Two pieces of fortune bless us, Tama Narath. It is my honor to report that I can confirm that we have detected multiple detonations on the surface of the heretic home world's moon."

Tama Narath gave a silent prayer of thanks to the Creator before returning his attention to the team leader. "You said you had two pieces of news?"

310

"From our readings of the heretic fleet's drive sources they are showing a definite increase of power. I believe that they will break orbit imminently."

Tama Narath closed his eyes as he felt the familiar presence of the Lesser Coltus enter his consciousness.

Our time is at hand, Tama Narath. The path of the Ehita is clear. Close with the heretics. Destroy their fleet and cleanse their world in the name of the Creator.

Tama Narath spun to face his communications officer. "General order. The fleet will advance and engage the heretics with energy weapons."

#

"The Freibas are engaging now, ma'am. We're reading hits on the primary targets. Confirmed... the Goshawks are slowing. I see sixteen dropping out of formation."

Analisa's fist crashed down on her armrest in celebration. The Goshawks were the enemy equivalent of her own Agis missile defense destroyers. Designed specifically for an anti-missile role, the Goshawks were based on the hull of the Buzzard cruisers but carried little in the way of energy armaments. That role was left to the larger Vultures that were the main fighting strength of the enemy fleet.

"OK people, the Benii have played their part and stripped away the majority of the Others' missile shield. Tactical, how long till we reach optimum launch range?"

"Two minutes, twelve seconds, ma'am."

This was going to be the longest two minutes of her life.

#

"What we had thought to be personnel shuttles has in fact turned out to be armed attack craft, Tama Narath. They have attacked the anti-missile escorts with high-energy particle weapons and have caused significant

311

damage. The majority of the escorts report damage to their engineering sections and are unable to keep up with the fleet."

Armed attack craft! Curse the ingenuity of the heretics. No matter. We will have no need of the escorts once we have closed the range sufficiently with their major fleet units. He still outnumbered the heretic fleet almost eight to one and he had supreme confidence in his ability to wipe them clear of space. Yes, he would take casualties, but the result would be the same for their planet. The final embrace of nuclear fire.

"Do not slow. Continue the advance!" Tama Narath said confidently.

#

"Entering missile range now, Admiral."

"Execute Fire Plan Baker! Communications. The fleet will reverse course. Tactical. Hold the enemy at maximum range and continue to fire."

As one, Fifth Fleet flushed its missiles toward the onrushing enemy fleet. The 220 missiles that shot toward the enemy may have seemed a paltry number in comparison to the weight of missiles that had been fired at them in the initial exchanges, but the Benii space fighters had stripped away a large part of the enemy fleet's missile defenses and more than would have were able to avoid what anti-missile defenses were left as they began to explode in the heart of the fleet. Battle armor giving way to the unforgiving battering of X-ray lasers and close in nuclear detonations.

#

The Path of the Creator shrugged off the concussions of the enemy fire as it raced along with its fellows to close the distance to the retreating heretic forces. The blue-and-white gem of the planet was nearly within reach. Tama Narath gritted his teeth as one by one, ships of the people were destroyed or too badly damaged to continue. He consoled himself in the knowledge that his followers were going to a better place. Into the warm, loving arms of the Creator. The steadily retreating heretics were remaining outside his energy weapons range but he could still reach them with his missiles and in the end, his sheer weight of fire would be enough. The heretics could only retreat so far and soon, once again, they would have their backs against the planet and have nowhere left to run.

"Incoming missiles bearing 162.4!"

What! Impossible! There were no enemy ships there! That was the wrong side of the heretics' planet's orbit!

\#

"Admiral. Signal from First Fleet. Remain at your current position. You are the anvil to my hammer."

Analisa Chavez gripped her seat's armrests as she forced herself against the restraints. "Fleet order. All stop. No ship is to give an inch. Hold the line!"

\#

TDF *Horizon* and her three sisters emerged from fold space less than 500,000 kilometers from the trailing Goshawk.

"Missiles away, sir. Detonation in thirty seconds. Mark."

Gavin Glandinning could have leaned forward and touched his tactical officer's chair. It wasn't that the retrofitted Talos cruisers were short of space. The advanced artificial intelligences that had replaced the majority of the crew meant that instead of requiring some 710 sailors to man her, the *Horizon* got by with less than 100. But the scientists and engineers who had done the modifications obviously didn't understand that an admiral may simply want the room to pace up and down his bridge.

313

Maybe he would have a word with Jeff Moore when he returned the ships to Zarmina, thought Gavin. Time to consider that later.

"Sound the collision alarm."

The hooting throughout the ship was an unnecessary reminder to the small crew to ensure that they were securely strapped into their seats for what was to come.

"Five. Four. Three. Two. One. Detonation!" For a fraction of a second it all seemed an anticlimax, then the blast wave of ten anti-matter warheads going off in unison, wiping an area of space nearly a million cubic kilometers in size clean of anything made by man or otherwise. The massive explosion left a gap in the Others' gravity drive-defying bubble. The shock wave rolled outwards and seemed to pick the *Horizon* up like she was nothing more than a leaf on the wind instead of a 24,400 ton cruiser. Alarms began going off all over the ship but this wasn't unexpected. The same thing had happened the last time they had detonated the experimental anti-matter warheads. Unfortunately, a few individuals had ignored the order to strap themselves in and were currently heavily sedated in the ships limited medical bay. This time, no injuries were reported.

"Tactical. Congratulations. Now what say we go test this new armor on those Goshawks before Third Fleet arrive in the hole we just tore them and have all the fun?"

The grin on his tactical officer's face was all the answer Gavin needed as *Horizon* increased speed to close with the enemy Goshawks.

#

John Radford gave his head a quick shake to clear it of the familiar swimming sensation of a completed fold space transit and forced his eyes to focus on the tactical display. The plan had worked like a dream. The slowly moving icons of damaged Goshawks led like breadcrumbs to the main Others' fleet as it hammered away at Analisa Chavez's ships. The steady missile barrage and energy weapons fire was turning Fifth Fleet into little more than useless scrap, but still they stood like an immobile cliff face.

First Fleet had just entered energy weapons range and its heavy Bismarck battleships were searing the enemy flanks while its missiles sought out the fleet command ships attempting to rip apart their command and control. Without the Goshawks that the Benii space fighters had disabled and with the unexpected arrival of First and Third Fleets, the Commonwealth forces had the upper hand and it was only a matter of time until victory was assured.

The four blue icons of Gavin Glandinning's cruisers were mixing it up with the already damaged Goshawks. Swooping down on them like scavenger birds on an injured animal. The pecks of the smaller cruisers wouldn't cause too much damage individually but just like the Benii fighters, the small pecks all added up and already two Goshawks had fallen to Glandinning.

"Communications. Fleet signal. Third Fleet will advance at flank speed. Tactical. I want a full missile and energy weapon spread on the Goshawks as we pass. Do enough damage that they can't escape, then leave them to Admiral Glandinning."

John eyed his tactical display. In his mind's eye he conjured up the image of the tumultuous battle raging before Analisa Chavez. "We have bigger fish to fry."

#

You have failed the Creator, Tama Narath. You have allowed the heretics to trick you. You are not worthy of your title as The Hand of the Creator.

The sense of failure and despair that filled Tama Narath was a physical thing. The fleet that the people had worked so long and hard to create was being destroyed piece by piece around him. What had once been massive armored leviathans were being reduced to bleeding, shattered corpses as the combined fire from two heretic fleets ripped its very heart and soul from it. Now a third enemy fleet had been detected approaching the rear. He was trapped. The situation was hopeless. He had failed his Creator.

Tama Narath had been a warrior of the Creator his entire adult life and his life was going to end in failure. He would never see Aseena. The Promised Land. Never share in the love of the Creator. His failure would mean his death and the deaths of those he had led here. His shoulders slumped beneath his blood-red cloak as his eyes fell to the symbol of the creator on his chest. The simple black circle with the red X. *No! No! I refuse to die in failure!*

"Signal the closest five ships. One ship will take up position directly ahead of us. The remaining four will take up flanking positions. When they are in position, we will advance at best speed. We shall blow a hole in their defenses big enough to allow The Hand of the Creator through and I intend to crash us down upon the heretic's home world, detonating our remaining weapons and our engines as we breach their atmosphere. They may have won the battle, but I will ensure they have no home to return to!"

#

A worried shout from tactical pulled Analisa's gaze away from the master plot.

"There's something strange going on at the heart of the enemy formation, ma'am."

"Define 'strange'?"

316

"Five Buzzards are converging on what we think is the fleet commander's Vulture. Their ECM is playing merry hell with my sensors but they are definitely changing formation."

What were they up to now? With the imminent arrival of Third Fleet, this battle was all but over. Fifth Fleet had held at a terrible cost in men and ships but it had held. Maybe the enemy fleet commander was going to make a run for it?

The strangled cry of "Oh my God!" came from Tactical.

Analisa's eyes fixed on the blood-red icons of the accelerating enemy ships. They were going to ram!

"Communications. All ships are to fire on the approaching enemy formation! Give them everything we've got."

Her orders given, Analisa could only watch in abject horror as the five enemy ships were pounded by the remains of Fifth Fleet. It didn't take a genius to work out what the Others had in mind and the surviving ships of Fifth Fleet quickly realized the danger and the fire on the enemy ships steadily increased. But on they came. Through the expanding nuclear fireballs and the searching grazers they kept coming. First one. Then another. And another dropped out of the last desperate forlorn charge. Until only the fleet commander's ship and a single remaining consort were still going. They were less than 2,000 kilometers from Fifth Fleet's battle line when the fleet commander's consort took its final victim. TDF *Perseus* realized the danger too late. Or maybe its captain saw the danger but chose to keep his ship in formation rather than allow the oncoming Buzzard to pass. Whatever happened, 220,000 tons of Buzzard moving at nearly 30,000 kilometers per hour struck the 37,000 ton Vulcan cruiser *Perseus*. When the fireball dissipated, there was nothing bigger than a ground car left, and what was left was a hole in Fifth Fleet's line; a hole the enemy fleet commander's ship bored through as fast as it could.

#

Tama Narath let out an exultant cry. They were through the last of the heretics' fleet! All that remained was the orbital defense platforms and he was sure that his ship's battle armor was strong enough to shrug off their weakened fire and punch through to the planet below. He sat back in his command chair and gave a silent prayer of thanks to the Creator that he had allowed him to complete his small part of the Ehita.

#

The Garundan Bassa class destroyer *Hortath* lay unmoving in high Earth orbit. Part of the visiting Garundan training flotilla, she had been ordered to fill a gap in the inner defense shell after the HVM and grazer platforms in this part of the shell had taken significant damage.

Captain Yaja was immensely proud of his little ship and of how its young crew had performed in the battle. Every order had been followed and executed flawlessly. Which, considering that this was the first inter system cruise of any Garundan ship, made him beam with pride. With the arrival of First and Third Fleets, victory was assured, so it was no surprise that he had allowed his mind to wander away from the tactical display. When the officer at tactical called to him, he began to berate himself. His heart stopped as his eyes settled on the display. Bearing down on the *Hortath* was vast bulk of an enemy Vulture.

"Tactical. Go active on ECM, let's see how many of his missiles we can confuse."

The small pause from Tactical was enough to let Yaja know that there was something wrong before he had a chance to focus on the confused face of the tactical officer.

"Sir. He hasn't launched any missiles... My plot shows that he is on a collision course with the planet and his speed's increasing. The local missile platforms are launching and the grazers are engaging, but..."

The officer didn't need to finish his sentence. Yaja could read the plot as well as the tactical officer could. The Vulture's course and speed could only mean one thing. He intended to crash into the planet and the firepower of the defense platforms even augmented by *Hortath* wasn't going to be enough to stop him. In his mind's eye, Yaja could imagine the destruction that would wreck on the humans' home world.

Yaja was a man of deep honor and he, like the majority of Garundans, felt they owed a debt of honor to the humans who had sacrificed so many of their own to protect his world when it was threatened by the Others. Now, it seemed, fate had decided to call in the debt.

His features became stony and his voice steely as he turned to his navigator. "Plot an interception course with the Vulture. Maximum thrust."

The *Hortath* leapt forward like the thoroughbred racehorse she was. Closing the distance between herself and the onrushing Vulture. Yaja raised himself from his command chair and brought himself to attention. The small bridge crew followed his unspoken cue and stood.

Yaja felt the emotion of the moment fill him as his heart swelled with pride. Not trusting himself to speak, he snapped out a parade-ground salute, which his crew returned. Holding the salute, he used his other hand to

319

flip the cover off the ship's auto destruct button. As the enemy Vulture filled his display, he smashed his thumb down on the button with all his might. Every remaining missile aboard the *Hortath* and the fusion power plants exploded as one. Ripping the Garundan destroyer and the Vulture into nothing more than boiling plasma and small pieces of hull, which flew into the Earth's upper atmosphere and burned up like small shooting stars.

Debt repaid in full.

CHAPTER NINETEEN

REPERCUSSIONS. MILITARY. POLITICAL. PERSONAL

CENTRAL COMMAND – MONT SALÈVE
EARTH – SOL SYSTEM

Deep under Mont Salève, the Pit was a hive of subdued activity. It was three days since the Others were defeated, and as the population of Earth fought to come to terms with how close they'd come to their own annihilation at the hands of an implacable enemy, the military leadership of the Commonwealth were busy taking stock of their surviving forces and planning their next move.

As Chairman of the Joint Chiefs of Staff, Keyton Joyce in particular was feeling the pressure from the politicians as they began the inescapable witch-hunt into who would eventually shoulder the blame for allowing the Others to come so close to victory. Keyton looked around the table at his fellow Joint Chiefs and the assembled fleet commanders. His eyes lingered for a moment on the one military person present who wasn't a member of the Commonwealth. High Commander Botac. When Fifth Fleet's back had been against the wall, rather than seek out a place of safety, High Commander Botac had committed her forces to the battle on the side of the Commonwealth. Forces that had undoubtedly allowed Fifth Fleet to hold on until rescued. They were all good men and women who deserved his unwavering support. They had all read the tactical situation the way he had. Third Fleet's opportunity to take out a major enemy naval base that threatened Garunda had been too good a possibility to pass up. The imminent enemy attack on Alona that had called for the only Commonwealth force available to come to the Empire's aid. The fact that that force had been First Fleet, Earth's primary defensive fleet, had been thought at the time as of no major concern. After all, the Others didn't have the gravity drive, so any enemy fleet approaching the Sol system would be detected in plenty of time for units of Second Fleet in Janus to fold into Earth's space and reinforce the understrength Fifth Fleet, and if that wasn't enough Third Fleet was only a fold away.

How completely they - Keyton gave himself a mental reproach - *he* had misread the situation. When First Fleet arrived at Alona, the Others activated their hidden buoys, which made the use of the gravity drive impossible. Admiral Jing had understood the implications of the situation immediately and fought his way past the enemy fleet and plotted a course for home, but that still left Admiral Chavez and her understrength Fifth Fleet to stand alone against the main enemy fleet that had appeared at the edge of the Sol system. If not for the selfless sacrifice of Admiral Catney who'd remained at his post to ensure his communications drones remained free from the dampening field and carried the call for help, then it could all have ended differently.

As it was, the tenacity of Chavez's defense and the quick thinking of Admiral Glandinning had saved the day. Chavez held long enough to allow Glandinning's cruisers to fold into Earth's space and use anti-matter warheads to clear an area of space from the enemy buoys large enough for First Fleet to arrive unobserved in Earth's orbit. First Fleet maneuvered into the perfect ambush position and used Fifth Fleet as the cliff face to dash the enemy's forces against. When Glandinning repeated his trick of clearing a large area of space of the enemy buoys to allow Third Fleet to fold in behind the enemy fleet, any hope of an Others' victory vanished. But he still had to try. In a last, desperate gamble, the enemy fleet commander had used his few remaining ships to blast a hole in Fifth Fleet's defenses that had allowed his flagship to make a suicide run at Earth. Just as it had seemed that nothing could stop him, a single Garundan destroyer, the *Hortath* appeared as if from nowhere. The *Hortath* was as a minnow to a whale but without hesitation, its crew set a course to intercept the enemy and rammed him. When the resulting fireball of expanding plasma had cleared, there was no sign of either ship. There were no survivors.

The weight of responsibility was heavy on Keyton's shoulders and before this meeting he had had a more private meeting with his fellow Joint Chiefs during which he had announced his intention to resign his position as head of the Joint Chiefs at the end of the day. Both Tolas and Horan had attempted to persuade him to remain, but Keyton knew that the political reality of the situation was that someone would have to take the blame for allowing the Others to come so close to destroying humanity's home. No matter how strongly Tolas and Horan protested that they would have both made the same decisions, the fact of the matter was that they also understood that the public, in their fear, was looking for a scapegoat and Keyton would rather they took his scalp than anyone else's. This war wasn't over and they would need good people to see it through and Keyton wasn't willing to allow someone else to take the fall so he could keep his post.

Keyton looked across the table and saw the indefatigable faces of his two fellow chiefs. Time to get this show on the road. Keyton caught the eye of the commander standing ready at the lectern and gave him a small nod. A single low tone sounded in the room and whatever whispered conversations had been taking place came to a hurried conclusion as attention focused on the commander who paused briefly as the room descended into attentive silence.

"Good morning, ladies and gentlemen. For those of you who don't know me, I am Commander Irene Spicer and I am attached to the Combined Joint Chiefs' planning staff. The briefing this morning will consist of three parts. Firstly, a quick round-up of current Commonwealth force levels and capabilities. Secondly, our proposed response to the enemy assault on the Sol system. And thirdly, an in-depth planning study which will involve you taking our proposals away with you and brainstorming with your own planning staffs. This third part must be completed in no more than twenty-four hours."

This last comment drew a few gasps from around the table. As of yet, none of them were aware of what the Combined Joint Chiefs were planning, but they all knew that twenty-four hours wasn't a long time to iron out the wrinkles in any plan on paper, never mind get it into actual operation.

Commander Spicer gave them a moment to catch their collective breaths before continuing.

"We now know that the Others' assault on the Alonan Empire was a ruse to draw forces away from the Sol system and trap them in Messier 54. However,

First Fleet quickly recognized the threat and was able to break through the blocking force the Others had placed in the system to hold them there. The latest post-battle analysis puts the enemy losses at fourteen Vultures, twenty-eight Buzzards, and eleven Goshawks. The remaining enemy ships…we believe three Vultures, six Buzzards, and only one Goshawk have reportedly made their way to the edge of the system and entered fold space. Destination unknown. The Alonan navy remains on high alert and is using its gravity drive-capable cruisers to comb the system in case the Others attempt a second sneak attack. First Fleet losses during the breakout amounted to one Bismarck battleship, eight Nemesis battleships, seventeen Vulcan heavy cruisers, twenty Talos cruisers, and twelve Agis destroyers. In addition, First Fleet lost another Nemesis to engineering damage on the voyage home. This ship is currently being recovered by fold-capable tugs and will be taken to Janus for repairs."

Keyton thought he detected a fleeting wince pass over the face of Ai Jing as his fleet's losses in his desperate dash back to the Sol system were made public for the first time before his face once more returned to its normal implacability.

"During the action in the Sol system, First Fleet suffered a further two Bismarcks, five Nemesis, eleven Vulcan and two Talos either destroyed or damaged beyond repair. In conclusion, First Fleet's current fighting strength remains at around fifty-five percent."

The silence in the room was a tangible thing. First Fleet. The pride of the Commonwealth navies had, in a single enemy operation, been reduced to nearly half its original strength.

A wave of the hand from Keyton urged Commander Spicer to continue.

"Third Fleet, however, remains at virtually full strength, minus BatFor 3.3 which is currently being held in Garunda for system security. That gives us three Bismarcks, six Nemesis, nine Vulcans, nine Talos, and nine Agis."

John Radford and his Third Fleet had arrived just a fraction too late to take part in the melee that had whirled around Fifth and First Fleet. What enemy ships remained were shattered husks of their former selves and what fight they had been able to put up had been met with overwhelming return fire.

Commander Spicer physically braced herself for what was coming next. "Moving on to Fifth Fleet. As of zero eight hundred hours this morning, Fifth Fleet in its entirety was designated non-operational due to combat losses..."

Keyton could only watch as with this single, sweeping statement he saw the shoulders of Analisa Chavez slump. Fifth Fleet had held against all odds and had paid the heaviest of prices. Not a single one of its battleships or cruisers was combat effective. A little over ninety percent of its ships had suffered major damage which would require them either to be scrapped or spend major time in the hands of the yards. Analisa's own flagship, TDF *Furious*, had more holes in it than a Swiss cheese. Keyton dragged his attention back to Spicer as she continued her rundown.

"With the arrival of elements of Second Fleet from Janus, it supplements our available units for further operations considerably…"

"I'm sorry, Commander, but exactly what further operations are you talking about?" interrupted Radford. "Surely we need time to consolidate and rebuild our defenses before we go looking to pick another fight."

Keyton held up a hand to stop Spicer. "Admiral Radford. It is the opinion of the Combined Joint Chiefs that, having reviewed the intelligence gained by your assault on the enemy naval base, and from the size of the forces which he has deployed in Messier 54 and here in the Sol system, that these two actions combined have severely depleted his naval strength."

John was shaking his head. "With all due respect, sir, that intelligence may be faulty."

A murmur of agreement went around the table. The other fleet commanders could see John's point. The Others' sudden ability to harness fold space could well allow them to appear at any time anywhere in Commonwealth space. Only Ai Jing remained silent.

Keyton leaned forward in his seat and perched his elbows on the table. "Your thoughts, Admiral Jing?"

Ai sat still for a few moments before he manipulated the controls embedded in the table. Above him, the holo cube came to life, displaying various star systems broken into blocks. "What you see in front of you is a representation of space which we believe to be controlled by the Others. This has been extrapolated from data recovered so far from the naval base secured by Admiral Radford's forces. As you can see, it is broken into fourteen sectors. Each varying in size and shape, but with one consistent string running through them."

The eyes in the room stared at the image, trying to discern what Ai could see but they couldn't. Another tap of the controls and names began to appear next to some of the stars.

Robert Lewis, Commander Second Fleet was the first to spot it. "Well, I'll be damned... these sectors contain either a planet we know the Others have destroyed or where we have encountered them... Look. There's

Garunda and there's 70 Ophiuchi. Each sector has two points highlighted." Robert was becoming more animated as he went on. "I'm willing to bet that one point is their naval base for the sector and the other is a target planet."

Ai nodded sagely. "Exactly, Robert. It appears to me that once the Others find a planet that holds sentient life, they establish a forward operating base in a secure location. Build up their forces then move on to the offensive."

Now it was John's turn to speak up as he looked quizzically at Ai. "Hold on a minute. If this is an accurate representation of enemy space, I don't see any colonies."

For the first time in what seemed like an age a smile tugged at the corners of Analisa Chavez's mouth. "They don't have any, do they?" She turned to Keyton and a feral smile formed on her face. "We know where their home planet is and we're going after it, aren't we?"

Keyton gave her a knowing wink. "Commander, if you would, please."

Spicer manipulated the holo controls and a single sector enlarged to fill the entire holo cube. This sector alone had a single planet highlighted. With a flair for the dramatic, Keyton announced in a loud voice: "Ladies and gentlemen, I give you the target of Operation Hades. The enemy's home world. At zero three hundred hours day after tomorrow, the massed fleets of the Commonwealth and our Benii allies will begin the biggest naval operation in history. The complete destruction of the enemy's ability to wage war!"

The various admirals all began to speak at once, only Analisa Chavez remained silent. With her battle damage she would have to remain on the sidelines as the remaining Commonwealth fleet avenged her dead. A subtle clearing of a throat caused her to turn to her left. High Commander Botac stood towering over the slight human admiral. "Admiral Chavez. As Benii forces are to be involved in the operation I feel it prudent to request a liaison officer of at least flag rank to accompany me on the bridge of the Koslla. Would you be available?"

Analisa could only look up at the Benii for a few shocked seconds as her mind scrambled to answer. "It would be an honor, High Commander." *I will have my revenge, you murdering bastards.*

#

CAPE TOWN - EARTH – SOL SYSTEM

The door of the holding cell slid silently into its recess as the cells lights flickered on, bringing the interior of the cell into stark relief. The disheveled figure lying on the single raised bed raised itself into a sitting position and drew a deep breath as it prepared to release a long and vocal tirade at whoever had entered the three meter by two meter room that had been its home for the past two days. The planned tirade stalled as the cells occupant's eyes focused on the visitor. A diminutive female figure in the uniform of a naval admiral. Recovering quickly from the unexpected sight, the cell's occupant decided to change tactics.

"Admiral Wilson, what a pleasant surprise. And may I ask what brings you to my spacious accommodation?"

Elizabeth Wilson eyed the fifty-something woman sitting on the bed and felt the tugging at the sides of her mouth as she tried to stop herself from allowing a satisfied smile to break her workman-like features.

"Ms. Thomas. You were detained trying to board a Zurich Lines private shuttle at Cape Town spaceport. A spaceport which at the time was under martial law, and your actions contravened orders from the federal government that all surface to orbit traffic was restricted to those of a military nature due to the ongoing emergency."

Daya waved a hand dismissively. "I had urgent company business on Janus which couldn't wait." An arrogant sneer appeared on her face. "When you military fascists eventually release me from this illegal detention I intend to see everyone involved in my arrest court martialed and drummed out of the service… No matter what their rank, Admiral."

"Well, at least we agree on one thing, Ms. Thomas, although you might find that our roles will be reversed." As Elizabeth paused to activate the PAD in her hand, two men in FIB uniform entered the cell. One was holding a set of arm and leg restraints in his hands. Daya felt the cold hand of foreboding touch her shoulders.

"Pursuant to Article 19 of the Emergency Powers Act, once a person is detained under martial law, they and all their belongings are liable to search without warrant…"

Daya made to speak but Elizabeth cut her off.

"During a search of your personal belongings, authorities came into possession of encrypted data files. These files have now been decrypted and their contents reviewed. They have been found to contain certain compromising information about a number of key political and legal figures as well as details of illegal payments made to political election funds and bribes made to employees of Zurich Lines competitors."

Elizabeth looked up from her PAD and she had a shark's smile on her face. "Another file held details of contacts within the Alonan Empire. A shipyard manager named Arnjad Harb. And the now-deceased ship's captain Jake Thackery. Although there are still some files awaiting decryption, it is the opinion of the Justice Department that there is sufficient evidence for you to be remanded into federal custody for the offenses of blackmail, industrial espionage, and my personal favorite… treason."

The wail that escaped Daya came from a deep, dark place within her.

Without a second glance, Elizabeth walked from the cell. One down, one to go.

#

PRESIDENT'S PRIVATE RESIDENCE GENEVA – EARTH – SOL SYSTEM

The select gathering in the president's private office late in the evening comprised her inner circle. Olaf Helsett, Secretary of Defense. Edvard Dietel, the Adjutant General. Gillian Rae, senator and chair of the Science and Technology Committee. Carol Manning, Secretary of Finance. Thomas Crothers, Governor of Janus, and lastly, Patricia Bath, Special Adviser to the President.

This esteemed group all sat in comfortable chairs around a low coffee table but no one present fooled themselves that they were gathered for anything less than a major policy meeting. What was decided here tonight was going to have far-reaching implications for not only the future of the Coston government, but how man's physical and political expansion into the universe was going to be dictated.

Rebecca looked over the rim of her steaming coffee cup at Olaf Helsett. The ex-admiral whom she had press ganged into the position of Secretary of Defense was chomping at the bit to get on. *No time like the present, Rebecca.* "Friends and colleagues. I've asked you to

331

gather here tonight because I believe that we have reached a crossroads of sorts. A crossroads which I do not feel comfortable in making a change of direction without advice and input from people I trust not to try and color my vision but to tell me straight-up their thoughts and feelings."

Rebecca placed her cup on the table and pushed her chair back as she stood, feeling the need to walk while she talked. The Others' attack on Earth has changed the people's mood in a radical way and has politicians from all sides baying for blood. The people want vengeance and whether or not you or I think this is a good thing, it is something that isn't going to go away."

"Operation Hades is scheduled to begin tomorrow. The day after at the latest," interrupted Helsett gruffly.

Rebecca stopped her pacing and turned to face them with a concerned look on her face. "But will it be enough, Olaf?"

Olaf's confused expression showed her the need to expand her question.

"Operation Hades is designed to destroy the Others' ability to wage war on us or anybody else, for that matter. But again I ask you. Is that enough?"

It took a few moments, but as Rebecca waited, the esteemed gathering slowly understood what she meant. Patricia Bath was the first to utter the words in a hushed tone, as her eyes searched the president's face.

"Surely we're not talking about genocide here, Madam President?"

Rebecca held her nerve despite the fluttering in her stomach. "Why not? They came to Earth with the intention of killing every last one of us. When they were finished here, they would have moved on and done the exact same thing to every other living world in the Commonwealth. God knows how many other innocent civilizations they have destroyed in the past. Don't they deserve the same fate?"

The shocked silence in the room held for a few seconds until it was broken by Gillian Rae. Of all the people in the room, Gillian probably had the most to hate the Others for. Her home, the Boreland Habitats, had been one of the off-world habitats unlucky enough to be on the Others' route to Earth. The first naval vessel to reach the once-thriving colony had reported no survivors. What had been a search-and-rescue mission quickly became one of recovery only. Nearly one and a half million men, women, and children had perished in the attack. If anyone had the right to demand a blood settlement, it was she. Gillian couldn't face her president.

"Madam President. If the purpose of this meeting is to advocate genocide, then I must withdraw. What you are suggesting is against all the principles that I have spent my life supporting. If you will excuse me, I can take no further part in this."

Gillian stood slowly only to be stayed by Rebecca's raised hand.

"Does anyone else feel that they could not support an order to completely eradicate the enemy home world?"

Without hesitation, each and every person present raised their hand. Rebecca felt the relief wash through her and a smile creased her weary face.

"Thank God for that. Gillian, please be seated."

The confused looks which crossed all her guests' faces invited explanation and was only exasperated by Rebecca's small laugh.

"Excuse me, friends. I just had to know where you all stood. As you can imagine, I am under a huge amount of pressure to end the threat from the Others and there are quite a few calls from politicians of all ilk to simply wipe them from the face of the universe once and for all. I, and I'm glad to see you, are not of that mindset. I have no intention of wiping an entire race out of existence simply for the sake of revenge. Operation Hades will proceed as planned."

The frown on the Olaf's face let Rebecca know that he had something more to say. "Care to share, Olaf?"

The gruff ex-admiral's mouth worked like he had swallowed something unpleasant. "It will not go exactly as planned, Madam President."

Now it was Rebecca's turn to be confused. "In what way, Olaf?"

Reaching into his inside pocket Olaf extracted an old-fashioned paper envelope and placed it in the center of the table. "Before I came here this evening, I had a visitor. With immediate effect, General Keyton Joyce has tendered his resignation as Chairman of the Combined Joint Chiefs of Staff and announced his intention to retire from military service."

Rebecca's shock at the announcement was reflected in the faces of the others. "His resignation is not accepted and you can tell him that from me," spluttered Rebecca. "No one can blame Keyton for the attack. I'll make a public announcement to that effect if I need to. No. You tell Keyton he's staying put."

Now it was Thomas Crothers' turn to hold his hand up and halt the president. "Madam President. Think about this logically. General Joyce understands that there's going to be a witch-hunt looking for someone, anyone, to blame for allowing the Others to come so close to killing us all. Joyce has done the honorable thing and has fallen on his sword." Thomas gave a quick glance in Olaf's direction. "If we are to believe the military estimates of what fighting strength the Others have remaining in their home system then whoever you replace him with will start their tenure with a crushing defeat of the enemy. And no matter what any senate investigation digs up, Joyce has already accepted ultimate responsibility for any actions of his subordinates, thereby protecting them and you."

Rebecca's face flushed red in anger even as the logical side of her brain accepted Thomas' explanation. "I don't need anyone's protection, Thomas."

"Don't you?" said Edvard Dietel quietly.

Rebecca spun on him. "What do you mean by that, Edvard?"

Edvard took a moment to collect his thoughts. "What about the arrest of Seaton Anderson? We may have conclusive proof that he was involved in the selling of military technology to Alona, never mind being implicated in the murder of Thackery, along with bribery and blackmail, but that man has a long reach and a lot of friends in the senate. There's no guarantee that what Daya Thomas was carrying at the time of her arrest was everything. I know if it were me, I wouldn't have put all my eggs in one basket. Anderson undoubtedly has more files hidden away somewhere that he'll pull out when the time is right."

Carol Manning found herself nodding slowly in agreement with the Adjutant General. "Zurich Lines' finances are a nightmare. My investigators are finding shell corporations within shell corporations. Anderson had his fingers in shipping, construction, defense, you name it. It could take years before we have enough to go to trial."

"And all the time, Seaton Anderson will be sitting in his estate in the Italian Alps. He'll have a lot of time to plan his defense... and revenge." Edvard sat back in his chair as he finished watching the president's mind at work.

Eventually, Rebecca gave a mental shrug. *Something to worry about on another day,* she concluded. *I have other more pressing issues today.*

"OK, let's get back on track. Olaf, whom do you recommend to replace General Joyce?"

Olaf didn't hesitate. "Admiral Jing. He's currently in operational command of Operation Hades and is probably your most respected and senior field commander."

Rebecca conjured up the face of the admiral in her head. Keyton Joyce had always spoken very well of Jing and he was already being hailed as the Earth's savior after his mad dash back from Messier 54. Even the Alonans were singing his praises and that was something that may come in useful in the longer term.

"Make it happen, Olaf. I want a draft announcement on my desk by tomorrow morning." Rebecca resumed her pacing. "That brings us to another sticky point and one which I feel we have to address as quickly as possible... the status of Janus."

Thomas Crothers had been expecting the subject to come up. Indeed, he had thought that it was the purpose of the meeting.

"We're not ready. Not yet," he said simply.

Patricia looked confused. "Not ready for what, Governor?"

Thomas gave her a lopsided smile. "Our independence, Doctor Bath."

Patricia looked open-mouthed from the governor to the president and back again.

#

LUNAR COLONIES - SOL SYSTEM

Nicholas Schamu endured the shuttle ride down from TDF *Cutlass* in stony silence. *Cutlass* had only been in lunar orbit for a few minutes when Nicholas received the call from Captain Vusumuzi Mkhize that the admiral had left his cabin and was headed for the shuttle bay. Nicholas expected as much and was already in his seat when Christos entered the shuttle and took his seat without saying a word. If Christos saw Nicholas or the silent hulking figure of Force Leader Verus and the six other equally impressive Persai accompanying her, then he chose to say nothing. The normally animated and smiling admiral that commanded SurvFlot One was gone. In his place was an unsmiling, unfeeling automaton who had barely functioned since learning of the attack on the lunar colony.

The shuttle shook slightly as the pilot fired his retro thrusters to bring the shuttle to a landing on the assigned pad. With a jolt, the landing pad slowly lowered itself below the lunar surface until it came to a halt with another small jolt. Christos unbuckled his restraints and moved to the hatch. The crew chief barred his way until the indicator went to green, signaling a good seal on the personnel tube. As the light went from red to green, the crew chief stepped to one side and half raised a hand as if to clasp the shoulder of his admiral but the deathly stare of Christos halted him. Instead he brought himself to attention as he stepped to one side.

Christos made his way along the personnel tube with Nicholas and the Persai at his heels. The small group entered the empty arrivals area. Empty but for one elderly, mousy woman hovering around two children. On seeing him, Maia and Odysseia broke free and ran for their father. Whatever had been holding Christos together evaporated as he dropped to his knees, taking his children into his arms, as he did so the tears flowed.

"She's gone, Daddy! Mama's gone!" wailed Odysseia.

Christos could only nod, his grief overwhelming him as he hugged them.

Verus gave a silent order to her fellow Persai who formed a protective circle around the grieving family. No one would be allowed to intrude on their moment of pain.

Nicholas nodded his thanks to Verus before making his way over to the woman who had been with the Papadomas children. If anyone had been paying attention, it would have surprised them to see Nicholas give the elderly woman an affectionate embrace before stepping back.

"Thank you for coming so quickly, Mrs. Brown."

Placing a small, seemingly fragile hand on his arm she replied in a soft tone. "Always so formal, Nicholas. How could I not come when one of my boys needs me?"

"It's just... Christos is a good man. He and Kayla invited me into their home and made me welcome..." Nicholas felt unfamiliar emotions well up in him.

Victoria Brown patted his arm. "When I got your message the first thing I did was call William. He told me what had happened, how the children's mother made sure they were safe in the deep mines before going back the hospital... William prioritized that impact area for search-and-rescue, but after a few hours any chance of finding anyone alive was ruled out and they decided the teams were needed elsewhere to help those who had a better chance of survival – I'm so sorry, Nicholas."

Nicholas looked down into the still-piercing blue eyes of the woman who had been more than a nanny to himself, his brother, and his sister. Victoria had looked after him from his earliest memory till the day he had left as a gangly, awkward teenager for boarding school.

It was Victoria who told him of his parents' death eight years before. Nicholas' parents had never been the intimate kind and always kept their children at arm's length, believing they would grow stronger and more independent for that. Victoria Brown, on the other hand, showered them with her love and affection and when Nicholas saw the effect the news of the death of Kayla had on Christos, he reached out to his brother William, governor of the lunar colony, to secure the Papadomas children and keep them safe until he could arrange for the arrival of his former nanny to care for them. The eldest Papadomas daughter, Philippa, had been looking at colleges in the American midwest when the attack by the Others had started and Nicholas had pulled strings to have her taken to his sister Madeleine's home, south of Geneva, until he could organize a shuttle to get her back to the lunar colony.

Nicholas put a gentle arm around Victoria's shoulders and guided her toward the solid circle of Persai that opened to allow them into the space holding the Papadomas family before once more closing around them.

Nicholas spoke gently to Christos who raised his head to look at him with tear-filled eyes. "Christos, this is Mrs. Brown. She's here to help."

CHAPTER TWENTY

OPERATION HADES

DURAV - 172 LIGHT YEARS FROM EARTH

In the blink of an eye, an area that had once been home to scattered particles of cosmic dust was filled with the massive forms of warships, bristling with weaponry as their sensors searched out targets. The Commonwealth fleet had arrived in the Durav system!

"Fold transit complete, Admiral. All units report ready to proceed."

"Thank you, Tactical." Ai Jing let a small sense of satisfaction creep into his normal wariness. But only a little. He was leading the largest fleet ever assembled by humanity and her allies into the very home of the enemy and he was taking nothing for granted. The Others had already shown themselves to be full of surprises and he wasn't about to give them any opportunity to spring another on him.

"Time till Benii arrival?"

"Ten minutes, sir. Admiral Radford has already broken off cruiser divisions 3.1.1 and 3.1.2 to sweep their arrival coordinates and provide escorts for the carrier's tugs."

The imminent arrival of five Benii carriers would provide Ai with 575 Freiba space fighters. The small but powerful Freiba had proven themselves to be a significant force multiplier in the battle that had raged around Earth only four days before and Ai had been reading everything he could about the American and Japanese tactics for employing fighter aircraft during Earth's World War Two in an attempt to ensure that he made best use of his new tool of war. His research had emphasized one thing in particular. The protection of the fighter's base. If you allowed the enemy to destroy the small space fighter's carrier, then you lost them as a fighting force. This point had caused no end of headaches for Ai's planning staff as he demanded they find a way to protect the carriers while still allowing them to take part in the assault on the Others' home world of Durav. One particularly bright lieutenant commander had come up with a simple but eloquent solution. The Benii themselves employed lighter units in their own space forces to protect the carriers, so why not copy them but up-gun the escort. Each carrier would get its own dedicated BatFor to act as both escort and strike force. With the forces that Ai had brought with him, that meant that five of his seven BatFors would have their own carrier. The remaining two BatFors would be stripped of their battleships, which would be evenly distributed amongst the five carrier BatFors and the battleships replaced with lighter, faster Persai Vitaros cruisers and Agis destroyers. The stripped-down BatFors, BatFor 2.1 and 2.2, Ai intended to use like light cavalry of old. To scout ahead of his main force and provide him with battlefield intelligence and a force to harass the enemy without forcing him into a full engagement. Their input may prove vital in the forthcoming battle.

Ai had brought his forces out of fold space on the outer edges of the Durav system. In the large main holo cube of the *Resolute's* flag bridge, the system lay before him. Sixteen planets orbiting a yellow G-class star. Highlighted on the outer edge of the Goldilocks zone was his objective. Durav. Home planet of the Others. As the fleet's sensors probed deeper into the system, the computer filled in the gaps in the intelligence picture. The large asteroid belt encircling the star was a hive of activity. Power sources were abundantly spread throughout the tens of millions of asteroids. *Mining and processing facilities no doubt*, thought Ai. Maybe some military bases but he couldn't be certain until he got closer. As he continued to survey the readouts, he was struck by the lack of space ship drives. Such a large mining operation should have ships continuously transiting back and forth to the inner system.

"Tactical. There seems to be a distinct lack of ship drives in the system, any ideas?"

The commander at tactical had been thinking the same thing and he had been searching frantically for an answer. Ah… found you.

The holo cube zoomed in on the area between Durav and its two orbiting moons. There. Clustered so tightly together that they obscured each other's drives were literally thousands of ships of all sizes. From small inter-system shuttles to massive cargo haulers.

Well, it looks like we were expected. "Try and clean up the readings, Tactical, I'd like to distinguish between warships and civilian."

"Aye-aye, sir. It might take me a while, but our readings should clear up as we get closer to the planet."

That would be soon enough, thought Ai. "Any indication of dampening buoys?"

"None yet, Admiral."

"Fold transit! It's the Benii carriers, sir. High Commander Botac sends her regards and requests permission to join the fleet."

"Very well. Fleet general signal. Fleet will assume formation Delta. Navigation. Shape us a course for the inner system. Fleet will advance at 0.1 of light. Tactical. Let's get BatFors 2.1 and 2.2 out in front, I need their eyes. BatFor 1.1 and 1.2 are to expedite the launching of half their Freibas equipped for an anti-shipping strike I want them on our flanks acting as a trip wire in case the enemy decides to try a sneak attack. All remaining Freibas are to go to a rotating thirty-minute alert status."

The officer at comms acknowledged the orders and began transmitting them to the fleet. *So it begins*, thought Ai.

#

As the Commonwealth fleet crawled through the outer reaches of the Durav system, the Others remained apparently motionless. It wasn't until the fleet passed through the system's asteroid belt that they detected any signs of enemy activity.

"Dampening fields detected, Admiral."

Ai stirred in the seat he had refused to leave in the hours since the fleet's arrival.

"Show me on the tactical display. Pinpoint the center of the field and its extent, if you please."

In Ai's tactical holo cube a patchwork of seemingly random spheres blossomed into life. The majority were in the path of the fleet's advance but some were clustered around one of Durav's moons while a few were in the wake of the fleet. An attempt to block his escape route? Ai continued to look at the display for another moment before coming to a decision. Tapping a key on his armrest, he waited patiently for a second while the link was established and the face of Gavin Glandinning appeared in the holo cube.

"Admiral Jing, sir."

"Admiral Glandinning, it appears that I require the services of your cruisers."

In the display, Gavin nodded expectantly. "Locate and destroy the dampening buoys, sir?"

Ai graced him with a small, tight smile. "Start with the buoys to our rear. Better safe than sorry, I think. Contact me again once you have destroyed them, I want to think about the ones in our path. They may appear random but if nothing else, our past experiences have taught us that the enemy doesn't do anything randomly, they always have a purpose. I just have to figure out what it is."

"Aye-aye, sir. Glandinning clear."

Ai went back to his contemplation of the tactical display, as if by staring long enough, he could divine the enemy's intentions. He didn't have to wait too long.

"Admiral. Movement. It looks like every enemy ship in the inner system has lit their drives off as one. We're getting thousands of returns. The computers are trying to clear up the picture but my initial take is that they're forming up into three waves and heading out to meet us."

Ai did his best to appear calm, but inside his stomach was doing somersaults.

"Estimated time to contact with the first wave?"

"If they continue on their current course and acceleration, BatFor 2.2 should be in contact in twenty-six minutes, with the main fleet entering effective weapons range in forty-two minutes."

"Understood." Ai ran the projected courses and speed through his tactical brain, the numbers crunching as fast as any computer. "BatFor 1.1, 2.1, and 3.2 will launch their Freibas for an anti-shipping strike timed to intercept the first wave two minutes before the enemy enters the missile envelope of BatFor 2.2. What is the time between enemy waves?"

The commander at tactical was still working his readouts furiously. "Sorry, sir. The first wave has turned on its ECM. At this distance, my sensors can't burn through the interference."

Ai mulled the problem over. He needed to know what the subsequent enemy waves were up to. Well, that was what he had stripped down BatFor 2.1 and 2.2 for. "Order BatFor 2.1 to make an immediate fold to system north. 2 AUs should be enough for them to get a good look down onto the enemy movements. Priority is to be given to identifying enemy command and control ships."

#

Wing Leader Yel Valat led her wing of ten Freibas into another set of tight, intricate turns as she and her fellow pilots sped toward the oncoming wave of enemy small ships. Her targeting display was filled with returns and even as she closed the range, the on-board computers were still having difficulty identifying individual targets as the enemy was flying so close together. No matter, she thought, as she warmed up the seeker heads of her anti-ship missiles. This was what any fighter pilot of any race would call a target-rich environment.

A low warbling tone in her helmet let her know that her missiles had pierced the enemy's ECM and had achieved a solid lock. Yel held her fire for another few seconds as the computer confirmed that each Freiba under her command had target lock and then as one, the entire wing loosed its load of missiles. Eight missiles per Freiba. Eighty missiles per wing. Thirty wings tasked to the strike. 2400 missiles streaked toward their targets. Inevitably, more than one missile locked onto the same target but there were so many missiles launched that it didn't really matter. Less than fifteen seconds after launch, the Benii missiles reached their targets and space was filled by the blinding light of nuclear detonations as the attackers' formation was decimated.

Yel let out a small, excited whoop before she regained control of herself. As her targeting display cleared and the tactical picture became clear, she saw that even through the maelstrom of destruction that she and her wing mates had released, there were enemy survivors who were still intent on reaching the fleet. Well, she wasn't about to let that happen.

"Waya Wing will break right and engage remaining targets with guns. Standby... Break! Break! Break!"

Arming her beam emitters, she executed another tight turn that had her restraints pulling her tight to her seat as she swooped down on the nearest enemy ship, her wingman tucking herself in tight. The first enemy ship. It looked like a small shuttle craft. Filled her targeting sights and she lightly stroked the trigger sending a line of deadly, highly charged particles into the center of the target. The beam emitters of a Freiba could do light to moderate damage to battle armor but to an unarmored shuttle it was like pushing a hot needle through wax. Her fire hardly slowed as it passed through the shuttle's hull without pause and it was then that the fleet learned of the enemy ships deadly cargo. The resulting detonation of the nuclear weapons that filled the shuttle's cargo bay to the gunnels not only wiped it from space but took Yel and her wingman with it into fiery death.

#

The barely disguised profanity that came from tactical grabbed Ai's attention like a physical thing.

"Report!" Ai demanded stridently.

"Admiral, it appears that the small craft are loaded with nukes. The Freibas killed the majority of the first wave with missiles, but when they engaged with guns they had to get in close and we've lost over sixty that were caught in the resulting explosions."

If Ai had been a man who used profanity he would have joined his tactical section. Instead he began firing out orders. "Order the Freibas to withdraw and re-arm with missiles. Get the second flight of Freibas away now to mop up the remaining enemy ships. I want each BatFor to reconfigure formation so they have a solid screen of Agis destroyers between themselves and the next wave. I have no doubt that our capital ships, in particular the carriers, will be the enemy's main target."

As the bridge crew bent to their tasks Ai reviewed the main holo cube. The feed from BatFor 2.1 was just starting to fill the cube. Yes, there was the second wave and... Ah-ha! Ai knew that the enemy wouldn't just randomly place its dampening buoys. The enemy second wave was breaking up into smaller formations and each was making a beeline for one of the spheres that indicated an area covered by the dampening buoy. If he let them reach the fields, he would lose the advantage of his GD missiles, which would force him to either expend Freibas to go in and get them or close tactical missile and energy weapon range with his capital ships. A prospect he didn't savor if each of those thousand-plus ships was filled with nuclear warheads. With the amount of destructive force aboard a single enemy vessel, even a near-miss detonation would cause severe damage and inflict heavy casualties. No. He had another idea. As one of his military predecessors had said, you either use them or lose them.

A tap of an armrest control and the inevitable wait for a secure link to be established. The face of a frowning John Radford appeared in the split screen.

"Admiral Radford, by your face I see you may have perceived my problem."

Although significantly younger than the senior admiral, the last few years had aged John in a way he wouldn't have believed possible and he returned Ai's sage-like look with one of his own.

"If you mean we're about to lose our most important tactical advantage to those dampening buoys, then we're on the same wavelength, sir. If I may make a suggestion?"

A nod from Ai and John continued.

"We launch a maximum effort GD missile strike now using the targeting data from BatFor 2.1. Target the second wave before they can reach the relative safety of the dampening fields."

"My thoughts exactly, Admiral Radford, but with one amendment. It will not be a fleet-wide maximum effort. I want to hold a strategic reserve. I don't think we've seen the last twist in this fight yet. I'm chopping operational control of BatFor 2.1 to you for the purposes of the GD missile strike…"

The commander at comms nodded as he acknowledged Ai's instructions and sent the order on to BatFor 2.1.

"I want you to flush all your available GD missiles as soon as you can…" A glance at the tactical display told Ai what he needed to know. "You have four minutes until the first enemy ship reaches the dampening field."

In the display John gave him a curt nod and cut the link.

Ai sat back and rubbed his eyes through closed lids. The fight wasn't over yet but he felt reasonably confident that if Third Fleet could destroy the second wave before it reached the relative safety of the dampening fields, then he would have more than sufficient resources to deal with the third and final enemy wave.

Radford had obviously been expecting an order to fire on the second wave as in under a minute Ai's tactical officer had received a preliminary strike package from his opposite number in Third Fleet. The arrival of the strike package was quickly followed by the first GD missile leaving the tubes of Third Fleet.

"Third Fleet has launched, Admiral. Admiral Radford's intentions appear to be to hold the first wave of missiles at a staging point while he gets a second wave away. Both waves will then target the enemy ships from opposite directions, spreading their defensive fire."

Ai waved a hand in acknowledgment. If Radford was going to get a second missile salvo into position before the first enemy ships reached the safety of the dampening field, then his crews would need to be quick.

"Second salvo of missiles away from Third Fleet, sir. Enemy ships should reach the dampening field in forty-five seconds. Time to missile impact… thirty-four seconds."

Ai's eyes were glued to the tactical holo cube as the two groups of missiles appeared momentarily in the feed from BatFor 2.1, only to disappear a fraction of a second later. Ai knew that the feed was as close to real time as he was going to get but still he wished it was faster. The missiles re-appeared less than 5000 kilometers from the enemy ships and bored in at maximum acceleration. Laser turrets swiveled to engage the approaching threat but there were simply too many of them for even computer-aided reflexes to react in time. It was a slaughter. Third Fleet's missiles tore into the enemy ranks. The exploding warheads caused a chain reaction and it was as if the gates of hell themselves had opened as the roiling, expanding, superheated plasma of the missiles and the enemy ships payloads combined. For just a moment it seemed like a new star had been born and when the destruction ended, over 1100 enemy ships ceased to exist.

Anyone who had witnessed the death dealt by Third Fleet would have to wonder at the dedication of the enemy crews as the third and final wave broke orbit and headed out to meet the Commonwealth fleet. Ai noticed immediately that again, the enemy was changing tactics on him as the ships formed up into four globes, civilian ships centered on what the computers were calling a core of Buzzards and Vultures.

"Tactical, let's get a GD missile strike package ready. I want the primary target to be the capital ships at the heart of each globe. Warn off all the Freibas for a follow-up anti-shipping strike on the enemy ships of the outer shell. We'll kill the capital ships with missiles then maneuver the fleet to hold the smaller ships at maximum range and pick them off. No sense taking casualties when we don't need to."

"Aye-aye, sir." The tactical section raced to prepare the package and Ai took the opportunity to review the battle so far. The first enemy wave had caused him to take casualties amongst his Benii fighters but the losses had been minimal and the enemy had shown their hand. They were lacking in real warships, so had used civilian ships to carry nuclear warheads with the intention of closing like the old Japanese Kamikazes and

350

detonating their weapons as close to his ships as they could get. A second strike by the Freibas and the protective shield of Agis destroyers had finished off the first wave. The second wave had tried a different tactic. They had headed for pre-deployed dampening buoys, which, if they had reached the fields, would have been safe from his GD missiles and he would have had to close with them to kill them but the quick actions of Third Fleet had dealt with them before they had been able to reach the cover of the dampening fields. Ai turned his attention back to the approaching third wave. The four globes were approaching the Commonwealth fleet in line abreast. They were presenting themselves as an easy target for Ai's GD missiles. Ai would be able to fire wave after wave of missiles at them without them being able to reply as long as he kept the distance to them open. Ai could feel a familiar tingling at the back of his neck as his hands formed an involuntary steeple. Why would they try to approach the fleet in a fashion that they knew could only result in their defeat? Ai began tapping away at his terminal, bringing up power readings from the core of each globe. Hoping that he was wrong. But as the computer spat out its reply, his expression hardened. The Others had sprung their next surprise.

"Tactical, get our GD missiles away now!"

The commander at Tactical turned to request more time to finish his work, but the look on Ai's face told him it wouldn't be forthcoming.

"Missiles away. I've had to let forty percent find their own targets, since the package wasn't complete. Sorry, sir."

Ai ignored him as he concentrated on his holo cube. The missile strike appeared in the display approximately 6000 kilometers from each of the globes.

The missiles took only a fraction of a second for their electronic brains to get their bearings but it was a fraction of a second too long. At the heart of each globe, a Buzzard towing a dampening buoy activated it. The entire missile strike was now nothing more than expensive metal cylinders floating uselessly in space as each and every gravity drive failed. The Commonwealth's greatest advantage was gone in one simple stroke.

In the display, the enemy globes accelerated toward the fleet. Protected now by their dampening fields. Ai closed his eyes and his mind to the chaos that was erupting around him on the flag bridge as officers rushed to prepare for the close-quarter battle that was imminent. Ai's eyelids snapped open as he came to a decision and his finger stabbed down on his armrest controls. Once more, the face of Gavin Glandinning appeared in his display.

"Admiral. The enemy has activated dampening fields at the heart of each of the attacking globes. I need those fields taken down. Split your four cruisers into two pairs. Identify the enemy ships with the dampening buoys and destroy them at all costs. If you do not then there is a very real chance that we may be forced to withdraw."

On the bridge of the *Horizon,* the grave face of Gavin Glandinning stared back into the holo pickup. Gavin had seen the globes form up. The computers estimated that each globe consisted of some 400 smaller ships around a tight core of a half dozen mixed Buzzards and Vultures. To fold into the heart of the globe with only another cruiser for support would be tantamount to signing his own death warrant. The look in Jing's eyes showed that the senior admiral was well aware of what he was asking of Glandinning and his crews.

"Understood, sir."

There was nothing more for Ai to say as the link to Glandinning was cut. Godspeed, Gavin.

#

Gavin Glandinning tightened the straps of his seat and placed a hand on top of his helmet in its rack on the side of the chair as he gave a silent prayer that the experimental armor on *Horizon* and her sister ships would be enough for them to survive in the maelstrom of fire that he was about to send them into. Gavin steadied his voice as he gave the order.

"Navigation, fold when ready."

TDF *Horizon* and her consort, *Daybreak*, disappeared from normal space only to blink back into existence a moment later, surrounded by enemy ships. The enemy gunners must have been expecting them, for *Horizon's* systems were still stabilizing themselves as the first lasers and grazers fired on her. If Gavin had ever been at the epicenter of an earthquake, then this is what it would feel like. The *Horizon* bucked like a wild stallion as the meta-materials in the experimental battle armor fought to bend and twist the mind-numbing power of the enemy fire.

The meta-materials developed by Moore and his teams were designed to reflect energy away from a ship's hull. The way Jeff Moore had explained it to Gavin was for him to imagine that he had stuck a straw into a glass of water. The parts above and below the water point in slightly different directions. That's a positive refractive index, and is the case for nearly all materials.

A negative refractive index occurs if you try to stick the straw into the water and it bounces back at the exact but opposite angle it enters the water. Now imagine the straw is instead a powerful laser. A ship made of conventional materials struck by such a laser would be sliced in half. But a ship made with meta-materials would reflect the beam. And the more powerful the beam, the stronger the reflection would be. The breakthrough had been that, like all optical meta-materials, their unique properties work only if the size of the structure is smaller than the wavelength of light being used. The Persai advances in nano-technology had allowed the teams at Zarmina to develop these microscopic structures. Hence the meta-material coating *Horizon* should in theory reflect any coherent light weapon used against it. Great in theory. Time to see if it actually worked in practice.

"The armor is holding, Admiral. We have a firing solution on the buoy. Engaging now with primary grazers… target destroyed."

Gavin pumped his fist in the air. "Great shooting, Guns. Navigation, let's get the hell out of here. Take us to target two."

Horizon and *Daybreak* disappeared once more into the safety of fold space.

In less time than it took to realize it had happened, the two cruisers re-appeared in the center of the second globe. And once more, the pummeling started.

As *Horizon*'s systems stabilized, Gavin noticed that *Daybreak* wasn't where she should be. Whatever had happened she had emerged from fold space out of position and her current location was closer to the small ships that formed the outer edge of the globe. Without hesitation, three of the smaller enemy ships darted toward her. *Daybreak* attempted to maneuver away but the enemy was simply too close. Short-range missiles fired desperately and laser defensive clusters fired frantically, but *Daybreak*'s defenses were swamped and within seconds Gavin felt his heart chill as the friendly blue icon of TDF *Daybreak* briefly blinked red before disappearing altogether.

The lieutenant at tactical was too engrossed in her own small battle to notice the loss of *Daybreak* and her crew. "Target identified. Firing now! Target destroyed."

Without waiting for an order, the navigator engaged the cruiser's gravity drive and took the *Horizon* safely away.

#

On the *Resolution*, a relieved cheer went up as the enemy's dampening fields went down and even Ai struggled to keep his relief in check. In the holo cube the enemy ships raced on and the distance to the first two globes was now such that his longer-range GD missiles would be wasted on them. This fight was about to get down and dirty.

"Tactical, target the fleet's remaining GD missiles on globes three and four. Maximum effort. Order the Agis destroyers to slow their speed enough that they move into the defensive fire envelopes of their respective capital ships. Signal the Benii. I want the remaining Freibas to engage globes one and two and punch a hole through the small craft to allow us to close with the remaining enemy warships. The fleet will execute fire plan Gamma on my order."

AI ignored his subordinates' acknowledgments of his orders as he tapped a control on his chair and the face of John Radford appeared in his holo cube.

"Admiral Radford. It's my intention to allow our remaining GD missiles to take care of globes three and four. Unfortunately, that means we'll have to engage globes one and two directly. You will take command of half the fleet while I retain the remainder. The Benii will clear a way for our ships into the heart of each globe while the Agis hold off the Kamikazes."

Ai looked into the impassive eyes of the commander of Third Fleet. "It's not going to be pretty, John, and we will take casualties. Hold to your course and we will be victorious."

John nodded once slowly in understanding before replying in the only way he knew how. "Aye-aye, sir." It would only be later that John realized that for the one and only time he could remember Admiral Ai Jing, the most senior admiral in the Commonwealth, had called him by his given name.

With the link cut, Ai gave the order he knew would commit his ships and crews to their greatest battle. "Communications. Fire plan Gamma. Execute! Execute!"

The vast Commonwealth armada broke into two parts and each headed for an enemy globe. The Benii Freibas took up position in front like the tip of a spear and Agis destroyers hugged close to their designated battleships like Remora fish attaching themselves to sharks.

The Freibas reached firing range and missiles leapt from weapons rails and flashed toward the enemy small craft. Space itself seemed to disappear as fire ravaged the outer edges of the enemy globes. The enemy small craft were packed so closely together that as one exploded, it would invariably cause another to explode sympathetically. As the Freibas peeled away, they left a gaping hole in the enemy globe, which the Commonwealth ships forged through. Enemy small craft maneuvered radically to reorient themselves into position from which to fling themselves on their prey, but as the opposing forces slammed together and inter-penetrated, short-range weapons fired, ripping and tearing with titanic fury, extinguishing the small craft like moths in a candle's flame.

Now it was time for the big guns of the battleships to fire and uncountable amounts of coherent light energy crisscrossed the emptiness of space as grazers, lasers, and plasma cannon fired continuously. Ships from either side staggered under the weight of fire being exchanged and systems were blinded by the explosions of multi-megaton munitions as hundreds of thousands of tons of starship turned itself into nothing more than lifeless, spinning hulks of junk. For what seemed like hours but was really only minutes, each side hacked away at the other then, like a butterfly exploding from a chrysalis, the Commonwealth fleets burst from the rear of the enemy globes. In their wake was not one surviving enemy capital ship. Like hungry wolves, the Freibas fell on the remaining small craft that were still attempting to immolate themselves and whatever Commonwealth ship they could reach. The Benii pilots had learned their lesson. Instead of closing with the nuclear-equipped small craft, they attacked in packs. Their combined fire guaranteed a hit even at extreme range and as the main Commonwealth fleet re-formed, the last vestiges of enemy space-borne threats was destroyed.

#

The flag bridge of TDF *Resolution* was strangely still as all eyes were on the snow-shrouded planet in the main holo cube. Durav lay at their mercy but it had come at a price in the blood of their fellow ship mates. Three more Bismarcks and five Nemesis battleships had been lost in the last cataclysmic battle. More had been left bleeding air and leaving a trail of debris behind them as damage control teams fought to save their ships. But now. At last. With Durav below them, it all seemed worth it.

Ai Jing allowed himself a moment of satisfaction as he slowly looked around the battered flag bridge. The damage repair teams had managed to find and repair the damage done by the enemy grazer, which had penetrated the *Resolution's* armor and caused the explosive decompression that had killed his tactical officer and nearly all his team. Ai spared a glance at the younger-than-should-be lieutenant who was his last remaining trained tactical officer. The lieutenant had been blown off her feet by the impact of the grazer but had had the good sense to have attached her helmet to her leg by its strap so when the flag bridge had decompressed and the life-giving oxygen had fled into space, she had survived. Not that a helmet would have done anyone else in the tactical team any good. The grazer had passed right through their section and where it touched, nothing survived. Eight crew member had simply ceased to exist in the blink of an eye. As the last of the oxygen escaped into space, the young lieutenant had dusted herself off and brought up one of the secondary engineering terminals and re-configured it to allow the ship to carry on the fight. As Ai continued to watch, the lieutenant tentatively touched her left shoulder. Ai suspected that it was at the very least dislocated, but when the medics arrived on the bridge, she shrugged off their ministrations and carried on. Ai would ensure that her dedication would be rewarded once they returned home. Ai gave himself a shake. Back to business.

"Is Third Fleet in position, tactical?"

"Yes, sir. All fleet units now report ready to begin the bombardment."

Ai gave a satisfied grunt. With the enemy space threat negated, he dispersed the fleet. Commonwealth ships now sat in high orbit above every major city. Industrial targets had been quickly identified and Ai ordered them destroyed with Kinetic Energy Missiles.

The use of KEMs would produce the same destruction as an equivalent nuclear missile strike but with a lot less collateral damage. Ai was here to destroy the Others' ability to wage war, not to lay waste to the planet.

"Very well. Begin the bombardment."

#

Deep inside a mountain, the High Coltus opened a file and reviewed its instructions. In the way only a dispassionate electronic intelligence could do, it put into place the orders that would ensure its own destruction.

#

Lieutenant Martha Grey fought to ignore the dull pain in her left shoulder as her terminal demanded her attention. The sensors had detected a massive power build-up in the planet's northern continent. Martha forced her left arm to bend to her will as she punched commands into the terminal, suppressing the urge to swear loudly at the pain her movements caused her. The computer displayed the results and they weren't what Martha had expected. She brought the area up on the tactical display and turned to face Admiral Jing, who sat as unmoving as a stone statue in his command chair.

"Admiral. Sensors are indicating a power build-up in a mountainous area on the northern continent."

"A buried weapons system?"

Martha shook her head. "The computer is calling it a communications array, sir. The computers are still working on it, sir but the array appears to be massive. At least several square kilometers in size."

Jing was staring at her incredulously when he remembered a briefing paper he had read somewhere that had identified a powerful ULF signal that had been generated by some kind of central computer system on enemy ships. This signal had supposedly been responsible for killing the ship's crews. Jing's mind reeled in horror at the thought that entered his brain. No. It couldn't be. Ai lunged out of his seat shouting as he did so.

"Emergency re-tasking! Any ship within range is to fire on that mountain. Nuclear weapons are authorized!"

The shouted order had barely left his lips when the sensor board lit up with the release of a powerful ULF signal. The signal raced around Durav and wherever it passed, the Chosen People felt an intense pain emanating from the Gift Stone. The pain was only fleeting and they were dead before their bodies touched the ground. Beneath each and every Atistes, house of the Creator, a building found in every village and city, the nuclear demolition charge was activated. The entire surface of Durav was wracked by nuclear detonations. Any member of the Chosen People not touched by the ULF signal died in rolling nuclear fire. The last act of the unfeeling High Coltus was to activate the thermobaric devices spread throughout its mountain complex. Within seconds, there was nothing left but ashes.

Aboard the orbiting Commonwealth fleet, a blanket of stunned silence settled. Ai Jing slumped into his seat, not trusting his trembling legs to hold him. In the holo cube, he watched as Durav and its entire population died in front of his eyes. Slowly a question formed in his brain. Why?

#

Systems long lying dormant were fed power and slowly came to life as the ever-watching sensors had registered the ULF signal from the planet below. The drive engines throbbed with power as the camouflaging dust and debris that had accumulated over the centuries were cleared from the hull by the freshly awakened repulsion systems. More power flowed to the engines and as the levels reached acceptability, the ship breached the moon's surface and accelerated rapidly until it entered fold space and vanished.

CHAPTER TWENTY-ONE
MORE QUESTIONS THAN ANSWERS

CARON CITY – EARTH – SOL SYSTEM

The steady beeping of the computer eventually broke through the tired dreams of Ensign Terrance Wilson. The beeping brought Terrance swimming slowly back to wakefulness. How long had he been asleep? Terrance regarded the clock on the wall of his small office through narrowed eyes. What had seemed like an age had actually only been an hour. Making the effort, he raised himself out of his seat and poured himself a cup of coffee from the carafe in the corner of his office. The coffee was steaming hot. Sometime during his sleep, some Good Samaritan must've come in and topped it up, for he was sure he had finished the last dregs of the coffee hours before. Looking down at his rumpled uniform, Terrance ran a hand through his hair and gulped the coffee in a vain attempt to kick his tired brain into action.

Settling himself back in front of his terminal, he tapped a key to bring up the results of his latest computer search of the Saiph database. The news of the destruction of Durav at what appeared to be their own hands had been met with both a sense of relief and disbelief throughout the Commonwealth. Admiral Jing had been hailed as a hero on his return to Earth but in every news vid that Terrance had seen, Jing emphasized the bravery of his men in the battle that had raged as the Others had fought to stop the Commonwealth fleet from reaching Durav and the humanity that they were still demonstrating as they conducted search-and-rescue operations throughout the system, in particular in the asteroid belt, as they tried to convince the remaining enemy outposts that the Commonwealth had been victorious and they should lay down their arms and surrender. It was with growing despair that marine boarding parties were finding that the Others had chosen death rather than capture. There was a growing sense of realization amongst the upper echelons of the government and the population in general that what the Commonwealth was watching was the extinction of an entire race at their own hands. All, seemingly, in the belief of this Creator and the path of the Ehita. A supposedly holy crusade to cleanse the stars of everything not of the Creator in preparation for his return.

Terrance put the thoughts to one side as the computer brought up its results and Terrance stopped in his tracks. The fresh coffee in his hand forgotten. Displayed in the center of the screen was a black circle with a red X at its center. Beside it was a phrase in Saiph and below that an English translation. The translation said "Military Prisoner."

###

About the Author

Paul was born in Johnstone, Renfrewshire, Scotland in 1967. He joined the British Army in 1985 at the grand old age of seventeen and a half. After completing his initial training he joined elite parachute force, 5 Airborne Brigade, spending four years there until moving on to various intelligence and signals units for the remainder of his twenty-two year's service. During his career he served in many areas of operations including: Africa, the Balkans, Central America, Northern Ireland, the Middle East and South East Asia. He continues to work in the security field and write part-time.

He has been a fan of science fiction since his school days, although his reading tastes have developed to include all things military, past, future and alternate history.

He began writing his own stories in 2013 and self published his first science fiction novel DISCOVERY OF THE SAIPH in 2014.

Want details of my new releases?
www.ppcorcoran.com/subscribe.html

Other Books

SCIENCE FICTION NOVELS:

The Saiph Series (4 book series)
Discovery of the Saiph, book 1
Search for the Saiph, book 2
Hunt for the Saiph, book 3
Legacy of the Saiph, book 4

The K'Tai War (3 book series)
Invasion, book 1

~

ANTHOLOGIES:

The Empire at War: British Military Science Fiction
Explorations: Through the Wormhole
Explorations: First Contact

~

MILITARY THRILLER SHORT STORIES:

The Province, Ghost Soldiers 1

Most books also available in ebook and audiobook.
Visit www.ppcorcoran.com for more.

Connect with Paul Corcoran

I really appreciate you reading my book! You can find me here:

Facebook Fan Page: http://facebook.com/ppcorcoran
Visit my website: http://www.ppcorcoran.com
Join my mailing list: http://www.ppcorcoran.com/subscribe.html

Printed in Great Britain
by Amazon

46426060R00222